PORTRAITS IN LITERATURE

Other books by Hava Bromberg Ben-Zvi

Eva's Journey: A Young Girl's True Story

The Bride Who Argued with God: Tales from the Treasury of

Jewish Folklore

Under an assumed name, Hava Bromberg Ben-Zvi survived the Second World War in Poland and arrived in Palestine in 1946. As a teacher of new immigrants she experienced the growing pains and joys of the new State of Israel.

Educated in Israel and the United States, she earned a Master's degree in Library Science and served for twenty-seven years as the director of the Jewish Community Library of Los Angeles.

Following retirement, Ms Bromberg Ben-Zvi pursued new goals as a writer. *Eva's Journey: A Young Girl's True Story* and *The Bride Who Argued With God: Tales from the Treasury of Jewish Folklore* are the products of her later years. *Portraits in Literature: The Jews of Poland. An Anthology* is a lavish, historically informative and poignant panorama of life that was, and a tribute to the Jews of Poland.

Portraits in Literature: The Jews of Poland.
An Anthology

Compiled, Edited and with an Introduction by
HAVA BROMBERG BEN-ZVI

VALLENTINE MITCHELL
LONDON • PORTLAND, OR

in association with

THE EUROPEAN JEWISH
PUBLICATION SOCIETY

First published in paperback in 2013 by Vallentine Mitchell

Middlesex House,
29/45 High Street, Edgware,
Middlesex HA8 7UU, UK

920 NE 58th Avenue, Suite 300
Portland, Oregon,
97213-3786 USA

www.vmbooks.com

British Library Cataloguing in Publication Data

Portraits in literature : the Jews of Poland : an
anthology.
1. Jews, Polish--Literary collections. 2. Holocaust,
Jewish (1935-1945)--Poland--Personal narratives.
3. Holocaust, Jewish (1939-1945)--Poland--Sources.
I. Ben-Zvi, Hava.
808.8'03529240438-dc22

ISBN 978 0 85303 923 5 (paper)

Library of Congress Cataloging-in-Publication Data
An entry can be found on request

Printed by CMP (UK) Ltd, Poole, Dorset, BH12 4NU

A loving tribute to the memory of my husband
Dr Ephraim Ben-Zvi
and for my son Henry Ben-Zvi, my daughter-in-law Molly
and my grandchildren Sarah, Daniel and Michael

Contents

List of Plates   xi

Acknowledgements   xiii

Praise for *Portraits in Literature: The Jews of Poland*   xxi

Introduction   xxv

The Jews of Poland in Legendary Tradition   xxxvii

PART I. OUR WORLD OF YESTERDAY

1. *The Rebel* by Sholem Asch. Excerpts from a Novel   3

2. *The Mother's Reward* by Sholem Asch.   11
   Excerpts from a Novel

3. 'Olke' by Kadya Molodowsky. A Poem   22

4. 'The Tale of the Washtub' by Kadya Molodowsky.   27
   A Poem

5. *The Teacher Reb Mendele* by Lili Berger. A Short Story   30

6. *Time of Peace* by Leon Weliczker Wells. A Memoir   37

7. *The Bride* by Israel Joshua Singer. Excerpt from a Novel   43

8. *The Wedding Night* by Israel Joshua Singer.   53
   Excerpt from a Novel

9. *A Jew in the Polish Army* by Siegfried Halbreich.   59
   A Memoir

10. *The Circumcision That Wasn't.* A Jewish Folk Tale   63

11. *The Recipe of Rabbi Yenuka of Stolin.* A Jewish Folk Tale   66

12. *My First Day in the Orphanage* by Israel Zyngman (Staszek). 69
    A Memoir about Janusz Korczak

13. *The Lamed Vovnik* by Isaac Loeb Peretz. A Short Story   81

Polish Voices
14. *Mendel Gdanski* by Maria Konopnicka, a Polish writer.   87
    A Short Story (Selections)

15. *Links in a Chain* by Eliza Orzeszkowa, a Polish writer.   95
    A Short Story (Selections)

16. *Ziselman of Honcharska Street* by Nina Luszczyk-   101
    Ilienkowa, a Polish-Belarus writer. A Memoir

17. *Rivka* by Nina Luszczyk-Ilienkowa. A Memoir   105

                PART II. YEARS OF FLAME AND FURY

The Ghettos
18. *Yossel Rakover's Appeal to God* by Zvi Kolitz.   109
    A Short Story

19. 'And the Earth Rebelled' by Yuri Suhl. A Poem   119

20. *A Shomer Pesach in the Ghetto* by Ruszka Korczak.   123
    A Memoir

21. Two Eyewitnesses: An Unknown Woman and   126
    Adam Sokolski

22. Eyewitness Testimonies. Siedlce, Poland, 1942   129

23. *From the Diary of a Young Shomeret* by Aliza Melamed.   132
    A Memoir

24. 'Cracow Autumn' by Natan Gross. A Poem   139

25. 'Kaddish' by Charles Reznikoff. A Poem   143

Children
26. 'The First Ones' by Itzhak Katzenelson. A Poem: Excerpt   147

27. *How Granny Saved Helenka From the Germans*   150
    by Ella Mahler. A Memoir

28. *We Will Not Hand Over the Children Alive*   155
    by Fredka Mazia. A Memoir

29. *Jewish Children on the Aryan Side*   159
    by Emanuel Ringelblum. An Essay

30. *Janusz Korczak Marches to Death with His Children*   169
    by Azriel Eisenberg. A Biographical Vignette

31. *Little Partisans* by Lena Kuchler-Silberman. A Memoir   173

32. *Books in the Ghetto* by Rachel Auerbach. A Memoir   177

33. *Poems by Children in the Warsaw Ghetto*   181
    by Motele, Natasha and Martha

Resistance
34. *Chief Physician Remba* by Yuri Suhl.   185
    A Biographical Vignette

35. *Little Wanda with the Braids* by Yuri Suhl.   188
    A Biographical Vignette

36. *Rosa Robota – The Heroine of the Auschwitz Underground*
    by Yuri Suhl. A Biographical Vignette   192

37. *Mordecai Anielewicz and His Movement*   197
    by Emanuel Ringelblum. An Essay

38. *The Last Wish of My Life Has Been Granted*   203
    by Mordecai Anielewicz. A Letter

39. *To Arms!* The Proclamation of the Rebels in the   205
    Ghetto of Vilna

40. 'Shlomo Jelichovski' by Itzhak Katzenelson. A Poem   207

41. *The Letter of the Ninety-Three Maidens*   213

42. *Jewish Resistance in the Warsaw Ghetto* by Vladka Meed.   216
    An Essay

Other Voices: Testimonies of Those Who Helped
43. *A Pole in the Ghetto* by Ruth Baum.   227
    A Biographical Vignette

44. *The Hiding Place* by Leon Weliczker Wells. A Memoir   233

45. *Polish Friends* by Vladka Meed. A Memoir   245

46. *Their Brothers' Keepers* by Philip Friedman.   249
    An Essay and Biographical Vignettes

47. *Survival on the Aryan Side* by Mieczyslaw Rolnicki.   256
    Vignettes

PART III. TO LIVE AGAIN

48. *Liberation* by Leon Weliczker Wells. A Memoir   261

49. *The First Letter from America* by Leon Kobrin.   265
    A Short Story

50. *I Discover America* by Abraham Cahan.   270
    Excerpt from a Novel

51. 'The Sweatshop' by Morris Rosenfeld. A Poem   275

52. 'Bread and Tea' by Morris Rosenfeld. A Poem   279

53. 'Yiddish' by Morris Rosenfeld. A Poem   280

54. *In the Catskills* by Abraham Cahan.   282
    Excerpt from a Novel

55. *The Name (Yad Vashem)* by Aharon Megged.   285
    A Short Story

56. *The Polish Wife* by Anna Cwiakowska. A Short Story   299

Glossary   317

Bibliography   325

Plates

1. Sholem Asch, probably 1940s. Photograph courtesy of the Sholem Asch Estate. 1. *The Rebel.*
2. Janusz Korczak with children, 1936. Photograph courtesy of Benjamin Anolik, the Janusz Korczak Association in Israel. 12. *My First day in the Orphanage.* Dr Janusz Korczak was the Director of the Jewish orphanage in the Warsaw Ghetto. See also 30: *Janusz Korczak Marches to Death With His Children.*
3. Maria Konopnicka, 1879. Photograph courtesy of Magdalena Wolowska-Rusinska, Muzeum Marii Konopnickiej, Suwalki, Poland. 14. *Mendel Gdanski.*
4. Eliza Orzeszkowa, probably 1900/10. Photograph courtesy of Ludowa Spoldzielnia Wydawnicza, Warsaw, Poland. 15. *Links in a Chain.*
5. Nina Luszczyk-Ilienkowa, 1999. Photograph courtesy of Anna Engelking. 16. *Ziselman of Honcharska Street.*
6. Yuri Suhl, c. 1950. Photograph courtesy of Lawrence Bush, *Jewish Currents.* 19. 'And the Earth Rebelled'.
7. Natan Gross, probably 1995/2000. Photograph courtesy of Yaakov Gross. 24. 'Cracow Autumn'.
8. Janusz Korczak, 1940. Photograph courtesy of Dr Eleonora Bergman, The Emanuel Ringelblum Jewish Historical Institute, Warsaw, Poland. 30. *Janusz Korczak Marches to Death with His Children.*
9. Emanuel Ringelblum, 1939. Photograph courtesy of Dr Eleonora Bergman, The Emanuel Ringelblum Jewish Historical Institute, Warsaw, Poland. 37. *Mordecai Anielewicz and His Movement.*
10. Emanuel Ringelblum family: Ringelblum, his wife Yehudit and son Uri, c.1930/31. Photograph courtesy of Naama Shilo, Yad Vashem, Holocaust Martyrs' and Heroes' Remembrance Authority, Jerusalem, Israel. 37 *Mordecai Anielewicz and His Movement.* Note: The family was executed in March 1944.

11. Mordecal Anielewicz, 1936. Photograph courtesy of David Amitai, Hashomer Hatzair Institute for Research and Documentation, Archives, Yad Yaari, and Daniela Ozacky, Moreshet Archives, Givat Haviva, Israel. 38. *The Last Wish of My Life Has Been Granted.*
12. Ruth Baum, 1998. Photograph courtesy of Ruth Baum. 43. *A Pole in the Ghetto.*
13. Mordecai Anielewicz, 1937. Photograph courtesy of the Dr Eleonora Bergman, The Emanuel Ringelblum Jewish Historical Institute, Warsaw, Poland, Daniela Ozacky, Moreshet Archives, and David Amitai, Hashomer Hatzair Institute for Research and Documentation, Yad Yaari, Givat Haviva, Israel. 42. *Jewish Resistance in the Warsaw Ghetto.*
14. Mieczyslaw Rolnicki, probably 1990. Photograph courtesy of Mieczyslaw Rolnicki. 47. *Survival on the Aryan Side.*
15. Aharon Megged, c.1980s. Photograph courtesy of Aharon Megged. 55. *The Name.*
16. Anna Cwiakowska, 2000. Photograph courtesy of Anna Cwiakowska. 56. *The Polish Wife.*

Jacket photos of author's family, clockwise: grandfather, Akiba Lewartowski; grandmother, Chawa Lewartowska; mother, Dinah Lewartowska Bromberg; author Hava and brother Michael; husband, Dr Ephraim Ben-Zvi; brother, Michael Abir; father, Herman Bromberg. Photo restoration and cover design by David Oswald.

Acknowledgements

I have no words to express my gratitude to Giovanna Fradkin for her friendship and dedication, wisdom and competence in bringing this book to its completion; Irene McDermott for unfailing support, always; Kay Haugaard, my mentor and friend; Alice Shulman for her care, advice and support; Carolyn Coleman for support, assistance and friendship; Linda Rourman, my friend and supporter, and her family; all members of the Arroyo Writers' Group for encouragement and friendship; Jeff Plumley of the San Marino Public Library; the wonderful staff and resources of the Hebrew Union College Library in Los Angeles; the staff of the Pasadena Public Library; Dr Leon Schwartz for his scholarship and assistance; and to Jeanne Leiter, my editor.

I express my deepest gratitude to the individuals, organizations and publishers for their gracious permissions to reprint their materials. They are:

Liora Amitai and Rachel Pedatzur for 'My First Day in the Orphanage' from Israel Zyngman, *Janusz Korczak Bein Ha'Yetomim* (Bnai Brak, Israel: Sifriat Poalim, 1979). Originally published in Polish by the Janusz Korczak Association in Israel (1976).

The Anti-Defamation League, New York. See Vladka Meed.

Association for Promotion of Jewish Secularism, see *Jewish Currents*.

Dr Sophie Balk for selections from Dr Philip Friedman, *Their Brother's Keepers* (New York: Crown, 1957), pp.16, 17–19, 26–30. Copyright © Philip Friedman 1957.

Ruth Baum for 'A Pole in the Ghetto', in Ruth Baum, *Syn Dziedzica I Inne Opowiadania* [The Squire's Son and Other Stories] (Lodz: Oficyna Bibliofilow, 1999), pp.3–8.

Beit Lohamei Haghetaot/Ghetto Fighters' House and Hakibbutz Hameuchad for permission to reprint Yitzhak Katzenelson (1886–1944),

Canto VI, stanzas 1–15, 'Di Ershte' [The First Ones] in 'Dos Lid funem Oysgehargetn Yidishn Folk' [Yiddish: The Song of the Murdered Jewish People] (1945). Translation by Noah H. Rosenbloom (Israel: Beit Lohamei Haghetaot/Ghetto Fighters' House and Hakibbutz Hameuchad Publishing House, 1980).

The Archives of the Ghetto Fighters' House grants one-time permission to reproduce the above excerpt in the initial print edition of the forth-coming book: *Portraits in Literature: The Jews of Poland. An Anthology*. Any further use would require a new application to us: Yossi Shavit, Director of Archives, Ghetto Fighters' House, Western Galilee, Israel. 25 February 2010.

Black Sparrow Press and John Martin, publisher, for Charles Reznikoff, 'Kaddish', *Jewish Frontier* (November 1942), pp.2–5.

The Board of Jewish Education of Greater New York and Barbara Kessel. See Yad Vashem.

Commentary for excerpts from Ziviah Lubetkin, 'The Last Days of the Warsaw Ghetto', *Commentary* (May 1947), p.407.

Anna Cwiakowska for 'The Polish Wife' in Anna Cwiakowska, *Zony I Inne Opowiadania* [Wives and Other Stories] (Lodz: Oficyna Bibliofilow, 1999), pp.7–25.

Dimensions. See Vladka Meed.

The Dora Teitelboim Center for Yiddish Culture, sponsor of *The Last Lullaby: Poetry of the Holocaust*, edited and translated by Aaron Kramer (Syracuse, NY: Syracuse University Press, 1998) for permission to reprint 'The Sweatshop', translated by Aaron Kramer. See also Edgar J. Goldenthal.

Petra Eggers of Eggers and Landwehr KG and Mathilde Kolitz for 'Yossel Rakover's Appeal to God' in Zvi Kolitz, *The Tiger Beneath the Skin: Stories and Parables of the Years of Death* (New York: Creative Age Press, 1947).

Engelking, Anna, see Nina Luszczyk Ilienkowa.

Edgar J. Goldenthal for poems by Morris Rosenfeld in Edgar Goldenthal, *Poet of the Ghetto: Morris Rosenfeld* (Hoboken; Ktav, 1998). Copyright © Edgar Goldenthal 1998: 'Yiddish' translated by Edgar J. Golden-thal; 'The Sweatshop' translated by Aaron Kramer and 'Bread and Tea' translated by Max Rosenfeld.

Michel Grojnowski for Lili Berger, 'The Teacher Reb Mendele'. See Jason Aronson.

Natan Gross and The Judaica Foundation, Center for Jewish Culture and Joachim Russek, director, Judaica Foundation, for 'Cracow Autumn' by Natan Gross, translated by Dr Antony Polonsky in *The Jews of Poland*, edited by Slawomir Kapralski (Cracow: Judaica Foundation, 1999), vol. II, pp.9–11. Copyright Judaica Foundation 1999.

Siegfried Halbreich for 'A Jew in the Polish Army' in Siegfried Halbreich, *Before, During, After* (New York: Vantage Press, 1991). Copyright © Siegfried Halbreich 1991.

Hashomer Hatzair Institute for Research and Documentation, Yad Yaari, Givat Haviva, (Archives) and Dalia Moran for Aliza Melamed, 'From the Diary of a Young Shomeret', Ruszka Korczak, 'A Shomer Pesach in the Ghetto' and to David Amitai for Emanuel Ringelblum, 'Mordecai Anielewicz and His Movement' in *The Massacre of European Jewry; An Anthology* (Kibbutz Merchavia, Israel: World Hashomer Hatzair, English Speaking Department, 1963), pp.180–7, 191–3, 200–6.

Kathryn Hellerstein for 'Olke' and 'The Tale of the Washtub', poems by Kadya Molodowsky, *Paper Bridges: Selected Poems of Kadya Molodowsky*, translated, edited and introduced by Kathryn Hellerstein (Detroit, MI: Wayne State University Press, copyright © Kathryn Hellerstein 1999). See also Litman, Benjamin.

Israel Folktale Archives (IFA) Named in Honor of Dov Noy, University of Haifa, Israel, for 'The Circumcision That Wasn't', told by Aaron Shalit from Poland, in Fishl Sider (collector), *Seven Folktales From Boryslaw*, edited and annotated by Otto Schnitzler (Haifa: Haifa Municipality Ethnological Museum and Folktale Archives, 1968), IFA 2850, Series 19, Story No.1, pp.17–21, and for 'The Recipe of Rabbi Yenuka of Stolin' told by Jacob Rabinovitz from Poland to Yohanan Ben-Zakai, in *A Tale for Each Month, 1967*, edited by Edna Cheichel (Hechal), IFA 7912, Series, 22, Story No.4, pp.60–2, Haifa Municipality Ethnological Museum and Folktale Archives, Haifa, 1968.

The Janusz Korczak Association in Israel and Benjamin Anolik for 'My First Day in the Orphanage' in Israel Zyngman, *Janusz Korczak Bein Ha'yetomim* [Janusz Korczak among the Orphans] (Bnei Brak: Sifriat Poalim, 1979), originally published in Polish (1976).

Jason Aronson Publishers for 'The Teacher Reb Mendele' by Lili Berger in *Great Yiddish Writers of the Twentieth Century*, selected and translated by Joseph Leftwich, foreword by Robert M. Seltzer (Northvale, NJ: Jason Aronson, 1987), pp.543–7. Copyright © Jason Aronson 1969, 1987. See also Michel Grojnowski.

Jewish Currents and Lawrence Bush, editor and publisher of *Jewish Currents*, for permission to reprint the late Yuri Suhl's poem, 'And the Earth Rebelled'. The poem originally appeared in *Jewish Life* (April 1954), the predecessor of *Jewish Currents*, and was reprinted in *The Jewish Life Anthology 1946–1956*, pp.136–8. The permission grants non-exclusive rights to use the poem as part of my work in all languages and for all editions, including electronic rights.

Jewish Frontier for 'Poems of Children from the Warsaw Ghetto', p.26, 'Two Eyewitnesses', pp.14–15, and Charles Reznikoff, 'Kaddish', pp.2–5, *Jewish Frontier* (November 1942). See also Black Sparrow Press.

The Jewish Historical Institute, Warsaw, and Professor Feliks Tych for 'Eyewitness Testimonies, Siedlce, Poland', in E. Karpinski, *Wspomnienia z Okresu Okupacji, Jewish Historical Institute Bulletin*, 1, 149 (1989), pp.66, 70. See also Edward Kopowka. And for permission to reprint 'Shlomo Jelichovski' in J. Leftwich (ed. and trans.), *The Golden Peacock* (New York, London: Thomas Yoeloff, 1961), pp.519–23. Copyright © Barnes and Company 1961.

The Jewish Publication Society for 'The Lamed Vovnik' in Isaac Loeb Perez, *Stories and Pictures*, translated by Helena Frank (Philadelphia, PA: The Jewish Publication Society of America, 1906, repr 1936, 1943, 1947). Copyright the Jewish Publication Society of America 1906.

The Judaica Foundation, Center for Jewish Culture and Joachim Rusek for 'Cracow Autumn' by Natan Gross, translated by Dr Antony Polonsky. See also Natan Gross.

Mathilde Kolitz. See Petra Eggers of Eggers and Landwehr KG for 'Yossel Rakover's Appeal to God'.

Edward Kopowka for the following quotations from *Zydzi Siedleccy* (Siedlce, Poland: 2001), pp.69–70. Published and copyright by Edward Kopowka:

E. Karpinski, *Wspomnienia z Okresu Okupaciji*, Biuletin Zydowskiego Instytutu Historycznego (ZIH), 1, 49 (1989), pp.66, 70. See also Note

196 in Przypisy, *Zydzi Siedleccy*, p.111. Reproduced by permission of the Jewish Historical Institute in Warsaw and by Edward Kopowka.

M.T. Frankowski, J. Staszewski, *Musimy Zydow zniszczyc* in *Tygodnik Siedlecki*, 36 (1986), p.5. See Notes 197, 198 in Przypisy, *Zydzi Siedleccy*, p.111.

Sora E. Landes for Azriel Eisenberg, 'Janusz Korczak Marches to Death With His Children' and Fredka Mazia, 'We Will Not Hand Over the Children Alive', translated by Azriel Eisenberg, in Azriel Eisenberg, *The Lost Generation: Children of the Holocaust* (New York: The Pilgrim Press, copyright © 1982), pp.130–2, 54–7, including notes and sources. See also The Pilgrim Press. 'We Will Not Hand Over the Children Alive' first appeared in *Reim BaSa'ar* [Comrades in the Storm] (Jerusalem: Yad Vashem, 1964), pp.125–9.

Benjamin Litman for the Estate of Kadya Molodowsky, for Kadya Molodowsky, 'Olke' and 'The Tale of the Washtub'. See also Kathryn Hellerstein.

Nina Luszczyk-Ilienkowa and Anna Engelking for 'Ziselman of Honcharska Street' and 'Rivka' in *Regiony*, 1, 96 (2000), pp.14–16, 33–4, and a note by Anna Engelking in *Wiez*, 3, 521 (March, 2002), p.110.

Ludowa Spoldzielnia Wydawnicza and Jerzy Dobrzanski for permission to retell in English a legend from: R. Zmorski, *Podania i Basnie Ludu; wybor i wstep Henryka Syski* (Warsaw: 1956 [1902]). The legend used here originally dates from 1854, and for permission to use the photograph of Eliza Orzeszkowa, and to translate into English, extracts from Eliza Orzeszkowa, 'Ogniwa' (pp.345–64), and by Maria Konopnicka, 'Mendel Gdanski', (pp.189–211) in E. Orzeszkowa, ed. and comp., *Z Jednego Strumienia* (Warsaw: Ludwa Spoldzielnia Wydawnicza, 1960). Originally published by E. Wende I Spolka in 1905.

Vladka Meed and Dr Steven Meed for 'Polish Friends' in *On Both Sides of the Wall*, translated by Dr Steven Meed (New York: Holocaust Library, Vallentine Mitchell, 1979), copyright © Vladka Meed 1979, and Vladka Meed, 'Jewish Resistance in the Warsaw Ghetto', *Dimensions*, 7, 2 (1993), the Anti-Defamation League. Reproduced by kind permission of the author, Vladka Meed, and Dr Steven Meed.

Aharon Megged for 'The Name', *Midstream* (Spring 1960) and *Israel Argosy*, 6, edited by Isaac Halevy-Levin (New York: Thomas Yoseloff,

1959). By kind permission of the author, Aharon Megged. See also Julien Yoseloff and *Midstream*.

Midstream (Spring 1960) for Aharon Megged, 'The Name'.

The Pilgrim Press for 'Janusz Korczak Marches to Death With His Children' and 'We Will Not Hand Over the Children Alive' in Azriel Eisenberg, *The Lost Generation: Children of the Holocaust* (New York: The Pilgrim Press, 1982), pp.130–2, 54–7. English translation copyright © The Pilgrim Press 1982.

Dr Antony Polonsky for the translation of 'Cracow Autumn' by Natan Gross. See also Natan Gross.

Eva Rapkin for translations by Maurice Samuel of Israel Joshua Singer, 'The Bride' and 'The Wedding Night' in I.J. Singer, *The Sinner* (New York: Liveright, 1933), pp.72–86, 59–68. Copyright © Joseph Singer. Reissued as *Yoshe Kalb* by Harper and Row (1965) and Schocken (1988). By permission of Ian J. Singer. And for translations by Maurice Samuel of Sholem Asch, 'The Rebel' and 'The Mother's Reward', in Sholem Asch, *Children of Abraham* (New York: G.P. Putnam's, 1942), pp.107–13, 62–80.

The Reconstructionist and Rabbi Richard Hirsh, editor, for *The Letter of the Ninety-Three Maidens*, translated by Bertha Badt Strauss, including introduction by the editor and note by Dr Dora Edinger, in *The Reconstructionist*, 2 (5 March 1943). Based on a Hebrew version by Hillel Babli in *Hadoar*, XXIII, 12 (22 January 1943), p.186.

Mieczyslaw Rolnicki for extracts from *Krzak Gorejacy* [The Burning Bush. Notes on the Years 1939–1944] (Jerusalem, Lublin: M. Rolnicki przy wspoludziale [with the participation of] Wojewodzkiego Domu Kultury w Lublinie, 1999), Part II: 'Survival on the Aryan Side'. Stories: 'W Bramie', and 'Niemcy i Kolezanka', pp.51–2, 57–8. Copyright Mieczyslaw Rolnicki.

Jack Rosenfeld for Max Rosenfeld's translation of 'And the Earth Rebelled' by Yuri Suhl. For further details see *Jewish Currents* and Beverly Spector. I also thank Jack Rosenfeld for the translation of 'Bread and Tea' by Morris Rosenfeld, in Edgar J. Goldenthal, *Poet of the Ghetto: Morris Rosenfeld* (Hoboken: Ktav Publishing House, 1998), pp.163, 164.

Dr H.B. Segel for selections from Lucjan Dobroszycki, 'Jews in the Polish Clandestine Press', in J. Miegel, R. Scott and H.B. Segel (eds),

Poles and Jews, Myth and Reality in the Historical Context. Proceedings of an International Conference, in Collaboration with the Center for Israel and Jewish Studies, 6–10 March 1983. Sponsored by the Institute on East Central Europe (New York: Columbia University, 1986), pp.279, 280, 281.

The Sholem Asch Estate for permission to reprint 'The Rebel' and 'A Mother's Reward' from Sholem Asch, *Children of Abraham*, translated by Maurice Samuel (New York: G.P. Putnam's, copyright © 1942 by Ruth Shaffer, Moses Asch, John Asch and the representative of John Asch), pp.107–13, 62–80.

Beverly Spector for 'Little Wanda with the Braids', 'Chief Physician Remba' and 'Rosa Robota', including editor's notes and sources, in Yuri Suhl (ed. and trans.), *They Fought Back* (New York: Crown, 1967), pp.51–4, 82–4, 219–25. Copyright © Yuri Suhl 1967. I also thank Beverly Spector for 'And the Earth Rebelled' by Yuri Suhl, translated by Max Rosenfeld, see *Jewish Currents*.

Ian J. Singer for 'The Bride' and 'The Wedding Night' in Israel Joshua Singer, *The Sinner* (New York: Liveright, 1933), reissued as *Yoshe Kalb* by Harper and Row (1965) and Schocken (1988). Copyright © Joseph Singer.

Marek Szukalak, Lodz, Poland; Oficyna Bibliofilow. See Ruth Baum and Anna Cwiakowska.

Leon W. Wells, see the United States Holocaust Memorial Museum.

United States Holocaust Memorial Museum for 'Time of Peace', 'The Hiding Place' and 'Liberation' (pp.12–17; 248–63; 265–8). Selected texts from the updated 1999 edition of the *The Janowska Road*, by Leon Weliczker Wells, published by and used with permission of the US Holocaust Memorial Museum, Washington, DC. Previously published in 1963 by the Macmillan Company as *The Janowska Road* and in 1978 by the Holocaust Library as the *Death Brigade*.

Yad Vashem Publications, Yad Vashem, The Holocaust Martyrs' and Heroes' Remembrance Authority Publications, for: 'Jewish Children on the Aryan Side' by Emmanuel Ringelblum, in *Polish–Jewish Relations During the Second World War*, edited by Dr Joseph Kermish and Dr Shmuel Krakowski (Jerusalem: Yad Vashem Publications, 1974). Including footnotes and a poem by Henryka Lazowert.

Yad Vashem, The Holocaust Martyrs' and Heroes' Remembrance Authority and The Board of Jewish Education of Greater New York for the following selections from *Flame and Fury*, compiled by Yaakov Shilhav, edited by Sara Feinstein, based on a publication of Yad Vashem (New York: The Board of Jewish Education of Greater New York, 1962): Mordecai Anielewicz, 'The Last Wish of My Life Has Been Granted'. Translated by David Kuselewitz, p.31; 'To Arms!' The Proclamation of the Rebels of the Ghetto of Vilna. Translated by David Kuselewitz, pp.43–4; Ella Mahler, 'How Granny Saved Helenka From the Germans', *Yad Vashem Bulletin* (1960), pp.77–9; 'Little Partisans' by Lena Kuchler-Silberman. Translated by David Kuselewitz, pp.62–5; 'Books in the Ghetto' by Rachel Auerbach. Translated by David Kuselewitz, pp.73–5.

Julien Yoseloff, director, and Associated University Presses for 'The Name' by Aharon Megged, *Israel Argosy*, 6, edited by Isaac Halevy-Levin (New York: Thomas Yoseloff, A.S. Barnes, 1959), and for 'Shlomo Jelichovski' by Itzhak Katzenelson in Joseph Leftwich (ed. and trans.), *The Golden Peacock* (New York, London: Thomas Yoseloff, © A.S. Barnes and Company, 1961), pp.519–23.

Praise for *Portraits in Literature: The Jews of Poland*

Finalist, National Jewish Book Awards

'It is a pleasure to comment on this remarkable anthology of important literature from a world that was nearly lost. The editor/translator has compiled a collection that combines the important figures of the canon with surprising and nearly unknown writers, biographers and chroniclers. We cannot get enough of this kind of material in the English speaking world which – sadly – is now the most populous Jewish center in modern life outside of Israel. The translations appear careful and yet imaginative, and the range of literature is stunning.'

Rabbi William Cutter, PhD
Emeritus Professor of Hebrew Literature, Hebrew Union College,
Jewish Institute of Religion, Los Angeles

'This is obviously a labor of love ... I was mesmerized by some of the selections. They give a broad sweep of the portrait of Polish Jewry.'

Deborah E. Lipstadt, PhD
Holocaust historian. Author of *History on Trial* and other books
Dorot Professor of Modern Jewish and Holocaust Studies, Rabbi
Donald Tam Institute for Jewish Studies, Director,
Emory University, Georgia

'An amazing variety of writing is found in these selections: historically informative, heartbreaking, amusing and more. Excellence of writing is their only common denominator. *The Mother's Reward* is touching and implicitly criticizes an elitist education system which is not accessible or of practical value to most people. *The Recipe of Rabbi Yenuka of Stolin* is a folk tale offering an insight of universal value. *My First Day in the Orphanage* and *Liberation* show glimpses of real life during World War II. *In the Catskills,* on the other hand, gives a vigorous and optimistic picture of American Jewish immigrants thriving in their new country. It is heart warming and reassuring. Every emotion is sensitively and skillfully explored in this fascinating anthology.'

Kay Haugaard
Emeritus Professor of Creative Writing,
Pasadena City College, California

'A most meaningful creative literary tapestry of the magnificent center of Jewish culture in Poland, a world of beauty and vibrancy that left an eternal indelible mark on the history of the Jewish people. Hava Ben-Zvi deserves the highest praise for this memorial for a world that was and is no more.'

Sam E. Bloch
President, American Gathering of Holocaust Survivors

'*Portraits in Literature* … is a delightful, comprehensive, and poignant anthology that brings to life the rich culture created by the Jews of Poland. Reading it is a reminder of the riches Hitler attempted to destroy. It is good to be able to recapture some of these riches, and proof that through books like this, the Jewish heritage of gifted writers will stay alive.'

Ruth Gruber
Author of sixteen books, including *Haven, Raquela,* and most recently *Inside My Time: My Journey from Alaska to Israel,* which has received a Pulitzer nomination

'Many people reading about the Holocaust are unaware that the Holocaust was the end of a thousand years of Jewish history in Poland. To them it begins in 1939 and ends with 1945. Your book is exceptional … It was of great interest to me.'

Leon W. Wells
Author of *The Janowska Road*

'Jews have lived in Poland since it was just a region of Slavic pagan tribes. But when the country organized itself and became Christian, it began a thousand-year harassment of its Jewish citizens. For much of that time, the persecution was intermittent and tolerable. But then, in five years starting in 1939, Hitler's army swept in and murdered almost all of the Jews in Poland. Indigenous anti-Semitism created the climate for indifference or collaboration in the country, though there were cases of Poles heroically helping their condemned Jewish compatriots.

Hava Ben-Zvi was one of the few to escape annihilation. In this collection, she rescues stories from her lost homeland and preserves them in English for appreciation by a wide audience. First, she offers tales that paint a varied, touching, and compelling panorama of the bygone world of Polish Jewry. Then she presents accounts of the Holocaust, its horror revealed in first-person intimacy. Finally, she selects stories of survivors adapting to their new lives in Israel and the United States.

Every one of these pieces is powerful in itself. Gathered together in Ben-Zvi's anthology, they stand as testament to the vibrant Jewish culture that once thrived in Poland. This book is a unique resource not only for those exploring Jewish heritage, but for anyone who seeks to understand the overall history of Europe.'

Irene E. McDermott
Librarian, Crowell Public Library, San Marino, California,
author of *The Librarian's Internet Survival Guide*

Ben-Zvi has selected some of the most affecting and enlightening passages from her remarkably diverse source material, and she makes them even more meaningful by providing her own annotations and illuminations. For example, she begins with a passage from Sholem Asch's novel 'The Rebel,' and she introduces the once-revered Yiddish writer to a new generation of readers who know little or nothing about him or his work. She points out that his novels about the life of Jesus, intended to show 'the common roots of Judaism and Christianity and to bridge the gap between them', resulted in a charge of apostasy. 'Misunderstood, he defended himself for the rest of his life', she points out, 'mostly without success' ...

'Jewish literature and culture did not perish from the face of the earth', Ben-Zvi concludes. 'Inherited and transformed by a new generation of writers, it was reborn, changed and enriched, finding new configurations, images and expressions'. Ben-Zvi's beautiful and stirring book is a superb example of the same phenomenon.

Jonathan Kirsch, *The Jewish Journal*, September 2011

One of its main strengths, aside from the selection of distinctive texts and emphasis on Jewish life and creativity in Poland, is the volume's foregrounding of stories by women and about female characters before, during, and after World War II. Most importantly, the book emphasizes the rich and long history of Polish Jewish literature and particularly its rebirth in the aftermath of World War II. It is indeed undoubtedly true, as Bromberg Ben-Zvi's *Portraits in Literature: The Jews of Poland* powerfully illustrates, that Polish Jewish culture did not perish, but changed and found new avenues of expression.

Justine Pas, Lindenwood University, *H-Judaic*, May 2012

This anthology, which could be subtitled 'Beyond Tevye', gives a broad picture of life in Poland from the late 19th century to contemporary times. Divided into three chronological sections which basically cover the pre-war, Holocaust, and post-war time periods, this collection contains stories, essays, letters, poems, memoirs and other literary forms. The topics cover many aspects of daily life and life cycle events as well as politics and war ... Hava Ben-Zvi has provided a note giving biographical information about the author and the context of each piece and a very informative introduction. This finalist for the National Jewish Book Award is highly recommended.

Sheryl Stahl, Hebrew Union College,
Association of Jewish Libraries, February–March 2012

The book – a finalist in the prestigious 2011 National Jewish Book Awards – is a collection of 56 short stories, eyewitness accounts, poetry, essays, folk tales and humor from a variety of Polish Jews from the 1800s to the present. ... it includes both fiction and nonfiction pieces she found in libraries in the U.S. and Israel that are accompanied by Ben-Zvi's own astute observations. Selecting the writings was not an easy task since Polish Jews were quite literate and prolific, she said. 'I needed stories that truly reflected their conditions, their problems, their joys and sorrows', she said. 'I didn't just pick any story. A story to me had to speak to the heart.'

Brenda Gazzar, *Pasadena Star News*, January 2012

The editor, Hava Bromberg Ben-Zvi, survived World War II in Poland and came to Israel in 1946, thus experiencing the challenges and joy of the new State of Israel. Her choice of writings and stories recaptures this unique period of Jewish history with unforgettable literary memories and emotional power.

Jewish Book World, Spring 2012

Introduction

My Jewish ancestors resided in Polish lands for approximately one thousand years. This book is the saga of Jewish life in Poland as reflected in the mirror of literature, and is an attempt to illuminate, through literary works, some of the conditions, joys, difficulties and sorrows of Jewish life and culture in the Polish homeland throughout a millennium. This anthology reflects different facets of the relationship between Jews and Poles, which began with reluctant acceptance and ended, tragically, with the almost complete annihilation of Polish Jewry by the German National Socialists during the Second World War. The Jewish community of that time suffered a tragic blow, even though there are some signs of resurgence of Jewish life today. Most of the selections reflect the Jewish perspective on the events described.

Speaking in many voices, including those of women and children, survivors and descendants, the collection brings together memoirs, short stories, poetry, eyewitness reports, fragments of novels, essays, letters, folktales and humour, reflecting life in this magnificent cradle of Jewish learning and culture. The works of writers, mostly Jewish but also Polish, well known and new, strive to present a true, valid, readable and compelling panorama of life as it was, ending with tales of rebirth and renewal in our own time.

In 1939 Poland had a Jewish population numbering approximately 3.5 million people. Not more than approximately 3 per cent survived the Second World War and lived to see its end in May 1945. It is accepted by historians that about six million Jewish men, women and children perished during the Holocaust years. Few stop to think that over three million, or half of those who died, were the Jews of Poland; their legacy lives on through their writings. I was one of those who survived.

It is difficult to determine precisely the date when Jews first arrived in Poland. Written evidence testifies to a Jewish presence in Polish lands as early as the twelfth century, but historians believe that Jewish traders travelled through Poland as early as the tenth century, predating Poland's acceptance of Christianity in 966, and before it was actually constituted as a nation.

In legendary tradition, the Jews resided in Poland as early as the ninth century, and were instrumental in the selection and crowning of Piast, the first king of Poland (even though, in fact, the Piast dynasty did not appear on the historical scene until the beginning of the tenth century).

KINGS, PRIESTS, PEASANTS, MERCHANTS, INVADERS AND DAILY REALITIES

The Jews came to Poland from the east, south and west, escaping the eleventh-, twelfth- and thirteenth-century crusades, the expulsion from France in 1306, and surviving the Black Death, a bubonic plague which spread over Europe during the fourteenth century, and for which Jews were blamed and persecuted. They came following the massacres in Germany between 1298 and 1348, the massacres in Christian Spain, and the expulsion from Spain in 1492.

Poland, a primarily agricultural land, needed commerce, banking and an infusion of capital. The kings were generally supportive of the Jews, beginning with Boleslaw V the Pious, of Kalish. He accepted the wanderers and issued a writ (their charter) in 1264, establishing the Jews as a people whose main business was to be moneylending against pledges. In spite of the king's apparently good intentions, designating the Jews as primarily moneylenders limited their options for economic survival and set the stage for future resentment and persecution.

These charters were generally preserved and sometimes expanded by future kings, and granted the Jews the rights to travel throughout Poland, to govern themselves and have their own schools and their own judicial system, to observe their religious customs, to engage in trade and not to be subjected to slavery or serfdom. Some scholars believe, however, that these protective measures isolated the Jews and laid the groundwork for their separation from the general community. In the early years of their life in Poland the Jews were peddlers, reaching villages located far from trading centres, and also acted as money-lenders, merchants, artisans, and were frequently employed by the wealthy nobility as tax collectors, lease holders of their lands (*arendars*), and tavern keepers. This meant that they frequently serving as a bridge, mediating between the landowners and the peasants, absorbing the hostility and resentment meant for their employers. But even the kings could not protect the Jews from attacks by the Church, the burgher-merchants, Christian artisans, the peasants and foreign invaders.

Records as early as 1267 reveal the Polish Church Council acting with hostility toward the Jews, aiming to isolate the 'abominable' Jews from the community, not only spiritually and socially, but literally, by establishing walls surrounding Jewish settlements. This attitude and practice was followed by subsequent Church Councils. To strengthen the Church, non-Christians could not be permitted to live together with Christians in peace, as friends and neighbours. In the fifteenth century the powerful Cardinal Zbigniew Olesnicki personally wrote a threatening letter to King Casimir IV Jagello about the Jews, the power and concerns of the Church, and the limited powers of the monarch, thus successfully urging the sovereign to repeal the Jewish charter.[1]

The insecure position of the Jews, exposed as they were to attacks, is most clearly demonstrated in their having to wear on their clothing a mark which identified them as Jews. Subsequent kings were more flexible and tolerant, as reflected in the decision of King Sigismund I, in 1564, that the Jews did not need to wear any longer the shameful identifying mark.

The peasants saw the Jew only as a peddler, a merchant and a tax collector – in a word, a parasite who did not work but lived off others who tilled the soil. The merchants regarded the Jew as an unwanted competitor; violent attacks, massacres and expulsions from the cities were not uncommon. Even though the conditions have changed, this unfavourable image of the Jew has persisted until our day.

And yet, for centuries, Poland was a safer and a better place to live than neighbouring countries; the Jews often had no other place to go, and in spite of all the hostility and barriers confronting them, they prospered economically and grew in numbers. Limited primarily to business contacts with Polish society, the Jews remained within their own communities, and focused on their religion and culture. The Jewish councils exercised considerable power over their people, attempting to guard the good name of Jewish merchants so as to ensure good relations with the wider, Christian community.

Jewish learning flourished, and Talmudic scholars residing in Poland were known far and wide. Jews were also engaged in the study of secular subjects such as medicine and science. The publication of Hebrew texts developed, and Poland became a great centre of Jewish culture, renowned for its *yeshivot* (academies of Jewish religious learning) and its scholars such as Moses Isserles of Cracow (1525–72) and Shalom Shakhna of Lublin, Solomon Luria of Lublin (1510–73), Eliezer ben Elijah Ashkenazi (1513–86) and many others. This proliferation of scholars gave rise to many religious disputes within the Jewish community; tensions and serious conflicts arose between orthodoxy and modernism, the *Haskalah* (Enlightenment) and the old-fashioned, Orthodox ways, the educated and the unlearned, the rationalists and the mystics, the rich and the poor. Particularly painful was the schism between *Hasidism* and its *Mitnagdim* (Opponents), who represented the Enlightenment. Hasidism (an eighteenth century movement) emphasized devotion, love of God, joy and purity of soul, rather than the pursuit of scholarship, which was the traditional Jewish attitude. After centuries of Talmudic *pilpul* (hair-splitting scholarly debates), Church persecution and scorn by their own Maskilim (Enlightened Ones), and especially after the Chmielnicki massacres, the impoverished Jewish masses flocked to this Hasidic message of hope.

In 1648 Bogdan Chmielnicki led an uprising of the Cossack and Ukrainian minorities against the Polish landowners, the Catholic Church and the Jews, resulting in the murder of hundreds of thousands of Jews and the total destruction of hundreds of Jewish communities.

Despite virulent opposition by the Jewish scholarly establishment, the Hasidic movement became widespread and powerful.

THE POLITICAL CONTEXT

Poland, geopolitically, was a nation that found itself perpetually threatened by its more powerful neighbours throughout the centuries, and suffered repeated invasion and partition at the hands of Russia, Prussia and Germany in 1772, 1793 and 1795. These partitions of Poland and the redrawing of borders profoundly affected Jewish life, since Russia imposed severe restrictions on Jews, their activities, their areas of permitted residence and even their freedom to travel. Raids carried out by Ukrainians and Cossacks left deep wounds upon the Polish landscape and people, and the Jews again became scapegoats, suffering repeated massacres. The Poles, humiliated and defeated, staged several revolts against the occupying powers. Many Jewish patriots fought on the side of the Poles, and for a while there were hopes of brotherhood, of a better relationship between the two communities and of a better future.

Sholem Asch (1880–1957), in his novel *Salvation* (1934), described the spirit of the times.[2] While repressive measures and endless arrests by the Russian invaders caused resentment, pain and sorrow, there was also a nationwide call for unity between all classes of society – the nobility, peasantry and the Jews. A recognition dawned that unity might bring victory against the hated Russian regime. But with defeat of the Polish uprising of 1831, and the consequent general disillusionment, anti-Semitism again raised its ugly head.

THE FINAL DECADES OF POLISH JEWRY

The end of the First World War in 1918 brought Poland independence. Between the years 1918 and 1939 the 'Jewish Question' became a common topic and pressing concern within Poland. In essence, the question was: What to do about the Jews? The rise of nationalism, and, consequently, increased anti-Semitism brought a series of punitive measures and even outright attacks on the Jews, such as boycotts of Jewish businesses, exclusion from employment in state-controlled institutions and monopolies such as the sale of tobacco and many others. The Jewish community endeavoured to improve their conditions, but to no avail. In spite of Jewish representation in the Polish *Sejm* (parliament) a spirit of hopelessness and futility prevailed, and emigration to Eretz Israel (the Land of Israel) increased.

Within Poland the majority of Jewish shopkeepers and artisans lived in poverty, practised Orthodox Judaism and spoke Yiddish as their everyday language; Polish, for them, was effectively an 'outside' language, used primarily for the purposes of commerce. But this period, from 1919 to 1939, also saw the rise of a Jewish middle class. Mostly professional and liberal, fluent in Polish, they became active in many areas of life including commerce, medicine, law, education, literature and the arts.

This assimilation, however, did not bring acceptance; they were, at different times, by unspoken or overt agreement, excluded from many areas of employment and social opportunities. There were, of course, exceptions. Never to be forgotten are those among the Polish population who later risked their own lives during the German occupation from 1939 to 1945 to help the Jews. Maria Dabrowska, in 'On a Beautiful Summer Morning' describes the execution of three women, two Christians and a Jew, for sheltering a Jew and an Englishman.[3] Jews and Poles had much in common: they were subject to the same global developments such as depressions, wars, pestilence and other natural and man-made disasters. By 1939 many shared a common language, a taste in clothing, food, literature, and art, and a common Judeo-Christian tradition of ethics and philosophical perceptions of right and wrong.

And yet there persisted a deep divide between Jews and Poles. In the common Polish perception, there was something loathsome and shameful about being a Jew. So much so, that the word 'Jew' was, and regrettably I believe still is, an insult in Poland, loaded with contempt. This deep-seated antipathy was supremely evident during the days of the Holocaust, when the Jewish population was annihilated by a foreign power.

There is no question that the destruction of the Polish Jews was caused by the occupying German power. But during our darkest hour, in 1942, when over 300,000 Jews had been deported to their death in Treblinka, a right-wing Polish underground paper, *Do Broni* [To Arms] had this to say: 'The Germans and the Jews have set the world afire. Therefore they must burn together.'[4] Another right wing paper, *Barykada* [The Barricade], in 1943: 'The liquidation of the Jews on Polish soil is of great significance for our future development, since it will free us from several million parasites. The Germans have greatly aided us in this matter.'[5]

Even a major mainstream Polish underground newspaper, *Narod* [The Nation] issued by the Christian Democrats in 1942 opined as follows:

> The Jewish question is now a burning issue. We must tell ourselves that the Jews cannot regain the political rights and the property they have lost. Moreover, they must in the future entirely leave the territories of our country. The matter is complicated by the fact that once we demand that the Jews leave Poland, we will not be able to tolerate them in the territories of Slavic nations. This means we have to have all of Central and Southern Europe cleansed of the Jewish element, which amounts to removing some eight to nine million Jews.[6]

However, other voices, even though a minority, were also to be heard. Czeslaw Milosz, the poet and future Nobel Prize winner, never forgave himself for not doing more to help the condemned Jews. He felt poetry was meaningless unless it served to save people. Much has been written about the merry-go-round and the music playing on the Krasinski Square in 1943, while across the wall the Ghetto was burning. To this, Milosz's Campo di Fiori is an unforgettable testimony.[7]

While the war was still raging, Zofia Nalkowska, a writer and novelist, and a member of the International Committee to Investigate Nazi Crimes, took part in an inspection of a special Nazi building in Poland, part of an Anatomical Institute. In *Medallions* (1947), a factual report, she described the abundant supply of corpses and separate human heads, the scientific machinery to extract fat from human bodies to produce soap, the processing of human skin for further use, and the matter-of-fact, calm testimony of witnesses who explained that, at that time, Germany needed fats.[8] This document needs no further comment.

The final exodus from Poland of most of the remnants of Jews who had survived the Holocaust was in 1968, following a virulent anti-Semitic campaign by the then communist government. At that time Jewish communal life in Poland had practically ceased to exist.

REFLECTIONS OF JEWISH LIFE IN LITERATURE

Jews were, and continue to be, a literate people, and culture, grounded in religious belief, has included, since ancient times, both oral and written records. The Jewish population of Eastern Europe, including Poland, was familiar with the Bible, biblical commentaries and exegesis, the Talmud, literal or homiletic translations of biblical tales into Yiddish. The *Tze'enah U-Re'enah* by Jacob Ashkenazi (1550–1620) of Yanov, Poland, deserves special tribute. A homiletic, warm translation into Yiddish of biblical narratives, it also included *midrashim* (commentaries), moral instructions, legends, historical events and proverbs. Beloved especially by women (and so known as the 'Women's Torah'), the *Tze'enah U-Re'enah* has survived and contributed to the Judaic education and entertainment of generations of children.

Also well known were rabbinical written responses to questions in all areas of Jewish life and thought, Hebrew and Yiddish liturgical literature (prayers), biographical works, wisdom literature and the Passover *Haggadah*. There were records of travel, memoirs, historical literature and drama, mysticism, romances and proverbs. There was poetry, drawing on religious and secular themes such as return to the Promised Land, hymns, love poems, morality books, parables and folk tales. One of the most notable texts from the folk literature was *The Ma'aseh Book*, an anthology of Jewish folk tales, its first-known edition published in 1602 in Basel. The tales, based on the Talmud, the *midrash* and authentic Jewish historical experience incorporated motifs absorbed from foreign folk literature. Jewish traders travelling between the east and the west, from India, Persia and Greece into Europe, contributed to the dissemination, transmission and mutual adaptation of tales to different environments, including their own.

Although few manuscripts of the thirteenth, fourteenth and fifteenth centuries have been preserved, Gutenberg's invention of printing by moveable type in the late fifteenth century wrought a cultural revolution and contributed to the availability of books and to the flowering of literature in the centuries that followed.

But it was not until the nineteenth century that talented writers, influenced by the Jewish Enlightenment movement, developed a genuinely Jewish literature worthy of world attention.

The founding fathers of Yiddish literature in Poland were Mendele Mokher Seforim (pseudonym of Shalom Jacob Abramowitsch, 1836–1917), Shalom Aleichem (pseudonym of Shalom Rabinovitz, 1859–1916) and Isaac Leib Peretz (1852–1915). After some initial attempts to write in Hebrew and (by Peretz) in Polish, these writers chose to express themselves in Yiddish, writing with familiarity and great sympathy about and for the Jewish masses, who adored them. This bond of appreciation between Jewish authors and their popular audience remains an enduring element of Yiddish literature. They were followed by giants such as Sholem Asch, Israel Joshua Singer, his brother Isaac B. Singer, David Pinski, David Bergelson and many others.

Anti-Semitism was endemic in Poland throughout most of its history, and this was inevitably reflected in the national literature. There were, however, periods when Polish writers presented positive images of Jews as honourable people, and sometimes as Polish patriots, and this was particularly the case during the nineteenth century. The leading example of a Jew as a Polish patriot and fighter is the image of Jankiel, the inn keeper in the epic poem *Pan Tadeusz* by the Polish poet Adam Mickiewicz (1798–1855); some even suggest that Jankiel is the real hero and subject of *Pan Tadeusz*.[9]

But the relationships were complex, and echoes of this ambiguity found expression in the works of numerous writers. J. Ignatius Kraszewski in *The Clever Woman or Jermola* (1891) presents an image of Szmula, the tavern keeper, a common Jewish occupation, as seen by the peasants he served:

> At first sight, this grave descendant of Israel was very pleasing, with his long beard and hair, his regular features, his serious and winning expression. One had a desire to study him closely, and to believe in his honesty. Nevertheless, his beauty and the sweet expression of his eyes were, as is so often the case, deceptive.
>
> In fact, there could be no more insatiable vampire, no more greedy blood-sucker, than the worthy Szmula of the village of

Popielnia. The constantly increasing profits earned by his deceit and tact did not render him above turning to account the smallest opportunities. Besides his bills of a thousand *roubles* and his coupons of government bonds, he deposited without shame in his chest the big copper money bathed with the sweat of the wretched peasants; and puffed up by his position and his wealth, he treated the poor villagers as though they were beasts of burden, and fleeced them without mercy.

The result was that when the villagers had any business to transact, they preferred to do so secretly, with the poorer Jews, who lived in the little town; and this aroused the deepest resentment in Szmula. He could not forgive them for being unwilling to allow him to cheat them.[10]

The 'bad Jew' depicted here is balanced by the reference to 'the poorer Jews' whom the peasants or villagers could trust. Kraszewski, one of the foremost Polish writers, must have been well acquainted with Jewish life, for we see, in *Zyd* [The Jew] (1890), an idyllic picture of the Sabbath in a Jewish home, as still practised by religious Jews today. The hero of *The Jew*, Jacob, an observant Jew, was nevertheless a Polish patriot, involved in underground political action, devoted to his homeland. He is the ideal 'Israelite', a model to follow. [11]

Sholem Asch (1880–1957) in *Salvation* (1934, 1951) described from the Jewish perspective the relationship between the Polish nobility and the Jewish tenant and tavern keeper in their service:

Shloyme-Wolf Pokrzywy (nettles) was Count Wydawski's only contact with the world outside his castle. Pokrzywy (nettles) was not his real name. It was a name bestowed upon him by his master.

Shloyme-Wolf fulfilled the function of an adviser and a counselor in estate management, delivered news, and was the trusted recipient of confidential, private information even about family members, interested only in the Count's health, all waiting for his death. The Jew was also a convenient, silent and helpless target of curses, humiliation and abuse, whenever needed and convenient.[12]

Eliza Orzeszkowa (c.1841–1910) was the author of *Meir Ezofovitch* (1898),[13] in which the hero, Meir, wishes to liberate himself from outdated Jewish prejudices, and is defeated by the rabbi and the Jewish community. In the same work, the young Polish lord of Kamionka tries to meet the rabbi of Szybow, only to discover that the acclaimed rabbi speaks only Yiddish, and that his followers live in a world of their own, unaware and unknowing of the culture surrounding them. The young lord of Kamionka leaves disappointed, surprised and angry, and his feelings are reciprocated by the rabbi's faithful followers.

Eliza Orzeszkowa was a distinguished Polish writer, a member of the nobility, and a proponent of the Positivism movement, who dedicated her life and work to promoting understanding among different social classes and minorities. Her *Ogniwa* [Links in a Chain] and other novellas speak eloquently in defence of the Jews, at a time of a rising tide of anti-Semitism and violent anti-Jewish riots in Warsaw. In fact, her defence of the Jews resulted in her being 'accused' of being herself a Jew!

Boleslaw Prus, a Polish writer (pseudonym of Aleksander Glowacki (1845–1912), in *Placowka* [The Outpost], originally published in 1885, describes a poor Jew, Yoyna Nietoperz, who comes to the aid of an unfortunate peasant, Slimak, who, attempting to hold on to his land, has reached the very end of his resources and hope.

> It was Yoyna Nietoperz, the poorest Jew in the neighborhood, who never had a thing, living with his big family in a small hut, half buried in earth, who traveled to the village hoping to find some work: patching cloths, running errands.
>
> He heard Slimak's thirsty cow lowing in distress, saw the two inert figures in the barn and understood the poor peasant's fate. Watering Slimak's cow, he rushed to the village to report the death of Slimak's wife and his dire condition. The poorest Jew, who dreamed about having a goat, was the one to experience a deep, profound compassion, and to call for help.[14]

In *Lalka* [The Doll] (1890) Boleslaw Prus realistically describes the prevailing emotions of his time at the turn of the century. He focuses on life in Warsaw, and the relations and conflicts between the nobility, the merchants and the Jews. The weak economy fuelled hostilities, and even the ancient fraud about the Jews killing Christian children for their blood to use in the baking of Passover matzot was still current. The author's sentiments, revulsion and empathy with the maligned Jews are clear.[15]

And what of our own times? Perceptions change slowly, especially those sanctioned by religion; they may bear little relation to actuality, but in the end can determine our feelings, reactions and sometimes our destiny. Many works written in Poland since the Second World War portray agonized, troubling images of Jews and Poles, and suggest, perhaps, the universality of human behaviour and the propensity for good or evil within us. Even though losses among the non-Jewish population in German-occupied Poland have been estimated at some 2.5 million lives, the realities undergone by Jews and Poles were vastly different, and their experiences and fates defy comparison. This anthology presents primarily the Jewish perspective.

Following the Second World War there has been a notable revival of Jewish literature in Poland. Among the new generation of writers identifying themselves as Jews are Hanna Krall, Henryk Grynberg, Ida Fink, Stanislaw Wygodzki and many others. Their themes reflect the authors' Jewish roots, and often portray the Holocaust years, frequently based on personal experience in all its pain and anguish, including images of childhood and life in the post-war years. These writers mirror the conflicts inherent in being a Jew who also embraces Polish language and culture. Particularly poignant are the images of Holocaust survivors in their encounters with the Polish community; these may portray endless cruelties, but they also demonstrate examples of the selfless courage of those who risked their lives to shelter their Jewish brothers and sisters.

Today the Jews of Poland are few, some living under assumed names; the Polish diaspora has ceased to exist. There is some evidence of rebirth and renewal of Jewish life, however miniscule, in the form of schools, synagogues, Jewish cultural festivals in Warsaw and Cracow, in commerce, and in diplomatic and other relations with Israel. A museum chronicling over a thousand years of Jewish history in Poland is scheduled to open in 2011 on the site of the former Umschlagplatz, the gathering point near railroad tracks for deportation to Auschwitz and other deadly destinations. Are these signs of a new page being written in the complex, tortured and multi-layered history of Polish–Jewish relationships? I hope that this book will help, in a small way, to recapture and preserve, through its selection of poetry and prose, the memory of a rich life that is no more.

I have used a number of criteria for inclusion in this anthology: authenticity of characters, problems and conditions; a realistic portrayal of relationships within the Jewish community and between Jews and Poles; authenticity of feelings, especially under trying conditions; literary merit; the availability of copyright heirs and the cost of permissions.

May this work bring pride and pleasure to its readers, and the realization that in spite of all that was lost, Jewish literature and culture did not perish from the face of the earth. Inherited and transformed by a new generation of writers, it was reborn, changed and enriched, finding new configurations, images and expressions in other parts of the world, especially in Israel and in a new, very receptive nation – the United States of America.

Translations from Polish, Hebrew and Yiddish are the work of many individuals, including myself.

NOTES

1. Szugski (ed.), 'Monumenta Mediaevi, Codex Epistolaris s. XV, T. II past posterior p.147', in *Encyclopaedia Judaica* (Jerusalem: Keter, 1972), vol.13, p.715, Poland.

2. S. Asch, *Salvation*, translated by W. and E. Muir (New York: G.P. Putnam's, 1934).

3. M. Dabrowska, 'On a Beautiful Summer Morning', in A. Gillon and Krzyzanowski (eds), *Introduction to Modern Polish Literature. An Anthology of Fiction and Poetry* (New York: Twayne, 1964), pp.150–69.

4. L. Dobroszycki, 'The Jews in the Polish Clandestine Press, 1939–1945', in J. Miegiel, R. Scott and H.B. Segel (eds), *Proceedings of the Conference on Poles and Jews: Myth and Reality in the Historical Context* (New York: Institute on East Central Europe, Columbia University, 1986), pp.275–86. Reproduced by kind permission of Dr H.B. Segel.

5. *Barykada*, in Dobroszycki, 'The Jews in the Polish Clandestine Press, 1939–1945'.

6. *Narod*, in ibid.

7. C. Milosz, 'Campo di Fiori', in Gillon and Krzyzanowski (eds), *Introduction to Modern Polish Literature*, p.447.

8. Z. Nalkowska, *Medallions*, in Gillon and Krzyzanowski (eds), *Introduction to Modern Polish Literature*, pp.130–6.

9. A. Mickiewicz, *Pan Tadeusz* (with translation by K. MacKenzie) (New York: Hippocrene Books, 1992).

10. J.I. Kraszewski, *A Clever Woman or Jermola*, translated by M. Carey (New York: The American News Company, 1891), pp.62–3.

11. J.I. Kraszewski, *Zyd*, translated by L. Kowalewska (New York: Dodd, Mead, 1890).

12. Asch, *Salvation*, pp.98–9, 115–16.

13. E. Orzeszkowa, *Meir Ezofovitch* (New York: W.L. Allison, 1898).

14. B. Prus, *Placowka* [The Outpost] (London: M.I. Kolin, 1941), pp.256–9.

15. B. Prus, *Lalka* [The Doll] (New York: Twayne, 1972).

The Jews of Poland in Legendary Tradition

Legendary tradition places Jews in Polish lands at an early date. There is a ninth-century legend about a poor Jewish gunpowder merchant (and some believe just a dust-covered peddler), Abraham Prochownik, who was to become the king of Poland.[1] Roman Zmorski, (1822–1867), a Polish poet, folktale collector and ethnographer, preserved the Jewish version of this tale about the beginnings of the Jewish presence in Poland:

> After the death of the cruel King Popiel who was eaten by mice and rats (they mistook him for a slab of lard), the nobles of Poland gathered in Kruszwica to elect a new king.
>
> They debated and debated, ate and drank, but could reach no agreement. Each one of the nobles believed he was eminently qualified and deserving to be king. They continued feasting till the food ran out. Then, the eldest and wisest of them said:
>
> 'Let us leave the decision to heavens. Let the first man to enter the gates of our town in the morning be our king.' The suggestion was enthusiastically accepted.
>
> The next morning a poor Jew, Abraham Prochownik, a gunpowder merchant, came through the gates at dawn.
> He was met by nobility and city officials dressed in white robes, with bells ringing, banners waving and songs.
>
> 'Long live the king.' They sang, and joyfully informed our ancestor he was to be the new king of Poland.
>
> Poor Abraham, frightened and astonished, knew he had no chance of escaping. The day of coronation drew near.
>
> 'I cannot be your king', he pleaded. 'I cannot fight.'
>
> 'If you cannot fight', they responded, 'then there will be no war.'

'I need time to pray and ask Adonai, our God, for guidance.'

They built a small shelter in the center of town. Abraham, in seclusion, contemplated his fate.

As a king, he thought, I could build a house with windows so high, no stone could reach them. I could have sweet noodle kugel and fish with eggs, as on the Feast of Tabernacles, every day.

The nobles waited and waited. Three days and three nights have passed, and Abraham failed to emerge from his shelter. Then Piast, a tall, strong, handsome farmer declared:

'Brothers, we can wait no longer. We cannot be without a king.' He took an axe, and broke the door.

Abraham took Piast by the hand.

'Piast is your king!' he announced to the waiting assembly. 'He was wise to wait no longer, and brave enough to break the door. He will rule wisely and kindly. He is your king. Remember this, and be thankful to Adonai, our God and to Abraham Prochownik.'

And so it was.[2]

The Piast dynasty ruled Poland for approximately five hundred years, ending with Kazimierz III (the Great) in 1370. Even though the story allegedly dates from the ninth century, according to historical records, the first kings of the Piast dynasty ascended to the throne not earlier than the beginning of the tenth century.

The legend reflects the fears and insecurity of the Jew's position in Poland. Abraham Prochownik is anxious to prove his harmlessness and lack of ambition. He is modest, wise and unable to fight, a truly non-threatening, ideal stranger. He knows 'his place'. The legend also hints at Jewish presence in Poland since times long past.

Another legend tells about Jewish refugees from Spain, expelled in 1492, arriving in Poland dust-covered and weary, seeking shelter in a dark, dense forest. A heavenly voice was heard: '*Po–Lin*', meaning, in Hebrew, 'Here, rest for the night.' They heard the message, stayed in Poland, and named the land 'Po-lin', in Yiddish and Hebrew.

But the most poignant and prophetic legend tells of Jews, arriving from Germany in the days of the second ruler of the House of Piast, humbly requesting asylum:

'We have a drought in the land', said the ruler, following the advice of his courtiers. 'If you can, through you prayers, bring us rain, you will be allowed to stay.' The Jews, wrapped in their prayer shawls, devoutly prayed through the night. Their prayers were heard in heaven, and the rains came, blessing the parched Polish lands. The Jews were permitted to stay.

This legend seems to foretell the fragility and insecurity of the Jewish millennium in Poland.

NOTES

1. Prochownik: derived from the Polish word *proch* for ashes and gunpowder, it perhaps refers to the traveller's dusty (unassuming) clothing or to gunpowder, any mixture of light power explosives.
2. R. Zmorski (Zamarski), *Podania I Basnie Ludu* (Warsaw: Ludowa Spoldzielnia Wydawnicza, 1902, 1956). The legend used in this retelling was originally published in 1854.

Part I
Our World of Yesterday

1

The Rebel

SHOLEM ASCH

Excerpts from a Novel

The mother came stormily out of the bride's room and fixed her blazing eyes on her husband, who was seated at the dinner table rolling breadcrumbs and waiting to say grace.

'You go talk to her! I haven't an ounce of strength left.'

'Rachel Leah the mother, Rachel Leah the educator of children!' muttered the husband, speaking of his wife instead of to her. 'The whole world's going to laugh at you! The whole world will point at you.'

'At me!' shrieked the mother. 'Oh, no, not at me. At *you*. Why didn't *you* stay home and bring the children up? Where were *you* all the time? It's you they'll laugh at.'

'Quiet, woman!' said the husband, sternly. 'Is this a time to stand there quarreling with me?'

'What shall we do, Menasseh, what shall we do?' wailed the mother.

'Bethink yourself, woman! There is a God in heaven! We shall go in once more to our daughter and plead with her not to disgrace us before the whole world.'

The father rose from the table and went into his daughter's room, his wife following him. On the little sofa near the window sat a girl of eighteen. Her hands clutched wildly at her thick, black hair in which she was hiding her face. The girl must have been weeping, for her breast rose and fell, but no sound came from her. On the bed opposite her were laid out the white silk wedding dress, the black silk dress for the visit to the synagogue, and the black woolen dress for everyday wear – all three delivered that morning by the trousseau-tailor. Near the bed stood a woman, with a pair of scissors in her hand, and at her feet lay several open boxes with wigs in them.

'Hannah, daughter, how shall we live down the shame of it?' began the father. 'How shall we show our faces among people?'

No reply came from the girl. The father changed his tone.

'Look at her!' he said. 'Menassah Gross's daughter! Genendel Freindel's daughter wasn't too high and mighty to cut her hair off for her marriage and wear a wig. But Menassah Gross's daughter thinks it beneath her. Why?'

And as the girl did not answer, the mother took up the theme.

'Yes, indeed! Genendel Freindel's daughter is more educated than you, her parents gave her a larger dowry, she has every reason in the world to be stuck up. But *she* didn't refuse to cut her hair off.'

Still there was no answer.

The father went back to his first tone.

'See, daughter', he implored, 'what you are doing to us. How much labor and worry and love it cost us to bring you up and to reach this day, which should be a day of fulfillment and rejoicing for us, your parents. And now you would turn our rejoicing into mourning, and our fulfillment into disaster. Is there no fear of God in your heart? We shall be put under the ban! Decent folk won't talk to us! And your husband-to-be will leave you! He will scurry away from this town as fast as his legs will carry him.'

'That's enough foolishness, daughter', the mother seconded her husband, half in command, half in entreaty. She picked out a wig from one of the open boxes and approached her daughter. 'Try this wig on, child! The color is exactly the color of your hair' – and she laid the wig awry on her daughter's head.

The eighteen-year-old girl felt the weight of the wig on her head. She unclenched one hand, felt the top of her head with it, and shuddered. Among her own, soft, smooth, living hair was the stiff, cold hair of the wig. One thought kept hammering in her young brain. 'Whose hairs were those? Where now is the head from which they were shorn?' She was filled with horror, as if she had touched an unclean thing. Suddenly she grabbed at the wig, flung it to the floor, and ran out of the room.

The parents stared at each other dumbly.

*   *   *

The morning after the wedding the bridegroom's mother rose early and unpacked the wig and the hat which she had brought with her from her home as a present for her new daughter-in-law. With these in one hand and a pair of scissors in the other, she made her way to the bride's room to prepare her for breakfast.

But she remained standing outside, for the bride had locked the door and would let no one in.

The bridegroom's mother, scandalized and terrified, ran off to find her husband who was still asleep, along with ten or fifteen others – cousins, uncles, brothers, and in-laws of all degrees – after the exhausting festivities of the previous day. She banged on the door where these were all asleep, until her husband sorted himself out and answered he was coming. She went in search of the bridegroom, who had left the bridal chamber early. He was of the same age as the bride, a timid youth, his lips still wet with his mother's milk. Knowing of the scandal that was brewing, and unable to face it, he had hidden himself in the kitchen. But his mother found him, cowering in his silk gabardine behind the stove. Then she went off screaming for the bride's mother, and the two women besieged the bride's door.

'Daughter dear', began the bride's mother, 'why do you lock us out? You don't have to be ashamed before us.'

'Assuredly not', chimed in the bridegroom's mother. 'It happens in all Jewish homes.'

There was no answer from the other side.

'Your mother-in-law has brought you two lovely presents, a wig and a hat, in which to go to synagogue', pleaded the bride's mother.

From the other room, where the guests were reassembling, was heard the sound of the orchestra tuning up.

'Now, bride, sweet, darling bride', cooed the bridegroom's mother. 'Let us come in. The guests are ready to go to synagogue.'

At this point the door yielded, and the two mothers almost fell in. But as the bridegroom's mother approached the young wife, shears in hand, the bride flung herself on her mother's bosom with a great cry:

'Mother, mother darling, I can't do it. My heart won't let me.'

And as her mother tried to disengage herself, the young wife covered her head protectively with her hands.

'Daughter, daughter!' said the mother. 'Have you forgotten there is a God in heaven?'

The mother-in-law was losing patience. 'What?' she said. 'Keep your own hair after your marriage? Do you know what punishment is reserved in the world to come for such sinners? Demons will tear the locks from your head with fiery tongs.'

'Mama, mama, darling', sobbed the young wife, and held on convulsively to her hair. Her hair! It had grown together with her, it was part of her. And if she let them cut it off, it would never, never grow again like this. She would be wearing, for the rest of her life, someone else's hair, hair that had grown on some unknown woman's head. Who knew if that woman was alive? And suppose the dead woman, long since rotting in the grave, would rise out of it, and come to haunt her, demanding her hair. She could almost hear the dead voice: 'Give me back my hair! Give me back my hair!' An icy wave passed down her spine.

Then suddenly she heard the click of the shears above her head. With a scream, she grabbed the shears from her mother-in-law's hand, flung them to the floor, and cowered back in a corner.

'No, no!' she screamed in an inhuman voice. 'My own hair! I'm going to keep my own hair, and let God punish me if He wants!'

There was nothing they could do. That same morning the outraged mother-in-law packed up and departed, taking with her the roast geese, the sponge cake and the other good things she had brought along for the marriage breakfast. She also wanted to take along her son, but here the bride's mother had something to say:

'Oh, no, not my son-in-law! It's too late. He belongs to me now.'

And on the Sabbath Menassah Gross's daughter was conducted to the synagogue as unshorn as any heathen woman. The whole village knew that the lovely black coils under the big new hat were her own; and one-tenth of the curses that were hurled at the wicked woman would have sufficed to obliterate the village, if the powers that be had paid any attention to them.

*   *   *

Late one summer evening, four weeks after the wedding, the young man came home from the *Chassidic* meeting house, and went into his and his wife's room. Hannah was already asleep. The pale lamplight fell on her upturned face, which was partly hidden by her coal-black hair. Even in sleep she had her hands on her hair, so deep was her terror of losing it.

The young husband had come home perturbed and unhappy. In the four weeks since his marriage he had not once been called up during Sabbath services to a reading of the Scrolls of the Law. This was the punishment for the wickedness of his wife. And this evening Chaim Moishe, one of the zealots, had shamed him in public.

'Do you call yourself a man?' Chaim Moishe had asked, when the meeting house had been crowded. 'You're not a man! You're a worm, a chicken-livered image of a man! What sort of excuse is it that your wife won't let you cut her hair? Is it not written, specifically: "And he shall rule over her?"'

The young husband had returned home determined to have it out with his rebellious wife. He was going to say to her: 'Woman! This is the law of Israel! You are married and must not wear your own hair. And if you insist on wearing your own hair, you are divorced without a bill of divorcement! It is the law.' Having said which, he was going to fling from the room, pack his things, and depart. But when he saw her asleep under the dim lamplight, the black hair awash over her pale face, his heart was filled with pity. He approached the bed softly, looked down at his wife a long time, and called in a whisper:

'Hannah! Hannah! Little one!'

She opened her eyes sleepily and, only half awake, she murmured:

'Nathan, were you calling me? What is it?'

'Nothing', he replied. 'Only your night-cap's fallen off.' And he bent down, picked up the white lace night cap from the floor, and gave it to her.

'Hannah! Little one', he said. 'There's something I have to tell you.'

The soft, pleading words went straight to her heart. In the four weeks of their marriage he had hardly ever spoken with her. In the daytime he was away, either in the synagogue, or in the *Chassidic* meeting house. When he came home to supper, he sat down wordlessly. If he needed something he would address, not her, but some invisible person. And if he did address her, he would do it with downcast eyes, as if afraid to look her in the face. This was the first time that he had really spoken to her, and his voice was tender and persuasive in the intimacy of their own room.

'What is it that you have to tell me?' she asked, in low tones.

'Hannah, my sweet, I beg you, don't put me to shame before the whole world; and don't put yourself to shame, too. God Himself brought the two of us together; you are my wife, I am your husband. It isn't fitting, it isn't proper, it isn't seemly, that a married woman should wear her own hair.'

Her body was only half asleep, but her mind, her energies, her will, were wholly asleep. She was weak, she longed to yield, and when he sat down by her side and lifted her head on to his breast, she let it lie there.

'Child', he said, still more tenderly, 'I know you aren't as wild as they make you out to be, you aren't bad and spoiled. I know you are a sweet, loving daughter of your people. And God will be good to us, and send us children, decent, God-fearing children. Leave these follies, my sweet one. Why should we have the whole world against us? Are we not husband and wife, and isn't your shame my shame?'

It seemed to her that somebody new; somebody at once remote and yet indescribably intimate had approached her and was speaking to her. No one had ever spoken to her so gently, with such endearing, homely words. And he was hers, her only one, her husband, and she would live with him for so many years to come, so many years, and they would have children, and she would be the mistress of a household.

'I know', he went on, 'how it hurts you to lose your hair, the crown of your beauty. I saw you for the first time when they brought me to your house, when they told me you were to be my bride. And I understand. I know that God has given you beauty and grace. It will cut into my heart just as much as into yours. But what can we do? This is the Jewish law, and there is no escape from it. We are Jews, are we not, and who knows how we shall pay in our children for the breaking of the law, God help us and save us and keep us!'

She did not speak. She only lay lightly in his arms, and the perfume of her hair ascended to him and bathed his face. There was a soul in his wife's hair; he knew it and felt it. He looked at her long and earnestly; there was an entreaty in his eyes, and the entreaty was for her happiness, and his, and those to come.

'Let me', said his eyes, and she did not answer, saying neither yes nor no.

He went quickly to the dresser, opened the top drawer, took out the shears, and returned to her. She put her head in his lap, as if she were bringing an offering and a sacrifice, redemption, for her, and for him, and for those that were to come. The shears flashed palely above her head, the black tresses fell one by one. She did not dare to move. She lay thus, her shorn head in his lap, dreaming through the night.

In the morning she awoke and cast a glance at herself in the mirror, which hung opposite her bed. A dreadful fear rose in her heart. She thought for a moment that she was in a hospital. On the little table at her side lay the black tresses, dead. The soul that had been in them only the night before, when they had still been part of her, was gone from them, and the shadow of death was in the room.

She buried her face suddenly in her hands, and the sound of her weeping filled the little room.

Sholem Asch, *Children of Abraham*. Translated from the Yiddish by

Maurice Samuel (New York: G.P. Putnam's, copyright © 1942 by Ruth Shaffer, Moses Asch, John Asch and the representative of John Asch), pp.107–13. Reproduced by kind permission of the Sholem Asch Estate.

NOTES

The story focuses on the prevalent custom of clipping or shaving the bride's hair at the time of her marriage. A woman's hair was considered her beauty, an intimate and erotic part of her body, not to be beheld by unrelated males. To prevent provocation and temptation to sin, as early as Talmudic times (second century) married women were required to cover their hair.

Since the Middle Ages observant Jewish women in Europe traditionally covered their shorn heads by wigs, scarves, shawls and most frequently, by simple kerchiefs. The custom of covering the woman's hair (and beauty) is still observed by some Orthodox women, and wigs are still in use, but the wigs, catering to women's innate need for beauty, are charming and becoming.

Asch feels and conveys the young bride's trauma at losing her beauty and individuality, and her inevitable submission due to the subtle (and not so subtle) ways of community pressure and coercion. This difficult issue features elsewhere in Jewish literature, notably in Fradel Schtok's story, 'The Shorn Head'.[1]

Sholem Asch, a novelist, short story writer and dramatist was one of the foremost and best loved Yiddish writers of the first half of the twentieth century. Born in Kutno, Poland, in 1880, into a well-to-do, educated and religiously conservative innkeeper's family, he received a traditional Orthodox Jewish education. Discovering secular European literature, he taught himself and read extensively in German, English, Russian, Polish and Hebrew. Coming to Warsaw in 1900, he met some of the most prominent Yiddish writers, among them I.L. Peretz.

Success came early to Sholem Asch. His drama *God of Vengeance* was staged in Berlin, Paris, London and New York, bringing the young author, still in his thirties, international recognition and acclaim. Numerous novels, short stories and plays followed, opening new vistas and introducing new attitudes into Yiddish literature, winning recognition on the world literary scene. He wrote about Jewish life in all settings, from the shtetl to the metropolis, and at all times, from the biblical era to scenes of contemporary life, never hesitating to explore even the most squalid phenomena of Jewish life.

Talented, outspoken, handsome, proud and wealthy, almost a legendary figure in the Yiddish literary world, he easily provoked envy and was not prepared for the stormy Jewish reception of his Christological novels, *The Nazarene* (1939), *The Apostle* (1943) and *Mary* (1949). Accused of apostasy and of fostering anti-Semitism, he insisted these works were an attempt to illuminate the common roots of Judaism and Christianity and to bridge the gap between them. Misunderstood, he defended himself for the rest of his life, mostly without success.

Always faithful to his background and creed, he described Jewish life, from the idyllic (*Salvation*, 1934) to the profane (*Motke the Thief*, English translation, 1935).

The portrayal of Jewish characters, and especially of women, in the selections included in this anthology have been drawn with deep understanding, sensitivity and sympathy, without minimizing the pressures and values of the times. Sholem Asch died in 1957, in London.

1. F. Schtok, 'The Shorn Head', in M. Kantrowitz-Kay and I. Klepfish (eds), *The Tribe of Dina; A Jewish Women's Anthology* (Boston, MA: Beacon, 1986, 1989), pp.190–3.

2

The Mother's Reward

SHOLEM ASCH

Excerpts from a Novel

The four sides of the square-shaped marketplace consisted of little whitewashed houses. The one opposite the well was the bakery; a thick cloud of smoke issued from its chimney and spread a veil between the marketplace and the blue sky. White pigeons flew through the veil, and at the door of the bakery stood a tall youth and whistled to the pigeons.

On the other side of the well the women had their 'stands', doors lay on trestles, and on the stands were displayed fruits and vegetables. The women wore shawls and kerchiefs even on the hottest days; and their faces were tired with years of waiting.

At this moment two of the women were quarrelling.

'I don't know why I take the trouble to talk to a piece of dirt like you! You low-down washerwoman, you! You haven't a kopeck to your name!'

Yente, a hard-faced woman of some forty-odd years, uttered the words venomously, flapped her dirty apron with both hands, as if she were shaking off an unclean thing.

'And you?' called back Toibe, to whom the words were addressed. 'Do you think you've got hold of God Almighty's beard? You'll get yours, don't you worry.'

And Toibe the widow shoved her kerchief up over her head, as if preparing for battle.

A customer approached Yente's stand, and Toibe, who stood idle, continued to curse.

'What's the good of all your dirty money? When you die there won't even be a dog to say a prayer over you.'

There was a bitter implication in these words, as both women knew. Toibe was referring to her own son Isaac and reminding the other of her childlessness. Realizing that she had gone too far, and that to boast of her children was to invite the evil eye, Toibe became silent.

'Oh, yes!' cried Yente, measuring out a quart of pears for her customer, but keeping her eyes fixed on Toibe. 'And if you hadn't been the kind of thing you are, your husband wouldn't be dead, and your son wouldn't be ashamed of you. Because everybody knows he's ashamed of you.'

Toibe crimsoned with rage.

'Liar!' she screamed. 'My son isn't ashamed of me. And how dare you mention him? Your lips are too dirty to utter his name!'

She was on the verge of tears, and it was only by an extreme effort of will that she kept them back, lest the other should have the satisfaction of seeing her weep. But she said no more, and the other, knowing that the shaft had gone home, also held her tongue.

Evening drew on. Jews hastened across the marketplace toward the synagogue alley. Boys returning from the Hebrew school gathered about the well.

Toibe picked up her baskets of fruit and vegetables. She left the stand where it was – no one would bother to steal it – and muttering a last curse under her breath she turned homeward.

She could not get Yente's poisonous words out of her mind – those about her son. What Yente had said concerning her husband, that he had died because of her had not touched her at all. The whole village knew how she had tended him, slaved for him and over him. But that remark about her son being ashamed of his own mother rankled deep; because, more than once, she had brooded over the fact that when her Isaac came home nights he seldom touched the food she had prepared for him.

'Father in heaven', she panted, as she struggled along under her burden, 'choke her with that lie.'

It seemed to her at this moment that it would never have occurred to her that her son was ashamed of his mother if Yente had not put the idea in her head.

'My son, my Isaac!' she went on. 'What business has she to mention his name?' And she raised her voice in a wail: 'Father in heaven! They call you the help of widows, the guardian of orphans. Remember me, remember my son. And remember that woman and punish her as she deserves!'

'Toibe! Toibe! Whom are you cursing so?'

Neche, the rich merchant's wife, was standing at the door of her shop; it was she who called out the question to Toibe.

'Whom should I be cursing, dear lady, if not that loudmouth, the Yente?' answered Toibe, without even lifting her head.

Trudging on, Toibe remembered how that same morning she had entered Neche's house by the back door and had delivered a hen to the kitchen. For on this day of the week her Isaac took his meals with Neche's children; every day of the week he ate with another house-holder, according to the custom. And Toibe had brought them a hen, so that her Isaac would have chicken soup. He was so weak he needed a good, nourishing, strengthening soup. And standing in the kitchen, the slaughtered hen still in her hand, she had heard her son's voice on the other side of the wall. Her Isaac was arguing with the children of Neche, the rich merchant's wife; he was arguing with them about a point in a holy book, and very clearly he was having the better of the argument. She knew that at once. And why shouldn't he have the better of the argument? Who was there among the children of Neche, or for that matter in the whole village, to compare with her Isaac? Standing thus in the kitchen, her heart full, she had said to herself: 'I'd better go away, lest they come in here and see me. A fine picture for my Isaac! His mother, the market-woman, standing in the kitchen with a hen!' And then again she had thought, in a surge of pride: 'I've never been able to spend a kopeck on him, and he outshines them all! How much money hasn't Neche spent on her children! If I had what my Isaac's learning should have cost, I'd be a rich woman!' So she remained standing listening ecstatically to her Isaac's dominating voice.

'If only *he* were here, and heard that voice! He would get up from his bed a strong man!'

She stood there so long that at last the door opened, and the chil-dren saw her – Neche's children, and her own Isaac. Isaac's cheeks flamed.

'Good morning!' he said to his mother, in a weak voice, before the door closed again. She knew she had done wrong. She should not have embarrassed her boy like that. But how could she help it? It was her son, her Isaac; he had fed at her breast. Who were Neche's children, to come between her and her son?

All this Toibe remembered as she neared her home, and she poured out the bitterness that was in her on the absent Yente's head, because Yente had dared to say that Isaac was ashamed of his mother.

'God!' she said aloud, 'take up my quarrel with her, and punish her as she deserves, this very night, before morning comes!'

It was dark by the time Toibe reached her house. She dragged her-self up the steps and opened the door. An outburst of children's voices greeted her out of the darkness. 'Mama! Mama! It's Mama! Mama, where have you been so long?'

The single room that was home to Toibe and her children was filled with smoke and dust. Toibe put down her burden at the door, and cried:

'Quiet! Let me catch my breath.'

For a minute or two she stood still, and panted, while the children clustered about her, some laughing, and some crying. When she had come to, she lit the lamp on the mantelpiece, and the darkness retreated a little distance toward the corners of the room. Now one could see the dust-covered sewing machine (all that her husband, the tailor, had left her) and one half of the bed. The bed was covered with straw, on which lay various fruits and vegetables, part of Toibe's stock. The remainder of the room lay in darkness, beyond the reach of the feeble rays of the lamp.

Less than two years had passed since the death of Lazar the tailor; but it was much more than two years since Toibe had been the sole support of the family. What had she not done? In whose home had she not worked? Month after month she had watched her husband's decline, hearing his cough become dryer and harder, seeing his eyes sink deeper into his head, before the light died out of them forever.

In those closing days, when the last illusion of hope was gone – whether they admitted it or not – Lazar the tailor had one consolation, his oldest son, Isaac. Isaac had a good head; he was cut out to be a scholar. Some day he might achieve fame. Lazar the tailor could feel that he had not lived in vain. The son that would say the *Kaddish* for him would plead the cause of the dead father in the courts of heaven. When Lazar died at last, the leading householders of the village met and took council as to what should be done. They collected a little money to set up the widow in business; and they honored Lazar's dying wish in regard to his gifted son. Isaac was taken into the school of the synagogue, and his days were portioned out among the well-to-do householders, according to the ancient custom. Every day he ate with another family, so that he could give his time to his studies.

It did Toibe's heart good to know that her son ate daily at the tables of the rich, where the best was served. He was a weak child; he needed something more than she could offer. But she suffered, too. Her son was everywhere a stranger. And she did not know whether, in the long run, it was a good thing or bad.

Sitting one morning at her stand in the marketplace, she saw her Isaac go into the house of Sundel the wheat merchant, for his breakfast. The sight of it stabbed her, and she turned to Yente, with whom she was then on good terms, for it was soon after Lazar's death and everyone was kind to her, and said:

'Yente, believe me, I just don't know what to think. Why should I have anything in my heart against those rich people? They've done nothing but good to me and to my Isaac. They've given him a place at their tables, they treat him like one of their own children, and not a bit as if he were the son of an ordinary market-woman. And yet every time I give my children supper, I set a plate for Isaac, and when I remember that he doesn't eat in my house I cry like a child.'

'Silly woman!' answered Yente, scolding her in a friendly way. 'Would you really prefer to have him eat with you? Much good that would do him! What can we offer our children, God help us?'

'Yes, yes, Yente, I know you're right. But every time I cut bread for the children, and not for Isaac, it's as if I were cutting my heart.'

And it was still the same, though she had had two years of it. She still had to hold back her tears this evening as she served the other children, and she still could not help feeling that the rich people, with their goodness and kindness, were robbing her of her child.

When she had put the children to bed she seated herself near the lamp and by its feeble light mended a shirt for Isaac.

Before long the door opened, and her son came in. Isaac was a tall, thin boy of fourteen. His white, serious, almost stern face stood out against his black gabardine and his black cap.

'Good evening', he said, quietly.

His mother moved away from the table, to make room for him. She felt that her son was entitled to respect, though she could not have said why. More clearly, however, she felt that she, with her poverty and her low occupation, was a calamity for her son.

Isaac sat down at the table, opened a book, and read. His mother turned up the wick of the lamp and wiped the glass with her apron.

'Will you have a cup of tea, son?' she asked in a low voice.

'Thank you. I've just had one.'

'Or perhaps an apple.'

He did not answer. Toibe wiped a plate, put on it two apples and a knife, and pushed it over toward her son. Very slow, very deliberately, just like a grown-up man absorbed by his thoughts, Isaac peeled the fruit, made the benediction, and ate. Toibe, seeing him eat something she had prepared for him, felt nearer to him, more as if she were really his mother. She moved her chair closer to the table.

As he peeled the second apple Isaac spoke in a low, grave voice.

'I had a talk today with the Rabbi about my going away. Here in our synagogue study house there is nothing to do. We haven't the teachers. The Rabbi himself says as much. He advised me to try the Talmudical college at Mokeve. He said he would give me a letter to Reb Chaim, the head of the college, who's a good friend of his, and Reb Chaim would befriend me.'

This was the first time that Isaac had ever mentioned the subject of his departure for another town, and a shock of fear passed through Toibe. But his grave way of talking, and the expressions he used – 'the Talmudical college' – 'the head of the college' – 'befriend me', expressions which in the Yiddish retain their original Hebrew form, and have about them a ring of culture and piety – impressed her, and filled her with a vague fear. But as he went on talking she found a little reassurance. So far, after all, they had only been talking about it.

'Well, if that's the Rabbi's opinion', she said hesitantly, a pious look coming into her face.

'Yes', continued Isaac. 'Over there in the Mokeve Academy, they have regular formal hours and lessons, with all the best commentaries. Reb Chaim, the head, is the head author of "The Glory of the Torah" and a celebrated scholar. At Mokeve a man can hope to become something.'

The high words fell like a soothing balm on Toibe's heart. A sweet exaltation brought a new light into her eyes. This was her son, she was the mother of such a son, and were it not for her there would not be this Isaac in the world. But behind the exaltation something frightening stirred, a premonition of loss.

She remembered her husband, and tears began to flow down her cheeks.

'If he were only alive', she sobbed. 'If he were only here to taste this joy.'

Isaac kept his eyes steadily on the book.

It was only in the night, when she tried to compose herself for sleep, that the reality of Isaac's impending departure came home to her. A dreadful emptiness opened in her heart. Toward morning, between sleeping and waking, she had visions of processions of great Rabbis, with vast fur hats on their heads and long earlocks dangling down their cheeks, leading her Isaac away to a remote place. Her Isaac, too, wore a vast fur hat and had long earlocks like the Rabbis; he carried a thick, leather-bound book. She stood at a distance and watched him go away with the Rabbis, and she did not know whether she ought to be happy or whether she ought to weep.

She woke up later than usual the next morning. Isaac was gone. She gave the children their breakfast and hurried off to her stand in the marketplace. But because she had not slept well she was pursued into the day by a dreaminess that she could not shake off. She kept thinking of Isaac. She saw herself sitting, not at a wretched stand in a market-place but in the house of her son Isaac. He was a Rabbi in a great city. There he was, seated in his big leather chair; he had on good stockings and a stout pair of shoes. A rich fur hat covered his head. He held an open book in his hand, and read in it silently. She sat at his right hand and knitted a stocking. The door opened, and Yente the marketwoman came in carrying a fowl; she was afraid there was a defect in the dead bird; she wanted the Rabbi to tell her whether the fowl was *kosher* or not.

A customer tore Toibe out of her daydreams.

Night after night Toibe sat at the table in her one-room home and by the light of the smoking lamp mended and patched the linen that her Isaac would need in the new town. With every stroke of the needle she reflected that she was doing this for her Isaac; her Isaac was going away to study in a Talmudical college; there he would begin a great career; and every Friday he would put on a fresh shirt, which his mother had prepared for him.

Isaac himself sat on the other side of the table, his eyes glued on a book. His mother would have liked to say something to him, but she did not know what.

On the morning of the departure Toibe and Isaac rose before dawn. Isaac kissed his sleeping brothers; and to his sleeping sisters he only said, in a low voice, 'Good-by, little sisters'. One of them, Goldie, woke up suddenly, perceived at once that her brother was setting out on a journey, and began to cry. She wanted to come along. Toibe soothed her, lulled her to sleep, and then stole out of the house with Isaac.

The street still slept as they came out, Toibe carrying her son's heavy box. All the windows were shuttered. The brilliant morning star glittered above the steeple of the church and shimmered in the dew that lay on the roofs of the houses. Silence rested on the street and on the village. It was only when they came to the marketplace that they saw the first signs of life. A peasant's cart had already arrived with the first load of fruit and vegetables. The market women were gathered round the cart, and from a distance Toibe and Isaac heard Yente's shrill voice: 'Five gulden and ten groschen for the whole load.' And Toibe carrying Isaac's box across the marketplace, straightened up, and as she passed Yente looked at her proudly and defiantly.

They went out of the village and took the road to Lentchitz; there Isaac would get a lift as far as Kutno. The sky began to grow gray above them. A cold, hard light filtered down through the low-hanging clouds, and a dewy mist went up from the fields to meet it halfway. The wide, curving road stretched away in front of them between silent fields. On the crossroads near Lentchitz they set down the box and waited for the diligence. Toibe took out a little bundle of coins from the pocket of her apron, and tied it around Isaac's neck. When the diligence arrived she bargained for a place on it for Isaac – forty kopecks as far as Kutno. She lifted the box on to the diligence.

'Good-by, my son. Don't forget your mother', she said, weeping. Isaac could not answer.

She would have liked to kiss her child, but she knew that it was not proper for a grown boy to be kissed in public, so she restrained herself. Isaac climbed on to the diligence and the passengers made room for him.

'Good-by, Mother', he said at last, as the vehicle began to move.

'Good-by, son. Study hard and don't forget your mother', shouted Toibe.

She stood there, watching the diligence grow small and smaller. Slowly it climbed up the little slope and disappeared on the other side. She kept on looking at the spot where the vehicle had disappeared. Only when several minutes had passed did she tear herself away and return to the village. But she did not go straight to the marketplace. She made a long detour, skirting the village till she came to the enclosure of the Jewish cemetery. A row of wooden palings separated the cemetery from the open field. The gate was locked, and Toibe could not force her way in. She managed, however, to thrust her head in between two palings, and her anxious eyes sought out the familiar little tombstone.

'*Lazar! Lazar!* Your son Isaac has gone away to the *Yeshivah* to study *Torah*!'

She waited till she was certain that the message had gone home, and only then did she bethink herself of the marketplace and the day's business. It was late. No doubt Yente had already supplied all of her, Toibe's, morning customers; but no matter. She had been busy with matters of high importance, and her spirit was at peace.

*   *   *

Two weeks later the first letter arrived from Isaac. Since she was unable to read, Toibe took the letter to Reb Jochanan, the Hebrew teacher, and asked him to read it out to her. Reb Jochanan put on his glasses, coughed impressively, and began: '*L'imi ahuvati ha-tzenua –* '

'What is that, what is that?' asked Toibe, eagerly.

'It's Hebrew, of course. A title of respect for a mother.'

Toibe's face was irradiated with joy. She put her apron to her eyes and wept. Reb Jochanan paid no attention, but went on heading in Hebrew.

'What's that? What is it?' sobbed Toibe.

'It's still Hebrew.'

'But what does he say?'

'You wouldn't understand if I told you. It's a very neat little piece of Talmudic argument.'

How wonderful! Toibe wept afresh, controlling her sobs so as not to lose a single syllable of the marvelous Hebrew words. Then, toward the end of the letter, in plain, intelligible Yiddish, was added:

'I send my greetings to my beloved mother, to my sisters Sarah and Goldie, to my brothers Joseph and Jacob, and I bid my brothers to be attentive to their books and to study diligently.'

Ah, that was good! Something she understood. Toibe took back the letter, folded it reverently, put it in her apron pocket, and went back to her stand. 'Tonight', she said to herself, 'I'll go to the Rabbi, and ask him to read the Hebrew part and explain it to me.'

That evening after feeding the youngsters and putting them to bed, she rushed to the Rabbi's house. They admitted her to the study, where she saw long rows of books on shelves that reached to the ceiling, and the Rabbi himself, grave, white-bearded, seated in his arm chair.

'What is it?' asked the Rabbi, 'A ritual question?'

'No.'

'What is it, then?'

'A letter from my son, Isaac.'

The Rabbi rose from his chair, came over slowly, took the letter, and began to read it to himself.

'Excellent! Excellent! He murmured with a pleased look. The boy will go far!'

The tears poured again down Toibe's cheeks. 'If only *he* were alive!' she whispered.

'According to Maimonides, however …' the Rabbi murmured, reading from the letter, 'while on the other hand the Tosaphists say – ' He pulled down his brows. 'Extraordinary!' he exclaimed.

'That's my Isaac', thought Toibe, 'Isaac, the son of the ordinary market-woman, Toibe.'

'Well, well', said the Rabbi at last. 'Here's your letter. I've read it through.'

'Yes – but – ' stammered Toibe.

'But what?'

'What's in the letter?' she asked, in a low voice.

'Bless my soul!' said the Rabbi astonished. 'These things are not for you.' He smiled. 'You would not understand them.'

*   *   *

Isaac's letters arrived regularly every fortnight. From one letter to the next the Yiddish section became shorter, the Hebrew section longer and weightier. Invariably Toibe took the letters to Reb Jochanan the teacher, and the same scene was re-enacted. Reb Jochanan read aloud the few Yiddish words of greeting, keeping the Hebrew for himself.

One day she brought a letter to Reb Jochanan, who read it with great absorption, and said nothing.

'Nothing for you', he said at last.

'How can that be?'

'That's how it is. There's nothing for you.'

'Please, read me whatever there is.'

'It's all in Hebrew. You wouldn't understand.'

'So I won't understand.'

'Good woman', said Reb Jochanan, patiently, 'I haven't time for that nonsense.'

That evening she went to the Rabbi.

'Rabbi', pleaded Toibe, timidly, 'just translate the Hebrew words for me.'

'It's Talmud, difficult Talmud. You wouldn't understand.'

'Then please read the Hebrew words for me, in Hebrew, so I can hear what he writes.'

'You won't understand a word', said the Rabbi, smiling.

'So I won't understand', answered Toibe.

The Rabbi thought a moment, shrugged, and began to read. The strange haunting syllables sent a thrill through Toibe. She strained her ears, as if by greater attentiveness she could penetrate to the meaning of the words.

The Rabbi looked up and was startled. He stopped reading and handed her the letter.

'There now, that's enough', he said, compassionately.

Toibe went out, thinking: 'It's my Isaac's letter, it's my Isaac's learning in it. Why shouldn't I hear what he writes, even if I don't understand?'

When she came home she took down the lamp from its hook and set it on the table. She sat down, took out the letter, and looked at it long and earnestly. Then she lifted it to her lips and kissed it but immediately she regretted the act, as a desecration. A letter filled with such holy learning ought not to be touched by the lips of an ordinary sinful woman.

She went over to the bookcase and took out the prayer book of her dead husband. She opened it, added this letter to the others that were already there, closed the prayer book and replaced it. Then she sat down at the table and looked at the bookcase.

Sholem Asch, *Children of Abraham*. Translated by Maurice Samuel (New York: G.P. Putnam's, copyright © 1942 by Ruth Shaffer, Moses Asch, John Asch and the representative of John Asch), pp.62–80. Reproduced by kind permission of the Sholem Asch Estate. For information about Sholem Asch, see 1. *The Rebel*.

3

'Olke'

KADYA MOLODOWSKY

A Poem

In the back streets of Warsaw, at the end of desire,
A yard filled with mire,

There lives Olke
With her blue parasol-ke.

Her father's a blacksmith,
Her mother boils peas.

The roof tilts aslant; in a hollow
Beneath the roof lives a swallow.

In the house, a table and a bed,
And a garret hung with laundry, a washshed.

And spoons and platters, pitchers, pans, and a pot,
And a baby in its cot.

And this girl Olke
With her blue parasol-ke.

A maid, six years old,
With hair like spun-gold.

Outside it's bright and mellow,
And the sand is yellow,

Olke picks up some sand to knead –
She wants to invite her friends for bread.

But her mother yells to the maid
So that the window panes quake,

And her father, the blacksmith, then
Joins in:
'Get into the house!
Little brother needs rocking,
Pots and pitchers need washing.

Water needs bringing,
Shirts need rinsing,
Potatoes need peeling.
Stories need telling.

A little to read,
A little to write –
Remember, I'll drive you out of the house tonight.'

When Olke goes to bring
Water for shirt-rinsing,
She sees:
Geese walking:
The goose walks proud and fine,
And the goslings in a line,
Feathers of white,
Feet of red,
Then comes the gander, that noodlehead.

Right then and there, Olke
Opens up her blue parasol-ke,
And she has a roof and a house
And geese numerous.

Olke wants to walk with geese all the way
Until the sun sets at the end of the day.

But her mother yells to the maid
So that the window panes quake,
And her father, the blacksmith, then
Joins in:
'Get into the house!

It's the workaday week,
There's kasha to cook,
Wood to split,
Matches to be lit,
A baby to hold,
Diapers to fold,

A little to read,
A little to write –
Remember, I'll drive you out of the house tonight.'

When Olke goes out to split the wood,
To hold the child,
She sees:
Birds flying
In a line as long as a train,
And, above them, an airplane.
Wings of white,
Birds up high,
And above them clouds,
Like blue smoke in the sky.

Right then and there, Olke
Opens up her blue parasol-ke,
And she has a roof and a house
And birds numerous.

Olke wants to stand there stock-still
Until the sun sets over the hill.
And her mother yells to the maid
So that the window panes quake,

And her father, the blacksmith, then
Joins in:
'Get into the house!
Socks need darning,
Thread needs turning,
Knots need tying,
Buttons need sewing,
A little to read,
A little to write –

Remember, I'll drive you out of the house tonight.'

When Olke unwinds some thread
To sew on buttons,
Suddenly the buttons spill down
And strew themselves all across town.
Each button turns into a wheel,
And the wheels begin to dance a reel.

One of them races across the cobbles,
Rolling as fast as a runaway barrel.
Two spin a bicycle, straight and narrow,
Three wheels on a plank make a wheelbarrow,
Four wheels get themselves into a brawl
And harness themselves as a wagon to haul.

Right then and there, Olke
Opens up her blue parasolke,
And she has a roof and a house
And wheels numerous.
Olke wants to stand there stock-still
Until the sun sets over the hill.

But her mother yells to the maid
So that the window panes quake,
And then her father, the blacksmith, then
Joins in:
But Olke does not want to hear or to know,
The wheels stir and bow to her and greet her, 'Hello.'
Then Olke hitches all the wheels in a harness
And makes a long train to go further than farness.
Then the train whistles, and Olke travels away,
Far, far away on a glowing, white way.

Kathryn Hellerstein, *Paper Bridges; Selected Poems of Kadya Molodowsky*. Translated, edited and with an introduction by K. Hellerstein, (Detroit, MI: Wayne State University Press, 1999), pp. 27–8, 181, 183, 185, 187, 189, 523. Reproduced by kind permission of Kathryn Hellerstein and Benjamin Litman for the Estate of Kadya Molodowsky.

NOTES

Kadya Molodowsky was born in 1894 and brought up in a traditional, observant Jewish family in a small town in the vicinity of Grodno, part of Russia at the time of her birth, which then became Poland during the period between First World War and Second World Wars, and is today Belarus. Unusually for her times, Kadya received an extensive education in Jewish as well as in general, secular subjects.

She lived and worked as a teacher in the Yiddish secular schools in Warsaw, and was deeply involved in Jewish education in Bialystok, Odessa and in other centres of Jewish life. She wrote from her earliest years, and at 26 (in 1920) saw her first poems published in Kiev. She continued to write stories and novels, with an ever-growing appreciation and awareness of the emotional sources and the cultural importance and function of poetry and other forms of literature.

Her poems and stories reflect her background in Biblical studies, Jewish history and experience, the Holocaust, the return to Zion, and especially, the realities of Jewish women's life: poverty and oppression. Her first book, *Nights of Heshvan,* published in Warsaw in 1927, lyrically reflects, as do her other books, the sadness and darkness of the days of autumn, the roles and destiny of women restricted by Jewish law and custom, death, deprivation and their destitution and sorrows.

As a teacher, Kadya knew, loved and understood children. Her children's poems brought relief and joy to the teacher and her young charges, and were enjoyed and translated, becoming, with the passage of time, modern classics. Some were set to music. The two children's poems included in this anthology mirror life in dusty, impoverished courtyards in Warsaw, and yet, they express humour, joy and hope.

Kathryn Hellerstein commentary on 'Olke' and 'The Tale of the Washtub' in *Paper Bridges* (1999) is inspiring and should be read. Olke lives in a dilapidated, dusty, grimy courtyard in the predominantly Jewish section of Warsaw. She is already 6 years old, 'with hair like spun-gold', and, accordingly, carries a full range of responsibilities:

> 'Little brother needs rocking,
> Pots and pitchers need washing.
> Water needs bringing,
> Shirts need rinsing ...'

But Olke, this Jewish Cinderella of Dzike Street, is not without resources. She has the Jewish child's heritage of strength and spirit to rely on. A survivor, she opens her blue parasol, and imagines a world of difference. Buttons transform themselves into wheels, and take Olke away 'to go farther than farness, far, far away, on a glowing, white way.'

'The Tale of the Washtub', this symbol of women's drudgery and enslavement to endless hard work, has undergone a magical, dramatic and delightful transformation into becoming an agent of change, and is now doing everyone's laundry, thus relieving all the women in the courtyard, including the Gentile neighbours, of their back-breaking, daily labour. The washtub travels from cellar to attic, knowing who needs and deserves help. Kadya, in 'The Tale of the Washtub', drew a true, loving, joyful and compelling picture of life in the courtyard, and of the demographic, economic, social, and even religious conditions and attitudes of the poor Jews of Warsaw in her time.

Kadya Molodowsky emigrated to the USA in 1935, and came to occupy a very prominent place on the Jewish literary scene. She died in 1975.

4

'The Tale of the Washtub'

KADYA MOLODOWSKY

A Poem

One bright day, at a lucky hour,
When the sun was dozing on table and bed,
Khantsche bought a wooden trough for kneading bread.

But knead as she might, today and tomorrow –
As long as the sun stayed up in the skies,
The dough simply refused to rise.

So this was what Khantsche said:
If the kneading-trough is spoiled
I'll make it a washtub where laundry is boiled.

Now came the wonder of wonders:
The tub scrubbed every spot, speck, and stain
From the children's clothes! With no soap, with no drain!

How did that happen?
A shirt rolled three times around, like a hoop,
The tub became soap.
Turn to the left,
Turn to the right –
Out of the washtub, clean and bright.

Neighbors popped up from cellars, from attics:
Khantsche dear, with seven children, it's always wash and
scrub!
Please, just for today, lend me your new washtub.

So the washtub traveled like gossip

From cellar up to a floor on top,
Down to the yard's darkest nook, didn't stop.

After that:
Up to an attic in a house with no door,
Like a windmill, whirled up the steps, one-two-three-four.

After that:
Into a room with an oven that's blue,
From there to Gentile neighbors too.

And the story went on
So long and so slow
That the washtub itself knew which way to go.

And it dared to set out
All alone, just like that,
Rolling and bumping from flat to flat.

Worriedly, the washtub thought:
There's Feyge-Beyle in her men's mackintosh –
On Sunday I have to go do *her* wash.

Because she has small children,
She must wash diapers much more often.

And Monday, I'll launder blouses and garrets.
And Tuesday, no offense intended,
I'm due to wash breeches stained with carrots.

And on Wednesday, the tub noisily rolled
To wash jackets, socks, and a coat
For Sore-Zlate, who sells milk from her goat.

Thursday was all push and shove
As the washtub rolled, expanded its girth,
And washed shirts for everyone on earth.

Friday, the children wore clean underwear,
Friday, the washtub became quite devout,
And did nothing but wash itself out.

Kathryn Hellerstein, *Paper Bridges; Selected Poems by Kadya Molodowsky*. Translated, edited and introduced by K. Hellerstein, (Detroit, MI: Wayne State University Press, 1999), pp. 25, 28, 195, 187, 199, n. p.523. Reproduced by kind permission of Kathryn Hellerstein and Benjamin Litman for the Estate of Kadya Molodowsky. For information about Kadya Molodowsky, see 3. 'Olke'.

5

The Teacher Reb Mendele

LILI BERGER

A Short Story

There was once a Jew by the name of Mendel. That's the name his father and mother gave him. But he had other names, as many as Jethro. He was red-haired. So of course he was called 'Redhead.' People don't as a rule like redheads. They call such a one 'redhead robber', even if the man is as far as heaven from being a robber. This Jew named Mendel was an exception. If someone referred to him behind his back as 'the redheaded Jew', it was said almost with deference. It may have been his beard that saved him. God went wrong there – making the hair on his head red, like new-baked brick, and his beard a different color, a kind of dark gray, and a special shape – like a triangle. So wags used to speak of him as 'The Little Beard', but again without any disrespect. Just like that.

So there were two names derived from his physical appearance. The others had to do with the ways he made his living.

The Jew with the name Mendel was a dealer with all sorts of books. He didn't have a shop. He was a traveling shop himself. He carried a kind of rucksack, half suitcase, and half sack, which could be carried over his shoulder or held in his hand.

So Mendel traveled with his 'shop' from town to town, from community to community, offering a prayerbook (a *siddur*), a *Ze'enu U-Renu*, a *Techina*, a *Selicha*, a *Haggadah* – according to the season – and sometimes various storybooks. For that reason they came to call him *Mocher Seforim*, the Bookseller. But though they say that Torah is the best goods a man can have, he didn't make much of a living at it. His cup certainly didn't run over.

So the Jew with the name Mendel also wrote letters, put addresses on envelopes for people who couldn't write, composed applications and petitions to the authorities. It wasn't necessary to explain every detail to him. If a poor widow had to turn to relatives in America it was enough for her to tell him just a few words and he produced an epistle that could move a stone to tears. And his handwriting! His script was like pearls. If he wrote an address it came from his hand smooth and polished. He honestly earned the name 'Letter-Writer.'

That would, one imagines, have been enough names. But God sent him another livelihood, so he got another name. His new livelihood fell down indeed from heaven, but the one who was responsible directly was Sheine (Belle), Israel the Tailor's wife. The name Sheine wasn't very well suited to her appearance, but she had a lot of other qualities. Most important, she had a head on her shoulders.

Sheine also had an old little house, sunk low in the ground, and a husband who was thin and pale and more often ill than plying his needle, and two grown sons who worked with their father at his tailoring, and a girl of twelve named Rashke, who was full of life.

Suddenly Sheine was left all alone. She took her husband to the cemetery, and they buried him. Rashke had to go to a relative as a nursemaid to their child, and the two sons she sent to America – she had prepared for that a long time before.

This brought Sheine into close acquaintance with the Bookseller – he conducted her correspondence with her sons. Whether it was his letters that did it or the sons' skilled hands and devoted hearts, Sheine was soon put on her feet.

The first thing, she took Rashke back home. The next thing, she decided that Rashke must learn to write, not be 'blind', as she herself was. And as Sheine now had not only dollars in her pockets, but also a sense of what is right in her heart, she started persuading mothers and their grown-up daughters who had to ask somebody to write their letters for them, that they must learn to write, and should take their lessons from the Bookseller. Sheine promised to do all she could to help. She would see to it that it would cost them next to nothing. They could have her room for the classes, and she wouldn't charge for the kerosene in the lamp.

'What, is a girl supposed to grow up like a dumb beast? If you can't write it's as if you were blind. Go without food, but don't grow up like a dumb beast!'

The mothers nodded their heads. Some of them saw what was meant immediately.

'You should be able to write an address yourself. Not have to ask somebody to do you a favor.'

So her husband Israel's tailor workshop became a school, and the Bookseller became 'the girls' teacher'. But the name he was called by was '*Reb* Mendele'.

Reb Mendele was a teacher blessed by God. Nowadays a teacher with a bunch of girls like that from eight to seventeen years of age would soon have found himself under a nerve specialist. But again God had gone wrong – *Reb* Mendele was a man who simply had no gall. Quietly, unruffled, he went from one pupil to another, with a gentle smile on his face, explained what was necessary to each of them separately. He was always soft-spoken. And when it was required he knew how to set their fears at rest.

There was for instance Breina the servant girl, who was in despair that she would never get the hang of this reading and writing that he was trying to teach her.

'You'll be all right!' he assured her. 'With God's help you'll learn to write! You'll be able to read! Don't worry! You'll manage fine!'

I wasn't getting anywhere with my lessons either. Everything I did was a flop. God must have gone wrong with me too. Instead of a right hand He had given me a left. And a left instead of a right. I wrote with my left hand, and all the girls giggled, and laughed at me. So I made up my mind that no matter how hard it was I would write with my right hand. It was terribly hard; but I did it. The only trouble was that the letters came out all pothooks and hangers, scrawling all over the place, above the lines and below the lines, and refusing to stand up straight in an orderly row.

The teacher, *Reb* Mendele, looked at my pothooks and hangers, and smiled quietly and said, 'Never mind! Never mind! You'll write! If it's easier for you, write with your left hand.'

But I was determined not to give in. I persisted in writing with my right hand. But my writing got no better. It was like nothing on earth. But I did well at reading. While the whole bunch of girls stammered and stuttered over their reading I read smoothly and fluently and without a fault. The girls listened enviously. The teacher, *Reb* Mendele, loved to hear me read. And Sheine concluded that this business wasn't so simple. The way she saw it, when I was writing, a bad angel stood by my hand; and when I read, a good angel stood beside me and put a blessing on my lips. How could I tell her that before I started learning to write the alphabet I could already read the *Ze'enu U-Renu*, the *Techina* and the storybooks – that reading was a kind of disease with me. I had to pick up any bit of paper on the ground and read it right through.

The teacher, *Reb* Mendele, was apparently a better psychologist than Sheine. He looked with wondering eyes at this pupil who couldn't write a decent stroke of the alphabet, and said:

'Take this! Read it and return it to me. Put it away now.'

I ran all the way home. But the temptation was too much for me and I stopped in front of the door, and by the light of the moon and the glitter of the white dazzling snow I opened the book, turned to the title page, and read: *The Little Man.*

How many tears I shed over Golda, Michael, Sheindel, and the old mother. I grew to love them! That I hated Isaac Abraham is another story, into which I won't go now.

I read the book, and I read it again – twice and three times, and I thought about it, and considered it, and finally I concluded that *The Little Man* had been written by no other than my teacher *Reb* Mendele. There were so many things in the book that pointed to it – his name was Mendel; they called him *Reb* Mendele; he was a bookseller, and that's what they called him – Mendele *Mocher Seforim*, Mendele the Bookseller. He made no secret of it. He told us at the opening of the book who and what he is. Not everything tallied, of course. That would have been photographic. So he didn't say for instance that he had red hair. But everything else agreed. Even his age. Sheine said he was in his fifties. I looked again at the book: 'In the passport they give my age as fifty-two.' Further on, 'Medium height – eyebrows gray; cross-eyed. Nose and mouth normal. High forehead, heavily lined. When I look at anything I half-close my eyes, as shortsighted people do, and I purse my lips, as though with a biting ironic smile. I make my living selling books – Pentateuchs, festival prayer books, daily prayer books, penitential prayers, *Techinas*, all sorts of books like that. I also have every kind of storybook, and a few books in the modern style. I've had many different occupations in my time. In the end I took to books.'

Heavens! It's him! I'd love to tell somebody what I've found out! My joy at having made this discovery is simply bursting out of me. I must share my joy with somebody. There's enough for all to enjoy. Only suppose it isn't so? That ironic smile – but the teacher *Reb* Mendele does purse his lips, only his smile is sweet as honey.

There I go again – he's not supposed to tell us everything about himself in the book.

Before my eyes my teacher *Reb* Mendele grew to be the greatest man of the generation. I started comparing him to ... even Moses, who took up the cause of the Jews with Pharaoh when they were his slaves. He strives for the poor, for the sick, for widows and orphans, tells the whole world how Isser learns to be a little man. And somebody like *Reb* Joseph Markil, his father-in-law, and the whole assembly of the town leaders – he has described them so that people should know their dirty tricks and refuse to allow it! Poor Golda, when she didn't know that Isaac Abraham looked at her 'like a wolf at a sheep'. Oh, what a great thing my teacher *Reb* Mendele has done by publishing such a book, and at his own expense.

In *Reb* Mendele's little pupil's mind it is not only certain that her teacher had published the book, but that he had written it. It was all settled. As clear as day. Except for the little horse and cart. That Mendele traveled about with a cart; he had a horse – this one went around with his books in a sack. The child's mind was working hard. Searching for an explanation. And found it.

It's winter now. And the book says in black and white that it was 'autumn time.' It was then and in summer that *Reb* Mendele traveled around with his horse and cart. When it was warmer.

That put an end to all doubts. He was the man. Now I saw *Reb* Mendele traveling around in the summer, sitting on the box of his cart, whipping up his horse, such a wise little horse, carrying *Reb* Mendele to Glupsk at the right time – a dumb tongue, but with plenty of sense. How I would love to see that horse! I wouldn't tear a single hair out of her tail – it would be a sin!

Where was the horse now? Where did he keep it? I wanted to know – at once! I had to return the book to him. I would ask him at the same time, and then I would know everything.

A silvery evening in early winter. The little pupil hid herself in good time behind the house. Everybody was on the go inside. They all came before time, young and old, waiting for the teacher. I too was waiting – for Mendele *Mocher Seforim*. Here he comes! I steal out of my hiding place, approach him with tremendous respect, produce the book, and stammer:

'It's a … love-love-ly book. But where's the horse? Where's the horse?'

'What horse?'

'Your horse, that carried you to Glupsk – your little horse.'

My teacher *Reb* Mendele gave me a sidelong look with his kind eyes. He smiled, laughed softly, but not an ironic laugh. He looked at me happily, as though the whole thing amused him.

'You take me for that Mendele? Oh dear, the things a child gets into its head!'

I must have looked lost. I stammered: 'But you are – the book says you are – '

'What am I, what am I compared to him? Mendele Mocher Se-forim is dead; he died long ago. Oh dear, the things a child gets into its head! But I see that you like him, that other Mendele, you like him, eh? There aren't many Mendeles like him. His books ... I'll let you have another one tomorrow.'

I had never known my teacher *Reb* Mendele so talkative. But I still didn't get the hang of it all. His words got tangled in my mind. That evening in 'school' my pothooks and hangers were more re-bellious than ever; they ran up and down all over the place; they wouldn't stay still. Two Mendeles kept turning in front of me. I saw them both riding on the cart, talking to the horse.

J. Leftwich, (ed. and trans.) *Great Yiddish Writers of the Twentieth Century* (Northvale, NJ: Jason Aronson, 1969), pp.543–7. Reproduced by kind permission of Michel Grojnowski and Jason Aronson, publishers.

NOTES

Shalom Jacob Abramowitsch (1836–1917), born in White Russia, was known by his pen name, Mendele *Mokher Sephorim*, Mendele the Bookseller, in Hebrew. A prolific writer, journalist and a translator of the Torah into Yiddish, he wrote orig-inally in Hebrew, then turned to Yiddish. He felt deeply for his people, portraying their oppression, misfortunes and conflicts, often in humorous, satirical images. Considered, along with I.L. Peretz and Solomon (Shalom) Rabinovitz (Sholem Aleichem), one of the 'fathers' of Yiddish literature, he pioneered a new, colloquial style in Hebrew and Yiddish writing, resembling natural, spoken language. Mendele *Mokher Sephorim*, the author of unforgettable classics, such as The *Travels of Benjamin III*, *Fishke the Lame*, *The Nag* and countless stories, remains a beloved figure in Jewish memory.

Lili Berger, a novelist, journalist, short story writer, literary critic and transla-tor of wide acclaim was born in Poland, in 1916, and received a traditional Jewish religious education, in addition to attending a Polish-Jewish gymnasium. Ms Berger emigrated to Paris in 1936, contributing to local Yiddish serial publications. Residing in Paris, her articles have been published in numerous magazines, worldwide.

6

Time of Peace

LEON WELICZKER WELLS

A Memoir

I shall begin with the time of peace, before the Germans came. On Saturdays the inner part of the city was deserted. Hardly any grownup walked on the streets, and if one did so, he was filled with the silence. He would hurry to get quickly to the outskirts, where there was more life.

Here and there, one would see children playing in front of their homes or in the marketplace, and their voices were muffled. Laughter was rarely heard from the windows.

Only, from the nearby synagogue, the old songs of the pious ones: a thin monotone threading the silence.

'A psalm, a song for the Sabbath day.'

The Sabbath really began on Thursday. That afternoon Mother would go to the stores and markets to shop for the weekend. In the evening the poor came to those who were better off to borrow money for the Sabbath supply. On Thursday, too, Father would cut the children's fingernails, and his own, wrap them in a piece of paper, add wooshavings, and burn them. Because, as it was said, fingernails resume their growth on the third day, it was the custom that the paring of the nails be done on Thursday. Therefore, the nails wouldn't start to grow on the Sabbath, but on the first day of the week. It was also believed that the nails must be burned so that one's soul would have peace after death. Otherwise the soul would have to gather up all its lost fingernails.

The whole of Friday was taken up with preparations for the next day. Mother arose early – in the winter, when the day is short, as early as two o'clock in the morning – to bake, cook, and clean for the next day, for Saturday, our Sabbath day. On Friday the food was different from that of any other day. In the morning there was a fresh buttered *pleztel*, an oval-shaped, baked, thin dough covered with seeds and onions. I especially liked the *bube*, a potato cake one ate with meatballs and sauce for lunch.

The younger children did not have to go to cheder (the lower grade of religious school) on Friday. After lunch we boys accompanied Father *schwitzen* (sweating) in the steam bath. This bath with its steam, its *reisigbesen* (the scrub brush) to rub our hot bodies with, the people lying on the wooden boards, sighing, enervated by the steam, was an ever-new and exciting event for us boys.

On our way home we passed a stand where we would stop for a glass of fruit juice and seltzer. We could see the little girls in front of their houses, already dressed for the Sabbath, their hair freshly washed and combed, and shiny from the kerosene used to wash it.

At home Mother, dressed in her holiday outfit, greeted us, and we felt the house filled with a holiday atmosphere. We hurried to change from our everyday suits into special ones.

Then came the evening. About half an hour before sundown the *shames* (sexton), a short, long-bearded old man in a shabby *bekeshe* (a long, silky black coat), ran hurriedly through the streets and rapped on the house doors with a wooden hammer as a signal that the Sabbath was about to begin.

Our house now came to life. Everybody ran around trying to get ready to 'bench the lights' (the benediction over the Sabbath candles) exactly on time. On the street one could see belated business people desperately hurrying to reach their houses for the ceremony.

My mother covered her head with a white kerchief and went to the table on which two covered *challahs* (Sabbath bread) were placed. Also on the table were two silver candlesticks and one three-armed brass candelabrum. She lit the candles, covered her eyes with her hands, and said the blessings. For a while there was complete silence in the room; then we heard her soft voice saying 'Good Sabbath.'

The lighted candles within the houses shone out into the street, and the entire inner part of the city was illuminated by thousands of candles one could see glimmering through the windows.

We boys now left with Father for the synagogue. He was dressed festively in a black coat with a velvet collar and a black velvet hat. Each of us boys carried a prayer book and marched solemnly abreast of Father without exchanging a single word.

All the Jewish men of the city were assembled in the synagogue, which was aglow with candles. The faces of the people shone from beneath their velvet hats or the *Straimeln* (a fur-edged hat). The beards, which practically all the married men wore, were shiny and combed, and some were freshly trimmed. Some of the men even wore black silken coats, as festive as their mood, carefree, happy, ready for the coming Sabbath. We children, too, felt the holiness of this hour that elevated us above everyday life.

After the prayers the out-of-town beggars gathered at the exit. Father always took one of them home; he was the *oirach* (guest) for the Sabbath.

In front of our house Mother waited for us, sitting on a bench with her daughters and neighbors, discussing the hard work all of them had done in preparation for the Sabbath. When she saw us coming she would rush in ahead of us. We greeted everybody with 'Good Sabbath', and, following Mother into the house, we all sat down around the table. Father poured the raisin wine into the tiny silver cups that stood next to each of our plates, and began to sing 'Shalom Alaichem' (Peace be unto you), the greeting of the Sabbath angels. Next song of 'The Woman of Worth' was chanted. We children joined in the singing. Afterward Father made *Kiddush* (the blessing over the wine) and drank the wine. After him each child made the blessing and drank his wine. Then Father poured water over his hands and spoke the blessing over the *challah* (Sabbath bread), cutting it, dipping each piece in salt, and giving everyone a piece of it. The dipping of the *challah* in salt symbolizes the salty Red Sea that divided into two parts, letting the Jews pass through on their exodus from Egypt.

My Mother served gefilte fish, which we children liked especially, followed by a wonderfully aromatic soup with noodles, then meat and dessert. Father and we children sang *Smires* (Sabbath mealtime hymns) between the courses. Tea was served last, and after it we said 'After-Meal Grace'.

When dinner was over, my parents liked to sit and read. My father usually had his newspaper, while my mother read a book which, when I was older, she would send me to get for her on Friday from the library. We children ate nuts and played until it was time for saying our night prayers and going to bed.

The next morning, on Saturday, after breakfast, Father again went with us boys to the synagogue. Here, sometimes, there was excitement during the morning prayers. It was an accepted custom that if anyone had any grievance against the community or any member of it he could step up to the podium just prior to the reading of the Bible, with the Holy Scrolls lying on the table on the podium. The man had the right to announce that he wouldn't let the scrolls be read until the entire congregation listened to his grievances. Everyone would sit down, and there would be grave silence in the synagogue. Everyone knew that it must be a serious grievance; otherwise no one would take the responsibility for stopping the reading of the Holy Scrolls. The grievances varied. On one occasion a friend of a widow accused the community of not taking proper care of her; on another, a man complained that a member of the community had opened a store next to his and was taking away his already meager livelihood.

I remember a time when the butcher, with his loud and raucous voice, complained that there was gossip that he cheated with his scales; that would mean to everyone, of course, that he was not true to the Jewish religion, and therefore could not be trusted to be selling truly Kosher meat. He could lose his livelihood through the rumor of dishonesty, of course, and wanted to know who was responsible for it. He wouldn't leave the podium until the community leaders promised to investigate the whole problem.

The airing of grievances was employed mainly by the poorer members of the community, because the well-to-do and influential had other means of letting the community know of their complaints. When grievances came up at the synagogue, they became the chief topic of conversation for the whole of Saturday, and often for weeks to come. This method of laying one's problem before the community is very ancient; a description of it can be found in the Talmud of two thousand years ago.

Sometimes a *Magid* (storyteller) came to the synagogue. He spoke in fables or in instructive parables. The *Magid*'s visit and what he had said were a basis of discussion for weeks. He would go from town to town, preach in the synagogue on Saturday, and on Sunday would collect offerings from house to house. This was his livelihood.

When my Father and we boys returned home at noon on Saturday Mother took the *tschulent* out of the oven. This is a type of bean and meat casserole that is cooked on Friday and kept in a hot oven until the next day. On Saturday, too, we ate a special dish, the *kugel* (round), so named because of its shape. It was normally made of macaroni and raisins or grated potatoes, and in rich homes sometimes out of rice and raisins. The *kugel* was a symbolic dish showing that in life everything is round – today one is rich; tomorrow one can be poor, or the reverse. After the meal my parents, as did all the others in the city, took their naps.

Now we children rushed out to the street to play with the neighborhood children. We were never as noisy on Saturdays as on other days, so as not to awaken our parents; moreover, we were permeated with the holiness of the day. We could play until about four o'clock.

As much as we disliked parting from our playmates on weekdays, today's parting was even worse, because we knew that the *rebbi* (religious teacher) would be waiting for us in the house, ready to test us in front of our father to find out how much we had learned during the week. If we couldn't answer the *rebbi*'s questions, a good beating awaited us, followed by reproaches from my father that lasted all the next week.

After the 'testing' we all visited my father's parents, for Mother's parents didn't live in the same town. Grandmother sat in front of her house in a long black dress, with a white scarf on her head, reading the Bible.[1]

When she saw us she would get up, greet us with a happy smile, and lead us into the house. Here, too, it looked different than on weekdays. The floor was scrubbed, and the table, which boasted brass candlesticks, was covered with a white tablecloth.

Grandfather, who was a tall, well-built man with a long white beard, was sitting, in his black silken coat, his *Straimel* on his head, in front of a Talmud, studying. When he saw us he would get up and invite us to the table where all my other uncles and aunts were already sitting. Grandfather would then inquire about our lessons in *cheder* and about the portion of the Bible we had studied that week. Father shone with pride when I knew the correct answers.

Then we children would go into another room, and Grandmother would give us sweets and fruits. Generally there was great fighting among us, everyone thinking that he didn't get the right share. Grandmother, who was smaller than some of her grandchildren (being a tiny four-foot-eight), smilingly would try to satisfy everyone. Then, the quarreling over, we would start to play while the ladies, sitting on one side of the table in the next room, conversed in low tones in order not to disturb the men, who liked to revive old memories or discuss politics. Sometimes we stopped our games and gathered around the adults to listen to their talk. Even though we usually didn't understand much of it, we felt grown-up being able to listen at all.

On Saturday evenings Grandfather and Father and the rest of the men went to the synagogue. We went home where we waited impatiently for Father's return. When he arrived, he poured wine into a cup, making *Havdalah* (meaning separation – the separation of the holy day and the workday), and so the Sabbath ended.

The festive hours were now over, and 'everyday' life begins. Another week had begun. Mother made a fire in the oven, and my older sister Ella, who went to school, had to do her homework.

The next day Father, as usual, took the train from Stojanov, the name of our town, to Lvov on one of his various business enterprises.

Selected text from the updated 1999 edition of the *The Janowska Road*, by Leon Weliczker Wells, published by and used with permission of the US Holocaust Memorial Museum, Washington, DC (pp.12–17). Previously published in 1963 by the Macmillan Company as *The Janowska Road* and in 1978 by the Holocaust Library as the *Death Brigade*.

EDITOR'S NOTE

1. In Yiddish.

NOTES

Leon Weliczker Wells was born in Poland, in Stojanow, near the city of L'viv, today in the Ukraine, in 1925. His book, *The Janowska Road*, speaks of his life between the ages of 16 and 20 as a prisoner in the Janowska Road concentration camp. He escaped a number of times, and after the war testified at the Nuremberg Trials. *The Janowska Road* was initially published in France, to great acclaim. Dr Wells lived in the United States from 1949, earned a doctorate in engineering and held several patents. He wrote two other books about his Holocaust experiences, *Who Speaks for the Vanquished* (1988) and *Shattered Faith* (1995). Leon Weliczker Wells died on 19 December 2009.

7

The Bride

ISRAEL JOSHUA SINGER

Excerpt from a Novel

During all the festive Seven Days of the Seven Benedictions, the aunt and uncle of Malkah lived in an agony of fear. Malkah was gunpowder! Malkah could explode at any moment! Malkah could get up in the middle of everything, leave Nyesheve and disappear without a trace.

From the day on which the stammering uncle came back from Nyesheve and announced that the great Rabbi wanted Malkah to be his bride, he and his wife had not known peace. Side by side with the incredible joy of the event – they, the obscure, the fallen, the penniless house of a long-dead Rabbi, were about to be lifted into an alliance with the world-famous head of the dynasty of Nyesheve! – together with that joy, almost intolerable in itself, there was the unremitting fear of their niece, Malkah Spitfire. Their lives were in her reckless hands. One characteristic gesture of hers, and they would be back in the dust from which the Rabbi of Nyesheve had raised them. And there was not one moment in which their happiness was not overshadowed by distrust and anxiety.

When the stammering uncle came home, and imparted the news to his wife, she looked at him pityingly, contemptuously, and answered in one word:

'Idiot!'

Aunt Aidele wore the trousers in that house. She considered herself the brains of the family. The proposal made by the Rabbi of Nyesheve, and brought home enthusiastically by her husband, was ridiculous.

'*The* match for our Malkah Spitfire', she said, mockingly. 'And if you want to have your beard torn out by the roots, just tell her about it, that's all.'

But in the first momentum of his joy, the stammerer rushed straightway to Malkah. Without preparation, and only fearing that his wife would interrupt and silence him, he broke the news.

'*M-m-mazel-tov,* good luck! Congratulations!' he babbled at his niece. 'You're g-going to be the wife of the Rabbi-bi of Nyesheve!'

Aunt Aidele rushed after him in time to hear these words, and she became quite white with fear. But Malkah Spitfire only laughed. She laughed naturally at first, as at a good joke, but gradually her laughter worked itself up into an uncontrollable spasm. She could not stop. And when the laughter exhausted itself for a moment, she did not ask what kind of man this famous Rabbi of Nyesheve was, what he looked like, how old he was; she only panted until the fit of laughter returned and doubled her up.

'Oh, Mama!' she cried, and continued to laugh.

They stared at her.

'Are you mad?' her uncle stammered. 'Don't you want the Rabbi of Nyesheve?'

Malkah mastered herself for a moment. 'Of course I want him! Only you've forgotten the cake and brandy to celebrate with ...'

The stammerer looked at his wife. This was the first victory he had ever scored over her, probably the first he had ever scored over any one. In his exultation he forgot his fear. He became aware suddenly of qualities of manliness. He approached his wife, tucked his thumb between two bent fingers, and thrust it derisively under her nose.

'Well!' he crowed. 'Aristotle! Who's the wise one now?'

Taken aback, Aunt Aidele turned up her eyes to heaven and murmured: 'God grant it!' Then she turned them back on her husband and said, warningly: 'But be sure to get your bear before you skin him!'

And so the match was arranged.

When the news became public, every relative of Malkah, close and distant, took on a new dignity. But everywhere, mingled with that dignity, was uncertainty. They could only explain Malkah's acquiescence to the fantastic match with the aged Rabbi as one of her characteristic, mad tricks. Malkah was capable of anything – just like her mother. By the time she was sixteen years old Malkah had run away three times; and three times she had been brought back, and the matter had been hushed up.

'Wicked blood!' they said of her in the family. 'She has it from her mother. She took it in with her mother's milk.'

Malkah's mother, a daughter of a Rabbinic house, and daughter-in-law of a Rabbi, had also run away – but successfully. She had been, in all, fifteen years older than her daughter. They had married her off at the age of fourteen and within a year she had given birth to Malkah. Eleven years after the mother's marriage, when Malkah was already ten years old, and marriage proposals were already coming in, the great tragedy took place. The twenty-five-year-old wife of the Rabbi of Prze-mysl left her husband and her daughter to run away to Budapest with a cavalry officer of the local garrison.

The family cursed her and wiped her name from their records. Her husband, a sickly scion of a Rabbinic house, died of loneliness and humiliation. Bur no one outside the family knew the truth. It was given out that the Rabbi's wife was a very sick woman, and that she was living abroad in a sanitarium under the constant care of doctors.

Malkah the orphan was taken over by her aunt Aidele. Aunt Aidele had had no children by her husband, the stammerer; and as she was widely known for her irreproachable religious life, the family decided that she should have the upbringing and education of the orphan. Malkah was to be made by her aunt and uncle into an example of Jewishness and God-fearing piety.

The stammerer set to work at once. The ten-year-old girl received, every day, long instructions in the duties of a daughter of Israel. For hours at a stretch her uncle explained the laws to her, and read her fearsome passages from morality books, in particular the descriptions of hell and its fires. The stammerer was a scholar and an authority on the infernal regions; he knew all the paths, fiery river and lakes, all the instruments of torture, the grids, the blazing pitch and sulfur baths, the white-hot prongs of the devils, and all the beds with their upright spikes. His wife, not as learned as he, had her own way of instilling reverence and dutifulness into the little girl. Lazy by temperament, too poor to have the many servants she would have liked to have, she taught the girl obedience by making her fetch and carry, by turning her into a mixture of scullery maid and personal attendant.

But the little girl already had a character of her own. She stood up against her aunt and uncle, and gave as well as she got. She would listen once to any story her uncle told her about hell and its compartments. The second time she rebelled.

'I've heard that!' she said sharply, and turned her back on him.

After the first instant of submission, she ignored her aunt's orders. She had to be called a dozen times before she answered. And when her aunt, emulating her husband, began to recount stories of the saintly lives of Rabbis and their chaste spouses, Malkah exploded.

'I don't want to hear that! I want to hear about my mother in Budapest!' she cried, right in the middle of a tale about the Master of the Name and his battles with a spirit from nether regions.

Aunt Aidele tightened her lips and answered frigidly: 'Don't ever dare to mention her name. You have no mother. I am your mother.'

'No, you're not!' Malkah shouted, stamping her foot. 'My mother is my mother. You're only my aunt!'

The family began to be afraid of the little spitfire.

'Her mother!' they murmured, horrified. 'The dead image of her mother, may her name be blotted out!'

Like her mother, Malkah grew swiftly into a tall, slender woman. She had blazing, dark eyes, but with all their darkness they were not Jewish. They had the wildness of the gypsies in them. Her hair was thick and black, with a blackness that glimmered blue. It lay on her head straight and smooth, without a suggestion of a curl. Equally black and thick and smooth were her eyebrows, which met above her thin, straight nose. Only toward the tip her nose broadened slightly, curving into the wide, sensitive nostrils.

As her aunt combed the little girl's hair, and braided it, she sighed.

'Nothing Jewish about *you*: the same smooth black hair, the same straight Gentile shoulders as – as *she* had.'

'She' was the mother, who was never mentioned by name. She had had a sharp tongue, and had spared no one; Malkah was the same. Malkah was wild and obstinate and rebellious. There were times – days at a stretch – when Malkah behaved like some young untamed animal. She laughed at the top of her voice, without rhyme or reason, ran from room to room, shouted, leaped on and off chairs. And there were times when, equally without rhyme or reason, she sat silent, obdurate and motionless.

'There's something evil in that child', the aunt said frequently to her husband. 'A devil, a spirit out of hell!'

That something evil showed itself whether Malkah was in high spirits or in low. Her playfulness was not like the playfulness of other children. It was furious, ungovernable. She would fill the house with children, upset the leather chairs, shove the furniture around, pull the drawers out of the desks and scatter her uncle's papers on the floor. Her favorite games were to build a train, seat the children on it, and set out on a journey to Budapest, to her mother, or to make marriages.

Next to this she liked most to play at marriage. She would pull out her aunt's dresses and furs and crinolines and hats, and deck herself out as a bride. She would unearth her aunt's jewelry – brooches, chains, necklaces, stickpins – and cover herself with them from head to foot.

Her aunt, coming in, would scream: 'Malkah! You'll ruin me! Malkah! Am I not poor enough already?'

Malkah was unmoved. As soon as her aunt left the house, she was at it again. She infected the other children with her own spirit. She yelled, danced about the room, sang, and turned the house into a bedlam. 'Shout!' she commanded. 'You're on the train! We're getting near Budapest!'

The 'marriages' were as noisy as the 'train-rides.' On one occasion a neighbor came to Aunt Aidele, confused and horrified. Malkah had made herself a bride, and had chosen an eight-year-old boy to be her bridegroom. After having gone through a mock ceremony, Malkah had commanded two of the little girls to conduct bride and bridegroom to their bed! The children, going home, told their mothers, and the bridegroom's mother came in weeping.

'I can't understand that', she complained. 'Where does that child get it from?'

For a long time Aunt Aidele tortured Malkah to find out who had told her about bride and bridegroom going to bed. But Malkah set her teeth and did not answer. In the night Aunt Aidele, unable to sleep, woke her husband.

'Listen, you', she said tugging at his skull-cap. 'That little demon will bring shame on us, as her mother did.'

Malkah developed an intemperate love of little children, a love so wild that children ran away from her, and mothers were frightened. Whenever she could lay her hands on some tot, she would press it so fiercely to her bosom, kiss it so rapturously, that the little one began to scream.

'The demon!' mothers exclaimed, when they saw her in the distance. And they pulled their children into the house. Under their breath they muttered: 'Salt in your eyes! Pepper in your nose!'

It came to such a pitch that whenever a child fell sick in the village, the mother would come to Aunt Aidele, and beg her for a thread from one of Malkah's shawls. A thread from the shawl of a possessed woman was a specific against the evil eye. Aunt Aidele wept with the shame of it.

At the age of thirteen Malkah ran away for the first time.

With nothing but the clothes she had on, without a coin in her purse, she boarded the train for Budapest where she knew her mother lived. What her mother was doing there, she did not know; nor did she have an address. She only knew that she was going to find her mother.

She was stopped by the train police and turned back home. Aunt Aidele thought that, on being brought back, the child would weep, would be frightened and ask to be forgiven. But Malkah was hard as stone. She stared at her aunt out of eyes that already showed the first hunger of adolescence and said:

'Wait! I'm going to do it again! I'm going to find my mother!'

Then Aunt Aidele and her husband explained things to Malkah. Day after day they spoke against her mother, explained what an evil woman she was, how she had brought shame and humiliation on the family and how, because of her, Malkah's father had died before his time. That woman, they said, had a forehead of brass and a heart of stone. She had cared nothing for her husband, nothing for her child.

Malkah was unmoved. 'I'm going to my mother', she repeated.

'If you go to your mother, they make you eat swine.'

'I'm going to my mother.'

'You'll have to live with non-Jews.'

'I'm going to my mother.'

'They'll make you wear a cross.'

'I'm going to my mother.'

Malkah was as good as her word. She ran away twice. But she did not find her mother. The woman had disappeared, had been swallowed up, and Malkah had to return to her aunt and uncle. And after her last attempt something came over the girl. Her silences became more obstinate. She no longer played with other children. She sat at the window by the hour, staring at the garrison officers as they passed down the street, staring mutely at them as they approached and as they receded into the distance.

It was at such a moment that her uncle burst in on her with the great news from Nyesheve. No wonder he and his wife were beside themselves with joy, for, apart from the good luck which it meant for them in the way of prestige – and something more substantial than prestige – it also meant that they would be relieved of their impossible niece. What hope had she? Poor, friendless, eccentric, evil-tempered, she might well stay on with them until her hair turned gray or until (God forbid!) she stooped to marry some laborer.

They could hardly believe it.

'If it was only over! If I only could see her standing under the canopy!' her aunt repeated. And she prayed to all her ancestry, to the Rabbis and pious wives in paradise, to stand by and see the match through.

They stood by, and Aunt Aidele saw her niece standing under the canopy side by side with her bridegroom, the Rabbi of Nyesheve. She went along to Nyesheve herself, and took part in the Seven Benedictions. And she was still incredulous. *Something* was going to happen. Malkah *always* had something in reserve.

'I don't understand it', she said nervously to her husband. 'It's too good to be true. My heart tells me something is going to happen.'

But nothing happened. During the months that passed between the announcement and her marriage, Malkah asked no questions about her bridegroom. She danced with joy over every present he sent her. He sent her a great many – diamond rings, earrings, brooches, bracelets and even diadems set with precious stones. One or another of the three wives he had buried had worn all of these. As each one of these had died, her respective daughters had claimed their mother's jewelry. But the Rabbi had accumulated a three-fold store, and even when the third wife died he still refused to divide the heritages. He locked the jewels away in the big iron safe, which stood in his room, and he never let the keypads out of his possession. He was in no hurry. He had calculations of his own. Now he sent the jewelry piece-meal to Malkah, and Malkah danced with joy. She covered herself with precious stones from head to foot, and tried to see herself all at once in the single half-size mirror, which stood in her aunt's room. She strutted from one end of the room to the other, and made great gestures, such as she imagined proper to a princess or a coun-tess. Besides the jewels, the bridegroom sent large sums of money for her trousseau. At first he tried sending her some of the costly clothes that had been worn by his three wives, priceless satins, silks and furs. But Malkah would not have them. It took a long time to make Rabbi Melech understand that clothes may be made of the finest materials, and may be as good as new, but if they are no longer in the fashion, they cannot be worn.

'So?' he said in astonishment to the stammerer, who repeated from memory, phrase by phrase, what his wife had told him to say. 'Not in the fashion? There's no understanding these strange creatures.'

He therefore sent money, and plenty of it. All day long Malkah flitted from one shop to another, buying silk, velvet, satin, wool and linen. She brought the brightest and most striking colors, materials as stormy as her own moods. She bought at first glance, luxuriously, in fantastic quantities. And she refused to let her aunt bargain.

'Lunatic!' her aunt exploded. 'What do you need all that stuff for? You're throwing money out.'

'I want it!' was the sharp answer.

The tailors brought their sewing machines into the house to make her wedding clothes. The older men sat with crossed legs, crooning melodies; the younger men sang snatches of German songs that had been carried by devious routes into the village, and made eyes at the bride. The whirring of the machines, the singing, the constant dressing and undressing, the measuring and re-measuring, filled Malkah with happiness. She even caught her aunt around the waist and kissed her furiously on both cheeks.

'Lunatic!' her aunt panted. 'Let go of me! You're leaving red marks on me.'

The idea of the wedding, too, filled her with ecstasy. She did not think of her husband to be. She knew he was old; and therefore she demanded that the wedding be held in another town. Then she forgot Rabbi Melech completely. When the wedding came, she liked it. She had always liked the game, and here she was, playing it on a grand scale, with real clothes, real ceremonies, real banquets and wine and musicians. Even the preliminary clashes with her husband did not upset her. The first time, when he asked her to let them shave her head, he had given way easily. The second time – in the dark room there – he had been terribly angry, an angry, scolding old man. It did not matter. She was even pleased by the spectacle; she had almost laughed aloud.

She did not look into the future. The excitement of the moment, the crowds of Hasidim, the flattery, the noise, the good wishes, the importance bestowed on her – everything was good while it lasted.

She liked, too, the long ride from Kiteve to Nyesheve. It was jolly. The Jews of the villages on either side of the road came out to see the Rabbi of Nyesheve and his bride pass by in state. They asked for his blessing and they brought presents. They brought their children to be blessed, and they paid for it with bottles of wine and jars of honey. The wives of the village Jews begged to be allowed to kiss Malkah's hand.

'Like a queen!' they exclaimed. 'The Spirit rests on her face.'

Wherever the procession stopped for the evening, there was a public festival; lanterns were hung up; there was dancing, drinking and singing. Malkah was in a continuous fever of excitement. She jumped up and down, and clapped her hands. Her attendants, the pompous womenfolk of the Rabbinic court of Nyesheve, blushed for her.

Her reception in Nyesheve was all love on the surface, all hatred underneath. Daughters, daughters-in-law, grandsons – all sorts of relatives of the Rabbi who had not come to the wedding – met her with smiles and compliments which did not conceal their envy and hatred. One after another the daughters of former wives of the Rabbi approached her, looked at her ornaments and sighed:

'Oh, that was mother's, blessed be her memory. May you wear it many, many years.'

Malkah was not at all displeased. She felt the envy and liked it. She realized at once that this place was filled with hatreds and intrigues and gossip, that the court was divided into hostile cliques that watched each other venomously. She had not been there one day before attempts were made, by flattery, by ill-natured reports concerning the attitude toward her, to win her into some of the cliques. She liked it all. Malkah Spitfire felt at home in this atmosphere; it appealed to her love of mischief and her hunger for domination. She was happy, and Aunt Aidele – if she had but known it – had as yet no grounds for anxiety. These, in fact, came into existence only when, satisfied and reassured, she returned with her husband, the stammerer, to Przemysl.

After the seven days of tumult and excitement came days of quiet and boredom. The visiting Hasidim scattered to their homes, the orchestras were silenced, and Malkah was left to her own devices in the big Rabbinic court, in the huge bleak rooms with their naked walls and their old-fashioned wardrobes filled with the moldering dresses of her three predecessors who had lived and died there. The big unwashed windows stared out upon the yard – a prospect of cracked plaster and mud. Malkah pulled aside the curtains and glued her eyes to the pane. She saw the crooked walls, the shapeless attics, the patched roofs and the rusty well that creaked from morning till night. She saw mangy cats and dogs, and Hasidim in filthy rags loitering at the doors. She felt the burden of all the years to come; forever and forever she would have to look out on this scene. And suddenly she was aware of an acute longing for Przemysl, for the windows of her aunt's room through which she had watched the garrison officers approaching and receding. She longed for distant things, the hooting of the trains, the swinging lanterns of the conductors in the night; she longed for Budapest and for her half-forgotten, far-off mother.

In all her apartment there was not one mirror; such vanities were forbidden the wife of the Rabbi of Nyesheve. When she put on her jewelry she could admire herself only in the silver trays and boxes on the tables, and the little hand-mirror she had stolen from her aunt before leaving. She looked at herself and bit her lips when her eyes rested on her own head, shaven and diminished.

She thrust her tongue out at herself.

'Monkey!' she said spitefully into the mirror.

She drew the black silk kerchief down till it touched her heavy eyebrows and pulled faces at herself. Then she wearied of the game and sat down to think.

What was she going to do with herself in this place? She remembered that she had jewelry – lots of it. And dresses. She took out the jewels, weighed them in her hand, let them run through her fingers. 'With these', she thought, 'I could travel a long way. Some night, when I can't stand it any more, when I'll be dreaming about Budapest …'

The thought of the horror which would descend on the place when they found the nest empty, the thought of the white faces and the gabbling, and the thought of her aunt and uncle in hysterics when the news reached Przemysl, made her shout suddenly with laughter. The bare walls redoubled the strange sound, and Malkah's servant, a stumpy, gray-haired elderly maid, came running in.

'I got such a fright', she panted, one red, scratched hand under the left breast.

'Fright?' Malkah asked. 'Why?'

'The others – the ones before' – the maid stammered – 'they never used to laugh.'

The maid's half-incoherent words lay like stones on Malkah's spirit. A chill settled on her, and the laughter died on her lips. The room became intolerably close; she heard the far-off voices again.

And then, one day, something happened – something astounding and unexpected and impossible – something that changed the whole Rabbinic court for Malkah, and made it the one place where, she felt, she could spend the rest of her days. Her longing for distant places died; it was as if it had never been. Here, in the ugly court, among the bleak, peeling walls was her happiness and destiny. She had seen a face.

Israel Joshua Singer, *The Sinner* (Yoshe Kalb). Translated by Maurice Samuel (New York: Liveright, 1933), pp.72–86. The work was reissued as *Yoshe Kalb* by Harper and Row (1965) and Schocken (1988), copyright © Joseph Singer. Reproduced by kind permission of Ian J. Singer and Eva Rapkin, for the translator, Maurice Samuel.

NOTES

Israel Joshua Singer (1893–1944) was a playwright, journalist and one of the leading Yiddish novelists of the twentieth century. Born in Bilgoray, Poland, a scion of a rabbinical family, he lived in Warsaw and became very prominent on the Yiddish literary scene. Some of his best known works are *Yoshe Kalb* (The Sinner), reflecting the world of the Hasidic courts in Poland, and *The Brothers Ashkenazi*, set within a rich merchant's family in the industrial city of Lodz. Migrating to the USA in 1933, he worked for the *Jewish Daily Forward*, and is especially remembered for his reports from Poland and his memoirs: *Fun a 'Velt Vos Iz Nishto Mer'* (From a World That Is No More). He was the older brother of Isaac B. Singer.

8

The Wedding Night

ISRAEL JOSHUA SINGER

Excerpt from a Novel

The marriage of Rabbi Melech of Nyesheve and the orphan girl Malkah was celebrated with great pomp soon after the Sabbath of Consolation.

When the Ninth Day of *Ab* – the day of mourning for the destruction of the Temple – had passed, thousands of Hasidim set forth for the village of Kiteve, in the Carpathian mountains, where the marriage was to take place. The young bride did not want her bridegroom to come to her in her home town of Przemysl. Her uncle had tried to impress her with the extraordinary honor that was being conferred on her, when the Rabbi of Nyesheve, with thousands of his followers, came all that distance for her sake. But she would not hear of it. She was ashamed to have the entire town, and all her friends, see with their own eyes the graybeard husband she was going to take; and she threatened to run away on the day of the marriage if the ceremony was not arranged in some distant village.

Her uncle, the stammerer, heard her and trembled. He was afraid of the anger of the Rabbi of Nyesheve; but he was still more afraid of the bride. He knew his niece only too well, and he knew that she had earned honorably her nickname – Spitfire. She could be as good as her word. Nor would it be the first time that she had run away from home. And therefore the uncle would rather try to make his peace with her than with the Rabbi. He tried to explain to the latter. In carefully chosen words, with hints and remote suggestions, he conveyed the situation, softening the impression. His embarrassment made him stammer more than usual, and as he talked the sweat ran down his face. But to his astonishment the Rabbi of Nyesheve showed no anger.

'Well, well', he said, 'she's only a child. We mustn't be hard on her.'

He had picked out for the wedding the remote and obscure village of Kiteve, far up among the mountains. The Jews of Kiteve were plain folk, of simple faith. Kiteve was a sacred place. Among these mountains the

Baal Shem, Master of the Name, founder of Hasidism, had dug lime; and along these roads he had driven his wagon to market. In the little river, which ran through Kiteve, the Baal Shem had bathed; the river was narrow and shallow and level, and it ran swiftly and noisily down its stony bed between rocky banks. Only in one place it was deep enough to reach a man's chin; and in this place the Baal Shem used to wash the crusted lime off his body. Sick women and barren wives came to bathe here, in order that the Baal Shem might help them. Rabbi Melech, too, intended to dip himself here. Not that, God forbid, he did not feel himself in full possession of his manly powers; but it would certainly do him no harm to steep his body in these holy waters – the more so as he was looking forward to the begetting of men children.

The wedding was celebrated in grand style. Apart from the thousands of Hasidim and local Jews who attended, the Gentile mountain folk, shepherds and peasants, turned out by the hundred. They came in hay carts, yokels in feathered hats, rosy peasant girls in balloon blouses, with heavy folds of beads on their bosoms. They danced in the Jewish inns, and shot off their guns to the health of the young couple. The peasants brought their flocks with them; lean, long-mustachioed peasants took their horses from the plowing, carpeted their clumsy wagons with straw, and transported Hasidim to the wedding. Such an opportunity came once in a lifetime; they earned such large sums that in the night they held celebrations of their own, lighting big bonfires of dried branches. Several Jewish orchestras, and a number of wedding-jesters, had come to town; there was even a non-Jewish orchestra, consisting of fiddles, shepherd flutes and a *kozba* – a sort of bagpipe made of goatskin, played by an old, barefoot peasant in sheepskin.

The morning after the wedding a long caravan set out from Kiteve and descended the winding roads and paths toward Nyesheve. Several peasant carts had to be hired for the wedding presents. These headed the procession; immediately behind came the Rabbi and his intimates, in a superb coach. After him, in less pretentious coaches, came the wealthier Hasidim; after them, in peasant carts padded with straw, the plain folk; after them, on foot, in rags, with bundles, the beggars and hangers-on. At the end of the caravan came the young bride, surrounded by women and servants. The dust went up, the sun shone, the Hasidim sang without pause.

But neither the magnificence nor the jollity could rejoice the heart of the sexagenarian bridegroom, Rabbi Melech.

He was an unhappy man. He was returning from Kiteve to Nyesheve not as if he had just celebrated his own wedding, but as if he had just

buried a near and dear relative. The singing of his Hasidim and the min-
istrations of his attendants made him feel bitter.

Melech, the great Rabbi of Nyesheve, had reason to be sad.

On the very day of the wedding, his young bride, Malkah, had given
him a hint of what he might expect.

The Atropos of the party, the official bride-shearer, a hard-faced,
scrawny old woman, with a pointed chin and a single tooth in her hideous
mouth, grinned at the bride. 'That's all right', she mumbled. 'They all
fight. They all fight but it does them no good.'

She flashed her scissors. 'God in heaven! If I only had as many gulden
as the heads I've shaved. Come, bride, come, darling.'

Malkah cowered in her corner like an animal at bay.

Women were sent for, and they pleaded with Malkah, soothed her,
and promised her all sorts of presents – a hundred gulden if she would
only submit quietly. But Malkah gripped her hair convulsively and
shrieked: 'I won't let you. You'll have to cut my hands off first!'

'But child, what's the difference?' they urged. 'You know you'll have
to give in before you go under the canopy. Why make all this fuss for the
sake of one day?'

'I'll let you do it tomorrow', she said, between her teeth. 'Not today.
And if you try to come near me I'll scratch your eyes out, I'll bite!' And
she showed her long white teeth in a snarl of rage, so that the women
shrank away from her.

The Rabbi himself came to plead with her.

'Bride!' he said with dignity. 'You are about to become the wife of the
Rabbi of Nyesheve! You must conform to the customs of Nyesheve. It is
my will that your head be shaved today.'

'It is my will that my head shall not be shaved today', she snapped
back, and glared at him unafraid.

A sudden chill contracted the Rabbi's heart. It was the first time in his
life that any one had dared to oppose him, or had even dared to talk back.

Malkah's uncle, the stammerer, almost fainted. Something terrible
was going to happen! He was certain that the Rabbi would fly out in a
towering rage and give immediate orders to pack up everything for an
immediate return to Nyesheve. But nothing happened. Rabbi Melech
only smiled softly and said:

'An obstinate child, the true daughter of a scholar. Well, it isn't a *law*
that her head should be shaved the day before the wedding. It's only a
custom, nothing more. Let be. Tomorrow will do.'

But this little prelude was as nothing to what took place later. All day
long Rabbi Melech prepared himself for the bridal night. Marriage was

no new experience to him; three times he had stood beside a 'destined one' under the canopy; every time the destined one had been a virgin. But never before had he felt so uneasy, so excited and confused. Hours at a stretch he pored over the laws of bride and bridegroom on the night of the wedding, for the entire world like a young and unripe boy. He repeated prayers; not ordinary ones, such as are to be found in the usual prayer books, but obscure ones, printed only in special volumes, and that only in old editions. He began suddenly to comb his thick beard and ear-locks with his stubby fingers; he had not used a comb for years. He did not fast through the whole day, as is the law; he excused himself on grounds of weakness, and took some cake and some brandy. He had an old Jew come in to exorcise from him the evil eye. The old Jew washed his hands and intoned:

'*Sholosh noshim* – three women stood on a cliff. One of them said, "Sick!" The other said, "There will be neither sickness nor weakness". If any woman has done thee evil, may her teeth and her breasts drop out. As the water has no path and the fish and the mosquito have no kidneys, so may neither sickness nor weakness nor pain nor harm nor evil eye come into Melech, the son of Devorah Blumeh, for he is sprung from Joseph the Just, against whom the evil eye could not prevail. I therefore abjure all eyes: evil eye, dark eye, bright eye, green eye, narrow eye, deep eye, bulging eye, eye of a man, of a woman, of a graybeard, of a girl that has not yet known a man; I abjure you that you may find no approach to Melech, the son of Devorah Blumeh, neither when he is awake, nor when he sleeps, nor in any one of his two hundred and forty-eight parts, nor in any one of his three hundred and sixty-five veins …'

While the Rabbi prepared himself, the women prepared Malkah, the bride. For the hundredth time they explained to her the incredible, the unexpected good fortune that had befallen her; thousands of women would have given years of their lives to change places with her who was about to become the wife of the great and powerful Rabbi of Nyesheve.

'The angels in heaven', they said, 'must have wrought this wonder for you. You should be dancing with joy.'

Over and over again – until she was sick of it – they explained to her what was due to her husband, the illustrious Rabbi.

Then they caressed her head, and spat out piously against the evil eye. At night they were very tender to her. They dressed her in a long white gown that reached from her toes to her throat, so that no part of her was visible. Malkah did not oppose them; passively she let the women do whatever they wanted. And for that reason the women forgave her for whatever she had done before, and said only sweet things to her. They combed her coal-black hair with their fingers and covered her head with a blue kerchief tied with satin ribbons. They tucked in every separate strand of hair saying:

'Hide it away, bride. At least let not your shame be seen.'

Then they kissed her head and stole out backwards from the room, murmuring: 'Good luck! Good luck! In nine months may we celebrate the birth of your first son!'

And when the Rabbi came into her room, she still said no word. She only watched his every motion with alert and curious eyes. She saw him throw off his velvet *capote*, and draw his ritual fringes over his head with trembling fingers. She saw his lips in motion; he was muttering prayers to himself. She heard his heavy sighing, and behind him she also saw the grotesque, mocking shadows on the wall. But when he put out the light, and began to rub his skull-cap back and forth on his head, she leaped out of bed with the swift motion of a young goat, and poised herself right in the middle of the room, her black eyes fixed on him with a phosphorescent gleam.

For a little while the Rabbi stood there paralyzed. Something, a confusion of ideas, passed through his old, weary mind.

'Spirits! Evil spirits! They always come to poison Jewish festivities!'

He shook from head to foot. His helpless hands looked for the protective ritual fringes. But soon he came to himself, and his eyes opened so wide that the eyeballs might have fallen out.

'God save us!' he muttered. He was lost! He had not the slightest idea of what to do now. He was prepared for everything but this. In his long career as husband, which stretched back half a century to his thirteenth year, he had met all sorts of situations. His wives had not all been alike. Now, in his aged mind, a variety of thoughts, memories, experiences, all kinds of nights, all kinds of situations, recurred. There had been nights of great joy and nights of weeping, nights of tormenting inadequacy, and nights of womanly abandonment, lightheadedness. But *this*! Such – such – mockery! Such contempt! And directed against him, against the Rabbi of Nyesheve!

If only her uncle had been here, her uncle, the stammerer! Rabbi Melech would have turned on him and rent him limb from limb. The pauper! The beggar! Did he know how lucky he was to have the Rabbi of Nyesheve as his relative by marriage? Had he ever explained to this penniless orphan girl how lucky *she* was? Had he ever made her understand what was due to her husband, the Rabbi of Nyesheve? But the uncle, the stammerer, was not here! It was with her, the orphan niece that he would have to talk now, this ungrateful, disrespectful, penniless bride of his, who did not know what honor had been bestowed on her. And Rabbi Melech did not know how to argue with a female. He had never done anything but command. He had never carried on a conversation with any one of his wives; and the only other women he had ever talked to at all were the mothers who came to him for his intercession with the powers above, weeping women who trembled in his presence. What was there to *say* to a woman?

He did not want to argue with her. How can you argue with a woman? And such a young, brainless one, too. But – but he could say something about her health, could he not?

'You can't stand in the middle of the room', he growled. 'You'll catch cold, God forbid.'

She did not answer. She only glared at him with her phosphorescent eyes.

This subject being exhausted, Rabbi Melech bethought himself of Jewish piety.

'Come, come! A Jewish daughter! A Jewish wife! A family of Rabbis. No, no! It is a great sin to torment a bridegroom.'

But this did not help either. And finding nothing else, Rabbi Melech passed into a towering rage. His beard and ear-locks danced in the darkness.

'Impudent!' he yelled. 'Ignorant, impudent creature! Have you no respect, no reverence?'

In his fury he forgot who he was and where he was. He began to crawl out of bed to catch her, to teach her, with his own hands, the insolent woman, how the Rabbi of Nyesheve ought to be treated. For the world was not yet coming to an end … The world … But at this point his strength deserted him. His arms and his legs shook as in a fever. He suddenly felt all his age, and he began to groan and whimper. He was old, broken, not like a bridegroom on the bridal night, but like a grandfather who needed rest and peace.

And as he lay there, almost sobbing, his bride approached him, and began to stroke his skullcap quietly. But he was too weak, too broken, to stretch out his hand to her. She tucked him in carefully under the thick, heavy cover, placed a big cushion over his feet, and watched him sleep.

Israel Joshua Singer, *The Sinner (Yoshe Kalb)*. Translated by Maurice Samuel, (New York: Liveright, 1933), pp. 59–78. The work was reissued as *Yoshe Kalb* by Harper and Row (1965) and Schocken (1988), copyright © Joseph Singer. Reproduced by kind permission of Ian J. Singer and Eva Rapkin, for the translator, Maurice Samuel. For information about Israel Joshua Singer, see 7. *The Bride*.

9

A Jew in the Polish Army

SIEGFRIED HALBREICH

A Memoir

In the fall of 1930, I was drafted into the Polish army. The Poles didn't like Jews serving their army, especially since many of the Jews had graduated from gymnasium, which entitled them to serve in the officers' school instead of being inducted into the regular army. Usually, the Poles found reasons to disqualify Jewish graduates. Most of the Jews didn't want to serve anyway, and we could easily be exempted by bribing an official. My father offered to bribe them: that's how Isidor got out of the army.

'It won't be so bad for me', I told my father. 'I am a well-known soccer player and a state team tennis player. They will at least respect my athletic abilities.' I wanted to prove to the Poles that Jews were not weaklings.

My first real contact with anti-Semitism was in the army. It didn't come so much from fellow cadets, but from the commanding officers. After my physical at the induction board in Tarnowskie-Gory, I was assigned to serve in the medical corps for reserve officers, but the sergeant wrote S.A.P. (Sapper Corps) instead of S.A.T. (Sanitary Corps). To this day, I still don't know if that was intentional. I ended up in Krakow, as an 'engineer' with another Jew who didn't belong in that division either. Our jobs were more like those of glorified laborers: we mostly built bridges on pontoons over the Vistula.

The drill sergeants did their best to make me and the other Jewish man feel unwanted and less capable than the other soldiers. Occasionally, we built bridges from platforms on the water. We carried heavy loads from the bank to the platform. A couple of times one of the sergeants 'accidentally' pushed me off the platform. The water was very cold and being fully dressed, it was hard for me to get out, so the other soldiers had to pull me out. At other times, when I should have served honor guard duty in the city, I was sent to an armament fort to stand guard. Later, when it was my time to serve as a sergeant, they never called on me to perform the functions of a sergeant.

Fortunately, I was athletic. During the night alarms, when we were suddenly awakened, we'd have to rush out in front of the barracks fully dressed. I was always first. This sometimes confused the Polish officers – they didn't quite know whether to regard me as a Jew or a German.

While on leave once, I found out from other Jewish soldiers that the officer on duty was supposed to read us an ordinance that allowed all Jews to attend Friday night services and take Saturdays off. It was similar to the one they read to the Christian soldiers, instructing them to go to church on Sunday. Never had the officer in charge read this to us! I came to the conclusion that if we didn't stand up for our rights, no one else would. So I went to the captain of our school and told him we were allowed to take the Sabbath off, that this was stated in the ordinance. He denied ever seeing it. Then I went to the colonel, our battalion commander.

I told him, 'Listen, there's a law that we are free to go to services on Friday nights and can have Saturdays and Jewish holidays off.' Colonel Modzelewski, a big Russian man, had no choice; he had to submit and he hated it. From then on I made sure all of the Jewish soldiers took time off on Jewish holidays. During Passover, when we had to eat special food, their kitchen couldn't accommodate us so they gave us furlough instead.

The colonel got used to seeing me. Whenever I knew the Jews had certain rights that weren't being granted, I went to him and complained. He couldn't stop me because what I was asking for was in compliance with their rules.

One Sunday night, after serving for eighteen months, I was suddenly awakened by the officer on duty.

'Corporal Halbreich, get dressed and report immediately to the officer on duty at the gate.'

'Yes.' I quickly got out of bed and dressed in my holiday uniform. In the hall, waiting for me, was a courier who led me to the gate. I had no idea what this was about.

'Corporal Halbreich, here is a night pass.'

'But I didn't ask for one.'

'There is a man waiting for you in front.'

It was dark out. A short, round man wearing a straw hat and a lighter colored suit than I was accustomed to seeing was waiting for me. His clothes had a different cut, even his eyeglasses looked different. Not from Europe, I thought as I walked toward him. Then I remembered that my aunt and uncle from the United States were coming, but I hadn't expected them to visit me.

'I'm your Uncle Samuel, Aunt Sallie's husband, from America.' He spoke in Yiddish.

After I introduced myself in Yiddish (my Yiddish is more German than Yiddish), he asked me where I would like to go. I suggested a restaurant in my favorite part of Krakow – Kazimierz, the Jewish section. We had a bite to eat; then I showed him around. I told him about my failed plans for medical school and the mix-up that prevented me from serving in the medical corps.

The following week I got a pass and went to visit him and Aunt Sallie in Tarnowskie-Gory, where they were staying with my parents. We were all curious about America. My uncle was an optometrist with his own practice in Cleveland. He had a home with a yard and he owned a car. It sounded interesting, but didn't inspire me to want to go there. I had plans to move to Palestine once I had a profession.

About six weeks later, a small miracle happened. I was called to the colonel's office.

'Halbreich, starting next week, you'll start working at the military hospital in Krakow in the pharmacy.'

It was incredible! This was unbelievable.

It took forty-five minutes by streetcar to get to the hospital from the barracks. Every day, for the remaining six months of officers' school I worked in the pharmacy at the hospital. While on furlough, I saw my uncle again and told him what happened.

'I wanted to see if I could help, so I asked for an audience with General Mond. He is the highest-ranking Jewish officer in Poland. He's in charge of the Krakow garrison. He couldn't transfer you to another division, but he could arrange for you to be transferred to the hospital.'

By the time I left officers' school in 1932, I was a corporal. Every second year, I had to return for four weeks of training in the reserves. By 1939, I was a lieutenant.

I returned to Tarnowskie-Gory and took some part-time work at the pharmacy. I began dating Marila Schneiderman, who was renting an apartment with her father's sisters who lived in Tarnowskie-Gory. They owned a small food market. We saw each other almost every day until I moved to Krakow to finish my studies in pharmacy. We had gotten to know each other very well and decided to get married, but my Zionist beliefs ended our relationship. Marila came from a very orthodox Jewish family and her parents didn't want her moving to Palestine. We stopped seeing each other.

I wanted to finish getting my credentials as a pharmacist. I had completed my two-year apprenticeship in Beuthen and my father was now able to pay for my education, so I registered at the pharmacy school at the Jagiellonska University in Krakow.

It wasn't easy for a Jew to attend a Polish university. The Polish government had established a quota system, the 'Numerus Clausus'. Since only 10 percent of the population was Jewish, only 10 percent were allowed to attend. We never reached the 10 percent quota. It wasn't official policy, but certain universities didn't allow Jews in at all. The pressure and hatred from the students and some of the faculty was so great that being Jewish was dangerous; it just wasn't worth attending these universities. Lots of Jewish students whose parents could afford it went to universities in Germany, Czechoslovakia, Austria, France, Italy or elsewhere.

I spent three years at the university in Krakow. Fellow students didn't allow us to sit down during lectures. We had to stand in the back. Sometimes, we were denied entrance into the lecture hall so we borrowed notes from other students. Often, just to get into the building, we had to fight our way past students. The authorities always looked the other way. Fortunately, attendance wasn't mandatory All that mattered was that we registered, passed our final exam, and continued to apprentice during summer breaks.

I graduated in 1935 with the degree of 'Magister'. It was like a doctor's degree but without the medical title. I was twenty-six.

Siegfried Halbreich, *Before, During, After; Surviving the Holocaust* (New York: Vantage Press, 1991), pp.13–16. Reproduced by kind permission of the author.

NOTES

Siegfried Halbreich is a Holocaust survivor. A former prisoner at the Auschwitz concentration camp, he lived to testify at the Eichman trial in Jerusalem, at the trial of one of the Kommandants of Auschwitz and at other trials of Nazi war criminals. He is an activist, donating his time to lecture to high school and university students about those tragic years.

10

The Circumcision That Wasn't

A Jewish Folk Tale

In the early days of our century, before the First World War, there lived in Otynia, a small town in Poland, a very wealthy man.

He derived much income from his inn, his mill and his stores. He bought and sold all manner of merchandise: lumber, grain, eggs and fine fabrics. And even the Polish landowner purchased wares and carried on commerce with him.

His neighbours both admired and respected him, and rarely referred to him by name. Rather, they called him 'The Master'. The Master was generous and pious. He helped the needy and maintained, in his spacious home, a synagogue with a Torah scroll and an Eternal Light burning, for all the town's Jews to pray in on Sabbaths and holidays. His sons and daughters married well into scholarly families, equal to them in status, and recently, his youngest daughter was betrothed to the son of the rabbi. It was not a minor matter to marry into the family of rabbinic sages, and the young bride and her family were the envy of all.

'May such luck and riches happen to all of us', women blessed one another.

One day a baby boy was born to one of the village girls, and she let it be known that no other but the Master was the father of her child! The gossip spread like fire: imagine the most respected man in town involved in a scandal!

The Master and his family were shocked and devastated, as if the sun no longer shone for them. His friends were full of compassion for that innocent man, facing shame and misfortune. How could a sixty-five-year-old grandfather be involved with a girl? Unbelievable!

On the other hand, how could this maid attack a totally innocent man? Why did she not accuse us, or anyone else, for that matter? There must be some reason for her claims.

On the Sabbath no one came to pray in the Master's home.

Wrapped in their prayer shawls, the pious preferred to travel and pray in a far-away city.

The Master's future in-laws returned the *tenaim*, the premarital agreement, and even the Polish landowner threatened him with expulsion.

In the Master's house the family moved as if in a nightmare, and the atmosphere was as sad as on the ninth day of the month of Av, the eleventh month of the Jewish year, commemorating the destruction of the Temple in Jerusalem. Such a shame ...

The Master himself could neither eat nor sleep, and frequently wished himself dead.

The girl persisted in her accusations, bringing her case to court, and the Master had no choice but to turn to a lawyer, Dr Herman Liberman, pouring his heart before him. The lawyer listened carefully.

'I assure you', he said, 'that I will do all I can to reveal the truth, and save your reputation and your honour.'

On the day of the trial the maid arrived in court with an infant in her arms. Serving as a maid to a Christian priest, her employer arrived in court as a character witness. As the priest entered, all rose to their feet, in reverence and homage, while the bailiff seated him on the podium, next to the judge.

Following the custom, the plaintiff's case was heard first. The Master refused to acknowledge his guilt.

The maid insisted on her story, and the defence's questions were often dismissed as embarrassing and immoral.

The maid swore her story was true, and was believed by the court, and the Master was sentenced to six months in prison, and to monthly payments till the child reached the age of 21. The judge commented that the judgment was light, due to the age of the accused, and to his flawless record.

The verdict stunned the Master, his family, and the Jews in town.

As the judge was leaving, the defence attorney approached the maid:

'Is it then true that this Jew is the father of your child?' he asked, pointing to his client.

'Yes', said the maid.

'If so, then the child is a Jew and must be circumcised', he said. In an instant, producing a sharp circumcision knife from his pocket, he ordered the maid to put the baby on the table, to be circumcised then and there.

The frightened maid, bursting in tears, fell at the priest's feet.

'Holy Father!' she cried. 'Will you permit your child to be turned into a Jew and to be circumcised?!'

Dr Liberman needed no more. The maid's words were heard by all and were part of the written protocol of the court.

The Jew was freed of a false accusation, and was found innocent. The truth was out, and the maid revealed the story of her love affair with the priest.

The Jews breathed a sign of relief, as if a verdict of death were lifted, and the Master continued to live his life of piety and good deeds.

F. Sider (collector), *Seven Folktales From Boryslaw*, edited and annotated by Otto Schnitzler (Haifa Municipality, Israel: Ethnological Museum and Folktale Archives. Israel Folktale Archives (IFA), 2850. Publication Series No. 19, Haifa, 1968). Told by Aaron Shalit from Poland, Story 1, pp.17–21. Reproduced by kind permission of the Israel Folktale Archives Named in Honor of Dov Noy and by permission of Edna Cheichel (Hechal). Many versions of the story have been preserved in IFA from different lands of the Jewish diaspora. Translated from the Hebrew and retold by Hava Bromberg Ben-Zvi.

NOTES

Herman Liberman (1870–1941) was a very prominent and talented Jewish lawyer in Poland, and a socialist leader. Active in politics, between 1919 and 1930 he was a member of the Polish parliament. Escaping to London in 1940, Liberman was appointed to a prominent position in the Polish Government in Exile.

The many versions of the story from different lands testify to the vulnerability of the Jews to attacks in the various lands of their dispersion. It was not uncommon to weave historical figures into folktales.

11

The Recipe of Rabbi Yenuka of Stolin

A Jewish Folk Tale

Rabbi Yenuka of Stolin, a small town in Poland, served his congregation with love and devotion. He knew, understood and cared for their needs. He exchanged a word of sympathy with Aaron, the porter, discussed a verse of Torah with Samuel, the old *melamed* (teacher), and shared a saying of wisdom with Rachmiel, the *shamash*, caretaker of the synagogue. He carefully listened to their words and complaints, and, when needed, wrote a healing recipe.

One day, during the spring days of Passover, a poor Jew came to the rabbi.

'Rabbi', he said, 'I am a cart driver. I work hard carrying burdens and driving people along hot, dusty roads. I feel faint and my head hurts at the end of day. Please help me.'

The rabbi listened, then tore a page from his notebook and wrote a recipe in a foreign tongue.

'Take this. It is a tested recipe against headache, and may the Almighty be with you and help you.'

The man thanked the rabbi, and was on his way.

The summer passed, and in the fall the Days of Awe were upon us. The same man appeared before Rabbi Yenuka. The cart driver's countenance was pale and full of pain.

'Shalom Aleichem' (peace be with you), said the rabbi. 'How are you and why do you look so sad?'

'Rabbi', said the man, 'my head hurts again. Please write me another recipe, and my headaches will stop.'

'But I wrote you a good and tested recipe for headache on Passover. Go to your pharmacist and ask him to repeat your dose.'

'Rabbi', said the man, 'may you live a long life. Do you think I would let your precious note out of my hands, and give it to a pharmacist I don't even know? I would do no such thing!'

'You did not give my recipe to a pharmacist?' asked the surprised rabbi. 'What did you do with it?'

'Rabbi, may you merit a good life, what do you mean? I opened a seam in the lining of my leather hat, put your note deep inside, and have sewn it back, strong and secure. As soon as I wore the hat, my headaches were gone, and I felt better. And I have had no pain for the last six months.'

'And where is your hat now?' asked Rabbi Yenuka.

'May you live a long life, Rabbi. As winter came upon us, rains and storms drenched me day by day, and furious tempests tore at my clothes. And the wind blew my hat off my head, and carried it off, stealing from me the priceless note you wrote with your own hand. Now I suffer headaches again all day long. Please have mercy upon me, and write me your note again, so my pains will pass.'

Rabbi Yenuka sighed, whispered a prayer, wrote the man a new recipe, blessed him and sent him on his way.

Yohanan Ben-Zakai (collector), *A Tale for Each Month* (Hodesh Hodesh Ve'sipuro), 1967. Edna Cheichel (Hechal), ed. Haifa Municipality. Ethnological Museum and Folklore Archives. Israel Folktale Archives, (IFA) 7912. Publication Series No. 22, Haifa, 1968. Collected by Yohanan Ben-Zakai from Jacob Rabinovitz (Poland). Reproduced by kind permission of the Israel Folktale Archives Named in Honor of Dov Noy and by Edna Cheichel (Hechal). Other versions of the story have been preserved in IFA. Translated from the Hebrew and retold by Hava Bromberg Ben-Zvi.

NOTES

The above humorous story is rooted in the deep belief of the *Hasidim* in their rabbis as holy men and miracle workers. The word *Yenuka* means 'babe' in Hebrew. Rabbi Yenuka (Israel Perlov), the 'Babe of Stolin' was the grandson of Rabbi Aaron of Karlin, and the son of Rabbi Asher.

Rabbi Yenuka, born into a distinguished, scholarly, rabbinic-hasidic dynasty of Stolin-Karlin, in the vicinity of Pinsk, today Belarus, continued his family's tradition of leadership, devotion and service to his community. According to historical sources, he lost his father and grandfather in quick succession while still in his early childhood. The story of his birth is retold in Ziporah Kagan, *A Tale for Each Month 1963*, Story

No.2, pp.16–19. Heard by Yohanan Ben-Zakai from his late father, Benjamin Globerman from Poland. Haifa Municipality. Ethnological Museum and Folklore Archives. Israel Folktales Archives Named in Honor of Dov Noy (IFA 4923). Publication Series No. 6, Haifa, 1964. The family perished in a mass execution of Jews during the Second World War.

12

My First Day in the Orphanage

ISRAEL ZYNGMAN (STASZEK)

A Memoir about Janusz Korczak

INTRODUCTION

Janusz Korczak (pronounced Yanush Korchak), the literary pseudonym of Henryk Goldszmit, physician, writer and educator, was born in 1878 into an assimilated Jewish family in Poland. The son of a prominent lawyer and an educated mother, he grew up in luxury, in an age of Polish-Jewish Enlightenment. The Polish language and culture were his own. His father's sudden illness had reduced the family to poverty, and young Henryk had to support his family by tutoring even while still in high school.

He was drawn to medicine, graduated from medical school in Warsaw, and served as a military physician during the First World War. While practising medicine he came to know many charitable organizations and orphanages, and to love children.

A talented writer of books for and about children, and a Polish radio personality, he became a celebrity early in life. But being a physician to the rich and being well paid and renowned failed to meet his innermost needs and to him, justify his existence.

And so, in the ensuing years, Janusz Korczak founded and directed an orphanage for Jewish children in an impoverished area of Warsaw, at 92 Krochmalna Street. The Orphanage became a model institution of love and care that was renowned worldwide, of new educational trends, of self-government by children, with a Parliament, a Children's Court of Justice and a Code of Laws to guide its functioning, a newspaper and a variety of other circles, maintained by children, reflecting children's needs and interests, paralleling adult society. The guiding principle was respect for children.

With the outbreak of the Second World War on 1 September 1939 the orphanage was forced by the Germans to relocate into more meagre quarters in the Warsaw Ghetto. Janusz Korczak's heroic efforts to provide food, clothing, warmth and care for 'his' children are well documented. But the Germans were not satisfied with decimating the Jewish population through starvation and disease. The 'final solution' called for deportation to death camps and the annihilation of an entire people.

Janusz Korczak was repeatedly offered escape into the Aryan (Polish) side of Warsaw. He declined the offers to leave the orphanage and be rescued. Not unexpectedly, on 5 August 1942, the orphanage was raided by the Germans. Approximately two hundred orphans, aged between 5 and 17, led by Janusz Korczak were seen driven, under guard, through the streets of Warsaw, to the dreaded *Umschlagplatz*, a gathering place near the railway tracks, where they were loaded into cattle cars, and transported to the gas chambers of Treblinka. According to the stories told, Janusz Korczak, the man and 'Father of the Orphans', was given permission to leave. He refused, and chose not to abandon his children in their final hours. He and the entire orphanage staff went with the children to their death. They remain a legend.

Israel Zyngman (Staszek), according to this memoir, was admitted to the orphanage as a 9 year old, following the death of his father. The year was, approximately, 1928. The description of his first day in the orphanage sheds light on the remarkable character of Dr Janusz Korczak.

STASZEK'S STORY

As the day of my entering the orphanage drew near, my anxiety increased. The frequent threats to send me to an 'educational institute', meaning 'A House of Correction for Youthful Offenders', along with descriptions of the harsh educational methods practiced there, took permanent root in my consciousness.

Following a conversation with the Lvov family, I was convinced I was being sent to an orphanage, instead of a house of corrections. And not to any orphanage, but the famous one, directed by the well-known friend of children – Janusz Korczak. In spite of that, during the week preceding my leaving my mother's house I saw before my eyes the wooden cot displayed at the gate of the House of Corrections, number 69 Targova Street. It was pointed out to me as the bed of the 'institute's' children, without a mattress or a cover, a bed in which children slept always in the same lice-infested clothing ... I was 9 years old.

I revealed my fears to no one, but my mother divined, nevertheless, my distress and suffering: I hardly left the house, and, deep in thought, I ate as if forced to do so, and all questions regarding my future were answered evasively.

My mother used every spare moment to talk to me to calm my doubts and fears, and to restore my self-confidence, mostly in slow afternoon hours, with few clients in our little store. Mother sat by my side, gently and lovingly describing the new life awaiting me. She told me about Janusz Korczak, and about the great achievement and honour granted to our family by my admission to his children's home. To prove it, she obtained several of Janusz Korczak's books, asked me to read the author's name, and proceeded reading aloud the most interesting parts. Mother's efforts bore fruit: she not only succeeded in convincing me, banishing my fears, but in eliciting some pleasure and joy.

The long anticipated Friday arrived. I woke up early after a sleepless night. After breakfast Mother planned a trip to the barber to shave my head smooth. I greatly regretted it, having carefully grown and cared for a shock of hair, a partition on my left and a forelock on my right side ...

My cousin had promised to substitute for Mother in the store, but she did not arrive at the appointed time, and Mother decided to send me to the barber alone. She emphasized again and again I was to go to the barber Richter on Florian Street and no other. I intended to do so, but in passing the barber shop of Mr Yazombek, who was my barber and friend until then, I saw him standing in front of his shop. When asked where was I going, I replied, for some reason, that I was coming to him.

'But I cut your hair recently', he said.

'Please cut all my hair, everything, till it's all gone!'

'No ...! What did you say?!'

'Exactly what you have heard, Mr Yazombek.'

'Have you lost your mind? You grew and tended your hair to have this forelock, and now, toward winter ... had it been summer, I would understand ...'

'Boss, he probably has scabs on his head!' exclaimed his apprentice, who until then sat in a corner. An insolent lout.

'And you, shut your mouth!' I yelled at him. 'Your duty is to clean my clothes, and that is all!'

'He is right', said the barber. 'Don't interfere while I converse with a client!'

'Well then, Mr Yazombek', I said, 'will you cut my hair?'

'Oh yes, I am beginning, but first, tell us the secret. How is it, that until today you had argued with me about every hair, and today, suddenly, to cut it all? ... Like a prisoner! Or, perhaps you have a rash on your head?'

'To tell you the truth, I have nothing to hide or to be ashamed of: I am to enter an orphanage today. You have probably heard of Dr Janusz Korczak's orphanage, at Krochmalna 92?'

'He is lying!' exploded the apprentice again. 'I saw children from the orphanage! They don't have shaven heads unless they have lice or leprosy; but just like that ...? You are going to Korczak, you?! To the 'Institute' they will send you! You will see, you will see if there is no policeman to welcome you at the gate!'

The barber, hearing this, twisted the apprentice's ear. 'You piece of filth! If you say one more word, I will throw you out!'

'Leave him alone, Sir', I said magnanimously, 'I will see that he gets what he deserves.'

'Listen, Srulek', said the barber. 'There is something to his words. Watch out: If you see a high, iron gate, and a policeman by it, know it is no orphanage but the House of Corrections. Then, my friend, pick up your feet and run! That is my advice.'

'Slow down, Mr Yazombek, my mother doesn't lie!'

'Fine. In that case, I will leave you a few locks in front. I am certain that a hairdo like that will be accepted in every orphanage, and you will look like a human being.'

'And really', I thought in my heart, 'Why not?' All the children I knew, even the most well bred among them, had a haircut similar to the one suggested by the barber. I agreed.

Mother noticed my haircut did not conform to the orphanage's directions, and ordered me to go back to the barber shop and return with my head completely shaved. I objected strenuously, claiming that only in the House of Corrections were the children's heads shaven.

Mother backed down, but I was obliged to wash my head thoroughly.

We ate our meal and were on our way. At the last moment I darted into my room to send a farewell glance to my lovely goldfinch, rocking in its cage by the window. My mother promised to take very good care of my bird, and so she did.

We left. The weather was muggy and cloudy. Waiting at the tramway station we heard the sound of thunder and, boarding the vehicle, we felt the falling rain.

The heavy rain stopped as we arrived at a street corner close to the orphanage. The sky turned light and gray again, as did my mood. My mother held my hand and in a few minutes we reached Krochmalna Street. Even though I fully trusted my mother, I still harboured some doubt in my heart, and I searched for number 92 to see if the gate was tall and made of iron and if there was a policeman nearby. I discovered there was, indeed, such a gate, so even though there was no policeman in sight, my fears returned. I decided not to go through the door if I saw a police guard.

The gate was closed, but Mother's light push opened it wide. The courtyard in front of the large building was empty.

Suddenly, from an unknown location, a tall, elderly, slightly bent woman came to meet us. She was dressed in black: a black skirt, black shoes and stockings, a dark gray, almost black blouse or sweater, and a shawl on her shoulders, also black. She held a bunch of keys in her hand. Her face was wrinkled, and her right cheek carried a wart the size of a coin.

Our eyes met. The contact lasted no more than a few moments, for I could not stand her glance. Unthinkingly, I pressed my mother's hand.

'Good morning!' said Mother.

'Good morning!' replied the lady, not taking her eyes off me, with a look that completely confused me. I could utter no sound.

'And where is your "good morning?"' she turned to me. 'Did you leave it at home?'

'Good morning', I said, with considerable effort.

'Finally', said the lady. 'And what is your name?'

'Srulek', I said, not lifting my eyes.

'Are you really that shy, Srulek, that you cannot lift your head?' she asked, lifting my chin with her finger. 'Srulek', she added calmly, 'is really a very nice name, but we already have two boys by that name in our home, we shall have to change your name.'

I stood numbly in my place, my glance riveted to the strange lady's face. My eyes filled with tears, and the large wart on her cheek began to grow ... I suddenly saw two warts, then three and four, and they turned and turned, my head turning with them ... Suddenly I felt I was no longer myself, – 'Srulek from the store', almost 10-years-old, Srulek known for his heroic feats among the neighbourhood children, – but a small child, 'Shaye-Shmaye the crybaby', defeated completely by a woman. In spite of all my efforts, my tears flowed like water, streaming down and wetting my whole face. I snuggled close to my mother to stop the river of tears, lifting my face higher and higher. A flock of black crows, wings spread wide, circled above me, flying closer and farther, in a criss-cross dance, under the gray, cloudy skies.

'Come in', said the lady. 'The rain is coming.'

Here something terrible happened. My mother, attempting a hug of encouragement, accidentally touched the peak of my cap, thus revealing the forelock on my forehead ...

'What?! You did not shave him as directed?' she shouted at my mother.

'We did, we did', Mother hastened to reply. 'Just on the forehead remained a small forelock, which probably makes no difference ...'

'No forelocks! Were you not told that all the hair had to be shaved?'

'Yes, we were told, but ...'

'Well, all right, we will take care of that ...'

By this time we had reached the building's entrance. Only a few stairs remained, and I decided I had had enough: I would not go in. I wanted to go home ...

The lady's explanations and Mother's entreaties were of no avail. I was firm in my decision. At the end, exhausting her patience, the lady in black declared she had no more time for me, and left the problem of convincing me to my mother.

'In fact', she said, 'I will send Binem, who will be his guide. He will explain everything to the boy.'

As soon as the lady disappeared from our sight, I explained to Mother, that even though there were no policemen here, this was not the lovely Dr Korczak's children's home she told me about. And therefore – back home!

Binem appeared, and, in spite of his limp, he made a good and calming impression on me. He verified that everything mother told me about the orphanage was true, even though at this time I could not meet the doctor. He had gone out, but would return soon, and would surely wish to speak with me, for he liked to know every new child joining his orphanage. And Mother added her promise that if meeting the doctor did not change my mind, we would return home. I agreed and went in.

We stood in a large hall, with a door to the right. I remained where I was.

'Well, is this not an orphanage?' asked Binem.

'I want Mister Doctor to speak with me', I said.

'Don't worry. He will be back soon. Meanwhile, I will show you around.'

'I will go nowhere!' I said in self defence. I feared this was a ruse to send my mother away.

'As you wish', he said. 'Wait here until the Doctor returns. He will pass this hall, and I shall go, in the meantime, to prepare everything.'

You can do as you wish, I answered silently. I will not stay here anyway.

Mother stood by my side silently, allowing me time to look around, and, hopefully, to get used to the place. My eyes roamed the hall, absorbing details around me.

First I saw the elevator. Then, a small stage with a large black piano, adorned with a vase of flowers. At that moment a boy, his hair beautifully combed, approached the piano, removed the vase of flowers, and, opening the lid, filled the hall with music melodious and light.

I saw before me three rows of tables, five tables in each row, all identical, except the one by the window, with a rough surface. Around each table there were eight chairs. I counted one hundred and twenty chairs in all.

Children of different ages passed us by, some indifferent to us, others throwing measuring glances before continuing on their way. A girl approached us wearing a black apron with a white, starched collar, her hair plaited in braids and coiled at the back of her head, like other girls. Hasia.

'A new boy?' she inquired bluntly, and without waiting for an answer, added:

'Why do you stand like that by your mother? Are you afraid, or, perhaps, shy?'

I really liked the girl, but her direct talk angered me, and I almost answered rudely, but I held my tongue, for she was so pretty, and her smile so sweet. I gave her an angry glance for her insensitive words.

At that moment the door opened and a middle-aged man entered.

'Oh, here is Mister Doctor', called the girl. 'Did you hear about Doctor Korczak?'

I turned to look, and, truth be told, I was disappointed: just a man, like any other. He had a small goatee, but so did many others. The music box owner, with the fortune-telling white parrot, who appeared at every market day, had a goatee even nicer than that ... At the very least, had he been dressed nicely, but – no! Why then all the respect surrounding him? I could not understand.

'Good morning, I already heard.' The man turned to Mother, as he passed by us. 'I will be back shortly.' And he was swallowed behind the door at the left of the hall.

He just came in, spoke to no one, how could he already have heard? I thought to myself. Perhaps the lady in black already told him everything.

He soon returned, wearing a green apron, his head bald. He looked different now, and younger, without his overcoat, hat and scarf.

The Doctor spoke with Mother while caressing my head. I lifted my eyes to catch his glance, but his eyes were upon my mother's face. A softness enveloped me and I thought: did anyone ever caress me like that, his hand soft as velvet? Perhaps my mother or father, but their hands were hard and rough from labour, and I felt no softness or joy, as I did from this touch.

'I see', he said, as Mother told him about my father's death and the circumstances surrounding my being brought here.

'Come with me, please', he said, leading us into the depths of the hall. I continued to walk by my mother's side, but without holding her hand. I was interested in nothing but the Doctor himself. He opened a door at the end of the hall and we entered a small room. 'Now, my dear boy, take off your shirt and undershirt and I will examine you', he addressed me for the first time. 'As you see, we care, first of all, for the health of our children. Health is most important in our lives, and children, in their years of growth are very susceptible to diseases.'

Mother helped me undress. Instead of a stethoscope, the Doctor used his ear.

'Breathe … more … more … deep … yes, yes … so, deeper, again … that is it, now the other side … he listened and listened, and the examination ended.

I dressed, and the doctor opened a square metal box, offering me candy. I refused at the beginning, out of politeness, but the Doctor encouraged me:

'Don't be bashful, take it. You never ate such candy!'

I took and tasted one piece of candy. Indeed, it was especially good, and he urged me to take another one and keep it for later.

'Now tell me, why were you so obstinate about not coming in?' he asked.

'Look, Sir, my name is Srulek. That lady said that right away they would change my name' …

'True', he interrupted me, 'we already have a boy named Srulek, and another named Srul. Imagine the confusion and misunderstanding caused by another name, so similar.'

So what? Perhaps I should be called Shaye? There is, on our street, a cry-baby by that name, and everyone laughs at him. How they would laugh at me if I returned and told the gang I am now called Shaye! It is enough that I have already quarreled with Leon about my name. I tried to convince the boys my name was nicer than other names, and Leon angered me by saying that my name was not even in the Polish calendar, and, anyway, Srulek was no name at all. And so, one word led to another, we came to blows ... So how, after all this, can I be called Shaye?'

'Wait, wait', interrupted the Doctor, 'who said that would be your name? We would not call you 'Shaye' at all. Simply, we have already a boy by that name, and I am certain you would be good friends. There are more than enough names beginning with 'Sh' or 'S', and we will choose a name you like.'

'Perhaps "Shmulek"', suggested my mother.

'No, I am afraid he would not like that', said the Doctor. 'What do you think about calling you "Staszek?"' he added, after a moment of thought.

'What ...?!' I cried, unbelieving, my eyes open wide with amazement and joy.

'You will then be called Staszek', he repeated his suggestion. 'This name also appears in the calendar. Agreed?'

My mother was about to comment, but seeing my excitement, and fearful of causing damage, she kept silent.

'Agreed', and how! Staszek! Of course! That is truly a fitting name, and similar to Srulek! I was wild with happiness. The Doctor won my heart.

'Well then, one matter has been resolved in a most satisfactory way. And now', added the Doctor, 'you are obstinately insisting on leaving the forelock on your forehead? We will not argue about that. We will do as you wish. But remember not to come to me later with complaints about it. All the children, except the oldest, who have proven they can keep their hair perfectly clean have their heads completely shaved. Imagine a boy with a forelock appearing among them. They would immediately respond by attaching some nickname to him. You know how it is with children. They may call you 'a cock', boasting of his cockscomb, or, maybe 'goat', for your forelock looks like a goat's beard ... Or, perhaps, they would make fun of the new boy, and on purpose play jokes with your name. Instead of Staszek, a nice, strong name, 'Staszek the Little Goat' … He looked at me with an expression so funny, I burst into laughter. 'It is funny, isn't it', he continued. 'Now you understand why I have warned you, so you would not come to me with complaints. So, is everything settled? Can Mother go home now, or is there any other grievance?'

I was silent, for I had no answer. I turned to my mother, saying: 'You may go home. When I come home, I will tell you everything.' Turning to the Doctor, I continued: 'Where is the barber who shaves the children?'

'Why do you need him?'

'To shave off the forelock, of course.'

'He stands before you. Sit down.'

The Doctor took a razor out of a drawer, and before I could think again, my head looked like the heads of the rest of the children.

My mother left, and the Doctor introduced me to my guide. I went with him willingly now, listening with interest to all his explanations. We went through the entire building, till shower time. The guide took care of all my needs. It was warm and merry in the showers and I enjoyed it, and then it was supper.

Fresh and clean and dressed in new clothes, I sat with my guide at table 11, by the door leading to the second courtyard. Eight children sat at the table and I soon made new friends. In the general silence a boy wearing a hat recited the Sabbath prayer and the meal began.

Of the meal we ate that night I remember only an egg, fried whole, on one side only, called here 'The Persian Eye.' I had never eaten an egg like that before, for at home, in winter, on the iron stove, we used to fry the eggs into an ordinary 'scrambled' omelette. In summer, we used a paper-burning stove, whose heat was insufficient for frying, and we ate our eggs soft-boiled.

After the meal, my guide took me to the upper floor. There were two bedrooms there, side by side, the boys' and the girls'. Fifty-one beds, all covered with clean bedspreads! The cleanliness, the order, the fresh air blowing through the open windows, all these pleased me so much! I forgot about myself, about my fears at the sight of the miserable cot at the gate to number 69 Targova Street, and I thought: What a fool I have been to be so afraid!

Before sleep we washed carefully: the hands, the face, and especially the teeth. At home, except for special cases, I did not pay attention to them, and mother had to urge me to brush my teeth.

I received a number: 41, and found my bed. After a while the noise of bedtime preparations subsided, and Mr Ezekiel, a staff member whose turn it was, began a story:

'The story I will tell you tonight is entirely new, and no one has ever heard it before. I will not reveal its author, but you all know him. It is the story about "The Wild Eagle and the Bald Vulture".

Far, far away, beyond the mountains,
Where the rocks kiss the sky,
Deep inside a cave
Lived a wild eagle ...'

The tale continued. Then Mr Ezekiel stopped, and left the room. Returning, he changed the subject.

'The eyes of the entire world focus today on Italy. The leader of the Fascist party, Il Duce Mussolini, accompanied by his black-uniformed troops, with the symbol of death's heads on their caps, broke into the royal palace and forced the king, Victor Emmanuel, to give up the rule of the land to them. In this way the murderers of the deputy Matteoti and other socialist fighters succeeded to crowning themselves dictators of Italy.'

I did not understand much of what was said, and I fell into a deep sleep.

Israel Zyngman (Staszek), *Janusz Korczak Bein Ha'Yetomim* (Janusz Korczak among the Orphans) (Bnai Brak: Sifriat Poalim, 1979). Reproduced by kind permission of Liora Amitai and Rachel Pedatzur. Translated from the Hebrew by Hava Bromberg Ben-Zvi.

NOTES

Israel Zyngman, born in 1919, was admitted to the orphanage between 1928 and 1929 at the age of 9. It is not clear how long he remained there, but his attachment to Dr Korczak was deep and long-lasting. With the outbreak of the Second World War in September 1939, following the German occupation of Warsaw, and the increasing persecution of the Jewish population, the 20-year-old Zyngman visited his old mentor and father figure, asking for advice before escaping to the east, into the heart of Russia. He came to rescue his mother, but she refused to go.

Israel Zyngman survived the war, married and arrived in Israel in 1948. Some of the information has been provided by his daughter, Liora Amitai. His book, *Janusz Korczak Bein Ha'Yetomim*, a final tribute to his hero, was originally published in Israel, in Polish, in 1976, by the Janusz Korczak Association in Israel. For additional information about Janusz Korczak, see 30. *Janusz Korczak Marches to Death with His Children*.

13

The Lamed Vovnik

ISAAC LEIB PERETZ

A Short Story

'In every generation there are thirty six righteous, upon whom the sight of the Shechinah (God) rests.' The Talmud, *Sanhedrin* 97b.

There is a legend based on this Talmudic verse that in every generation there live thirty-six righteous persons by whose merit the world exists. These *tzaddikim* (the Righteous) are among us, unrevealed and unsung, living their humble lives as poor cobblers, laborers, and even beggars. In folklore, one of them may be the Messiah. Their identity is unknown to us, and some believe, even to them. In times of stress and danger they step forward to save the Jewish community, then disappear to continue their unassuming existence.

Lamed Vov (in Hebrew) means, literally, 36, the numerical value of the Hebrew letters Lamed (30) and Vov (6). Many folktales have been woven around the Lamed Vovniks, as they are called in Yiddish, some of which feature the *Baal Shem Tov,* and other Jewish heroic figures. These legends feed upon the fundamental Jewish idea that the poor deserve assistance, and that charity is no more than justice. The beggar at our door may be one of the Lamed Vovniks, or even the Messiah ...

THE LAMED VOVNIK

'We (the story is told by a teacher of small children) once had a real Lamed Vovnik!'

'He said so himself?' I ask.

'Well, he would have been a fine Lamed Vovnik if he had! He denied it "stone and bone". If he were questioned about it, he lost his temper and fired up. But, of course, people got wind of it, they knew well enough! Yes, "kith and kin", the whole town knew it! As if there could be any doubt! People talked, it was clear as daylight! In the beginning, there were some who wouldn't believe – they came to a bad end!'

'For instance: Yainkef-Yosef Weinshenker, a man of eighty and much respected, I can't quite explain, but he sort of turned up his nose at him. Did he say anything? Heaven forbid! But there! Like that ... turned up his nose as much as to say: Preserve us! Nothing worse! Well, what do you think? Not more than five or six years after, he was dead. Yainkef-Yosef lay in his grave. Poor Leah, the milkwoman! One was sorry for her. It was muddy, and she did not step off the stone cause-way to make room for him. Would you believe it, the milk went wrong at all her customers' for a month on end! And there was no begging off! When approached on the subject, he pretended to know nothing about it, and scolded in the bargain!'

'Of course', – I wish to show off my knowledge – 'though a scholar declines the honor due to him ...'

'A scholar? Is a Lamed-Vovnik a scholar? And you think he knew how to read Hebrew properly? He could manage to make seven mistakes in spelling Noah. Besides, Hebrew is nothing. Hebrew doesn't count for much with us. He could not even read through the weekly portion. And his reciting the Psalms made nevertheless an impression in the highest! The last Rebbe, of blessed memory, said that Velvil (that was his name, the Lamed Vovnik's) cleft the seventh heaven! And you think his psalm singing was all! Wait till I tell you!

Hannah the Tikerin's goat (not of you be it said!) fell sick, and she drove it to the Gentile exorcist, who lives behind the village. The goat staggered, she was so ill.

'On the way – it was heaven's doing – the goat met the Lamed Vovnik, and as she staggered along, she touched his cloak. What do you think? Cured, as I live! Hannah kept it to herself, only what happened afterwards was this: A disease broke out among the goats; literally, there was not a house in which there was not one dead. Then she told. The Lamed Vovnik was enticed into the marketplace, and all the goats were driven at him.'

'And they all got well?'

'What a question! They even gave a double quantity of milk. The Tikerin got a *groshen* a goat – she became quite rich!'

'And he?'

'He? Nothing! Why, he denied everything, and even got angry and scolded – and such a one may not take money, he is no "good Jew" – he must not be "discovered"!'

'How did he live?'

'At one time he was a shoemaker (a Lamed Vovnik has got to be a workman, if only a water-carrier, only he must support himself with his hands); he used to go to circumcisions in a pair of his own shoes, but in his old age he was no longer any good for a shoemaker, he could no longer so much as draw the thread, let alone put in a patch – his hands shook: he just took a message, carried a can full of water, sat up with the dead at night, recited Psalms, and was called up to the *Tokhekhot*, and in winter there was the stove to heat in the house-of-study.'

'He carried wood?'

'Carry wood? Why, where were the boys? The wood was brought, laid in the stove, he gave the word, and applied the light. People say: A stove is a lifeless thing. And yet, do you know, the house-of-study stove knew him as a woman (*le' havdil* – to make a distinction) knows her husband! He applied a light and the stove burnt! The wind might be as high as you please. Everywhere else it smoked, but in the house-of-study it crackled! And the stove, a split one, such an old thing as ever was! And let anyone else have a try – by no means! Either it wouldn't burn, or else it smoked through every crack, and the heat went up the chimney, and at night one nearly froze to death! When he died, they had to put in another stove, because nobody could do anything with the old one.

'He was a terrible loss! So long as he lived there was *Parnosseh* (livelihood), now, heaven help us, one may whistle for a *dreier* (coin)! There was no need to call in a doctor.'

'And all through his Psalms?'

'You ask such a question? Why, it was as clear as day that he delivered from death.'

'And no one died in his day?'

'All alive? Nobody died? Do you suppose the death-angel has no voice in the matter? How many times, do you suppose, has the "good Jew" himself of blessed memory wished a complete recovery, and he, Satan, opposed him with all his might? Well, was it any good? An angel is no trifle! And the Heavenly Academy once in a while decided in the death-angel's favor. Well, then! There was no doctor wanted; not one could get on here. Now we have two doctors!'

'Beside the exorcist?'

'He was taken too!'

'*Gepegert* (died)?'

'One doesn't say *gepegert* of anyone like that – the "other side" is no trifle, either.'

I.L. Peretz, *Stories and Pictures*. Translated from the Yiddish by Helena Frank (Philadelphia, PA: The Jewish Publication Society of America, 1906, reprinted 1936, 1943, 1947), pp.295–99. Reproduced by kind permission of The Jewish Publication Society.

NOTES

Isaac Leib Peretz (1852–1915) is considered one of the 'fathers' of modern Yiddish literature, along with Mendele *Mokher Seforim* and Shalom Aleichem. Born in Zamosc, Poland, he received a traditional Jewish religious education, beginning, as was the custom, at the age of 3. At 6, he was already studying the Talmud. A brilliant student, Peretz taught himself Polish, Russian, French and German. Having access to a large library, he read voraciously all available literature. He also taught himself law, passed the bar and established a flourishing legal practice. Later moving to Warsaw, he became a functionary of the Jewish community. According to scholars, Peretz started to write at the age of 14 in Polish and Hebrew, but much of his early work has been lost. Soon, however, aiming to be read and understood by the general Jewish population, he turned to writing in Yiddish.

In his stories Peretz reflects the period between approximately 1850 and 1914, coinciding with the outbreak of the First World War, drawing on his people's history and experience, portraying their poverty, oppression by the authorities, their customs and internal struggles. He wrote about the conflicts between rich and poor, about the tailors, cobblers and water-carriers, about true charity and faith, about family devotion, posturing and pretensions.

Familiar with the trends of the *Haskala*, or Enlightenment, he nevertheless sympathized with the mystical, Hasidic movement, bringing upon his head the ire of its opponents, the *Mitnagdim*. Employing common Yiddish idioms, he brought modern Yiddish writing to a level equal with the best of world literature.

Peretz died in 1915, and it was said that 100,000 people attended his funeral. He is remembered with love, reverence and pride. His works were read in the ghettos during the Second World War to bring comfort to his people during their last days on earth, and are still read and loved today.

I.L. Peretz was my father's contemporary. My father, active as an educator in the Jewish schools in Warsaw, told me that one day Peretz was in a coffee shop with a mutual friend, who was writing a letter to my father. Peretz added a note:

Ikh drick iyer hand	I shake your hand
Unbekant	Unknowing
Oif credit	On credit
Und bleib demit,	And remain,
I.L. Peretz	

The friend gave the note to my father, who cherished it and showed it to me.

In August 1941, in the town of Lachowiche (Poland), my father, Herman Bromberg, his brother Abraham Bromberg (Romek) and approximately fifty other Jews, mostly teachers and other educated people, were summoned by the Germans for a day of compulsory labour. They never returned. This was the German way: at the beginning of their occupation they destroyed all potential leadership that might have organized resistance.

Polish Voices

14

Mendel Gdanski

MARIA KONOPNICKA, a Polish Writer

A Short Story (Selections)

His hair is mostly gray, and his beard – completely gray. His chest, concave under the quilted kaftan, is sometimes out of breath, and his bent spine somehow impossible to straighten, but nothing to worry about, as long as the legs and the eyes suffice, as long as the hand is strong. When out of breath, with his back wracked with pain, old Mendel fills his small pipe with tobacco from a blackened, string-tied bag, and smoking, rests a while. The tobacco he uses and which is to Mendel's taste is not of prime quality, but emits such a lovely, blue smoke. The blue smoke has another peculiarity: one can see in it things far away, and events long past.

He can see Resia, his wife of thirty years, with whom he lived, contented, and his sons, who, in search of bread, dispersed as wind-driven leaves, and his son's children, and various sorrows, and consolations, and cares. And for the longest time he can see his youngest girl, Liya, married so young and so early extinguished, who left him only with one grandson. When old Mendel lights his pipe, his mouth emits a quiet mutter. As he smokes, seeing distant visions and those never to return, his murmur increases, grows louder, turning almost into a moan. The soul of the man, the old Jew, has its sadness and yearning, deadened by work.

Meanwhile a neighbour brings, in one hand, a crock of broth, with pieces of a softened roll, and in the other, a covered plate of meat and vegetables. Old Mendel accepts the modest meal. He eats not, though, but puts it on a small iron stove, and waits.

He does not wait long. At two o'clock the door opens loudly, noisily, and in it appears a small *gimnasist* (a *gymnasium* student), in a long coat allowing for growth, a large, pushed back hat, a satchel on his back. This is a boy, perhaps of 10, who from his mother, Mendel's youngest daughter, inherited hazel eyes with a golden glow, long, dark lashes and a small mouth, and from his grandfather an aquiline nose and a narrow, high forehead. This slim, small child seems even smaller and thinner after removing his coat, remaining in his wide-belted school blouse.

Old Mendel is constantly anxious about him. His transparent complexion, frequent cough, his frail chest and bent shoulders cause his grandfather unceasing worry. He selects for him the best meat morsels, adding to his plate, and, at end of meal, pats him on the back, encouraging him to play with the children in the courtyard.

The little lad seldom follows his prompting. He is tired of his lessons, his heavy coat, of sitting in school, his long travel to school, of carrying his heavy satchel. He also has much homework for tomorrow. He drags his feet, and even when smiling his hazel eyes convey some melancholy.

A few minutes after dinner the boy sits down at a simple pine table, and pulls out of his bag books and exercise notes, while old Mendel returns to his workshop.

At twilight, the fat watchmaker, wearing his gray coat, squeezes through the low door of the room.

'Did you hear the news?' he asks, sitting down on the table's edge by the little student.

'Nu', replied Mendel, 'what do I care about news? Good news I will hear anyway, later, and bad news, nu, why should I hear?'

'There is a rumor abroad they will beat the Jews', says the fat watchmaker, dangling a foot in a cut-out shoe, with a shining steel buckle.

Old Mendel's eyes blinked nervously, his mouth trembling. He controlled himself, though, and assuming a tone of jovial good nature, says:

'Jews? What Jews? If those that are thieves, that they harm people, that they rob people on the highways, that they fleece poor people, nu, why not? I will go myself and beat them!'

'But no!' laughs the watchmaker. 'All Jews.'

Mendel's gray pupils suddenly flash. He dims them, however, with his turned-down lids, and seemingly unconcerned, asks:

'Nu, why do they have to beat all the Jews?'

'Why?' replies the watchmaker with an easy manner, 'Because they are Jews!'

'Nu', says Mendel with half-shut gray eyes, 'and why don't they go to the forest and beat the birch for being a birch, and the fir tree for being a fir?'

'Ha! Ha!' laughs the watchmaker. 'Every Jew has his quibbles! After all, the birch and the fir are ours, grown from our soil!'

Mendel almost choked, and the answer, by itself, comes to his lips. He bends toward the watchmaker, looking deeply into his eyes:

'Nu, and what did I grow from? What soil did I grow from? You, my good Sir, have known me for a long time. For twenty-seven years you have known me! Did I come here like to an inn? Ate, drank and did not pay? Nu, I did not come here like to an inn! I grew into this town like the birch in the woods! I ate here my piece of bread, true. And drank the water, also true. But for this bread and for this water, I paid. With what did I pay? You, my good Sir, want to know with what I paid?'

He stretches before him his toil-worn, shrivelled up, venous hands. 'Nu', he called with some vehemence, 'I paid with those ten fingers! My good Sir sees these hands?!' Again, he bends down, shaking his scraggy hands before the watchmaker's shining face.

'Nu, these hands did not carry the bread and the water to the mouth idly! These hands were twisted by the knife, by pliers, by screws, by the hammer! Nu, I paid with them for every piece of bread and every cup of water that I ate and drank! And I also applied these eyes that see well no longer, the back that would not straighten, and the legs, that would carry me no longer!'

The watchmaker listens indifferently, playing with his watch chain. The Jew is inflamed by his speech.

'Nu, and where is my pay? My reward is in school, with children, with the masters and the misses that learn from the book, that write in the notebooks, nu. It is also in church, where people go with books. Nu, it is also with the priest, for I bound his books, may he be well!' Here he doffs his *yarmulka* and says: 'My pay is in good hands!'

'But, as the saying goes', countered the watchmaker diplomatically, 'a Jew is always a Jew.'

New sparks catch fire in the eyes of the old bookbinder.

'Nu, and what should he be? A German? Frenchman? Perhaps he should be a horse? Nu, because a dog he became a long time ago, that he is already!'

'That is not the point', says the watchmaker pathetically. 'The point is not to be a stranger!'

'What is the point?' replies the Jew, bending backward, drawing back his elbows. 'Nu, let the good Sir tell me quickly. This is a word of wisdom! I like to hear a wise word! A wise word is like a father and a mother to a man. Nu, I would walk a mile for a wise word. When I hear a wise word, it is like bread to me. If I were rich, a big banker, nu, I would give a ducat for every wise word. My good Sir says that the

Jew not be a stranger? Nu, I say the same. Why not? Let him not be a stranger. Why should he be a stranger, why make him a stranger, when he is, anyway, to himself, one of you. My good Sir thinks that when it rains, the Jew doesn't get wet, for he is a stranger? Or, perhaps, the good Sir thinks that when the wind blows, the Jew gets no sand in his eyes, for he is a stranger? Or, perhaps the good Sir thinks that when bricks fly, they will by-pass the Jew, for he is a stranger? Nu, I will tell the good Sir, that they will not by-pass the Jew, and the wind will not by-pass him, and the rain will not by-pass him! Look at my hair, my beard! They are gray, they are white. What does that mean? It means they saw many things, and they remember. I will tell my good Sir, they saw great fires, and great storms and thunderbolts in this town, and if the Jews were free of these, I did not see it! And when night comes upon this town, the Jews have no sunlight either!'

'My Dear Mr Mendel', said the watchmaker in a tone of superiority, 'people say this and that, but every Jew, as long as he has money ...'

The old bookbinder does not let him finish, but raising his hand shakes it, as if banishing an annoying insect.

'Let the good Sir not speak to me like that! That is the talk of stupid people. If money were everything to the Jew, God would have made, in his skin, a pocket or two. And as God did not make a pocket in his skin, nu, then money is to the Jew like to anyone else.'

'Should be!' shouts the watchmaker triumphantly, raising his fat chin and stroking it. 'But it isn't! That is the point, that it isn't! In theory, anyway', he adds seriously, 'you may be right, but practice shows differently. You Jews breed like the locust, and always are a foreign element!'

'Nu, my name is not only Mendel. My name is also Gdanski. Nu, what is Gdanski? That is a man or a thing springing from Gdansk. The good Sir knows? There is vodka Gdanska, and a Gdanski chest, and a Gdanska wardrobe. As they can be of Gdansk, so am I Gdanski. I am not of Paris, not of Vienna, nor of Berlin – I am Gdanski. My good Sir says I am a stranger. Nu, how can that be? If I am Gdanski, am I a stranger? What does the good Sir say?'

The door opens violently, and the gaunt university student from the garret shoves him (the small boy) back into the room.

'Run away! They are beating the Jews!'

The old man is transfixed with horror. But soon, coming to his senses, his face on fire, like a wildcat he jumped at the student:

'What run away?! Where should he, my boy, run away?! Did he steal anything, that he has to run away?! Is he in a stranger's house?!

A stranger's home? He is in his house! In his home! He did not steal anything from anyone! He is going to school! He will not run away!'

Mendel springs up to the student standing in the doorway, tense, strained, hissing, snorting, shaking his beard.

'As you wish!' The student retorted roughly. 'I told you …'

Louder and louder, a more distinct uproar is heard at last in the deserted street. Then a thunderous explosion of screams, whistles, laughter, curses, abuse.

Hoarse, drunken voices blend with the devilish squeals of callow youths. The very air seems drunk with this roar of the rabble. An inhuman wantonness overwhelms the street, drowns it, wildly over-flowing, with a deafening clamour. The cracking of broken shutters, the rumble of rolling barrels, the jingling of broken glass, the clatter of stones, the grinding of iron crow-bars – they all seem to come to life in this hideous scene. Like flakes of thickly falling snow the feathers fall from ripped pillows and feather beds. Only a few flimsy stalls separate Mendel's room from the unruly crowd.

The little boy ceases sobbing, and, shaking feverishly, joined his grandfather. His large, dark eyes have darkened even more, and shine mournfully in his pale, small face.

A strange thing! This snuggling of the child and the nearby danger fortifies the old Jew. He puts his hand on his grandson's head, breathes deeply, and with his face still as pale as a sheet, his pupils project life and fire.

'Sh …', he whispers, soothingly. Only now he calms the boy's crying. Only now the former weeping of the child penetrates his consciousness.

At that moment into the long, narrow hallway burst several women: the rope-maker, the caretaker, the stall-keeper.

'Away, Mendel!' yells the caretaker from the doorstep, 'get away from their eyes! I will put a holy picture in the window, or a cross. They have already done that in other rooms … They don't go there!'

She catches the little boy by the hand: 'Away, Kubus, into the alcove!'

The women surround them, shield them with their own bodies, pushing behind the crimson curtain. They have known this Jew for a long time; he is a good, neighborly man. Following the women, other tenants of the small apartment building begin to slip in. The room fills up with people.

Old Mendel leans with one hand upon the shoulder of the boy, with the other moving the women aside. In a moment he regains control.

'Stop that, Janowa!' his voice sounds hard, like a bell. 'Stop that!

I thank you, for wanting to give me your holiness to save me, but I don't want to put a cross in my window! I don't want to be ashamed of being a Jew. I don't want to be afraid! If they have no mercy, if they want to do harm, nu, then they will not care about the cross or the picture ... Nu, then they are not people. They are completely wild beasts. And if they are people, if they are Christians, nu, then for them, such a gray head of an old man, and such an innocent child will also be holy.'

'Come, Kubus.'

Pulling the child behind him, in spite of the noisy protests of the people, he approaches the window, opens both its shutters with a push of his hand, standing in it in his open kaftan, a leather apron, shaking his white beard, his head high, hugging to him the little *gimnasist* in his school blouse, whose large eyes open wider and wider, fastened on the howling rabble.

The sight is so moving that the women burst in tears.

The mob notices the Jew standing in the window, and passing the stalls, rushed toward him.

This heroic courage of an old man, this silent appeal to the human feelings of the crowd is perceived as an affront, a mockery. Here they no longer look for another barrel full of vinegar to roll, another pack of merchandise to smash to pieces, another feather bed to rend, another basket of eggs to break. Here explodes that wild lust to torture, that instinct of cruelty, hidden in the individual, and like a fire envelops the crowd.

They have not reached the window, when a stone is thrown from the middle of the mob. It hits the boy's head. The boy cries, the women rush to him. The Jew releases the child's shoulder, does not even look back, but, raising his both his hands high, his eyes fixed upon the howling mob, lips pale, whispers:

'*Adonai* (God), *Adonai*', – while heavy tears stream down his wrinkled face.

When the first of the crowd reach the window, they find there an unexpected obstacle in the person of the lanky student from the garret.

Hair dishevelled, uniform unbuttoned, he stands before the Jew's window. He spreads his arms, tightens his fists, and spreads his legs. He is so tall he covers almost half of the window. Anger, shame, contempt, pity shake his uncovered breast, and like flames flicker on his dark, pock-marked face.

'Don't you dare! Hands off this Jew', he snarls like a mastiff at the first ones coming. 'Oh no, strike me, one and all, scoundrels, black-guards, good-for-nothings!'

His whole body trembles, his voice chokes with anger. His small, gray eyes seem to shed sparks.

He stands as handsome as Apollo!

Some of the more sober of the mob begin to retreat.

*   *   *

In the alcove, behind the crimson curtain, lies the small schoolboy with his head bandaged. A green lamp burns beside him. The slender student sits on the bed's edge, holding the child's hand.

In a corner sits old Mendel Gdanski, motionless, voiceless. Crouching, with elbows resting on his knees, face concealed by his hands, he has sat like that since noon, from the moment he had learned that the boy was out of danger.

This immobility, this silence of the old bookbinder makes the student impatient.

'Mr Mendel', he grunts, 'crawl out of that corner! Are you conducting a *Shiva* (Jewish mourning ceremony) or what? Just some fever and nothing more. The boy, in a week's time will go to school, as soon as the skin heals up a little. And you sit as in a nightmare, as if something has died.'

The old Jew is silent.

'You say that nothing has died. Nu, with me, has died that with what I was born, with what I have lived for sixty-seven years, what I have hoped to die with! Nu, with me the heart to this town has died!'

E. Orzeszkowa (ed. and comp.), *Z Jednego Strumienia* (From One Stream) (Warsaw: E. Wende I Spolka, 1905), pp.5–30 and by Ludowa Spoldzielnia Wydawnicza, 1960, pp.189–211. Selection translated from the Polish by Hava Bromberg Ben-Zvi. Reproduced here by the kind permission of Jerzy Dobrzanski, Ludowa Spoldzielnia Wydawnicza. This selection was translated from the 1905 edition.

NOTES

Maria Konopnicka (1842–1910) was one of the most prominent and popular Polish poets and writers. A contemporary and a friend of Eliza Orzeszkowa, she felt deeply for the maltreated Jewish community. 'Mendel Gdanski' is the literature of protest, and the author's answer to the wave of anti-Semitism sweeping Poland at that time.

Konopnicka was renowned for her sympathy with and interest in the underprivileged and the oppressed, who frequently served as characters in her poetry and prose. Educated in Warsaw and fluent in several languages, she was expelled from the capital city by the Russian authorities and lived in Italy, France and Switzerland, but returned to spend the last years of her life in her homeland.

15

Links in a Chain

ELIZA ORZESZKOWA, a Polish Writer

A Short Story (Selections)

The room was small, low ceiling to floor filled with a noisy, monotonous, quick murmur. There was no noise, but a murmur, never swelling nor subsiding, but endlessly, changelessly, without a second's pause filling the room from top to bottom. Nothing more had been heard: neither street noises, creak of shop signs, nor any sound from the land of the living. Nothing, but from ceiling to floor, and from wall to wall, talk or deliberation of clocks, hanging upon walls, and speaking, one after another, with a great many voices, dry and rattling: 'Tak-tak, tak-tak, tak-tak ...'

In the midst of this conversation or council, apparently everlasting, by a single window, by a small table lit by a long-chimneyed lamp, above a multitude of glittering circles, springs and hooks, there sat a man in a long, graying coat, with two snow-white patches, one upon his breast, the other above his bent neck: his gray beard and gray hair, escaping from under his velvet *yarmulka* (skullcap). Wearing large spectacles, a delicate tool in hand, he sat and worked at the sparkling trinkets, with a forehead wrinkled, lips curled, deep concentration in his eyes, a silver spark shining from under gray eyebrows, and reddened eyelids. Perhaps to his ear, so accustomed to the noisy conversation of clocks, other sounds penetrated with difficulty. He did not hear the stranger's entrance.

A moment later, a resonant voice erupted from the murmur, strangely alive and fresh, calling out: 'Koo-koo!' Then, with cadenced regularity repeating: 'Koo-koo! Koo-koo!', until, after the eighth time, it was silent, and the small room was filled again with the noisy, and in spite of its perfect regularity, hurried, restless conference of the clocks.

The old Jew, with the two snowy patches of age raised his head, his concentration-curled lips widened in a delighted smile, looked around him, and his glance, full of contentment met, the arrival's face, also wrapped in smiles.

'What will honourable *Pan* (Sir) …?'

Noticing, however, the expensive fur, the gold-framed spectacles, the slightly bent, but still towering posture, corrected himself: 'What does noble *Pan* desire?'

But the noble Sir, instead of answering, walked straight to the wall of the murmuring clocks, stopping before the clock emitting the sound of the koo-koo bird.

'Where did you get this clock? Old-fashioned … A peculiar dial …! Where did you get it? To whom does it belong?'

The Jew, as if jolted by a spring from his stool, jumped up and in two hurried steps stood side by side with the old gentleman, facing the tall, ebony wood cupboard. Through a door window emerged to the world the countenance of the koo-koo clock.

'Whose clock? Whose should it be? Mine! As a son is his father's, as a friend is his friend's, so it is mine! And the noble *Pan* thought, perhaps, that this clock was with me for repairs? That someone will soon come and take it away? Ay, ay! I would take a stick to who wanted to take this clock away from me! Anyone taking it away, I would make such a din and hubbub that people would come running and would drive away anybody who takes this clock away from me, for it is mine!'

He spoke very animatedly, with fervour and a playful smile, but suddenly was silent, intently fixing his gaze upon his guest, who, paying him no heed, with a raised head looked at the clock, exclaiming:

'Give me a stool and a lamp, since I cannot see the landscape on the dial. I see it is there, but cannot determine what it is.'

With that, he stepped nimbly up a stool pushed forward by the Jew, as if he had never dragged his feet.

'Bring a lamp!'

'Right away, right away, noble *Pan*!'

Uttering these words, the old Jew, lamp in hand, stood beside his guest, on another stool.

'Geneva!' called out the old *Pan* – 'yes, yes! A Swiss factory; do you know which?'

'Why shouldn't I know? Can I not know anything about it?'
Triumphantly, he mentioned the name of the factory, no longer in existence.

'This factory is no longer in this world!'

'True, oh, how true, that a factory like that exists no longer! And how is it turned on?'

They stood side by side, on stools, differing by posture, for the host was slimmer and shorter than his guest. The light of the lamp, which the Jew held high, fell upon two unlike faces, but covered uniformly by a great many wrinkles. Both wore glasses upon eyes glued, with identical rapture, upon the clock.

Suddenly released from inside the clock by a pressed spring, a metal bird flew above their gray heads and wrinkled faces, loudly and melodiously, calling out: 'Kookoo! Koo-koo!'

The Jew was first to descend the stool, and helped his guest to do the same. Then, forgetting to put the lamp away, again looked upon him.

'With permission of noble *Pan*' – he whispered timidly – 'perhaps I am mistaken, but I think that my old eyes recognized you …'

'Wait, wait', spoke the old nobleman with vivacity, 'I also remember something. Did I ever know you?'

'Noble *Pan* Ksawery from Strumienica?'

'And you? I cannot remember.'

'I am Berek, son of Shimshel, that in Strumienica held a tenancy.'

'Berek! Can this be? I remember it splendidly! My sister used you as a model for some picture.'

The Jew nodded his head and hands shaking, put the lamp on the table. Pulling out from a corner an old chair with a concave seat and a broken arm, he invited his guest to sit. He smacked his lips, laughed; his red eyelids blinked rapidly under his gray eyebrows, as if dazzled. Sitting down at last, he kept his eyes fixed upon his guest and uttered vague sounds, conveying joy and wonderment. But the old gentleman also gazed upon him with admiration.

'Can this be? You, Berek …! You, this Berek with curly, golden hair, with a blushing face, like a girl's, with eyes like turquoises? My sister took you as a model for some figure in a picture, and you have often come to the palace. So it is you?'

'I … It is I, noble *Pan*! And you, noble *Pan*, are the young Master, who had never climbed the stairs but jumped four steps at a time. When the noble count's daughter painted me, and Master Ksawery entered the room, it was as if the sun had risen. Ay, don't I remember how Master Ksawery rode on horseback, and how he danced with girls! No matter how many young masters rode on horseback, he outdistanced them all, and no matter how many girls there were, they all wanted to dance with him alone. I saw it all, standing by the fence, or by the palace window.'

'Exactly, exactly', called out the count, 'I remember you best standing by the rail fence in the courtyard or the garden, and looking at it all with eyes expressing a strangely naive curiosity and delight. More than once did we, my sister and I, talk about you, saying that you looked as if you enjoyed the whole world, and never had had enough merriment.'

'How did you fare my Berek? How do you fare now? Do you have a family and sufficient means of subsistence?'

The Jew thanked him for the kindly questions, replying in some length: rich he was not, and had accumulated no wealth, but he had some means and suffered no great poverty. He still worked, earning as much as he needed now, living alone but with one granddaughter, who looked after him, and earned some money by sewing. The family was large, several children, more than ten grandchildren but that was all.

He waved his hand.

'Does the noble *Pan* know something? There is a riddle, and I am most curious if the *Pan* knows it. How can it be, that a man may have a family, and at the same time have none?' Saying so, he peered into the count's face, his eyes playfully questioning.

'Nu, does the *Pan* know the riddle?'

The count smiled, ironically.

'I know this riddle, Berek. I know it well.'

The Jew hit his knees with both hands, exclaiming worriedly: 'Oy, what does the *Pan* know it for? It is better not to know! Nu, but since we both know it, then I will not tell the *Pan* about my family. They are all respectable and kindly people, and some are even educated and wealthy, but they are not mine, they are their own and of the world, not mine.'

The count seated himself comfortably on the chair, as if for a long chat, and from the murmur filling the room a bass voice was heard, very clear, ringing: one, two, three! At the fourth strike it was joined, like a mature man by a youth, by a high sound of violin, ringing: one, two! At the third strike more and more voices joined in, until an entire choir together stroked a few times, melting to three and then to two voices, finally announcing eleven o'clock.

*   *   *

This was one of the most splendid funerals ever to occur in this town.

Through the large glass of his spectacles and the perspective of a narrow street, Berek quietly watched the procession passing by, occasionally shaking his head, deep in thought. But when a few words from the crowd stroked his ears, he trembled, drew himself up and started to ask, no one in particular: 'Vos? What? *Vos? Ver?* Who? *Graf*?! What *graf*?! What happened? Who died?! Whose funeral?!'

These questions crowding his bloodless lips, he found himself on the sidewalk, barring the way of someone passing by.

'What of it? Do not hold me up, Jew! Whose funeral? Of Count Strumienicki! The father ...! The father ...! Old Count Ksawery! Let me pass, for I am in a hurry!'

He let go the stranger's coat-tails, tilted back his head, and, looking up at the blue skies, spoke, almost crying:

'He died?! *Pan graf* Ksawery died?! How can this be?! Why did he die? He was completely healthy when he came to me! He was once so young, and so handsome, and so gay, and now he died? Where did this come from, that he died?'

Perhaps he drew attention and surprise to himself. Where did he come from, and why was he going along? But he moved on. At the head of the procession, the dark outlines of crosses had risen in the radiant air, to the solemn sound of church music. And yet he went on. Soon, a thought occurred: 'Nu, how did I come here? Why did I run like mad? Why am I going?'

But he went on. As long as he ran, pushing through the crowd, he gave it no thought, following instinctively a feeling, unclear, and yet overpowering. Now he began to wonder about himself and the man after whose coffin he tottered, along the sides of family and close friends, stumbling upon the stones.

'Nu, why did he sit with me then for hours, almost the whole night? Why did he chat with me, like a brother? Why did I run after this wagon, when I learned he rode it? Why do I follow it now?

Thus he thought, wondering more and more about himself and the count, but he went on.

*   *   *

Upon the yellow sands a place loomed, surrounded by a low wall, and filled with protruding stones. It had no trees, such as were here, nor tombstones. Nothing but a multitude of prominent stones, reddish in the sunlight, yellow sands around. The Jewish cemetery.

'Here is the end, yours and mine!'

He stopped muttering, but stayed, sitting under the birch trees, gray among the surrounding greenery, the twitter of birds, by the violet strewn grave.

And the two cemeteries, one sheltered by trees and crosses, the other all protruding stones and yellow sands, remained welded together by the one high and wide sky.

E. Orzeszkowa (ed. and comp.) *Z Jednego Strumienia* (From One Stream) (Warsaw: E. Wende I Spolka, 1905), and by Ludowa Spoldziel-nia Wydawnicza, 1960, pp.345–69. Selection translated from the Polish by Hava Bromberg Ben-Zvi. Reproduced here by the kind permission of Jerzy Dobrzanski, Ludowa Spoldzielnia Wydawnicza.

NOTES

Eliza Orzeszkowa (1841–1910) was born near Grodno, Poland, into a well-educated family of Polish gentry. Married at a very young age, aware and interested in the issues of the day, her many novels and stories focus on social and humane issues.

Her concern and sympathy for minorities engendered an avid interest in the position and fate of the Jews of Poland. In the novel *Meir Ezofowicz*, and in many of her novellas, such as *Gedali*, *Silny* (Strong) *Samson*, *Daj Kwiatek* (Give Me a Flower) and *Ogniwa* (Links in a Chain) the famous author presents Jewish images, speaking eloquently and movingly for this, most oppressed of minorities in Poland, displaying a deep familiarity with Jewish life, concerns, customs, faith and philosophy. The novella in this anthology was part of the literature of protest against the anti-Jewish movements and riots she witnessed in her beloved land. She is an author to be remembered.

16

Ziselman of Honcharska Street

NINA LUSZCZYK-ILIENKOWA,
a Polish-Belarus Writer

A Memoir

Short was the life of my sister Lidia. Three years older than I, she was a beautiful child, with an angel's face, who started early to talk and sing. But her little heart was sick from birth, and she died at the age of three. Our parents, our older sister Valentyna and brother Vitaliusz were disconsolate in their despair. In addition, the family found itself in dire financial need. Father was employed by the State, but expenditures on doctors and medicines greatly reduced the family's means. Father expected no aid from our family in the Novogrodek area, and Mama's entire family was in the Soviet Union. My parents never were in debt before, buying nothing on credit or instalment.

They faced, therefore, a dreadful fact: there was no money to bury the deceased child. Having consulted his ill and distressed wife, father went to Miodova Street, to the Reverend of the church, with the painful request to bury the child, and the debt would be repaid in the near future.

And this was a grave error and a frightful, moral, life-changing experience for my father, a man of religious principles, brought up in a godly family. Grandfather Prokop, a village teacher, taught the little ones religion along with the alphabet, and Grandma Emilia, even though not Orthodox but Protestant, equalled her husband in devoutness, and so brought up their five children.

Until his death Father did not forget the day he stepped into the office of the Reverend. He took off his railroad engineer's hat with an eagle, and, his voice choking with emotion, asked: 'In God's name, bury my poor child.'

The Reverend, surprised, gazed at my father; always clean-shaven, with lovely, fluffy hair and eyes as blue as heaven, he did not look poor.

'What?' he roared. 'What? Will I do you a burial on credit? And he calls himself a railroad engineer! It is for you to pay, and if not you, who else?' Father, still in the posture of a supplicant, his work-worn hands clasping the brim of his hat, didn't believe he was denied. Denied a prayer and a last service on earth to a dead child? The clergyman's words hit my father as a whip, his eyes dimmed by tears.

'Close the door on the other side and bring money, then we will bury, do you hear, you filthy railway man! Do you hear? Away from here, pretending to be poor!'

Father closed the door, stepped down the porch and went away as a beaten dog, reviled by a man of the clergy, through no fault of his, because of the death of his little daughter. And why was he abused so? Why? He did not neglect his Orthodox Church[1] and his wife, Marfusha, with her fine alto voice, rare for a woman, sang in the choir, and read the Slavonic language *psaltyr*. And the Church, in the person of its spiritual leader, denied them? My father, passing from one street to another, knew not where he was going, as if pierced through the heart by a hot iron. My God, what shall I do? How can I tell my wife? No, no, she should not know it. His fingers clutched the fence, and he wept.

'Volodia, what is the matter with you, Volodia? It is I, Ziselman. Come to my house, or to the store, we will talk about what has happened.' The storekeeper from Honcharska Street, Ziselman, led father to his room, seated him, and holding in his palms the hand of the battered man, said: 'Nu sha, sha, Volodia, I hear you, tell me your trouble.' Father told Ziselman about the death of his little daughter, and about his financial straits. And he heard a reply: 'Your little girl died, but be of good hope, your wife will soon bear another daughter. And as soon as Ziselman grows a long beard, she will come and bring from her little garden the green chives that Ziselman loves. And she will not fear the old Jew, for her parents will not teach her so. And about the money for the Holy Father …' Here Ziselman got up, opened his small chest, taking out a leather bag. Asking not how much was needed he counted enough to pay for all rites, and for the family to live on till father's payday.

Asking no warranty of my father, this not wealthy man rescued our family at that tragic time. In addition, he restored my father's faith in the goodness and decency of man. God, the Father of all men, did not forsake my parents, and again, showed man where goodness dwells. And spiritual positions, when occupied by evil and greedy men, harm religion. Did God forgive the Holy Father? I don't know. Our family forgave him.

Ziselman remained a good friend for the rest of our lives. His prediction regarding the birth of a daughter was fulfilled to the letter. A girl was born, very small, but by the time she was 1 year old, she walked and talked. And at 3 she knew the good man Ziselman and feared not his long beard, his black *kapota*, nor his *yarmulka*. She loved him and dutifully brought him onions.

The money borrowed in an hour of need was repaid. And I, with this true story wish to leave a remembrance and respect of a good and God-fearing man, who foresaw my birth, spiritually contributed to, and lit, in the heart of a little girl, a candle of goodness and love for all people. She will carry this memory through her life, to write in her old age this story and to tell people: Be good. Only thus will we save our God given world.

24 June 1999

Nina Luszczyk-Ilienkowa, 'Ziselman z Honczarskiej', first published in the Warsaw quarterly, *Regiony*, XXV, 1, 96 (2000), pp.14–16. Reproduced here by kind permission of the author, Nina Luszczyk-Ilienkova and Anna Engelking. Translated by Hava Bromberg Ben-Zvi.

A peronal note:

> Dear Mrs. Hava Ben-Zvi,
>
> May the heroes of my texts live forever on the pages of your book.
>
> Nina Luszczyk-Ilienkowa,
> an author born and residing in the capital of Polesie, Pinsk.
> 22 March, 2002

NOTES

Nina Luszczyk-Ilienkowa (born in 1929), a resident and a patriot of Pinsk, approaching the age of 70, began to dress the experiences, observations and ruminations of her life in literary garb: stories, both told and written. The former, transcribed from magnetic tapes, as well as the latter, were edited preserving the author's individual linguistic traits, which used the local Polish idiom, with Russian inferences and dialect characteristic of her native area of Polesie.

Their content is history, on a macro and micro scale, viewed from the perspective of Pinsk: the annals of the multicultural community of the Old Grand Duchy of Lithuania lands, beginning with the twenty-year period of Polish independence between the wars, through the turmoil of the Second World War, and post-war life in the Soviet Union. Her tales were published by *Swiat Literacki*, edited by Anna Engelking.

Anna Engelking continues:

> Mrs Nina is an amateur in the field of literature. She is, first and foremost, a person who, in the autumn of her life, desired to express and transmit that which she, during many years, remembered and lived through. To those who wish to listen and to know, she tells about her land, aware that it is her duty to record and preserve the memories.

Anna Engelking, in N. Luszczyk-Ilienkowa, *Wiez*, 3 (521) (Poland, March 2002), p.110.

Note by Anna Engelking, reproduced here by kind permission of Anna Engelking, and translated from the Polish by Hava Bromberg Ben-Zvi.

1. The Eastern Orthodox Church: A group of churches including the Greek and Russian Orthodox, which evolved from the church of the Byzantine Empire, observing the Byzantine rite and acknowledging the primacy of the patriarch of Constantinople. Nina Luszczyk-Ilienkova, a Belarus writer, exemplified the complex, mixed religious and ethnic make-up of the area where Poles, Jews and other people of Belarus lived together.

17

Rivka

NINA LUSZCZYK-ILIENKOWA
A Memoir

A little store, a few steps, and the counter. Mistress Rivka and a drawer, and silver coins in it, but not many. In an old, emptied box of candy and sweets, a few pennies. And, wrapped in an oilcloth, a small, chubby booklet, full of tiny pencil writing. Names of foremen, locksmiths, cashiers, porters. Rivka writes in, adds up, and balances. The month ends – naturally, payday at the railroad. The drawer bursts with coins. The pencil crosses off, sets percentage, missing nothing.

And the purses are thin again, and conveniently light. When they are heavy – ba! Great inconvenience, and why wear one's pockets threadbare, and ruin purses? There is a little store, right by the tracks, and in it Rivka! And a shining, lustrous counter, and, of course, a booklet in a deep drawer.

And little shelves, high and full, heaped in fabulous disorder by a masterful hand. A picturesque whole! Courtesy. But the main thing, the credit, such a convenience. And at every hour the little store is open! And a smiling Rivka is a big enticement!

Soon we unlatch the door, the little bell ringing. Look, ladies and gentlemen, what we have here. Hats of Vilnius milliners, from Zamkova Street, slightly out of fashion, but at convenient prices. Christmas ornaments and colourful tissue paper, laces, beads, pins, ribbons, clasps for girl's braids. Tooth-combs, side combs, and gloves of fabric and wool, or lightly knit and transparent. Stockings of lisle-thread, silk, gauze, of many hues, plain and of quality. Thread to darn socks, thick thread for sewing buttons, for Singer sewing machines, of naturally coloured silk, woollen angora yarn for little hats – first class fashion.

On the other side, on little shelves, choice morsels galore. Halva with nuts, vanilla, chocolate. Crescent rolls straight from Chaim's oven, browned, amply sprinkled with poppy seeds. Bagels, naturally Pinsk style, not Smorgonian style. Kaiser rolls for five pennies, and little cinnamon *challahs*. And sweets a-plenty. Well, for example: lemon drops, almond and mint, chocolate bombs with filled centres, plum finger-candy. And excellent, Bakina brand baking powders, before holidays in great demand. Sugar cubed or poured straight into paper bags. Bags of salt and millet. To look further is unseemly. Ah, excuse me! A barrel of herring, fat herring, delivered just today by Berko Kuflik.

I would end here, for I swoon at the memory of the aromas long forgotten, not experienced for sixty years. But! But Rivka's famous sour cream can in no way be forgotten. Pardon me. This sour cream for *borscht*, stuffed cabbage, cucumber salad, and, naturally, potato pancakes. And where was this delicious, cool, snow-white, always fresh sour cream stored? In a large, earthenware, wire-bound pitcher, in a zinc bucket lowered repeatedly into the backyard well.

The shopkeeper smilingly used to say: 'Nu, wait just one moment, I will get a cup of sour cream for Mrs Wandechka, for her cool soup, with fresh dill.' Two minutes, and the sour cream by the pencil was noted, the cup travelled to Wesola or Panska Street.

Years pass. The puddles have long dried, or they are cold, Siberian, bathing no rainbows, and no new ones were sent by heavens.

The little house stands, where the store used to be. The window looks out at a different world. A new master of the house! Does he draw water from the well? Forgive me, forgive me, my dears, the well is dry, full of rubbish and dirt.

Rivka walks and walks. She asks, looks into our eyes: 'My lady, what offense did I commit, when and whom did I not please? I marked up only few percentages!' The years of peace were priceless, taken for granted.

Thunder was still unheard, but beyond Luniniets black clouds have gathered, and beyond the Odra River lightning flashed. On the shelves, someone meticulously arranged bullets.

And life was good, for there was sour cream and Rivka on Koleyova Street, by the chestnut tree.

My story completed on 19 April 1999. Saturday, a hot day. Cool soup with dill, but no more sour cream. It is too dear.

Nina Luszczyk-Ilienkowa, 'Rivka', first published in the Warsaw quarterly, *Regiony*, XXV, 1, 96 (2000), pp.22–4. Reproduced here by kind permission of the author, Nina Luszczyk-Ilienkowa and Anna Engelking. Translated from the Polish by Hava Bromberg Ben-Zvi. For information about Nina Luszczyk-Ilienkowa, see 16. 'Ziselman of Honcharska Street'.

Part II
Years of Flame and Fury
The Ghettos

18

Yossel Rakover's Appeal to God

ZVI KOLITZ

A Short Story

I believe in the sun even when it is not shining, I believe in loveeven when feeling it not; I believe in God even when He is silent.
(An inscription on the wall of a cellar in Cologne where a number of Jews hid themselves for the entire duration of the war.)

In the ruins of the ghetto of Warsaw, among heaps of charred rubbish, there was found, packed tightly into a small bottle, the following testament, written during the ghetto's last hours by a Jew named Yossel Rakover.

'Warsaw, April 28, 1943.

I, Yossel, son of David Rakover of Tarnopol, a *Hasid* of the Rabbi of Ger and a descendant of the great, pious, and righteous families of Rakover and Meisel, inscribe these lines as the houses of the Warsaw ghetto go up in flames. The house I am in is one of the last unburnt houses remaining. For several hours an unusually heavy artillery barrage has been crashing down on us, and the walls around are disintegrating under the fire. It will not be long before the house I am in is transformed, like almost every other house of the ghetto, into a grave for its defenders. By the dagger-sharp, unusually crimson rays of the sun that strike through the small, half-walled-up window of my room through which we have been shooting at the enemy day and night, I see that it must now be late afternoon, just before sundown, and I cannot regret that this is the last sun that I shall see. All of our notions and emotions have been altered. Death, swift and immediate, seems to us a liberator, sundering our shackles; and beasts of the field in their freedom and gentleness seem to me to be so lovable and dear that I feel a deep pain whenever I hear the evil fiends that lord it over Europe referred to as beasts. It is untrue that the tyrant who rules

Europe now has something of the beast in him. He is a typical child of modern man; mankind as a whole spawned him and reared him. He is merely the frankest expression of its innermost, most deeply buried instincts.

In a forest where I once hid, I encountered a dog one night, sick and hungry, his tail between his legs. Both of us immediately felt the kinship of our situations. He cuddled up to me, buried his head in my lap, and licked my hands. I do not know if I ever cried so much as that night. I threw my arms around his neck, crying like a baby. If I say that I envied the animals at that moment, it would not be remarkable. But what I felt was more than envy. It was shame. I felt ashamed before the dog to be, not a dog, but a man. That is how matters stand. That is the spiritual level to which we have sunk. Life is a tragedy, death a savior; man a calamity, the beast an ideal; the day a horror, the night – relief.

When my wife, my children and I – six in all – hid in the forest, it was the night and the night alone that concealed us in its bosom. The day turned us over to our persecutors and murderers. I remember with the most painful clarity the day when the Germans raked with a hail of fire the thousands of refugees on the highway from Grodno to Warsaw. As the sun rose, the airplanes zoomed over us. The whole day long they murdered us. In this massacre my wife with our seven-months-old child in her arms perished. And two others of my five remaining children also disappeared that day without a trace. Their names were David and Yehuda, one was four years old, the other six.

At sunset, the handful of survivors continued their journey in the direction of Warsaw, and I, with my three remaining children, started out to comb the fields and woods at the site of the massacre in search of the children. The entire night we called for them. Only echoes replied. I never saw my two children again, and later in a dream was told that they were in God's hands.

My other three children died in the space of a single year in the Warsaw ghetto. Rachel, my daughter of ten, heard that it was possible to find scraps of bread in the public dump outside the ghetto walls. The ghetto was starving at the time, and the people who died of starvation lay in the streets like heaps of rags. The people of the ghetto were prepared to face any death but the death of hunger. Against no death did they struggle so fiercely as against death by starvation.

My daughter, Rachel, told me nothing of her plan to steal out of the ghetto, which was punishable by death. She and a girl friend of the same age started out on the perilous journey. She left home under cover of darkness and at sunrise she and her friend were caught outside the ghetto walls. Nazi ghetto guards, together with dozens of their Polish underlings, at once started in pursuit of these two Jewish children who had dared to venture out to hunt for a piece of bread in a garbage can. People witnessing the chase could not believe their eyes. One might think that it was a pursuit of dangerous criminals, that horde of fiends running amok in pursuit of a pair of starved ten-year-old children. They did not endure very long in the unequal match. One of them, my child, running with her last ounce of strength, fell exhausted to the ground, and the Nazis then put a bullet through her head. The other child saved herself but, driven out of her mind, died two weeks later.

The fifth child, Yacob, a boy of thirteen, died on his Bar Mitzvah day of tuberculosis. The last child, my fifteen-year-old daughter, Chaya, perished during a *Kinderaktion* – children's operation – that began at sunrise last Rosh Hashona and ended at sundown. That day, before sunset, hundreds of Jewish families lost their children.

Now my time has come. And like Job, I can say of myself, nor am I the only one that can say it, that I return to the soil naked, as naked as the day of my birth.

I am forty-three years old, and when I look back on the past I can assert confidently, as confident as a man can be of himself, that I have lived a respectable, upstanding life, my heart full of love for God. I was once blessed with success but never boasted of it. My possessions were extensive. My house was open to the needy. I served God enthusiastically, and my single request to Him was that He should allow me to worship Him with all my heart, and all my soul, and all my strength.

I cannot say that my relationship to God has remained unchanged after everything I have lived through, but I can say with absolute certainty that my belief in Him has not changed by a hair's breadth. Previously, when I was well off, my relation to God was as to one who granted me a favor for nothing, and I was eternally obliged to Him for it. Now my relation to Him is as to one who owes me something, owes me much, and, since I feel so, I believe that I have the right to demand it of Him. But I do not say like Job that God should point out my sin with His finger so that I may know why I deserve this, for greater and saintlier men than I are now firmly convinced that it is not a question of punishing sinners. Something entirely different is taking place in the world. More exactly, it is a time when God has veiled His countenance from the world, sacrificing mankind to its wild instincts. This, however, does not mean that the pious members of my people should justify the edict that says that God and His judgments are correct. For saying that we deserve the blows we have received is to malign ourselves, to desecrate the Holy Name of God's children. And those that desecrate our name desecrate the name of the Lord; God is maligned by our self-deprecation.

In a situation like this, I naturally expect no miracles, nor do I ask Him, my Lord, to show me any mercy. May He treat me with the same indifference with which He treated millions of His people. I am no exception, and I expect no special treatment. I will no longer attempt to save myself, nor flee any more. I will facilitate the work of the fire by moistening my clothing with gasoline. I have three bottles of gasoline left after having emptied several scores over the heads of the murderers. It was one of the finest moments in my life when I did this and I was shaken with laughter by it. I never dreamed that the death of people, even of enemies – even of such enemies – could cause me such great pleasure. Foolish humanists may say what they choose. Vengeance was and always will be the last means of waging battle and the greatest spiritual release of the oppressed. I have never until now understood the precise meaning of the expression in the Talmud that states: Vengeance is sacred because it is mentioned between two of God's names: A God of Vengeance is the Lord. I understand it now. I know now why my heart is so overjoyed at remembering that for thousands of years we have been calling our Lord a God of Vengeance: A God of Vengeance is our Lord. We have had only a few opportunities to witness true vengeance. When we have, however, it is so good, so worthwhile – I've felt such profound happiness, so terribly fortunate – that it is like an entirely new life was springing up in me. A tank had suddenly broken into our street. It was bombarded with flaming bottles of gasoline from all the embattled houses. They failed to hit their target, however, and the tank continued to approach. My friends and I waited until the tank was almost upon us. Then, through the half bricked-up window, we suddenly attacked. The tank soon burst into flames, and six blazing Nazis jumped out. Ah, how they burned! They burned like the Jews they had set on fire. But they shrieked more. Jews do not shriek. They welcome death as a savior. The Warsaw ghetto perished in battle. It went down shooting, struggling, blazing, but not shrieking!

I have three more bottles of gasoline. They are as precious to me as wine to a drunkard. After pouring one over my clothes, I shall place the paper on which I write these lines in the empty bottle and hide it among the bricks filling the window of this room. If anyone ever finds it and reads it, he will, perhaps, understand the emotions of a Jew, one of millions, who died forsaken by the God in whom he believed unshakably. I will let the two other bottles explode on the heads of the murderers when my last moment comes.

There were twelve of us in this room at the outbreak of the rebellion. For nine days we battled against the enemy. All eleven of my comrades have fallen, dying silently in battle, including the small boy of about five – who came here only God knows how and who now lies dead near me with his face wearing the kind of smile that appears on children's faces when dreaming peacefully – even this child died with the same epic calm as his older comrades. It happened early this morning. Most of us were dead already. The boy scaled the heap of corpses to catch a glimpse of the outside world through the window. He stood beside me in that position for several minutes. Suddenly he fell backwards, rolling down the pile of corpses, and lay like a stone. On his small, pale forehead, between the locks of black hair, there was a spattering of blood.

Up until yesterday morning, at sunrise, when the enemy launched a concentrated barrage against this stronghold, one of the last in the ghetto, at sunrise, every one of us was still alive, although five were wounded. During yesterday and today, all of them fell, one after the other, one on top of the other, watching and firing until shot to death. I have no more ammunition, apart from the three bottles of gasoline. From the floors of the house above still come frequent shots, but they can hold out no more hope for me, for by all signs the stairway has been razed by the shell fire, and I think the house is about to collapse. I write these lines lying on the floor. Around me lie my dead comrades. I look into their faces, and it seems to me that a quiet but mocking irony animates them, as if they were saying to me, 'A little patience, you foolish man, another few minutes and everything will become clear to you too.' This irony is particularly noticeable on the face of the small boy lying near my right hand as if he were asleep. His small mouth is drawn into a smile exactly as if he were laughing, and I, who still live and feel and think – it seems to me that he is laughing at me. He laughs with that quiet but eloquent, penetrating laughter so characteristic of the wise, speaking of knowledge with the ignorant that believe they know everything. Yes, he is omniscient now. Everything is clear to the boy now. He even knows why he was born, but had to die so soon, why he died only five years after his birth. And even if he does not know why, he knows at least that it is entirely unimportant and insignificant whether or not he knows it, in the light of the revelation of that godly majesty of the better world he now inhabits, in the arms of his murdered parents to whom he has returned. In an hour or two I shall make the same discovery. Unless my face is eaten by the flames, a similar smile may also rest on it after my death. Meanwhile, I still live, and before my death I wish to speak to my Lord as a living man, a simple, living person who has had the great but tragic honor of being a Jew.

I am proud that I am a Jew not in spite of the world's treatment of us, but precisely because of this treatment. I should be ashamed to belong to the people who spawned and raised the criminals who are responsible for the deeds that have been perpetrated against us.

I am proud to be a Jew because it is an art to be a Jew, because it is difficult to be a Jew. It is no *art* to be an Englishman, an American, or a Frenchman. It may be easier, more comfortable, to be one of them, but not more honorable. Yes, it is an honor to be a Jew.

I believe that to be a Jew means to be a fighter, an everlasting swimmer against the turbulent, criminal, human current. The Jew is a hero, a martyr, a saint. You, our enemies, declare that we are bad? I believe that we are better and finer than you, but even if we were worse – I should like to see how you would look in our place!

I am happy to belong to the unhappiest of all peoples of the world, whose precepts represent the loftiest and most beautiful of all morality and laws. These immortal precepts that we possess have now been even more sanctified and immortalized by the fact that they have been so debased and insulted by the enemies of the Lord.

I believe that to be a Jew is an inborn trait. One is born a Jew exactly as one is born an artist. It is impossible to be released from being a Jew. That is our godly attribute that has made us a chosen people. Those who do not understand this will never understand the higher meaning of our martyrdom. If I ever doubted that God once designated us as the chosen people, I would believe now that our tribulations have made us the chosen one.

I believe in You, God of Israel, even though You have done everything to stop me from believing in You. I believe in Your laws even if I cannot excuse Your actions. My relationship to You is not the relationship of a slave to his master but rather that of a pupil to his teacher. I bow my head before Your greatness, but will not kiss the lash with which You strike me.

You say, perhaps, that we have sinned, O Lord? It must surely be true. And therefore we are punished? I can understand that too. But I should like You to tell me – *Is there any sin in the world deserving of such punishment as the punishment we have received?*

You assert that You will yet repay our enemies? I am convinced of it. Repay them without mercy? I have no doubt of that either. I should like You to tell me, however – *is there any punishment in the world capable of compensating for the crimes that have been committed against us?*

You say, I know, that it is no longer a question of sin and punishment, but rather a situation in which Your countenance is veiled, in which humanity is abandoned to its evil instincts. I should like to ask You, O Lord – and this question burns in me like a consuming fire – *What more, O, what more must transpire before You unveil Your countenance again to the world?*

I want to say to You that now, more than in any previous period of our eternal path of agony, we, we the tortured, humiliated, buried alive, and burned alive, we the insulted, the objects of mockery, we who have been murdered by the millions, we have the right to know: *What are the limits of Your forbearance?*

I should like to say something more: Do not put the rope under too much strain, lest, alas, it may snap. The test to which You have put us is so severe, so unbearably severe, that You should – You must – forgive those members of Your people who, in their misery, have turned from You.

Forgive those who have turned from You in their misery, but also those who have turned from You in their happiness. You have transformed our life into such a frightful, perpetual struggle that the cowards among us have been forced to flee from it; and what is happiness but a place of refuge for cowards? Do not chastise them for it. One does not strike cowards, but has mercy on *them*. Have mercy on them, rather than *us*, O Lord.

Forgive those who have desecrated Your name, who have gone over to the service of other gods, who have become indifferent to You. You have castigated them so severely that they no longer believe that You are their Father, that they have any Father at all.

I tell You this because I do believe in You, believe in You more strongly than ever, because now I know that You are my Lord, because after all You are not, You cannot after all be the God of those whose deeds are the most horrible expression of ungodliness.

If You are not *my* Lord, then whose Lord are You? The Lord of the murderers?

If those that hate me and murder me are so benighted, so evil, what then am I if not the person who reflects something of Your light, of Your goodness?

I cannot extol You for the deeds that You tolerate. I bless You and extol You, however, for the very fact of Your existence, for Your awesome mightiness.

The murderers themselves have already passed sentence on themselves and will never escape it; but may You carry out a doubly severe sentence on those who are condoning the murder.

Those that condemn murder orally, but rejoice at it in their hearts … Those who meditate in their foul hearts: 'It is fitting, after all, to say that he is evil, this tyrant, but he carries out a bit of work for us for which we will always be grateful to him!'

It is written in your Torah that a thief should be punished more severely than a brigand, in spite of the fact that a thief does not attack his victim physically and merely attempts to take his possessions stealthily.

The reason for this is that the brigand in attacking his victim in broad daylight, shows no more fear of man than of God. The thief on the other hand fears man, but not God. His punishment, therefore, is greater.

I should be satisfied if you dealt with the murderers as with brigands, for their attitude towards you and towards us is the same.

But those who are silent in the face of murder, those who have no fear of you, but fear what people might say (Fools! They are unaware that the people will say nothing!), those who express their sympathy with the drowning man but refuse to rescue him – punish them, O Lord, punish them, I implore You, like the thief, with a doubly-severe sentence!

Death can wait no longer. From the floors above me, the firing becomes weaker by the minute. The last defenders of this stronghold are now falling, and with them falls and perishes the great, beautiful, and God-fearing Jewish part of Warsaw. The sun is about to set, and I thank God that I shall never see it again. Fire lights the small window, and the bit of sky that I can see is flooded with red like a waterfall of blood. In about an hour at the most I will be with the rest of my family and with the millions of other stricken members of my people in that better world where there are no more doubts.

I die peacefully, but not complacently; persecuted, but not enslaved; embittered, but not cynical; a believer, but not a supplicant; a lover of God, but no blind amen-sayer of His.

I followed Him even when He repulsed me. I followed His commandments even when He castigated me for it; I loved Him and I love Him even when He hurls me to the earth, tortures me to death, makes me an object of shame and ridicule.

My rabbi would frequently tell the story of a Jew who fled from the Spanish Inquisition with his wife and child, striking out in a small boat over the stormy sea until he reached a rocky island. A flash of lightning killed his wife; a storm rose and hurled his son into the sea. Then as lonely as a stone, naked, barefoot, lashed by the storm and terrified by the thunder and lightning, hands turned up to God, the Jew, again setting out on his journey through the wastes of the rocky island, turned to God with the following words:

'God of Israel, I have fled to this place in order to worship You without molestation, to obey Your commandments and sanctify Your name. You, however, have done everything to make me stop believing in You. Now, lest it seem to You that You will succeed by these tribulations in driving me from the right path, I notify You, my God and the God of my father, *that it shall not avail you in the least*. You may insult me, You may castigate me, You may take from me all that I cherish and hold dear in the world, You may torture me to death – I will believe in *You*, I will always love *You*!

'And these are my last words to You, my wrathful God: nothing will avail You in the least. You have done everything to make me renounce You, to make me lose my faith in You, but I die exactly as I have lived, crying:

'Eternally praised be the God of the dead, the God of Vengeance, of truth and of law, Who will soon show His face to the world again and shake its foundations with His almighty voice.

'Hear, O Israel, the Lord our God, the Lord is One.

Into your hands, O Lord, I consign my soul.'

Zvi Kolitz, *The Tiger Beneath the Skin; Stories and Parables of The Years of Death* (New York: Creative Age Press, 1947), pp.83–95. Reproduced by kind permission of Mathilde Kolotz and Petra Eggers of Eggers and Landwehr KG, Berlin, New York.

NOTES

Zvi Kolitz, born in Lithuania and moving to Italy in 1936 where he was educated, a scion of a rabbinical family, was a playwright and a co-producer of films and plays. He lived in Israel from 1940, where he served in the British armed forces, was imprisoned by the British and was a representative to the Zionist Congress. Zvi Kolitz died on 29 September 2002.

He is best remembered for the story 'Yossel Rakover's Appeal to God'. For years this short story was believed to be an authentic report from the Warsaw Ghetto. As such, it was reprinted by many publications. The story is about the eternal question and conflict: Where was God during the Holocaust?

'And The Earth Rebelled'

YURI SUHL

A Poem

(News Items: 'A great number of Jewish prayer-shawls, many of them blood-stained, were given burial in the Jewish cemetery in Yavar, Lower Silesia ... Together with the prayer-shawls, there were also buried several small cakes of soap which the nazi murderers had made out of Jewish bodies ...')

The earth rebelled.
The good and patient earth,
Which knows so well
Death's varied look, its every shape and mold,
Had never taken to itself
A corpse of soap,
Enshrouded in a prayer shawl's bloody fold.

The Grave was stunned,
And beat the earth with frantic cry;
'And where is body? Where is bone?'
But earth had no reply.
The Grave insisted: 'I have always been
The confidant of Death, his trusted kin,
I know the turn of all his harrowed lines;
Death with gaping holes instead of eyes.
Death with shape of life, or cruelly torn,
And tender, cherished infants dead, newborn,
And those who died by gas, the 'peaceful' dead,
'Efficient' Death, with bullet-hole in head,
And Death imprinted with hangman's rope.
But never have I seen a corpse of soap,
Nor heard that Jewish prayer-shawls can die!'...

But earth had no reply.

The earth was stark
In soundless shock
From drop of dew to mountain mass;
And all the leaves on all the trees were numb,
And all the winds arrested in their paths.

The birds in all their secret nests
Were stricken dumb,
As though the Grave, by disbelief,
Had turned the pulse of earth to stone,
And now moaned lonely in his grief:
'Whence this *talis*? Why this soap?
And where is body? Where is bone?
But suddenly a blast of thunder split
The clotted silence of the earth to bits,
And over all of Europe's fields and seas,
From ocean beds to misty mountain peaks,
Was heard the throbbing of the Grave's demand:
'For every bit of soap there was a soul,
For every *talis* there was once a man!
Now earth and Grave must call the awful roll,
And never will the reckoning be done,
Till all the dead are counted,
One by one!'

And thus the Grave spoke to the Wondering Wind:
'Get ye into that land of frightful sin,
Where German nazi – forever cursed name –
Destroyed a people in a flame of pain.
Awaken all the martyrs, tortured, bled,
Bestir the crumbling ashes in the pits,
And ask the ashes, ask the restless dead,
And ferret out the traces, find a way
To recognize the *talis* and the corpse
Of human soap that came to me today!'

And thus it was that in a herald's guise,
The Wind pressed forward into Polish skies.

The grasses wept, and all the stalks of grain,
And every threshold, suffering memory's pain,
And all the splintered ruins, charred and burned,
And all the ancient hallowed streets, upturned,
And anywhere the searching Wind appeared,
Arose the sound of sobbing and of tears,
The Wind, perplexed, turned here and there.
So many graves on Polish earth!
Lublin or Lodz or Warsaw first?
Or maybe Maidanek? Or where?

'Where!' the echo came from far and near,
And from the disembodied multitude
A million-voiced reply resounded:
'Here!
Our corpse, an image of six million Jews!
The tortured dead of Warsaw, Vilna, Lodz,
The bitter weeping and the tears unshed,
Each smoldering ash, each drop of blood,
Are all one corpse, one body of our dead!'
But still the doubting Wind did not believe,
And tarried, unconvinced, to hear the truth.
Again the echoes cried, 'Go back!
And take along these signs as proof.'
And then the heavens shook
And from the emptiness
Came forth the witnesses;
A speck of glowing ash.
A letter from a sacred Book,
A last *Shema*.
And shifting in his course, the Wind returned
To tell the waiting Grave what he had learned.

But as the Wind moved past a Polish wood,
A voice arose: 'Your work is not yet done!
Add to the prayer, the ashes, and the Book,
The thunder of a Jewish Fighter's gun!'

Yuri Suhl, 'And the Earth Rebelled', translated by Max Rosenfeld. The
poem originally appeared in *The Jewish Life* magazine, which was the
predecessor of *Jewish Currents*, in April 1954, and was reprinted in

Jewish Life Anthology, 1946–1956, pp.136–8. Reproduced here by kind permission of Lawrence Bush, editor of *Jewish Currents*, and of Beverly Spector for Yuri Suhl, and Jack Rosenfeld for the translator, Max Rosenfeld.

NOTES

Yuri Suhl, a well-known novelist, poet and biographer was born in Podhajce, in Austria-Hungary, today Poland. One of his earliest memories is of him and his parents barricading themselves in their home to survive a Cossack attack on the Jewish community. He was six years old. Emigrating at fifteen to the United States in 1923, he was educated at the Brooklyn College of the City University of New York and the New York University.

As a writer of books for children, he won several awards for *Uncle Misha's Partisans*. Deeply interested in the Holocaust years, and particularly in Jewish resistance, he travelled widely to obtain authentic materials and information. His studies led him to Yad Vashem, The Holocaust Martyrs' and Heroes' Remembrance Authority in Jerusalem, to the Jewish Historical Institute in Warsaw, and to the Yivo, the Jewish Scientific Institute in New York. The results of his research, fully documented, were published in his book *They Fought Back: The Story of Jewish Resistance in Nazi Europe* (New York: Crown, 1967), one of the best-known sources of information about Jewish resistance between 1939 and 1945 and the source of *Little Wanda with the Braids*.

20

A Shomer Pesach in the Ghetto

RUSZKA KORCZAK

A Memoir

It was our first *seder* in the ghetto – and for many of us … the last. To this day, whenever I think about that evening, whenever those scenes rise in my memory, I am unable to free myself from a certain hidden, troubled feeling. Perhaps I shall never be able to rid myself of that feeling.

It comes back compulsively again: the memory of that *seder* comes back …

… There is a wonderful light in the room. How much whiteness and light is strewn over the long, laid tables! – And there are flowers: living flowers in the *ghetto*.

Taibl and Dinah stole them from the farm and smuggled them into the ghetto under their skirts. The guards at the gate did not notice the fact.

We bought potatoes and beetroots with the few pence that we had at our disposal. The girls prepared the 'raw materials' devotedly and imaginatively, and they turned into delicacies. Now, there are all kinds of salads made of beetroots, standing on the dazzling white background of the tablecloths, and translucent glasses full of red beetroot juice. It is like blood. I suddenly shudder – like our living blood. I thought, 'We shall be reminded of blood by everything.' On the walls were burning the words:

'Night's dark shadows increase their sway,
But sparks of light still show the way.'

There are many participants. This is the first time that we are all gathered together – from youngest to oldest. All of us have been transformed by this festival. I have never seen *chaverim* look like this before.

They begin to sing – and forget themselves in song: are intoxicated by it. The old words receive new content and are expressed with new meaning.

'Among ruins and corpses – yet we sing.'

For one moment, it seems as though it is still the same anthem that we used to sing at festive meetings of the groups, of the *ken*, at camp.

I clearly hear the words which broke the silence that came after the singing:

'Like every Jew on *seder* night, I ask myself and all those present, "*Ma nishtanah?*" – "What is changed?" What has changed that makes us different from other Jews? How do we differ from our comrades who were tortured by murderers – whose bodies are spread over all Europe and whose spilt blood cries and know neither rest nor redemption?

'I ask and I give myself the answer: We, we shall be different. If we fall – we shall fall fighting. We shall fall as free men, and our blood will bring redemption to that blood which cries for revenge.

'... *Pesach* – festival of blood. This white, festive unleavened bread (*matzah*) which is on the table before us conjures up a whole sea of spilt Jewish blood. Sometimes you can no longer recognize its gleaming whiteness and it seems scarlet, as though dipped in our blood.

'And I continue to ask: Is there anything special about the blood which has been poured out? And I answer: Yes; it is important where it was spilt.

'The thousands of humans who were exterminated and buried together in the hills of Ponar will leave nothing after them except bloody memories, tragic sighs, grief and a deep unhealable wound in our people's heart. All this because they fell on foreign soil.'

'The very same blood, which our comrades spill over there nourishes the soil, is absorbed by it and remains part of it for ever. Afterwards, new life springs forth from it, new men mature, and death is transformed into life.'

The faces of the *chaverim* fill with sad yearnings. *Eretz Yisrael*! How far away and unattainable it is!

There is silence. Someone reads the *haggadah*, our new *haggadah* that was compiled by Michael and Moshe Namzer. Once more we listen to those ancient yet living words, of Massada's last defenders.

Then they sing and sing – as though they want to pour out their souls to the very last drop.

The narrow alleyways of the ghetto were empty and wrapped in darkness when we returned to our homes. The high walls cast cold shadows. It seemed as though the heavy closed gate was mocking us. Our eyes were dying to tear aside the veil of darkness and to peep at the secrets of the future. However, the blackness was impenetrable. The petrified silence was broken only by the clatter of our youthful feet.

From *Sefer Hashomer Hatzair*, in *The Massacre of European Jewry: An Anthology* (Kibbutz Merchavia, Israel: World *Hashomer Hatzair*, English Speaking Department, 1963), pp.191–3. Reproduced by kind permission of Dalia Moran, Director, Archives, *Hashomer Hatzair* Institute for Research and Documentation, Yad Yari, Givat Haviva, Israel.

NOTES

Ruszka Korczak, also known as Rozka Korczak-Marla 1921–1988, born in Poland, was a youthful member of the *Hashomer Hatzair*, a leader, a founder of the youth movement, taking part in the underground Jewish action in Vilna. She was a member of, and fought with, the Jewish partisan group 'Vengeance' in the Rodniki forest. After the war she became a member of the kibbutz *Ein Hahoresh* and an author of the book, *Flames in the Ashes*.

For further information see: http://jwa.org/encyclopedia/article/korczak-marla-rozka

21

Two Eyewitnesses:
An Unknown Woman and
Adam Sokolski

1. Story of a Woman Who Lived in the Warsaw
Ghetto until April 1942

The prevalent impression that the morale of the Jews in the Warsaw ghetto is high, is not borne out by the latest reports. The severe winter the like of which Warsaw has not had for many years and the aggravated situation generally have brought about a feeling of despair.

The price of coal that used to be thirty odd *zlotys* per ton before the war reached two thousand last winter. Most Jews used only old furniture for heating or left their homes unheated, keeping the children in bed and covering themselves with rags to keep warm. Some few could afford to buy coal by the pound. Many families, depending on their children to provide their daily food, had to let them out in cold weather to trade on the streets, and many of these children were frozen to death.

The doors and the windows of the Jewish houses were covered up with boards and rags to keep out the cold. This made them dark during the daytime and the dreary feeling so induced did not serve to raise the spirit of their hungry inmates.

Electric illumination has been cut off from the ghetto. The electric bulbs in the houses remain as cruel reminders. Theatres and public institutions and the well-to-do use carbide lamps that give out a light not unlike gas, but the poorer Jews use small kerosene lamps or stay in the dark. The blackout imposed on the ghetto from 9 p.m. each evening – as compared to 10 p.m. elsewhere in Warsaw – is the easiest regulation to observe in the ghetto.

But the Nazis exploit the craving of the Jews for light to engage in their cruel sport. Thus they announced at the beginning of the winter that electric light would be reintroduced into the ghetto, but that this involved some expense which the Jews desiring electricity were asked to help cover. Contributions were taken up by officials, but the whole thing turned out to be a plain swindle.

The outbreak of the German-Russian War was received by the Jews of Warsaw as heralding the end of Hitler, but the past winter with its hunger, thirst, and increased terror brought about a spirit of dejection. Every Jew still believes that the United Nations will win, but he doubts if he will live to see the victory.

Contact between the ghetto and the outside world is strictly regulated. For a Jew to leave the ghetto often means death. Yet so desperate are many that they risk death. During last winter several mass executions were carried out against Jews who illegally left the ghetto. A special sadistic ceremony accompanied these executions: Jewish policemen were charged with blindfolding the victims, Polish police did the shooting and the Gestapo police was present to supervise and to give the orders to fire. Often the Nazis offer to spare the victims' lives on payment of ransom by the ghetto. In one case a million *zlotys* was raised to ransom the lives of three Jews who illegally left the ghetto. In the case of children the Gestapo men sometimes show signs of human feeling and look away when an eight or ten year old emaciated provider crawls from under the wall of the ghetto covered with mud and goes out to sell or to beg in Polish houses.

The Nazis keep account of the number of deaths in the ghetto and hasten to fill the vacant places with Jews or non-Aryans from outside. From two to three thousand Jews die each week in the ghetto and an equal number is brought in from other places to keep the population at the figure of 600,000. Those arrivals include Jews from Wilno, Lemberg and other formerly Polish territories first occupied by the Soviets and now by the Nazis, as well as German Jews or German non-Aryans, that is, Germans with one of their grandparents Jewish.

2. Testimony of Mr Adam Sokolski, a Polish-American Who Returned to America Recently After Spending Several Years in Warsaw

Mr Sokolski proudly asserts that he has never been an anti-Semite. But he adds that even those of the Polish middle-class in Warsaw who were anti-Semitic before the war, are now friendly to the Jews. The very fact that the Nazis advocate anti-Semitism is enough to condemn it in the eyes of every Pole. That the Poles are now friendly to the Jews is evidenced by their treatment of Jewish children who steal out of the ghetto to beg for food. The children are careful to avoid the houses of Germans where they are likely to be turned over to the Gestapo, but they never leave a Polish house empty-handed.

The Nazis seek to stop this traffic and are especially afraid that the children may spread epidemics. Mr Sokolski himself once witnessed the murder of a Jewish child by a Gestapo agent. This happened on the Zelazna Street when the tall broad-shouldered Gestapo agent noticed in the crowd a lean emaciated eight-year-old Jewish beggar. With a cry of *Donner-wetter* he collared him. The child wrenched itself out of the Nazi's hold and made a quick dash. The Nazi immediately whipped out his revolver and aimed at the child's shoulders. Soon a shrill cry was heard and the child's lifeless body lay in a pool of blood. The Gestapo agent smiled with satisfaction, calmly put back his revolver and walked on with his head raised high, without even looking at his victim. The crowd did not dare to stop.

'Two Eye Witnesses', *Jewish Frontier* (November 1942), pp.14–15. Reproduced by kind permission of Bennett Lovett Graff, editor, *Jewish Frontier*.

22

Eyewitness Testimonies Siedlce, Poland, 1942

O n Saturday 22 August 1942, in the early morning hours the Ghetto was surrounded by Germans, the 'blue' Polish Police and Ukrainians. Machine guns were placed on both sides of the Ghetto gates. That day Jews from Mordy, Losic and Sarnak arrived in Siedlce. Local Jews were issued an order to arrive, by 10 a.m., at the cemetery by the burnt synagogue. Compliance with this order, in addition to the formerly mentioned formations, was watched over also by the Jewish Police. The action of detecting and catching the hidden began. Some of them, especially those found by the Ukrainians, were killed on the spot.

The people gathered on the square and forced into a sitting position suffered terribly from lack of water, for it was a sunny day. The members of the *Judenrat*, Weitraub and Furman, who spoke German well, got up and turned in the direction of the main gate, where the officer direct-ing the entire Action stood. They did not reach him, though. A few shots were heard. They fell dead. At that moment the machine gun was heard in a series of shots, killing those who attempted to get up, or sit in an upright position.

Around 11 a.m. a special squad arrived, composed of Germans and Ukrainians. There was a brief verbal exchange between the commander of the squad and the chief of the local *Arbeitsamt*. The first one wanted to include in the transport all Jews, while the other wanted to retain a certain number of young men and skilled workers.

Ultimately, 'around two in the afternoon, the Germans ordered men between the ages of 15–40 to stand in a line, for selection of those capable of working. From all sides of the cemetery men rushed in a run, like wild animals, to the place where the line was being formed, trampling others. In the end, under the never-ceasing blows of the Gestapo men, the line was formed, moving slowly forward. The high-est-ranking Gestapo man pointed out with a stick who was to live and who to die. Those intended for work he asked about their occupation and inspected their hands, to prevent, by chance, a non-worker from slipping through. Whoever showed any papers or certificates as an official of the *Judenrat*, was irrevocably directed to the left, meaning death. (...) Those directed to death were beaten mercilessly.'[1]

The evening of that day the fire department was brought in, and ordered to drench the sitting Jews with water. Another eyewitness testified:

'The Gestapo men drank beer by a small table, set up on the ruins of the old synagogue. Around them crouched the Jews, person by person. (...) I saw Dube and other Gestapo men shoot into the crowd of Jews while sipping beer. (...) The bodies of the Jews shot were taken away by the Jewish police, and driven away in wagons (...) to the Jewish cemetery.'[2] All this time the Germans were shooting Jews at the Jewish cemetery, the *kirkut*, on Szkolna Street.

One of the eyewitnesses remembers those days thus:

'As we arrived at the prison's courtyard, I noticed there a group of Jews – men. They were well dressed, they even wore furs. (...) The Gestapo man announced to the Jews gathered in the courtyard that they would be sent west, to work, and that they were not in danger. Then these Jews were ordered to get into an automobile led by Domanski. (...) A Gestapo man took the driver's seat. I stood on the steps of the automobile. We drove to the Jewish cemetery. There I saw very many pits and many dead bodies of people of Jewish descent. There were bodies of men, women and children. The group of Jews brought by us to the cemetery were arrayed in three rows: the first stood in a row by the wall, the second row was kneeling, and in the third row the Jews half-lay, or sat. The impression was as if the group had been set up for a photographic picture. These Jews were shot at with machine pistols serviced by three Gestapo men and four *Sonderdienst* functionaries (...). Later, the same Gestapo and *Sonderdienst* men killed off the Jews laying on the ground with pistol shots. (...) From the prison we drove a group of women of Jewish descent to the Jewish cemetery, counting over thirty persons. All the women driven to the Jewish cemetery were shot by the same perpetrators. The women, while being shot, unlike the men, screamed loudly, lamented, and even resisted.'[3]

Edward Kopowka (ed.), *Zydzi Siedleccy* (Siedlce, Poland: Copyright Edward Kopowka, 2001), pp.69–70. The first and second accounts are reproduced by kind permission of Edward Kopowka, and the first by kind permission of Professor Feliks Tych, director, Jewish Historical Institute, Warsaw, Poland.

Translated from the Polish by Hava Bromberg Ben-Zvi. Hava Ben-Zvi's mother, Dinah Lewartowska Bromberg, was born in Siedlce.

NOTES

Selections were based on:

1. E. Karpinski, 'Wspomnienia z Okresu Okupacji', *Bulletin of the Jewish Historical Institute* (ZIH), 1, 149 (1989), pp.66, 70. See also note 196 in 'Przypisy', in Kopowka, *Zydzi Siedleccy*, above.
2. T.M. Frankowski and J.T. Staszewski, 'Musimy Zydow Zniszczyc' (We Must Annihilate the Jews), *Tygodnik Siedlecki*, 36 (1986), p.5. See also notes 197, 198 in 'Przypisy', in Kopowka, *Zydzi Siedleccy*, above.
3. Ibid.

23

From the Diary of a Young Shomeret

ALIZA MELAMED

A Memoir

DELIVERING LETTERS

From the first days of the ghetto, the members of *Hashomer Hatzair* worked voluntarily at various aid-institutions. They served in the public kitchens, organized appeals, and afterwards, from 1941 onwards, the Movement took the postal service upon itself: taking letters from the Jewish labor camps to the workers' families. The younger *chaverim* played the main part here. It was spring, and we used to scurry about the ghetto streets, delivering letters to their destinations.

The things I saw in the ghetto streets cannot be forgotten. The pavements were filled with people. It was impossible to get anywhere without clearing a way with one's elbows. People are pressed closely together. There is not enough room on the footpath and pedestrians therefore spill on to the road. The '*rickshaws*' and the horse-drawn buses fill the air with their honking and barely manage to move through the mass of humanity.

There is a long row of beggars leaning against the walls of buildings. Horrible sights! They have yellow swollen faces, with eyes peering like narrow slits out of spheres of flesh from which the human semblance has all but gone. Their legs are prominently displayed so that the gangrene that has attacked them should arouse pity. A specter like that stands there and does not even bother to stretch his hand out for a coin. He knows that no one will give him a thing. The people on the street pass these unfortunates by with complete indifference.

At distances of no more than a few steps there are naked corpses, covered with newspapers. In a short time the corpse cart will come and gather up the bodies. (The ghetto had a joke: someone who died was said to have handed in his food-card.)

During the autumn rains we used to run those filthy streets, to the slums, to the winding alleys, to deliver the letters. It often happened that we would arrive at a home only to find it empty. The whole family had wasted away and died. In another home the whole family would be down with typhus. We were in great danger of infection, for most of our work was in the centers of filth and disease.

LIFE IN THE CITY OF THE DEAD

In the spring of 1941, our group used to meet in the Jewish cemetery in Okopova Street. The cemetery was the only place in the ghetto where a sign of green could be found. There, in the city of the dead, we could feel the coming of spring.

We used to sit on the marble benches, among the flowers, and in this, of all places, we felt that we were really living our young lives, in a world that had turned into a cemetery. Death held no fear for us. We had accustomed ourselves to it. Not far from us were numbers of mass graves. The naked bodies that were gathered in the ghetto were laid out in long rows in the pits, and chloride of lime was poured over them. Then several more layers of bodies were systematically arranged above the first one, in the same manner, until finally they were all covered with soil.

During our discussions, we gave no thought to the death around us. The spring was with us there and it aroused the hope that the world as a whole would experience that spring, that season of rebirth, which we were certain would some day come.

But there were many days when doubt stole into our hearts. Then things were bad indeed. However, there was always someone who would cheer us up. Everyone had his day. There was not one of us who did not have his hour of despair, and there was hardly a person who did not console others in their moments of despair.

In those difficult days, the whole *Ken* assembled to commemorate the Spanish Civil War and to celebrate our *gedud's* admission to the Movement. Our *gedud* was born in the fire of war, and that was its name: '*Gedud Ba'esh*' [In the Fire]. The *kvutsot* of our *gedud* stood there with their leaders, each one with a name which symbolized its conception in the purifying fire: '*Avukot*' [Torches], '*Zikim*' [Sparks], '*Lehavot*' [Flames], '*Shvivim*' [Scintillations], '*Hasneh*' [The Burning Bush], '*Lemarom*' [Skywards], and all of us listened to the words of Mordecai Anielewicz:

'We are in the very midst of corruption and degeneration. Our struggle is taking place in the sphere of corruption itself. We must not forget that our most difficult struggle is the struggle with our-selves: not to accustom ourselves to these conditions and not to adapt ourselves to them! The person who adapts himself to these conditions has ceased to differentiate between right and wrong: he has become enslaved, body and soul. No matter what happens to you, always remember; do not accustom yourselves to these conditions! Do not adapt yourselves to them! Fight this kind of existence!'

I COMPLETED MY MISSION ...

Spring went by. So did summer. The terrible winter was approaching. Winter was the symbol of starvation and death for us. Winter meant unfired stoves, days of lying under the bedclothes, nights without light (there was no electricity; those who could get them used smelly carbide lamps), slices of fodder-beet for food, and perhaps some thin soup made of frozen potatoes.

The *gedud* used to come together in the apartment of the new *Kibbutz 'Gal-On'* at 23 Nalewki Street. The apartment was divided into two. One part served as living quarters for members of the kibbutz, and the other part served the Movement. There was a large dining-hall, the walls of which were decorated with pictures, a *Ken* kitchen, and one more room for *hanhaga* meetings. Members of the *Ken* used to come here to eat. Poverty ravaged our members, and the Movement decided to help its people as much as it could. The apart-ment was the center of the kibbutz's underground activities. The *Hanhaga Rashit* used to meet there, and in the large dining-hall meet-ings of the *Ken* and of the *gedudim* used to take place. In that house, where so many important Movement events occurred, we came together to listen to the report by Rivka, one of the few remaining *shomrim* from Vilna. She had managed to reach us from there.

It was a gray autumn evening. Rivka sat and spoke. I saw her out-lined in the evening's waning light. She had a wonderful face: the young face of a woman of twenty-three. Her eyes were like cold steel and her hair was completely gray. Only rarely would her tranquil eyes show a glint of sorrow. Her sentences were thrown piecewise into the space of the room:

'It was a night of horrors. We lay on our beds fully dressed and listened fearfully. At eleven o'clock at night we heard the noise of a long line of motorcars. They stopped in one of the streets. After that there were screams, shots and groans. The next morning, we were informed that the whole street had been emptied and the deportees sent to be slaughtered. They did not take much trouble with them – just finished them off with a few volleys of shots ...

'On one of those horrible nights, when screams and cries for help frenziedly broke the silence and mercilessly tensed the nerves of those of us who were awaiting our turn to be killed, we decided: "We, the members of *Hashomer Hatzair*, will not die like sheep taken to the slaughter. We will defend ourselves. If we do not have enough weapons, we will spit in their faces; we will jeer at them. We shall die, but our deeds shall not be forgotten." So the order was given. One half of us would die with weapons in our hands and the other half would break its way through and reach Warsaw, in order to bring our last will to its destination. My friends remained in the ghetto, in the fighting half. I was commanded to remain alive and take their last message to its destination. Of all those who set out for Warsaw, only another girl and I are left. The remainder fell on the way. I completed my mission.'

Rivka's words ended in tense silence. No one asked her anything. Everything was clear.

COMMUNAL LIVING

Sometimes Shoshanna, one of the leaders of *Gedud Tel-Amal*, would come and lecture to us. To us she was the embodiment of beauty and devotion of spirit. She was slim, with childish blue eyes and a crown of blonde hair. Her whole appearance was one of strength and of unshaken spiritual peace. She gave all her wages to the treasury of the *Ken*. She did not give only her money but devoted all her strength and all her soul to the Movement. After some time, she took charge of the *gedud* from our *Rosh-Gedud*, Mira Fucherer. Peace was always evident in her face. She was more devoted to the Movement than to herself, and when her turn came she went to her death imperturbably.

Tuvia Sheingot of *Gedud Tel-Amal* used to visit us sometimes too. It used to be so pleasant to look at him as he sat in his work clothes and talked to us about astronomy. He was an amateur astronomer, and after a hard day's work used to set out with us for distant worlds in the far heavens. We liked him very much. He was brave and fearless.

We had a dramatic group, a choir, and a verse-speaking group. We put on several small performances at *Purim* and *Chanuka* on the premises of the public soup kitchen at No. 8, Prosta Street. The choir was conducted by Aviva from *Gedud Tel-Amal* – a sprightly, energetic girl. Wherever she went, she brought joy and enthusiasm with her. Could she possibly have known that she would be among the first to be deported?

When winter was only a short while away, we – all the girls of our *kvutsa* – gathered our warm winter clothes together and held them in common. Those of us who still had food at home used to save half our meals for members who had nothing to eat. Of course, our parents were not very happy about what we were doing. However, we took the warm clothes whether they agreed or not. We were convinced of the rightness of our actions.

Our *gedud* grew older and we began to take charge of our own activity. A committee was elected, with a representative from each *kvutsa* in the *gedud*, which was directed by Mira Fucherer, the *Rosh-Gedud*.

Mira was serious and grave. She would sit with us listening to our discussions, and her slightly slanting eyes – with their steely glint – seemed to look right inside the speaker's head. When decisions had to be taken, she did not hesitate. Her face would acquire a particular peculiar expression and within a few seconds she would give her decision. Her sentences were short, logical and clear. She perpetually had a kind of halo of secrecy about her. All we knew about her was that she was Mordechai Anielewicz's girl friend, and that she was active in the *hanhaga*. That was all. To our young imaginations she seemed like a revolutionary from the days of the *Narodnaya Volya* [People's Will – an early Russian romantic-terrorist revolutionary movement – Trans.]. She had the personality of a leader.

BEGINNINGS OF THE UNDERGROUND

The days were filled with disquiet and fearful expectations. The murder of people near the ghetto's exits became common. Sickness and poverty increased unceasingly and 'snatchers' began to appear in the streets. Youths and girls who had reached the limit of suffering used the last vestiges of their strength to attack people in the street and snatch their parcels of food from them. When they had snatched the bread, they would immediately sink their teeth into it, without paying attention either to the blows that were rained upon them or to the cries of the robbed person. Some people used to leave their parcels in the 'snatcher's' hands, while others would beat them and hand them over to the police.

At that time, we went underground. The meeting of the *Ken* in the library hall in Tlomacka Street was the last of the large meetings. At that meeting *Gedud Sarid* was accepted into the Movement. Its leader was Shmuel Breslav. All the members of the *Ken* were wearing white shirts and the young *gedudim* wore blue Scout scarves and Scout fleur-de-lis badges. At first they sang a lot. Then performances on the stage began. The *Ken* choir and choirs of the *gedudim* appeared. Two plays in Hebrew were presented, as well as witty sketches and recitals on topical subjects in Yiddish. At that meeting, information about all the *Kenim* in Poland was read out and the last instructions were given: 'From this meeting onwards, our underground period begins. The Movement journals, circulars and even *kvutsa* diaries are to be burnt. All orders are to be destroyed immediately after being read.' We were forbidden to meet in our usual meeting places (every *gedud* used to meet in a particular street every evening). We were forbidden to walk the street in groups.

After that, we saw Mordecai Anielewicz very rarely. I remember him well. He always wore a gray coat, sports trousers and golf-socks; he had a thin face and greenish eyes with daring in them, which would sometimes smile, and then they looked so fatherly and forgiving. He had a strong chin, and his whole expression was one of energy and of will.

Our *gedud* held a meeting in complete secrecy, in a narrow lane on the fringe of the ghetto, near the cemetery in Okopova. We placed guards in the street. We sat on the cellar floor by the light of a candle. It was forbidden to sing. We were depressed by events that were taking place, and the difficult atmosphere choked the words in our throats.

Mira's quiet voice could be heard in the silence. It slowly became louder, and sharp, serious words were to be heard. Now and again her voice would falter from emotion, but she would recover and continue. The sentences were spoken with finality:

'The critical moments of our lives will soon be before us. It is possible that we shall be parted and scattered. We must be prepared for that. But up to the last moment our aim must be to be human beings, to be *Shomrim*. We must not sink in the mire of this degenerate, contaminated life: we must not defile our ideals. We must hold our flag high – the flag of our strivings and our belief in free man and in

Jews free in their own homeland as brothers to all men. We shall not bow, and we shall not humiliate ourselves before our enemies. We may have to part. Remember then: it is no great thing to be a man when you are with others and can rely on their support. Your great test will come when each one of you remains completely alone – face to face with the enemy. Let our motto be the words of the song: "We have been called to these ranks for life; only death shall release us".'

From Sefer Hashomer Hatzair, in *The Massacre of European Jewry. An Anthology* (Kibbutz Merchavia: World Hashomer Hatzair, English Speaking Department, 1963), pp.180–7. Reproduced here by the kind permission of Dalia Moran, Director, Archives, Hashomer Hatzair Institute for Research and Documentation, Yad Yaari, Givat Haviva, Israel.

NOTES

Aliza Melamed survived. After the war she became a member of the Kibbutz Ein Hamifratz in Israel.

'Cracow Autumn'

NATAN GROSS

A Poem

At this time of year chestnuts fall from the trees in Cracow.
But no one any longer hangs them in a *sukkah*.
Wawel stands as it always has. But at the dragon's cave
There are no Jewish children.

The leaves cover the ground with a thick blanket
Near the University, as always a favorite meeting place for lovers.
But today the student corporations are not to be seen
And no one cries 'Beat the Jews,' because there are no Jews.

The tower of the Virgin's Church still stands, so does the Sukiennice
And Mickiewicz still looks out over the *Rynek*.
The same houses, shops, churches and streets.
Only on Orzeszkowa you won't find *Nowy Dziennik*.

The dear pages of *Nowy Dziennik*,
The banner of Zion on the Cracow streets.
'Jerusalem' and 'the pogrom in Przytyk'.
'Hitler' and 'The White Paper'. 'Disturbances in Hebron'
and *kosher* slaughter and again politics,
And Bialik's poems translated by Dykman.
And an article by Dr Thon.

There is no more *Dziennik*, there are no more Jews.
In Kazimierz the ghosts of the past still walk.
The Old Synagogue is falling down from age
And perhaps from sadness and shame ...

On Jozef Street, on Ester, on Dietel

Jewish beggars no longer knock on the doors.
On Szeroka, Skawinska and Waska
The wind howls and weeps.
From Wawel to Stradom
The *tramway* runs
Along Krakowska Street.
Here you heard Yiddish,
Here you could smell Jewish sorrow,
Here were spread before you the Planty on Dietel Street,
Here the Jewish holidays were celebrated
With the help of God.

At this time on Miodowa
A happy, festive, holiday crowd
Went to the Ajzyk Synagogue, to Remu, to the Old Synagogue
And to the Tempel – the shrine of the progressive.
At this time in Cracow, you heard the yearning voice of the shofar
And the prayers of the faithful rose hopefully to heaven.

Today, there only remain
Desecrated scrolls
And *Azkarot*
Memorial Services for the departed.

A memorial service for Stradom and for Kazimierz,
For Jakub Street for Jozef, Szeroka, Miodowa.
For Rabbi Meisels Street and for Podbrzezie,
For Orzeszkowa, Skawinska and for Brzozowa.

For those who raised the standard of revolt in the ghetto,
For our Jewish fighters – the soldiers of hope
Thrown like a stone by God against the ramparts.
Thus they went in turn to their death
for the memory of the Hebrew School
for the theater on Bochenska
for years, months, weeks and days
for the whole of Jewish Cracow
for *Mizrachi* and *Beis Yaakov*
for *Makkabi* and the Jewish Gymnastics Club.
Where is Cracow? Where is the Vistula? What has happened to us?
'Where is Rome, where Crimea and where Poland?'

Our Cracow stretches for many kilometres

From Plaszow to the Urals, to Sverdlovsk.
From Auschwitz to Siberia it accompanies us,
To Paris, London, New York, to all corners of the world.
And we who still survive after so much, after so many years
We gather and we remember, we gather and we remember.

We gather like the chestnuts on the Planty of Cracow.
We thread a chain of memory longer than slavery;
Our idyllic Cracow Jewish childhood,
Days of struggle and exaltation, days of youth and pranks,
Days of love, days of happiness, days of disaster, days of sadness.
Who knows as well as you, you Cracow streets,
What once pained us, what still pains us –
Our Jewish fate.
At this season, the chestnut trees are wet from the rain in Cracow
It is already autumn on the Planty and winter in our hearts.
Darkness falls. It is time to return. The gates are closing.
It is slipping away, my unforgettable Cracow,
That Cracow which is no more.

Natan Gross, 'Cracow Autumn', translated by Dr Antony Polonsky, in S. Kapralski (ed.), *The Jews of Poland* (Cracow: Judaica Foundation, Center for Jewish Culture, 1999), vol.II, pp.9–11. Reproduced by kind permission of the author, Natan Gross, the translator, Professor Antony Polonsky and by Joachim Russek, director of the Judaica Foundation, Center for Jewish Culture.

NOTES

Natan Gross was a novelist, a poet, a film director and an author of literary studies. Born in Poland, he describes in prose and verse his experiences during the tragic years of the Second World War. His novel *Who Are You Mr Grymek?* was published in Polish, Hebrew, and in 2002 in English translation (London and Portland, OR: Vallentine Mitchell). Among his credits are the books, *The Jewish Film in Poland* (1992) and with his son, Yaakov Gross, *The Story of the Hebrew Film* (1991). He is the author of *Poets of the Shoah* (1993), a collection of essays on the Holocaust as reflected in Polish poetry. In the course of his research in 2000 he discovered eighty songs by the celebrated Jewish bard, Mordecai Gebirtig, and is known for his writings about the life and creativity of Gebirtig. Mr Gross was born in 1919 and died in Israel on 5 October 2005.

25

'Kaddish'

CHARLES REZNIKOFF

A Poem

'Upon Israel and upon the Rabbis, and upon their disciples and upon all the disciples of their disciples, and upon all who engage in the study of the Torah in this place and in every place, unto them and unto you be abundant peace, grace, loving kindness, mercy, long life, ample sustenance and salvation, from their Father who is in Heaven. And say ye Amen.'
> *Kaddish de Rabbanan*, translated by R. Travers Herford

Upon Israel and upon the rabbis
and upon the disciples and upon all the disciples of
their disciples
and upon all who study the Torah in this place and
in every place,
to them and to you
peace;

Upon Israel and upon all who meet with unfriendly
glances, sticks and stones and names –
on posters, in newspapers, or in books to last,
chalked on asphalt or in acid on glass,
shouted from a thousand thousands windows by radio;
who are pushed out of class-rooms and rushing trains,
whom the hundred hands of mob strike,
and whom jailers strike with bunches of keys, with
revolver butts;
    to them and to you
    in this place and in every place
safety;

Upon Israel and upon all who live
as the sparrows of the streets
under the cornices of the houses of others,
and as rabbits
in the fields of strangers
on the grace of the seasons
and what the gleaners leave in the corners;
you children of the wind –
birds
that feed on the tree of knowledge
in this place and in every place,
to them and to you
a living;

Upon Israel
and upon the children and upon all the children of
their children
in this place and in every place,
to them and to you
life.

Charles Reznikoff, *Jewish Frontier* (November 1942), p.25. Reproduced by kind permission of Black Sparrow Press and John Martin, publisher, and Bennett Lovett Graff, editor, *Jewish Frontier*.

NOTES

Kaddish: Derived from the root of the Hebrew word for 'holy' or 'consecration', the *Kaddish* is an ancient prayer, devoted in its entirety to praising and glorifying God. Known as early as the period of the Second Temple ending in 70 CE, the basic text is sometimes changed by adding a few sentences in Aramaic and Hebrew. Since the beginning of the second millennium, the *Kaddish*, in Aramaic, has been known as the mourner's *Kaddish*, and has been traditionally recited by the bereaved. Death is not mentioned in this most solemn of Jewish prayers, used daily in the synagogue.

Printed in the *Jewish Frontier* in 1942, in the midst of the Holocaust years, the poem reflects on the variety of ways in which the Jewish people have been abused, at that time and other times. The poem is a prayer for life, safety and peace. Unlike in the original *Kaddish*, God is not mentioned.

Charles Reznikoff, 1894–1976, was a prominent American author and poet, and the recipient of the Morton Dauwen Zubel award for poetry, from the National Institute of Arts and Letters, 1971.

Children

26

'The First Ones'

ITZHAK KATZENELSON

A Poem: Excerpt

The first to perish were the children, abandoned orphans,
The world's best, the bleak earth's brightest.
These children from the orphanages might have been our comfort.
From these sad, mute, bleak faces our new dawn might have risen.

At the end of the winter of forty-two I was in such a place.
I saw children just brought in from the street. I hid in a corner –
And saw a two-year-old girl in the lap of a teacher –
Thin, deathly pale and with such grave eyes.

I watched the two-year-old grandmother,
The tiny Jewish girl, a hundred years old in her seriousness and grief.
What her grandmother could not dream she had seen in reality.
I wept and said to myself: Don't cry, grief disappears, seriousness
  remains.

Seriousness remains, seeps into the world, into life and affects it deeply.
Jewish seriousness sobers, awakens and opens blind eyes.
It is like a Torah, a prophecy, a holy writ for the world.
Don't cry, don't … Eighty million criminals for one Jewish child's
  seriousness.
Don't cry … I saw a five-year-old girl in that 'home'.
She fed her younger, crying brother …
She dipped hard bread crumbs in watery marmalade
And got them cleverly into his mouth … I was lucky
To see it, to see the five-year-old mother feeding him,
And to hear her words. My mother, exceptional though she was,
  was not that imaginative.
She wiped his tear with her laughter and talked him into joy.

O little Jewish girl, Sholem Aleichem could not have done any
    better. I saw it.
I saw the misery in that children's home.
I entered another room – there, too, it was fearfully cold.
From afar a tin stove cast a glow on a group of children,
Half-naked children gathered around the glowing coal.

The coal glowed. One stretched out a little foot, another a frozen
    hand,
A naked back. A pale young boy with dark eyes
Told a story. No, not a story! He was stirred and excited –
Isaiah! You were not as fervent, not as eloquent a Jew.
He spoke a mixture of Yiddish and the holy tongue. No, it was all
    the holy tongue.
Listen! Listen! See his Jewish eyes, his forehead,
How he raises his head … Isaiah! you were not as small, not as great,
Not as good, not as true, not as faithful as he.
And not only the little boy who spoke in that children's home,
But his little sisters and brothers who listened to him with open
    mouths –
O no, you countries, you old and rebuilt European cities,
The world never saw such children before; they never existed on
    earth.
They, the Jewish children, were the first to perish, all of them,
Almost all without father or mother, eaten by cold, hunger and
    vermin,
Saintly messiahs, sanctified by pain … O why such punishment?
Why were they first to pay so high a price to evil in the days of
    slaughter?

They were the first taken to die, the first in the wagon.
They were flung into the big wagons like heaps of dung –
And were carried off, killed, exterminated,
Not a trace remained of my precious ones! Woe unto me, woe.

2–3–4.11.1943

Canto VI, 'Di Ershte' ('The First Ones'), stanzas 4–15, from 'Dos Lid
Funem Oysgehargetn Yidishn Folk' (Yiddish: The Song of the
Murdered Jewish People) by Itzhak Katzenelson (1886–1944), first
published in 1945. English translation by Noah H. Rosenbloom

(Israel: Beit Lohamei Haghetaot/Ghetto Fighters' House and Hakibbutz Hameuchad Publishing House, 1980). Reproduced by kind permission of The Archives of the Ghetto Fighters' House which grants one-time permission to reproduce the above excerpt in the initial print edition of the forthcoming book: *Portraits in Literature; The Jews of Poland. An Anthology.*

Any further use would require a new application to us. Yossi Shavit, Director of Archives, Ghetto Fighters' House, Western Galilee, Israel, 25 February 2010.

NOTES

Itzhak Katzenelson, a writer and a poet, was born in 1886, in the province of Minsk, then Russia (Poland between 1918 and 1939), today Belarus. The son of the writer Benjamin Katzenelson, he came to Warsaw as a youth to work on the Hebrew paper *Hazefira*. His poems for children have been well known and are popular to this day. During the Second World War, imprisoned first in the Warsaw ghetto, he was taken in 1942 with his son to Vittel in France. He was there for over ten months, where he wrote his poem 'The Song of the Murdered Jewish People', one of the most moving expressions of Jewish tragedy. He succeeded in hiding it in bottles, and told someone about it. He was then taken to Drancy, and two weeks later to Auschwitz, where he and his son were murdered on 1 May 1944. The poem was found after the liberation of the camp, aroused wide attention and was translated into many languages, including German.

27

How Granny Saved Helenka from the Germans

ELLA MAHLER

A Memoir

'Getting along fine', says Granny in that brittle voice of hers. 'Everybody in Beit Mazmil speaks Polish – the grocer, the baker, even the butcher ... though for all the meat we buy here, he could be deaf and dumb ... At the greengrocer's I use my fingers, he understands me all right. Helenka pays the bills. A smart girl my Helenka, as smart ...' The chiming of bells from across the hills stopped Granny in the middle of her sentence. She made a sign of the cross, and looked through the open window. The red roofs and stony steeple of St John's in Ein Karem glowed softly in the evening sky, right in front of her.

Granny pointed at St John's church: 'Went there once when we first came here, over a year ago ... Only once ... You have to take a bus going down and at the crossroads another one going up to the left to Ein Karem ... too much trouble ... At seventy, all a body can do is to creep around the house, keeping it straight. And to think that not long ago I was as strong as a horse ... She shook her head in annoyance. 'I was past fifty when left alone with Helenka, and she just a babe in arms ... and all around us the Germans a-swarming ... Accursed people those Germans ... fiendish people ... every one of them ...' The bells stopped tolling and Granny crossed herself again.

'I worked for Helenka's Grandfather since I was a young girl. And a rich man he was; everybody in Kovno knew him. I raised Helenka's mother from a mite. A stubborn little girl she was, to be sure. Never took "No!" for an answer. When she set her mind on marrying Helenka's father, marry him she did, poor as he was. Grandfather gave her a big wedding, fixed a nice home for her and I went with her to her new home.' She smiled indulgently: 'A fat lot did she know then about housekeeping.'

'When the war broke out and the Germans and the Russians divided the world between them, Kovno fell to the Soviets and the first thing they did, was to send all the rich men to the ends of the earth ... nobody knew where ... We never saw Grandfather again ... When the Germans picked a quarrel with the Russians and chased them out of Kovno, the first thing they did was to send all the young men to concentration camps. Helenka's father got caught too. Only women, children and old folks remained. And then the Germans started to lead us a dance! First they told the people of Kovno to hand their gold over to them; they could use it! And the people of Kovno were turning in; he a gold watch, she a wedding ring, a brooch, a pin ... till all the gold was gone. Finished with gold, the Germans took a fancy to copper. In two days all the copper kettles, pots, plates vanished from the kitchens. Through with copper, the Germans demanded furs, so they wouldn't be cold running after the Russians to the Urals, squeezing the life out of them. And the people of Kovno were hauling in all the furs there were, till not even the most stinking old sheepskin coat was left ... Then the Germans wanted babies' carriages. And the mothers of Kovno were wheeling in their babies' carriages, a mountain of them ... I and a few mothers hid ours, for what were we going to do without them?

'Everything taken, the Germans told the Jews of Kovno: "You got nothing more. Out with your lives!" and ordered them to come to Sosenki.' Granny smoothed out her apron and sat still for a while.

'There was behind the city a pine wood – Sosenki. That's where the Germans told the Jews to come. On the eve of the day the Ukrainians and the Poles dug a long ditch, and the next day the Jews of Kovno were dragging themselves to Sosenki. It was after their holiday – *Sukkot* – and a cold rain was drizzling. The sky was dark and wet, and the earth was cold and wet and clung to the soles of the crying Jews ...

'Came to Sosenki and stood over the open ditch, the Jews broke out in such a cry ... such a cry ... There was an old Rabbi among them ... He asked the Germans to let him talk to his people, and they let him: "Jews of Kovno", the old Rabbi said, "Jews of Kovno! Why do you cry? It was written above that we will die such a death ... So why cry?" Then the Germans started to shoot and the Jews to drop into the open ditch by the hundreds ... Some dead ... some wounded ... and some faint from fright. The dead were falling over the living and living over the dead, till no one was left standing ... The diggers put a thin cover of earth over the ditch, for it was late and they were in a hurry. And the earth over the ditch was moving up and down ... up and down … for three nights and three days … so many living were buried under it.

'Nobody got away from the ditch, only one baker. He saw his two children shot, and he saw his wife shot, and from all that grief and fright he fell on his side into the ditch, not a scratch on his body. At night he dug himself from under the dead and crawled on his hands and knees back to the city to the place where a few Jews were still living behind barbed wire. The baker was terribly hungry. But the Jews from behind the barbed wire said: 'Why should we feed you? When you were rich and we begged for bread, did you give us any? Why should we?' And the baker, from all that hunger and fright and grief – for he saw his children and wife shot – lost his mind and wasn't afraid of anybody any more … He ran around screaming and yelling, and the Germans shot him too …

'On that Judgment Day after *Sukkot*, Helenka's mother went with the others to her death, to Sosenki. Before she left, she tried to feed Helenka, but the baby would not take the breast … and cried … Such a little thing and she cried so … Helenka's mother said: "I have no gold, I have no money, but there are plenty of good clothes, linen and things in the house. You and Helenka can live on them for long. Take good care of my baby, Granny. God bless you both …" and she kissed the baby and she kissed me and closed the door behind her … Granny swayed lightly looking with unseeing eyes at the red glow over the hills.

'I was left alone with Helenka, but did not stay alone for long. A woman moved into our place. She told the Germans that she's a German too; can't speak their language because the Russians took her away from her family when she was still little. The Germans believed her. Once in the house, the woman grabbed anything she could lay her hands on – pillows, sheets, dresses … everything … and I had to keep my mouth shut.

'One day three drunken soldiers, two Germans and one Czech, stumbled into our place. I was feeding Helenka, holding her on my lap. The woman dug her finger into the child's arm squealing; "Jude! Jude!" I put my arms around Helenka. One of the German soldiers jumped over to me, trying to tear the child away. I let out such a yell that the German stepped back. The Czech soldier whispered something into his ear, he was a good man, the Czech, and the German laughed and kicked me and the baby out of the house … I stood behind the door crying and begging them to let me have Helenka's carriage. It was old and broken, but where was I to put her? After a while the Czech kicked the carriage out …

'I wheeled Helenka through back streets and lanes, empty lots, so nobody would see us, to my brother's place. He lived with his two married sons and a lot of grandchildren at the far end of the city. When my brother saw me, he wrung his hands: "Do you want us to get killed! Look for another place!" But what other place was there for me? Kovno was packed full with refugees from near and far and nobody wanted me with a Jewish child ... So my brother let me stay. He did not ask me to give up Helenka ... he knew better than to do this ... I stayed with my brother for three months, and for three months I kept looking for any little hole, any corner for Helenka and me, and could not find one ... The neighbors started to whisper ... my brother's sons and their wives stopped talking to me ... So I took the baby, put her in the carriage, and went away ...

'There lived at the other end of the city in a wooden shack, a very old woman. I went to her. Sick and alone as she was, she would not have me. "Go to the police and leave the child there", she said. "Then I'll take you in. Don't risk two Christian souls for a Jew-child" ... I could not do it. So I stood there and looked at her. Helenka raised her head and looked at the old woman too. And the old woman said: "Stay. There is not much life left in me. I can't lose much one way or the other ... Stay."

'I stayed with the old woman until she died and took good care of her. Now I had a place of my own. I whitewashed the shack for it was black with dirt. I kept Helenka hidden in the shack never letting her out. My cousin used to bring me food, and so did my brother on the sly. But there wasn't enough food to go 'round ... Some people knew where Helenka was, but they never told ... For a while the Germans were looking for me, and people would say: "There was such a woman with a Jewish brat, but she left long ago." And all the time I was living right under their noses, waiting for the war to end.

'The war over, letters started to come from Russia. Helenka's father wrote many a letter asking about his wife and child: one of them reached our midwife and the other the teacher. I took Helenka, and went to see the teacher. She was almost five then, quite a big girl. The teacher wrote for me a letter to Helenka's father. Pretty soon the father sent me a thousand rubles. It kept me going for quite a time. Then he sent us another thousand, but I never saw the money ... somebody had stolen it. And then Helenka's father came ...

'We lived for a while in one city, then in another ... and in still another ... eighteen months ago we came here ...' Granny got up from her seat and closed the window. 'Better keep the evening air out ...'

'A strange country here ... A lot of stones and rocks around Jerusalem ... few trees ... no water anywhere ... Well, people live here just as they live everywhere – working, worrying, hoping ... My brother died long ago ... I left behind me many graves and crosses ... and very few living I care about ... She's a good girl, my Helenka ... We went through the whole war together ... hungered together .... and together came here ... She's the one I want to be with at my last hour ...'

Y. Shilhav (compiler) and S. Feinstein, (ed.), *Flame and Fury* (New York: Jewish Education Press of the Board of Jewish Education, 1962), pp.77–9, Based on Yad Vashem, Holocaust Martyrs' and Heroes' Remembrance Authority, Jerusalem, *Bulletin* (June 1960). Reproduced by permission of Yad Vashem, Holocaust Martyrs' and Heroes' Remembrance Authority, and the Board of Jewish Education of Greater New York.

28

We Will Not Hand Over the Children Alive

FREDKA MAZIA

A Memoir

My new job was at the children's day-care home. We adjusted quickly to the new conditions ... We had to provide shelter and care for the babies and young children of hundreds of mothers, who were compelled to go to work and had no place to leave them. We acquired a two-story house consisting of six rooms and a kitchen. On the first floor we outfitted the rooms for the two-to-six-year olds, who were under the leadership of Zusha Gelbard, who, in the pre-war years, had studied early-childhood education in Warsaw. She gave of herself fully and selflessly from six in the morning, when the mothers brought their young, until six in the evening, when they took them home. She was teacher and mother; she washed them, dressed and fed them, played with them – always with a smile and cheerful song ....

She would sing while leading her group in a long line, their faces pale but their eyes alight and bright, tapping with their small feet and clapping hands. Zusha succeeded in restoring to them a bit of their blighted childhood, and in changing their sad surroundings into a magic retreat of freedom and happiness.

In the evenings, when the house was quiet, we would sit and talk. Around us were the playthings, which the children had used, and the drawings, which adorned the walls. We would ask ourselves, 'Until when will *they* let us go on like this?' Once Zusha burst out in a trembling voice, 'What will happen if *they* come and take them away?' I gasped. It was as if she read my mind, for this very question gave me no rest.

My 'dominion' was upstairs with the infants, where beds, covered in white, were arranged in two neat rooms that were painted in cheerful colors. The third room contained cupboards filled with infants' clothing and diapers. The second floor was equipped with a large table, a bath, a small kitchen filled with cereals, margarine, and powdered milk. How much effort, tears and cajoling were required to acquire all this 'wealth'?

The man who initiated and made the home possible was Dr Lieberman. He would scurry from office to office, from shop to shop, his hat askew and his coattails flying. He would burst in like a blast of wind, demanding, pounding on the table – and finally get what he wanted for the children. His counterpart, Dr Zufia, carried on her supervisory work with an inexorable determination. Her almost impossible duty was to provide nutritious menus, examine the children regularly, and take care of their physical well-being.

Through the long day, when the children were in the home, I had no time to think. The tasks were endless – cooking, bathing, feeding, toilet duties, changing from wet to dry underthings, and so on and on. The infants knew me and would smile when I came near their beds; they would stretch out their thin arms to be lifted and embraced and would gurgle and babble cheerfully. And when they pressed their heads to my breast, when I fed them, a deep warmth enveloped my whole body.

Only when the mothers returned after their day's work and took them home, when I rearranged the cribs and covered them with clean spreads in preparation for the next day, did the ever-recurring fearful question return to haunt me: What if the Germans come to take them away? What can I say to the mothers, when they return from work and find their children gone? Never had I expressed this fear to anyone – when suddenly Zusha put it to me in all its brutality.

We went to the garden surrounding the house and sought possible hiding places, should, God forbid, the need arise. But it was evident that we were deluding ourselves. Should this happen, we could, at the very most, hide a very small number. Nevertheless, we did not relent. We sought a way out. In the end we decided to confront the mothers with this problem. Theirs was the right and the responsibility to decide what to do.

When we put it to them, the reactions were varied. Some broke down, sobbing, and could not utter a word. One shrugged her shoulders, saying, 'What can we do? We are all doomed to die – some earlier, some later.'

'But what will happen when you do not find your child?' I retorted with great emotion.

'God will help', she responded.

Some tearfully implored, 'We beg of you, don't give them up. You are so kind. Watch over them. Save them.'

They reiterated these words despite our arguments and reproofs. However, there were a number of perceptive and courageous parents who responded, 'If and when this happens, give them an injection to put them to "sleep" so that they do not suffer. You know how to handle little ones. Take pity on them.'

'Am I capable of murder out of a sense of pity?' This thought gave me no rest. It was always with me in everything I did and wherever I was. And since I felt unqualified to act on my own, I turned for advice and guidance to my superiors. Dr Zufia blanched. She was silent for a long time and then answered in a whisper, 'You know that I handed over my daughter to a Polish family on the Aryan side before we were imprisoned in the ghetto. They took her. But they refused to accept my little boy. They feared that he would be discovered because of his circumcision. When I was with him I could not repress my tears. Should I let him suffocate in the jammed trains until he arrived at the death camp? Should I look on while they smashed his head and threw his body on the death pile? These horrors were ever with me day and night. I would wake from my sleep and hurry to his bed, feel him, hear him breathe. The nightmare would pass, and I behaved as if he was still in my care. Finally I decided I would not give him away alive. I would arrange that he go to sleep quietly, that he not suffer pain.' Her head dropped. Big tears rolled down her cheeks. I heard her whisper, 'Time was when they called this act "premeditated murder". Is there any act more monstrous?'

'Don't say it', I comforted her, as I patted her head, whose hair had turned prematurely gray. 'You did an act of great kindness and of self-sacrifice – a noble, merciful act of a mother who had given him life. But what shall I do with my little ones, whom I did not bear and whose fate I have not the right to determine?'

Finally I turned to Dr Lieberman for advice. I knew how much he loved the children. I would see him change from a despondent bro-ken-down shell to a new man as soon as he passed the threshold of the home. He loved the children and was their greatest protection. One day, as he went from crib to crib, amusing the children by removing his glasses and putting them on again, I stopped him. 'Have you a moment?' With a nervous gesture he looked at his watch.

'I shall not take up your time. Just one question.'

'All right. Has anything happened?'

'Not yet. But what if the Germans take away the children?'

He pushed his glasses up his forehead and directed his sharp blue eyes at me. 'Why this sudden question?'

'I cannot free myself of this thought. I am in constant dread. Every car that passes, every sound of a boot step, upsets my equilibrium. I cannot bear this tension any longer. I cannot carry this responsibility, to which I find no solution. Perhaps we should close up the home and not assemble the children conveniently for "them", ready for shipment to be murdered.'

The tension and fatigue of the last few days overcame my self-control as I banged my fist on the table, shouting, 'I do not want to give them the children. I cannot take that awesome responsibility. Let each mother act on her own.'

Dr Lieberman was silent for a long time while walking up and down the room, peering out of the window at the empty street. Then he turned to me, speaking tersely, 'Prepare a sufficient number of sleeping pills and capsules. We cannot burden the mothers with the children. If they do not report for work, they will be the first to be deported. But we will not hand over the children alive. We will not let them be subjected to torture. They will be put to "sleep" quietly. But remember: *only at the very last moment; only if there is no way out, when all is lost.*'

'With my own hands?' I asked as a great fear overwhelmed me. I repeated, 'With my own hands?'

'Yes, Fredka. *Your loving hands.* Not the brutal hands of barbarians. Be of strong courage and keep cool.'

He stood for a moment, hesitating. Then he rushed down the stairs.

A. Eisenberg, *The Lost Generation: Children of the Holocaust* (New York: The Pilgrim Press, 1982), pp.54–7,130–2. Reproduced by kind permission of The Pilgrim Press and Sora E. Landes.

NOTES

Fredka Mazia was a member of the Zionist Youth Movement and during the war served in many capacities as hospital nurse, governess, underground courier, and partisan. Her extraordinary narration begins in the fall of 1939. She was active in the three neighbouring cities of Katowice, Sosnowiec and Bedzin, in Upper Silesia, which were centers of Jewish population and culture. Her main base of operations was Sosnowitz. After the ghetto was liquidated, she managed to survive and finally settled in Eretz Yisrael in 1944.

The excerpt above describes Fredka's occupation as governess in 1943, in an infants' home in the Sosnowitz ghetto. The Germans had generously furnished and outfitted the children's home – another ruse to deceive the Jews. But the staff was not deceived.

A.E.

29

Jewish Children on the Aryan Side

EMANUEL RINGELBLUM

An Essay

Jewish families rarely crossed to the Aryan side together. First the children went, while the parents stayed on in the ghetto in order to mobilize the necessary funds for staying on the Aryan side. Very often the parents gave up the idea of going across to the Aryan side, as they did not have the money to fix up the whole family. The cost of keeping a child on the Aryan side in the summer of 1942, when the number of children being sent over was at its peak, was very high, about 100 *zlotys* a day. A sum was demanded for six months or a year in advance, for fear that the parents might be deported in the interim. Thus, a sum of several tens of thousands of *zloty* was required to fix up a child on the Aryan side and only very wealthy people could afford to do so. Parents of limited means and especially working intellectuals were forced to see their children taken as the first victims in the various 'selections' and 'actions'. Not all Jewish parents wanted to send their children to the Aryan side. There were those who weighed the question of survival for the children, especially the youngest ones, when no one knew what would happen to the parents at the next 'selection'. Some parents argued that a child deprived of its parents' care will wither like a flower without the sun. There were children who strongly opposed being sent to the Aryan side. They did not want to go to the other side alone, but preferred to die together with their parents. It took me a long time to convince my son that it is in the interest of our people that as many children as possible should survive the war. I know ten-year-old twins, who put up stiff opposition for several months and refused to go over to the Aryan side, despite the fact that there was a worker's family which was to keep the children at the expense of a workers' organization.

The children declared emphatically that they would not go over to the Aryan side without their mother, as they did not want to survive the war on their own, alone. After a long period of conflict, the mother prevailed, and the children went across to the Aryan side, where they are to this day. The mother died in a sewer trying to get through to her children during the 'action' of April 1943.

The majority of children, however, agreed to go across to the Aryan side, as living conditions in the ghetto were terrible. They were not allowed to leave their flats, they stayed for whole weeks in stuffy, uncomfortable hideouts, they did not see daylight for long months. No wonder then that they let themselves be tempted by the promise of going out into the street, of walking in a garden, etc., and agreed to go to the Aryan side by themselves.

I knew a twelve-year-old boy who jumped with joy at the ghetto wall, which he was about to cross to get to the Aryan side, and shouted, 'I'll survive the war'. This boy has suffered greatly on the Aryan side. Far away from his parents, whom he did not see for months, he did not go out into the street at all. He stayed in a one-room flat belonging to very noble people; if somebody came, he had to hide in a cupboard, behind a sofa, in the toilet, etc., and stay there for hours without moving until the guests departed. Though the boy was very much liked, he had to leave this flat, since the landlord's anti-Semitic relatives did not acquiesce in hiding a Jew and considered it a sin against the Polish people. The boy had been there throughout the 'hottest' time for the Jews, the April 'action'. When the ghetto where his father lived was burning and the explosions reverberated as walls were dynamited, the boy had to listen to anti-Semitic conversations, with the talkers frankly expressing their great satisfaction at the Nazi solution of the Jewish problem. This boy was clever and understood political problems, and he had to listen to this anti-Semitic drivel without being able to react. The boy is now together with his parents and they are staying in a hideout on the Aryan side. He has again been confined there for many months, among nervous people exhausted by their experiences. He is losing ground physically, but for all that he is lucky to have his parents with him.

I know an eight-year-old boy who stayed for eight months on the Aryan side without his parents. The boy was hiding with friends of his father's, who treated him like their own child. The child spoke in whispers and moved as silently as a cat, so that the neighbors should not become aware of the presence of a Jewish child. He often had to listen to the anti-Semitic talk of young Poles who came to visit the landlord's daughters. Then he would pretend not to listen to the conversation and become engrossed in reading one of the books that he devoured in quantities. On one occasion he was present when the young visitors boasted that Hitler had taught the Poles how to deal with the Jews and that the remnant that survived the Nazi slaughter would be dealt with likewise. The boy was choking with tears; so that no one would notice he was upset, he hid in the kitchen and there burst out crying. He is now staying in a narrow, stuffy hideout, but he is happy because he is with his parents.

The situation is much worse for the children who have lost their parents, who were taken away to Treblinka. Some of their Aryan protectors have meanwhile taken a liking to the children and keep them and look after them. But these are only a small percentage of the protectors, generally people of limited means in which Mammon has not yet killed all human feeling. People like these have to suffer on account of the Jewish children but they do not throw them out into the street. The more energetic among them know how to fix themselves up and receive money subsidies from suitable social organizations. We know of cases where the governesses of wealthy children took care of them after their parents had been taken away to Treblinka. They supported these children out of their beggarly wages and didn't want to leave them to their fate. Some of these Jewish orphans were fixed up in institutions, registered as having come from places affected by the displacement of the Polish population (Zamosc, Hrubieszow, Poznan, Lublin, etc.) A considerable percentage of the orphans returned to the ghetto, where the Jewish Council had them put in boarding schools; they were taken away in the 'resettlement actions'. There were frequent instances when the 'protectors', having received a large sum of money, simply turned the child out into the street. There were even worse cases where the 'protectors' turned Jewish children over to the uniformed police or the Germans, who sent them back to the ghetto while it was still in existence.

There were also cases of Jewish children, especially very small children, who were adopted by childless couples, or by noble individuals who wanted to manifest their attitude to the tragedy of the Jews. A few Jewish children were rescued by being placed in foundling homes, where they arrived as Christian children; they were brought by Polish police, who, for remuneration of course, report them as having been found in staircase-wells, inside the entrances to blocks of flats, etc.

There were no problems with Jewish children as far as the need for keeping their Jewish origin secret. In the ghetto Jewish children went through a stern schooling for life. They experienced a *gehenna* without equal in world history. They knew and felt that the sharp edge of Nazi hatred was aimed at them. The Jewish children went through the hard school of round-ups and 'selections'. They learned to control themselves, even outdoing adults in this respect. They learned to keep silent for hours at a time and even to hold their breaths when the enemy was approaching. They learned to sit motionless for hours at a time since the slightest movement might be heard by a Ukrainian or an S.S. man during a search and this could bring disaster to the whole hideout. They learned to stay in the hideout for months at a time and not see daylight, for fear of the S.S. torturers. They ceased to be children and grew up fast, surpassing their elders in many things. So when they were sent to the Aryan side, their parents could assure their Aryan friends and acquaintances that their little daughters or sons would never breathe a word about their Jewish origins and would keep the secret to the grave. I know of a young girl who was dying in an Aryan hospital, far from her parents. She kept the secret of her origin till her death. Even in those moments of the death agony, when earthly ties are loosed and people no longer master themselves, she did not betray herself by a word or the least movement. When the nurse who was present at her death-bed called her by her Jewish name, Dorka, she would not reply, for she remembered that she was only allowed to respond to the sound of the Aryan name, Ewa.

Even the youngest children were able to carry out their parents' instructions and conceal their Jewish origin expertly. I remember a four-year-old tot who replied to my asking him 'treacherously' what he was called before – a question often put to children by police agents – by giving his Aryan name and surname and declaring emphatically that he never had any other name.

In spite of this, 'give-aways' by children do occur, for several reasons. I know of a case of a five-year-old Jewish child, who had been living on the Aryan side for a long time and had been playing the part of a Christian very well indeed. One day there was a conversation at table about horse-drawn trams. The grandfather related that in his youth there were trams like these in the streets of the capital. The Jewish child present at the table said suddenly that he too had seen a horse-drawn tram, in … Zamenhoff Street. After this 'give-away', the parents had to take the child away and place him somewhere else.

A 'give-away' of a seven-year-old girl with a 'good' appearance, who had been living in a village for a long time, happened because of the non-sensical rumors spread by unknown persons to the effect that every Jew possesses enormous fortunes in gold, valuables, dollars, etc. All of a sudden a rumor spread through the village by word of mouth that the little girl from Warsaw was Jewish and that kilograms of gold had been handed over for keeping her. For fear of denunciation, the girl had to be sent quickly to her parents in Warsaw.

A 'give-away' can sometimes occur with a Jewish child because of so innocent a question as, 'Are you going to school?' A Jewish child, deprived of systematic schooling since the beginning of the war, has large gaps in his education and has difficulty in coping when asked questions like this by a visitor or acquaintance.

I have heard of a case of a four-year-old Jewish child who secured his return to his parents ... through blackmail *sui generis*. The child was longing for his parents, from whom he had been separated for a long time, and one day he declared that if he were not allowed to return to his parents, he would go to a German and tell him he was from the ghetto. The blackmail succeeded and the parents had to take the child back.

Unfortunately Jewish children were not spared real blackmail. There have been cases where they were kidnapped by blackmailers and held until the parents bought them out of the hands of the worst type of criminal.

The circumcision of Jewish children is a serious obstacle to their living on the Aryan side. The number of uncircumcised boys was very small. Pressure from religious parents and relations, together with the judicial difficulties presented by the Jewish Community and municipal authorities, were so great that very few parents, even the most progressive ones, could manage not to have their children circumcised. One simply was not given a birth certificate by the Jewish authorities, and the child was exposed to humiliations and difficulties in school.

I know an uncircumcised Jewish boy who has suffered a great deal on the Aryan side. He has been living there for ten month and has already moved to his fifteenth place. Something always goes wrong. He complains that anti-Semites harass him. He has had to listen to more than one Jew-hating lecture from his 'protectors', who were not informed of his Jewish origin.

Children of parents who are not well off are also to be found on the Aryan side. This dates from the first moment the ghetto was formed. Many poor parents managed to live off the smuggling done by their four-to-five-year-old children, who went across *en masse* to the Aryan side. Every day one could see hundreds of Jewish children hanging around the exit gates in masses in order to get through to the Aryan side. The children would wait for a 'good' guard so as to get through. Some went through holes in the walls or fences. To hide the things they were smuggling, the children would wear jackets or dresses with a double lining; after these had been stuffed with potatoes or other produce, they looked like crinolines. These children went through several times a day, laden with goods that often weighed more than they did. Smuggling was the only source of subsistence for these children and their parents, who would otherwise have died of starvation. Nothing could discourage the children from smuggling, not even blows by the Jewish 'Order-men'. The children were not frightened off by shots from soldiers vexed by their importunity, by their wanting to get to the Aryan side at any cost. Even when the *gendarme* or guard was shooting into the crowd and the pavements were wet with the blood, the children would only hide inside the entrances of the neighboring blocks of flats for a short while in order to attack the ghetto exit a moment later. Only a Frankenstein-type criminal, a mate of the Dusseldorf murderer, could pass indifferently by the bodies of innocent children. Pitiless soldiers would often stop the little smugglers and bring them to the sentry-posts, where they would take everything away from them and beat them mercilessly. The screams and pitiful cries of these innocent children could be heard all around, but this had no effect on the German soldiers, who were utterly brutalized and devoid of all human feeling.

The children who were smuggling had the most extraordinary and fantastic courage, which I often admired at the ghetto exits. Once, at the corner of Zelazna and Chlodna Streets, I saw how a soldier took smuggled wares away from a six-year-old boy. The boy was choking with tears and, despite the blows falling on his small shoulders, kept going back to the sentry-box where his treasure lay, treasure probably bought with his last pennies. The Aryan mobs that gathered on the other side of the exit were watching the fight between the soldier and the Jewish boy with satisfaction. The laughter of the street ruffians heartened the soldier and encouraged him to drive the boy off more and more violently. With everyone turned against him – the soldier, the uniformed police, the Aryan mob and even the Jewish Order Service – the boy did not give up the fight, and kept renewing his efforts to retrieve the confiscated wares. I watched the uneven struggle for quite a long time and saw in it the energy and endurance of the Jewish masses, who persist in the obstinate defense of their rights even when they know that excessive importunity may mean a bullet put through their heads.

The hard life of the smuggler children is reflected in this poem by a young Polish-Jewish poetess, Henryka Lazowert, who was taken to Treblinka during the 'resettlement action' of July 1942:

'The Little Smuggler'
Past walls, past guards
Through holes, ruins, wires, fences
Impudent, hungry, obstinate
I slip by, I run like a cat
At noon, at night, at dawn

In foul weather, a blizzard, the heat of the sun
A hundred times I risk my life
I risk my childish neck.

Under my arm a sack-cloth bag
On my back a torn rag
My young feet are nimble
In my heart constant fear
But all must be endured
All must be borne
So that you, ladies and gentlemen,
May have your fill of bread tomorrow.

Through walls, through holes, through brick
At night, at dawn, by day
Daring, hungry, cunning
I move silently like a shadow
And if suddenly the hand of Fate
Reaches me at this game
'Twill be the usual trap life sets.

You, mother
Don't wait for me any longer
I won't come back to you
My voice won't reach that far
Dust of the street will cover
The lost child's fate,
Only one grim question
The still face asks –
Mummy, who will bring you bread
Tomorrow?
Henryka Lazowert (1910–1942)

I heard a report from a woman working in the *Centos* about the life of a group of young smugglers. There were more than ten in this group, living at 28 Mila Street. They were full of energy and *joie de vivre*, and talked jokingly and with satisfaction about their life and its many thrills. In the beginning they made 200 to 400 *zloty* a day each. They engaged in 'looting' in the 'Little Ghetto' (the locality of Wielka, Ciepla, Twarda and Sienna Streets). In winter they lived by trading in wood, which they tore from the floors, attics, etc. of deserted houses. At that time they made

40 to 50 *zloty* a day each. The children shared between them the task of keeping house. Two of them would stay at home to prepare the meals and clean the room. When the *Centos* worker proposed that they move into a boarding school, the children refused, declaring that they were managing very well by themselves. They said that the *Centos* should put starving children in the boarding schools.

Many homeless children, orphans whose parents had died at the so-called refugee 'points' or in the 'death houses' where the very poorest lived, used to go begging on the 'other' side. They were well received there and were not refused alms or food. Even the Germans used to give them alms. Some children returned to the ghetto for the night, others would spend the night in attics, back yards, etc. The Germans, with the help of the Blue Polish Police and native anti-Semites, fought the swarms of Jewish children on the Aryan side. Every day they would drive them *en masse* to the Jewish gaol at Gesia Street. The prison director of 'Gesiowka', Rudnianski, whom the Germans later shot, tried to ensure humane conditions for the children; he taught them gardening and trained them for productive work. When the 'resettlement action' came in July 1942, 'Gesiowka' was the first victim that fell to the S.S. bandits, who sent the children to Treblinka. When the daily round-ups for children did not help much, and the number of smuggler children increased from day to day, rigorous repressive measures were employed. Children were drowned in the Czerniakow Lake – at least, so rumor had it.

'Looting,' that is stripping deserted houses of all their contents, done by the smuggler children, was a very dangerous occupation. The Germans considered the possessions of Jews taken to Treblinka their property, and looting was therefore punishable by death. S.S. men or *gendarmes* who caught people looting put them to death on the spot. Thus, looting was usually done at night or at daybreak. The children would afterwards sell the looted goods on the Aryan side for a few pence. Sometimes a homeless child like this would become adjusted to the Aryan side, which afforded him shelter. I knew a five-year-old orphan who had lost his parents in the 'action'. He lived on the Aryan side permanently and paid five *zloty*, for a night's lodging. The boy sold newspapers, which he smuggled into the ghetto from the Aryan side, making a profit of a few *zloty* on each copy. Some children earned their living by singing in the streets or courtyards. They assimilated to their environment to such an extent that they even sang the anti-Semitic songs that came into being during the war. Some children were able to live on the Aryan side thanks to the Jewish work-posts, which used them as errand-boys, sending them to do shopping in the streets, etc.

Attempts were made to settle a certain number of children as wards in institutions, but this activity had to be suspended after a short time because of fear of denunciation from their staffs. A few girls were placed in these institutions. The clergy took some children in their institutions, generally the very young ones. These few cases did not help the general condition very much. Polish Fascists and anti-Semites were to blame for the prevailing atmosphere which was not favorable for rescuing the children or adults. Fear of the anti-Semitic hue-and-cry was even greater than fear of the Germans and this discouraged attempts to rescue the children. We accuse the Polish anti-Semites and Fascists of spilling the blood of the innocents who could have been saved from the Huns of our time.

For the sake of history, we mention a project to settle a few hundred Jewish children in convents, in accordance with the following principles: the children would be aged ten and upwards; the annual charge of 8,000 *zlotys* would be paid in advance; a card-register would be kept of the children, recording their distribution throughout the country, so that they could be taken back after the war. This project was discussed in Jewish social circles, where it met with opposition from Orthodox Jews and certain national groups. The objection was raised that the children would be converted and would be lost to the Jewish people for good. It was argued that future generations would blame us for not rising to the necessary heights and not teaching our children *Kiddush HaShem* (martyrdom for the faith), for which our ancestors died at the stake during the Spanish Inquisition. The discussion on the matter among social workers reached no agreed conclusion, no resolutions were accepted, and Jewish parents were left to decide for themselves. The project was not carried out because of a variety of difficulties, but mainly because the Polish clergy was not very much interested in the question of saving Jewish children.

Emanuel Ringelblum, *Polish-Jewish Relations During the Second World War*, Joseph Kermish and Shmuel Krakowski (eds) (Jerusalem: Yad Vashem, 1974). Reproduced by kind permission of Yad Vashem Publications.

NOTES

Both Dr Joseph Kermish and Dr Shmuel Krakowski, were, in turn, directors of the Yad Vashem Archives, and while both have now retired, Dr Krakowski remains affiliated and active in Yad Vashem research.

Henryka Lazowert (1910–1942), Jewish Polish-language poet. She had earned fame before the war with her collections of poems, *Zamkniety pokój* (The Closed Room, 1930) and *Imiona swiata* (Names of the World, 1934). During the war, she participated in the work of the clandestine Ringelblum Archives. A victim of the great deportation from the Warsaw Ghetto, she perished in Treblinka in August 1942.

Dr Emanuel Ringelblum, a historian and the founder of the secret Ghetto Archives, known by its code name *Oneg Shabbat* in Hebrew (*Oyneg Shabes* in Yiddish) was born in Buczacz, Galicia, in 1900. A serious student since childhood, he read widely in the areas of sociology, Jewish history and literature, and joined the *Poale Zion*, a Zionist youth movement. He earned his PhD in 1927.

Interested in Jewish history, and particularly in the history of the Jews of Warsaw, he was associated with the Yivo Institute for Jewish Research, and taught in secondary schools in Vilna and Warsaw. With the outbreak of the Second World War and the German occupation and persecution of the Jewish population, Dr Ringelblum undertook the establishment of the Ghetto Archives, to collect and preserve documents, including those issued by the Germans, as well as diaries, eyewitnesses reports, newspapers, bulletins, songs, and other evidence of life in the Warsaw Ghetto and in other areas of Poland, all testifying to Jewish resistance and recording evidence of the relations between the isolated and besieged Jews and the Poles, on the other side of the Ghetto walls.

He and his many assistants wrote and disseminated throughout Poland and abroad reports about the conditions, the suffering and the underground resistance movement in the Warsaw Ghetto. On 7 March 1944 he was betrayed and severely tortured, never revealing any information about the underground, and a few days later executed, along with his wife and 13-year-old son, Uri. Ringelblum was 44 years old at the time of his death, in 1944. Two Poles who assisted and hid him were shot.[1]

The Ringelblum Archives were hidden in several locations in the Ghetto. Unfortunately, some of the documents were lost, but others survived and were found after war's end, under the ruins of the Ghetto. They are a priceless trove of information about the Holocaust years. In 2009 I received information from a private source that Emanuel Ringelblum committed suicide, but was unable to verify it.

1. S.D. Kassow, *Who Will Write Our History; Emanuel Ringelblum, the Warsaw Ghetto and the Oyneg Shabes Archive* (Bloomington, IN: Indiana University Press, copyright © 2007 by Samuel D. Kassow), pp.362–5, 383–5.

1. Sholem Asch, probably 1940s. Photograph courtesy of the Sholem Asch Estate. 1. *The Rebel*.

2. Janusz Korczak with children, 1936. Photograph courtesy of Benjamin Anolik, the Janusz Korczak Association in Israel. 12. *My First day in the Orphanage*. Dr Janusz Korczak was the Director of the Jewish orphanage in the Warsaw Ghetto. See also 30: *Janusz Korczak Marches to Death With His Children*.

3. Maria Konopnicka, 1879.
Photograph courtesy of Magdalena
Wolowska-Rusinska, Muzeum Marii
Konopnickiej, Suwalki, Poland. 14.
Mendel Gdanski.

4. Eliza Orzeszkowa, probably
1900/10. Photograph courtesy of
Ludowa Spoldzielnia Wydawnicza,
Warsaw, Poland. 15. *Links in a Chain.*

5. Nina Luszczyk-Ilienkowa, 1999. Photograph courtesy of Anna Engelking. 16. *Ziselman of Honcharska Street*.

6. Yuri Suhl, c. 1950. Photograph courtesy of Lawrence Bush, *Jewish Currents*. 19. 'And the Earth Rebelled'.

7. Natan Gross, probably 1995/2000.
Photograph courtesy of Yaakov
Gross. 24. 'Cracow Autumn'.

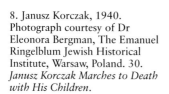

8. Janusz Korczak, 1940.
Photograph courtesy of Dr
Eleonora Bergman, The Emanuel
Ringelblum Jewish Historical
Institute, Warsaw, Poland. 30.
*Janusz Korczak Marches to Death
with His Children*.

9. Emanuel Ringelblum, 1939. Photograph courtesy of Dr Eleonora Bergman, The Emanuel Ringelblum Jewish Historical Institute, Warsaw, Poland. 37. *Mordecai Anielewicz and His Movement.*

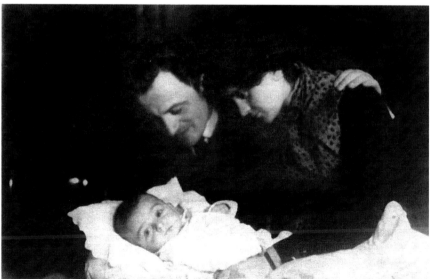

10. Emanuel Ringelblum family: Ringelblum, his wife Yehudit and son Uri, c.1930/31. Photograph courtesy of Naama Shilo, Yad Vashem, Holocaust Martyrs' and Heroes' Remembrance Authority, Jerusalem, Israel. 37 *Mordecai Anielewicz and His Movement.* Note: The family was executed in March 1944.

11. Mordecai Anielewicz, 1936. Photograph courtesy of David Amitai, Hashomer Hatzair Institute for Research and Documentation, Archives, Yad Yaari, and Daniela Ozacky, Moreshet Archives, Givat Haviva, Israel. 38. *The Last Wish of My Life Has Been Granted.*

12. Ruth Baum, 1998. Photograph courtesy of Ruth Baum. 43. *A Pole in the Ghetto*

13. Mordecai Anielewicz, 1937. Photograph courtesy of the Dr Eleonora Bergman, The Emanuel Ringelblum Jewish Historical Institute, Warsaw, Poland, Daniela Ozacky, Moreshet Archives, and David Amitai, Hashomer Hatzair Institute for Research and Documentation, Yad Yaari, Givat Haviva, Israel. 42. *Jewish Resistance in the Warsaw Ghetto*.

14. Mieczyslaw Rolnicki, probably 1990. Photograph courtesy of Mieczyslaw Rolnicki. 47. *Survival on the Aryan Side*.

15. Aharon Megged, c.1980s. Photograph courtesy of Aharon Megged. 55. *The Name*.

16. Anna Cwiakowska, 2000. Photograph courtesy of Anna Cwiakowska. 56. *The Polish Wife*.

Janusz Korczak Marches to Death with His Children

AZRIEL EISENBERG

A Biographical Vignette

First to be deported were the children. And among the earliest victims were the 'children of the streets' – the homeless and the orphans. Despite their sprightliness and elusiveness, they were rounded up for deportation. Thousands of refugee children trudged to the *Umschlagplatz*, and ultimately to their death.

The *Centos* staff, who provided shelter and aid to some 25,000 children, many of whom were housed in dormitories, was fully alert to the grave danger of concentrating children in specific places. To avoid imperiling the children's lives, they considered many proposals, such as scattering the children in the homes of relatives, friends, and families; registering the older children as 'productive shopworkers'; providing temporary day-care homes attached to shops (which were recognized and protected by the German military); smuggling children to the Aryan side; and other stratagems.

They knew that these steps were temporary, that the children would be living on borrowed time. Ultimately their end would be like that of their parents – annihilation …

The deportation of the children in orphanages began in August 1942. One of the first institutions whose children were rounded up was the Korczak Orphanage. The whole staff, including the director, Dr Janusz Korczak, and his associate, Stefa Wilchinska, would not part from the children and led the procession. Ringelblum noted in his diary (15 October 1942): 'Korczak (and his staff) set the pattern that the teachers accompany the children to the *Umschlagplatz*. Well did they know what awaited them, but they were committed not to desert their children. The teachers accompanied them to their death.' Two months later Ringelblum noted in his diary: 'We bow our heads in reverence to our educators, even though their self-sacrifice did not help or make any difference.'

These sentiments were also expressed by Dr Adolf Berman, head of the *Centos* organization. 'Many communal leaders were moved by the martyrdom of the educational personnel. Janusz Korczak headed the list of those who went to death with their pupils, even though they could have saved themselves. This lofty, noble act was motivated by psychological and moral considerations. They would not abandon their dependents on their last march. Their souls were bound up with the lives of their students … True, some communal leaders questioned the wisdom of their self-sacrifice: "Would it not have been preferable for men like Korczak to remain alive so that they might be of vital service to help rehabilitate the Jewish community after Hitler's downfall? Were they not sacrificing their lives in vain?"'

We are not in a position to pronounce judgment on their actions. Beyond all doubt they performed an exalted, incomparable historic act. They viewed themselves as the guardians of the precious lives that had been entrusted to them. Their consciences dictated their decision to live or die. Korczak's immortal act served as example to other directors of orphanages.

The reactions of the children during their final hours were mixed. The older ones knew well what awaited them, and yet they walked quietly and boarded the train with their teachers, fully aware that they were going to their death. The younger children did not know what was happening but were affected by the noise, the crowding, and the crying of the parents and relatives. They clung to their teachers and would not let go. Many wept and kept repeating, 'Will they drown us *there*?' Death by drowning seemed to frighten them more than anything else.

Thus some 4,000 children of orphanages were deported to death, a fraction of the 100,000 Jewish children of Warsaw who were exterminated. The march, led by Korczak, consisted of 192 children and eight staff members and, as stated, was headed by Dr Korczak and Stefa. It was a warm day, and the road was long. Witnesses reported that Korczak clasped the hand of a five-year-old.

Journalist Yehoshua Perla, a witness of the procession, noted in his memoirs: 'The scene was unforgettable. The children were silent; 200 innocent souls knew they were marching to their death. No one tried to hide or escape. The little ones hugged their teachers, like helpless birdlings, seeking to give them shelter and protection. Bareheaded Korczak, a leather belt around his waist, wearing boots, walked bent over, holding a little child by the hand. The children were dressed in their finest – sacrificial offerings brought to the Nazi Moloch. They were surrounded on all sides by German and Ukrainian guards and even Jewish police. The guards impelled them on with their whips and with their smoking revolvers ... The very stones weep at the sight of this procession ...'

Nahum Remba, secretary of the Warsaw Jewish Council, narrates how he and others tried to rescue the children: 'It was an unbearably hot day. I arranged for the older students to find benches far away from the train. I believed that I could save them by delaying their boarding the train until late in the afternoon. I suggested to Korczak that he go with me to urge the Jewish Community Council to intervene with the killers. He refused, because he did not want to leave his children alone even for a short while. The loading of the cars began ... The victims were beaten by knouts to hasten the packing of the over-loaded railroad cars ...

'Korczak, head erect, his eyes raised heavenward, walked at the head. This was an unforgettable march. The children walked in groups of four, Korczak leading the first group, Stefa Wilchinska second, and so on ... When the Jewish police spied Korczak, they saluted as one. The Germans asked, "Who is this man?" I could not restrain myself and hid the flood of tears that burst from my eyes. I was convulsed with sobs at our utter helplessness.'

Many were the stories circulating about Korczak. In the turmoil during the final procession, an SS officer made a beeline to Korczak and handed him a letter. It was rumored the letter stated that he was free to go home – but *not* the children.

Another rumor has it that when the children were already in the train a German officer approached him and inquired, 'Did you write *Young Jack?*' Korczak replied in the affirmative. 'A good book. I read it as a child. You may leave the train.'

'And the children?'

'The children will continue their journey. But you may remain in town.'

'You are mistaken', Korczak replied. 'Not everyone is a villain.'

The mother of twelve-year-old Halinka Pinchonson, who worked at the First Aid Station, which was conducted by the above-mentioned Nahum Remba, was summoned to save her daughter from deportation. Halinka refused to leave. 'When things were bad, you asked Korczak to admit me to the orphanage, and now you want me to leave them to their fate, and I am to remain alive. No! My place is with them.'

Korczak's martyrdom was a shattering experience to those who witnessed it, but to him it was a voluntary act performed without hesitation. It was the crowning moment of his noble life.

Anthony Shimansky, one of the Righteous Poles, a partisan of the Underground, noted in his memoirs: 'Cry aloud! Give honor to his valor, to his death that crowned his beautiful and multi-blessed life! Eternal shame to the executioners – the murderers of infants.'

Azriel Eisenberg, *The Lost Generation: Children of the Holocaust* (New York: The Pilgrim Press, 1982), pp.130–2. Reproduced by kind permission of The Pilgrim Press and Sora E. Landes. Based on accounts by Nahum Remba, Halina Pinchonson and Antony Shimansky, and on the book by Hanna Olczak-Mortkowicz, *Mister Doctor: The Life of Janusz Korczak* (London: Peter Davies, 1967). See also Shimon Frost, *Jewish Education* (Winter, 1963) and 12. *My First Day in the Orphanage.*

NOTES

Janusz Korczak was the celebrated pen name of a Polish Jewish physician who will be remembered as a lover of children, educator, and author. He devoted his life to home-less Jewish children, whom he raised in a world-renowned orphanage, which he founded and directed. When the children were deported to the Treblinka death camp in August 1942, he could have saved his own life, but he would not part from them.

To honor his martyrdom, two literary prizes were established recently by the Anti-Defamation League of B'nai B'rith and the Polish-American Catholic Committee, with Pope John II serving as honorary chairman. One is for books written for children and the other for books about children written for adults. To commemorate his contribution to child welfare, UNESCO designated 1979, the centenary year of his birth, as the Year of the Child.

A.E.

Azriel Eisenberg was a prominent author, anthologist and educator.

31

Little Partisans

LENA KUCHLER-SILBERMAN

A Memoir

'IT WAS I WHO WON!'

'No, I am not that old!' he answers with pride, and strikes his hips with the ruler. 'I look like an adult, that's because I am a boy from the woods. I had my own horse and gun when I was only twelve. When I was on horseback I used to shoot from both guns at the same time and hold the reins in my teeth … Like this!' And then he bestrides the only chair in the room, grabs the back of the chair in his splendid teeth, and shows how he held the reins.

'I killed Germans like dogs, my Lady (he decides to try and make an impression on me!), I threw hand grenades, I fired my guns right and left … Poof, poof, and I've already hit that German son of a gun … I avenged my brother and my mother …' he adds in a more subdued tone. 'And when we found out that a German troop train is about to pass we dismantled the tracks. Here, you see my Lady, we had a special wrench, one track this way and one the other way, and the train had to leave the tracks and to overturn. Or we used dynamite … That was the most beautiful thing to watch! The work was done at night, in the darkness, on hands and feet we sneaked up to the tracks and laid the detonator string … Then we ran back to the bushes where the horses were waiting for our quick getaway. Only one remained to light the fuse … I always begged for this job, but they didn't always give it to me. We lay at a safe distance and waited for the train to approach. And then it came around like a fiery snake with burning headlights, puffing and huffing like an old lady. Then I began a conversation with it. I said to the train: ' "Come a little closer, closer–quickly, don't be afraid! A little more, my fiery dragon! You think you'll swallow me, you monster! But you're mistaken. I'll get ahead of you and send you flying into the sky!" Another minute and the fuse is already sputtering. I jump back into the bushes, and suddenly the locomotive rears up, the cars pile up one on top of the other, a pleasure to watch! You see, you German sons of a gun, I have beaten you, and not you me! It was I who won!'

The boy became excited like an actor, and the other children left their teacher and sat around him in a close circle and listened with rapt attention to his story. In the meantime, Bronek, the one with the flax colored mane, returned to the group, and our performer slapped him on the back and said: 'And you, Bronek, do you remember how I dragged you off the tracks by your hair? You would have been chopped into mincemeat, or at least have lost an eye and an ear like Saul ...' And at this point he turns to a boy who had really lost an eye. 'For Bronek was very contrary – whatever anyone told him to do, he did the opposite, and when one told him not to do something, he went ahead and did it precisely. First he insisted that no one else but he must light the fuse; and then it turned out that he didn't know how to do it! The commander, Maxim, told him plainly: "After you light the fuse don't stay there gaping at the sky, but run as fast as your legs can carry you!" But he just stood there, that dope, in the middle of the tracks, and didn't budge. If I hadn't jumped and dragged him away by his hair he would already be pushing up daisies!'

'That's because my foot got stuck in the tracks', Bronek yelled out with such vehemence as if the whole thing had happened just then and not several months ago.

'In that case you pull your leg out of the boot and run! You don't stand there and wait for the train to arrive! But once a dope – always a dope, I say. His head is straw on the outside and straw on the inside ...'

'I THROW A BOMB'

Once an incident occurred which shattered the sense of security of all the Jews in Cracow, and in Poland generally (this was in post-war Poland, right after the liberation from the German occupation). Yet, this incident which so shocked the whole Jewish population restored Stepan's mental balance and self-assurance. And this is what happened:

One Sunday afternoon, as the thousands of Gentiles were leaving the churches, and masses of Jews were congregating in front of the Jewish Council House, a peculiar unrest was felt in front of the Council's gates. All the Jews standing there were suddenly running through the gate into the yard, yelling: 'Pogrom! Pogrom!' In a little while the yard, and all the rooms and corridors were filled with panicky, frightened people. Several of them broke into the office of the Council president, and began to pull him, and his secretary, by their sleeves, begging: 'Telephone immediately to the police, to the Ministry of Security ... They are going to murder us! They are rushing the gates of the Council! Save us!'

The president of the Council, and the other officials, began to telephone, and I rushed upstairs to the children's quarters. I saw through the window how our men were fortifying the gate with iron bars, and putting up barricades of boxes, barrels and old kettles, and anything else they could lay their hands on, while others were running around trying to find hiding places, and their faces were as white as cadavers.

Suddenly I heard the sounds of running and bounding down the stairs, from upstairs, from the direction of the children's rooms. The older boys were bounding downstairs three steps at a time, carrying chairs, a huge kettle which we used for cooking soup, and one bench.

With difficulty I managed to get out of their way, in order not to be tumbled down the stairs by their mad descent, and then I ran after them. The girls also pursued them, led by Mariussia, who soon joined the boys.

Meanwhile, we heard the sounds of knocking on the gate. The crowd outside pounded on the gate with sticks and stones, as was told to us by those who observed the scene from the upper stories, and soon began to fashion battering rams from some old poles lying about. The gate was made of old wood, and even the hinges were rusty. The hinges began to creak, and it seemed that soon the attackers would be inside the gate. We already heard the yelling of the crowd: 'Return the Polish girl! They have kidnapped a Catholic girl and are killing her to put her blood in their Matzoth! Kill all of them, not one must remain alive!'

The boys had brought additional material for the barricade from the kitchen. All the big pots and kettles. But the pressure outside increased from minute to minute, and the adults at the gate began to retreat, to look for hiding places in the building.

'If you break down the gate we will shoot you!' shouted Stepan with all his strength. 'We have bombs and grenades', yelled Bronek in a hoarse voice, as he was pulling a huge kettle and banging on it with an iron bar. But these shouted warnings were of no avail, and the mob continued to press against the gate.

Suddenly, Stepan jumped from the gate, picked up an empty can that was lying there, and ran with it as fast as an arrow to the second floor in the front of the house. With one smash of his fist he broke the window pane, and climbing up on the ledge he raised the can up high and yelled with all his might toward the surging crowd outside: 'Run, I'm throwing a bomb!'

'A bomb, a bomb!' the mob outside began to shout, 'The Jews have a bomb!'

And wonder of wonders, the 'heroes' began to run away! They left the gate and dispersed. The former inmates of the concentration camps inside began to crawl out of their shelters, to peek outside through cracks in the fence. The street was cleared, the danger was over. Soon it became known who the saviors were. The children surrounded Stepan and could not hear enough of the details of his wondrous act. And soon thereafter the older boys and Stepan in particular, became the talk of the day in the Council. But like true heroes they did not brag about their heroism. Not only that, but Stepan continued to tell about the clever inventions of his erstwhile commander, Maxim:

'He had better tricks than that! He alone knew how to scare and rout a whole company of German soldiers!'

'It would have been better if we had here, like in the ghetto, real Molotov Cocktails', said little Olga Podgorska, one of two sisters who absolutely refused to leave the big room and stay with the smaller children upstairs.

'A big deal – to make Molotov Cocktails – I can teach it to you in a jiffy!' said Bronek. 'It pays to set up a little workshop so that we'll have them in stock, for next time ...'

From that day on Stepan stopped talking about his impending journey to Russia, and Bronek always walked around with a bottle in his hand. Every now and then he would shake it up, and raise it to his ear to hear if the stuff inside was boiling and bubbling.

Lena Kuchler-Silberman, *My Hundred Children* (Jerusalem: Yad Vashem and Kiriat Sefer, 1959). Reproduced here from Y. Shilhav (compiler) and S. Feinstein, (ed.), *Flame and Fury* (New York: Jewish Education Press of the Board of Jewish Education, 1962), pp.62–5. Based on a publication of Yad Vashem. Reproduced by kind permission of the Board of Jewish Education of Greater New York and Yad Vashem, Holocaust Martyrs' and Heroes' Remembrance Authority.

NOTES

Lena Kuchler-Silberman was born in Poland. A young woman during the Holocaust, she lost her husband and child, and, dyeing her hair blond, survived the war on the Aryan side. During that time, assisted by Polish friends, she worked as a village teacher.

After the war Lena, one of the unsung heroines of the Holocaust years, dedicated her life to saving orphaned Jewish children in Poland, and was successful in gathering approximately one hundred children and bringing them to a new life in Israel. She movingly related her experiences in *One Hundred Children* (New York: Doubleday, 1961), including an anti-Semitic attack on her orphans in Zakopane. Her *We Accuse: Children's Holocaust Testimonies*, translated by Eliahu Porat, was published in Hebrew (Jerusalem: Sifriat Poalim, 1962).

32

Books in the Ghetto

RACHEL AUERBACH
A Memoir

For several years the librarians of the Ghetto were Leib Schur, the founder of the Vilna publishing house 'Tamar', and Basia Berman, who was later known as 'Pani Basia', the organizer of Jewish relief on the 'Aryan' side.

When other community workers were wracking their brains where and how to find bread and shelter for the homeless and hungry masses of Jews, these two were trying to find spiritual sustenance for the children. They were the first to appreciate the value of a book as a weapon against despair.

People had never shown such a ravenous appetite for books as in those days. This hunger derived, in the first instance, from an attempt to forget the constant peril that hung over people's heads, to bolster our sagging self-esteem.

And if this was so among the adults, all the more so among the children. The child in the ghetto was deprived of everything: the river, green trees, and freedom of movement. All these he found again in the magic world of books.

It was the winter and summer of 1940. Basia Berman worked in the clothing store. Others collected only old clothing to distribute to the destitute, but Basia mainly collected books for children. And in order to 'legalize' her activities she called her collection 'Toys and Booklets'. She discovered that many of the children still retained their pre-war books and toys, and that they were exchanging them with their neighbors. Thus the 'rich' had their own circulating libraries. There were even house committees that had organized clubs, and children's centers. But the most deprived were the unfortunate inmates of the refugee centers, the orphans, the homeless ones – they had nothing.

Together with Leib Schur, Basia began to move about with a valise full of books. From this store she supplied books to the homeless children.

It is November 1940, and the decree announcing the formation of the Ghetto is at hand. At Lishna Street there is the old Polish public library, where Basia used to work. But that institution was ordered to move to the 'Aryan' side. Basia, nevertheless, procured a permit to open the library of the ghetto in another place.

Yet the place must be camouflaged with children's paper-cut-outs, with little dolls and toys on the shelves, with colored leaflets and books, to give the impression more of a playroom than a place for reading and study. Yet, underneath this façade there was hidden a veritable treasure of books in Polish and Yiddish. These books came mainly from Schur's private library; he had simply donated all his books that were suitable for children.

'We must help Basia', he kept saying, and with genuine sincerity he cooperated in all of her ventures for the library. Another close friend who did much to help Basia was Rosa Simchowitz. After the latter's death, the library was named for her.

Thus, the library prospered. In a very short while it acquired over 700 youthful subscribers. Many of the children could not read Yiddish, or knew no Yiddish at all. But Basia had a method to attract those children as well. She would lend them two books simultaneously – one Polish and one Yiddish. Many times the Yiddish books opened a new world to the children; they gave them a key to their inner selves. And many of the children developed a passionate attachment to the Jewish books.

From time to time the library would arrange readings from Jewish books. The reader for the children was the teacher, Nathan Smoliar. The children themselves sometimes read aloud to each other. For the assimilated teachers lectures in Jewish literature were given. Here also met the Jewish cultural leaders in quiet and intimate discussions. There was a warm atmosphere in this house of the Jewish Child and the Jewish Book. Here I saw for the last time, Rosa Simchowitz and Menachem Linder, who was shot. I can still hear him humming the tune of 'Don and Donia', while the singer was performing in one of the concerts at the library ...

But Basia's best helpers were the children themselves, whom she trained for this work. I remember Sabshia Keitel, Roisele Schwartzberg, Paula Belzer – the first 16 years old, the two latter, fifteen.

Every time Basia would mention their names, she would sigh, and her face would darken like someone reciting the memorial prayers. The girls are now dead, yet I must smile when I recall them. They were so sweet, so fresh, so full of life ...

The most urgent and the most difficult task of the library was to supply special books to the unfortunate children in the quarantines, in the hospitals, in the jails, many of whom were infected with contagious diseases. The books they used could not be returned to the common pool, for sanitary reasons. Thus, for instance, there were special books for children afflicted with sores …

In the shelters the children lived in horrible conditions, in spite of all efforts to ameliorate them. They had no shoes and clothing, and there was no fuel to heat those places in the winter. Yet these children also borrowed and read books. They would send representatives dressed in whatever warm clothes they possessed in common. In the library these 'delegates' were immediately recognized by their bald heads, a souvenir of the sweatbaths they were forced to go through for sanitary control. Their eyes were often decorated with baggy swellings, the result of starvation, sleeplessness and tears. They would perform the act of exchanging the books with uncommon earnestness and skill. They would reach for the precious gift of books, the magic balm for their afflictions, with their outstretched, emaciated arms … In some of the shelters where there was no heat at all, we organized public readings. Basia especially appreciated the work of one housemother, Pashpiorka, at the shelter on Valnosz Street 16. The children would huddle under one blanket and listen rapturously to an adventure story that took place somewhere under blue skies in the sunny lands of Asia or Africa …

Among Basia's clients there was one who was known as a 'book swallower'. This boy, Merrel, once returned a book infested with lice. But, in the library, they did not scold him for that. It was not his fault that lice inhabited his body as well as his books … Books also played a pathetic part later, during the period of the 'actions'. For even in the first days of the 'actions' most children did not forsake their books, if they could help it. Basia remembered one little girl by the name of Simcha, who was very courageous. She was not afraid to walk in the street; her father worked in a protected factory, she said, and the Nazis would not take her. To prove it she showed her special pass. But we knew the worthlessness of these passes; the books borrowed that day were never returned. Some of them were, no doubt, packed into the little bundle that the deported ones were allowed to take with them on their trip eastward. They surely were scattered, together with the prayer books and adult books in the yards of Treblinka …

I can see now one boy whose mother had decided to join him, of her own free will, on his fateful journey to the *Umschlagplatz*. She collected a little food from her neighbors in the midst of the terrible confusion of a city suddenly besieged by a merciless foe ... But the twelve-year-old boy is absorbed in his own private world. He stands in a corner of the yard, hearing and seeing nothing of what is happening all around him. His head is immersed in a torn and tattered book with a shabby red binding.

Rachel Auerbach, *In the Streets of Warsaw*, translated by D. Kuselewitz (Tel-Aviv: Am Oved, 1945). Reproduced from Y. Shilhav (compiler) and S. Feinstein (ed.), *Flame and Fury* (New York: Jewish Education Press of the Board of Jewish Education, 1962), pp.73–5. Based on a publication of Yad Vashem. Reprinted by kind permission of Yad Vashem, Holocaust Martyrs' and Heroes' Remembrance Authority and the Board of Jewish Education of Greater New York.

NOTES

Rachel Auerbach was a very prominent member of the Warsaw Ghetto intellectual leadership, and worked closely with Emanuel Ringelblum on the Oneg Shabbat (Oyneg Shabes in Yiddish) Archives. She survived the war. For information about these Archives, see S. D. Kassow, *Who Will Write Our History? Rediscovering A Hidden Archive from the Warsaw Ghetto* (New York: Vintage Books, 2007).

33

Poems by Children in the Warsaw Ghetto

Translated from the Ghetto Newspaper
Gazeta Zydowska

MOTELE

From tomorrow on, I shall be sad
From to-morrow on!
To-day I shall be gay!
What is the use of sadness – tell me that?
Because these evil winds begin to blow?

Why should I grieve for to-morrow – to-day?
To-morrow may be so good, so sunny,
To-morrow the sun may shine for us again,
We will no longer need to be sad.

From to-morrow on, I shall be sad
From to-morrow on!
Not to-day; no! To-day I will be glad.
And every day, no matter how bitter it be,
I shall say:
From to-morrow on, I shall be sad,
Not to-day!

NATASHA – 8 YEARS OLD

It is twilight. I sit with my dolls by the stove and dream.

I dream that my father came back and will no longer go away.
I dream that my father lives with us now.

He comes home from work; he takes me on his knee.
He will tell me stories. He will play with me.

Mamma, mamma, how good it is to have a father.
I don't even know where my father is. Does he remember me?
If only a letter came from him.
Suddenly there is a knock at the door ...
I think – perhaps my father has come back.
I run to the door; I dance; I throw down my dolls!
My heart beats so – I think I hear my father ...
A beggar–man is standing at the door!

MARTHA

I must be saving these days,
(I have no money to save)
I must save health and strength,
Enough to last me for a long while.
I must save my nerves,
And my thoughts, and my mind
And the fire of my spirit;
I must be saving of tears that flow –
I shall need them for a long, long while.

I must save endurance these stormy days.
There is so much I need in my life:
Warmth of feeling and a kind heart –
These things I lack; of these I must be saving!
All these, the gifts of God,
I wish to keep.
How sad I should be,
If I lost them quickly.

Jewish Frontier (November 1942), p.26. Reproduced by kind permission of Bennett Lovett Graff, editor, *Jewish Frontier*.

Resistance

34

Chief Physician Remba

YURI SUHL

A Biographical Vignette

Editor's Note: *In their continuous struggle for survival, outwitting the enemy became a full-time occupation of the Jews in the ghettos and camps. The story of Nachum Remba, a communal worker turned 'physician', is an unusual but by no means isolated instance of Jews matching wits with their German tormentors. Y.S.*

Umschlagplatz was a dread word among the ghetto Jews. It meant transfer point for deportation, usually located near a railroad siding. There was only one place to go from the *Umschlagplatz* – into the cattle cars. And when these were crowded to suffocation the train left for what the Germans called 'Resettlement in the East'. Though the Jews did not know yet that they were heading for an extermination camp, they were full of dark forebodings about their unknown destination.

But one Jew from the Warsaw Ghetto attempted the impossible and succeeded in rescuing hundreds of Jews already on the *Umschlagplatz*, hours and sometimes even minutes before they were pushed into cattle cars. His name was Nachum Remba. A modest, retiring man, described by those who knew him as a 'saintly figure', he embarked on a rescue operation worthy of the most daring adventurer.

He set up a make-believe First Aid Station right next to *Umschlagplatz*. This 'hospital' was staffed with trustworthy doctors and nurses. Then Remba donned a long white doctor's coat and entered the *Umschlagplatz* as head of the 'hospital.' (As an employee of the Jewish Council, *Judenrat*, Remba enjoyed a freedom of movement which most other Jews did not.) He then pointed out to the German officers Jews he claimed were too weak to make the journey east, and demanded that he be permitted to take them into the 'hospital'. And the Germans who, after a while, began to refer to him as '*Haupt Artzt Remba*' – Chief Physician Remba – acceded to his requests.

The well-known Yiddish actor Jonas Turkow, whom Remba had saved in this manner, describes what the *Umschlagplatz* looked like in his memoir, *This Is How It Was*; 'Huge throngs of people are being pushed toward the barbed wires that divide the place in two. On the ground lie wounded men, women and children, valises, all kinds of possessions, bedding, prayer shawls, phylacteries, food packages and single shoes lost by some who were caught in the round-up. Police officers are running back and forth with orders from the little 'Napoleon', the convert Schmerling, who is Platz-Kommandant ... On the roofs are machine guns manned by SS-men and *gendarmes*. Bullets swish by your nose. Near me a woman falls, wounded. No one pays any attention to her. People pass by her, step over her, step on each other.'

And in the midst of this nightmarish scene, writes Turkow, 'Remba, dressed in his doctor's coat, went from one place to the next, from one German to the other, rescuing Jews, pulling them out of the *Umschlagplatz* and sending them back to the ghetto. Always calm, always smiling good-naturedly ... he would appear where no one dared set foot, where one could get shot for merely standing there. Fearlessly and with dignity he faced the German henchmen on the *Umschlagplatz* and demanded that they free this very sick one who is unable to make the "difficult journey east"'.

In the 'hospital' the rescued were ordered to lie on the beds. Some were 'bandaged'. As soon as the path was clear, they were taken by 'ambulance' back to the ghetto. The nurses wore especially wide coats under which they were able to hide the rescued children. Frequently it was necessary to chloroform the little ones and put them to sleep to make their rescue possible.

How was Remba able to put it over on the Germans? 'This is the irony of it', writes Turkow, 'that even the Germans, with their refined system of punctuality, were capable of being fooled, at least for some time. And until they caught on to the "Jewish trick" many a Jew was rescued.' Who knows how many more Jews Remba might have saved had he not been betrayed by members of the Jewish police, who saw in him a dangerous rival because he rescued Jews for nothing while they demanded heavy bribes from the victims.

Born in Kolna, Poland, in 1910, into a prominent Zionist family, Remba spent most of his adult life as a communal worker. Prior to Hitler's invasion of Poland in 1939, Remba was secretary of the educational department of the Warsaw Kehilla, the official administrative body of the Jewish community of Warsaw. Although himself an employee of the *Judenrat* – a German-elected body regarded by most Jews of the ghetto as an instrument of the Germans – he did not hesitate to join a committee to combat corrupt *Judenrat* practices, and he secretly organized the *Judenrat* employees into an association of which he was chairman.

Remba kept a diary of life in the Warsaw Ghetto, but it was lost. A few passages, however, are extant, thanks to the ghetto historian, Emmanuel Ringelblum, who quoted them in his sketch of the famed pedagogue and children's writer Janusz Korczak, who led the column of Warsaw Ghetto children deported to Treblinka.

'At night', Remba noted in his diary, 'I imagined that I was hearing the thump of children's feet, marching in cadence under the leadership of their teacher. I heard the measured steps, tramping on and on without interruption to an unknown destination. And to this day I see that scene in my mind. I see clearly the figures, and I see the fists of hundreds of thousands that will come raining down on the heads of the henchman.'

In the spring of 1943, Remba was again on the *Umschlagplatz*, this time not in his white doctor's coat in the role of savior, but as victim. The Germans caught him during the Warsaw Ghetto uprising and deported him to the death camp, Maidanek. There, too, Remba did everything he could to alleviate the sufferings of his fellow prisoners. He was especially close to the children, telling them stories, taking them for walks, making them forget, if even for a while, their horrible surroundings. In the end, like their beloved writer, Korczak, he went to the gas chambers with them.

Yuri Suhl (ed. and trans.), *They Fought Back: The Story of the Jewish Resistance in Nazi Europe* (New York: Crown, 1967), pp.82–4. Copyright Yuri Suhl. Reproduced by kind permission of Beverly Spector.

NOTES

For information about the author, Yuri Suhl, see 19. 'And the Earth Rebelled'. For information about Janusz Korczak and Nachum Remba, see 12. 'My First Day in the Orphanage' and 30. 'Janusz Korczak Marches to Death with His Children'.

35

Little Wanda with the Braids

YURI SUHL

A Biographical Vignette

Editor's Note: *In his* Notes from the Warsaw Ghetto, *Emanuel Ringelblum pays high tribute to the women couriers of the Warsaw Ghetto underground, who knew no fear and knew no rest. 'Every day they are exposed to the greatest of hazards ... They take upon themselves the most dangerous missions and carry them out without a whimper or moment's hesitation.' Niuta Twitelboim (Wanda) belongs to this category of brave women. Her story is drawn from sources listed at the end of this chapter. Y.S.*

One day a young woman walked up to the German guards in front of a Gestapo building in Warsaw and, lowering her large blue eyes demurely, whispered the name of an important Gestapo officer and added, 'I have to see him about a personal matter'.

She was twenty-four, but her slight figure, her long, blonde braids, and the flowered kerchief she wore on her head gave here the appearance of a sixteen-year-old girl. She was very attractive. The guards smiled at her knowingly, ushered her into the building and gave her the officer's room number.

She entered and remained standing hesitantly at the door. A tall, elegant-looking German rose from behind his desk. He stared at the girl for a long moment and then called out in wonderment, 'Gibt es bei euch auch Lorelei?' (Do you, here, also have a Lorelei?)

The girl did not reply. Instead, she quickly drew a revolver from her handbag and shot the German dead. Then she left the office and calmly walked toward the exit. As she passed the guards she smiled bashfully and lowered her eyes again. A moment later she was out of their sight. That was Niuta Teitelboim, a Jewish girl from the Warsaw Ghetto, whose underground name was 'Wanda'. This was not the only death sentence she had carried out for the underground. On another day she surprised a Gestapo officer in his own house when he was still in bed. When the startled German saw the girl with a revolver in her hand, pointed directly at him, he ducked under the eiderdown quilt. Wanda shot him through the quilt, and disappeared.

Though she operated mainly in the Warsaw area, Wanda became a legendary name throughout Poland, a symbol of fearless resistance to the German occupation forces. In Gestapo circles she was known as 'Die kleine Wanda mit die Zöpfen' (Little Wanda with the braids) and she was high on the list of wanted 'bandits', their term for underground fighters. They placed a price on her head of 150,000 *zlotys*.

Wanda was born in 1918, in Lodz, of a Hasidic family, but she did not follow in the footsteps of her Orthodox ancestry. She sought a place for herself in the secular world. She became a student in a Polish Gymnasium, joined the left-wing student movement, and soon became one of its most active members. Despite her excellent scholastic record, she was expelled from school for her radical activities.

But Wanda gained entrance into other institutions of learning, for in 1939 she was a major in history and psychology. That year Hitler's Wehrmacht marched into Poland. Wanda's studies came to an abrupt end. A year later she was one of half a million Polish Jews who were herded into the Warsaw Ghetto.

She joined the ghetto underground and became one of its most fearless members. An underground leader who worked closely with Wanda in those days remembers her telling him: 'I am a Jew ... my place is among the most active fighters against fascism, in the struggle for the honor of my people, for an independent Poland, and for the freedom of humanity.' To the very last minute of her life she tried to live up to this credo.

In the ghetto she organized a woman's detachment which later produced heroic figures in the Warsaw Ghetto uprising. The underground was divided into cells of five, and Wanda was an instructor of one such cell in the use of weapons. One of her surviving students recalls: 'Everyone who saw her giving instructions did not believe that until recently she had no knowledge of weapons ... Her innocent, jovial smile could fool the most suspicious German ... No one could lead Jews out of the ghetto or smuggle hand grenades and weapons into the ghetto past the vigilant guards as did Niuta.'

On July 22, 1942, when the Germans began the liquidation of the Warsaw Ghetto with mass deportations to Treblinka, the ghetto was completely cut off from the outside world. The Germans threw a heavy police cordon around the ghetto wall and cut the telephone wires linking the ghetto with the Aryan side of Warsaw. For the ghetto underground it was imperative to establish contact with the Peoples Guard and apprise them of the new situation in the ghetto. Wanda volunteered to hazard the risk and sneak out of the ghetto. A few days later she returned with new instructions from the Peoples Guard.

At the request of the Peoples Guard, Wanda left the ghetto to become deputy commander of the special task force in Warsaw that carried out the most daring acts of sabotage against the Germans. On the nights of October 7 and 8, 1942, they blew up the railway lines at several points in Warsaw, paralyzing for many hours vital communication lines to the German eastern front.

The Germans reacted with bloody reprisals. On October 16 they publicly hanged fifty Poles, active members of the PPR (Polish Workers Party), let their bodies swing from the gallows all day long, and then ordered them buried in the Jewish cemetery. In addition, they imposed a levy of a million zlotys on the Warsaw population.

Eight days later came the reply from the Peoples Guard. One group of the special task force, with Wanda participating, bombed the exclusive Café-Club on Aleje Jerozolimskie, which was a gathering place for Wehrmacht and Gestapo elite. Simultaneously another group attacked the German coffee house in Warsaw's main railway station, and a third group tossed a few grenades into the editorial offices of the collaborationist *Nowy Kurier Warszawski* (New Warsaw Courier). It was estimated that about thirty German officers were killed in these attacks. Later the Peoples Guard distributed leaflets, informing the Warsaw population that with these acts they avenged the hanging of the fifty Poles.

On November 30, Wanda, together with other members of the special task force, staged a spectacular raid on the KKO, the Communal Bank, in broad daylight, and retrieved the million zlotys the Germans had confiscated from the people of Warsaw.

In the fall of 1943 Wanda was sent, at her own request, to the forest to join the partisans, but was later recalled to Warsaw to resume her duties with the special task force of the Peoples Guard.

In the early hours of April 19, 1943, the Germans marched into the Warsaw Ghetto to liquidate the last remnants of Warsaw Jewry. In the evening of that same day, in a secret room in Praga, a suburb of Warsaw, the leadership of the Peoples Guard met to discuss how best to express its solidarity with the embattled Warsaw Ghetto fighters. It was decided to attack a German artillery emplacement on Nowiniarska Street from which the Germans bombarded the ghetto. A special group was selected to carry out the attack. Wanda was one of the group.

Twenty-four hours after the decision was taken, around seven o'clock in the evening of April 20, the artillery gun was silenced, and the crew, consisting of two Germans and two Polish policemen, was killed.

The Gestapo intensified its hunt for 'Little Wanda with the braids'. Her comrades in the underground pleaded with her to cease her activities and go into hiding because the Gestapo was on her trail. Wanda did not heed their advice.

One day in July, 1943, Wanda came home and found Gestapo agents waiting in her room. She tried poisoning herself to avoid falling into their hands alive, but did not succeed. She was arrested and taken to the torture cellars of the Gestapo. Before she was killed she managed to smuggle out a note to her comrades in the underground assuring them that she would not betray them.

In the spring of 1945, on the second anniversary of the Warsaw Ghetto uprising, the Polish Government posthumously awarded Niuta Teitelboim (Wanda) the Grunwald Cross, the highest battle decoration in Poland.

Yuri Suhl (ed. and trans.), *They Fought Back: The Story of Jewish Resistance in Nazi Europe* (New York: Crown, 1967), pp.51–4, copyright Yuri Suhl. Reproduced by kind permission of Beverly Spector. For information about the author, Yuri Suhl, see 19. 'And the Earth Rebelled'.

The story of 'Wanda' was drawn from the following sources: Ber Mark, *The Book of Heroes* (Lodz: 1947), I, pp.112–13; Ber Mark, *The Uprising in the Warsaw Ghetto* (Warsaw: 1955), pp.135, 137–8, 153; *Dos Neie Leben* (Lodz), 9 August 1946; Colonel G. Alef (Bolek), *Three Fighters for a Free Socialist Poland* (Warsaw: 1953), pp.13–14; Meilech Neustadt, *Destruction and Rising, the Epic of the Jews in Warsaw* (Tel Aviv: The World Union Poale-Zion (Z.S.), 1948), I, pp.37–8, II, p.328.

36

Rosa Robota – The Heroine of the Auschwitz Underground

YURI SUHL

A Biographical Vignette (Selections)

Editor's Note: 'The truth about Auschwitz? There is no person who could tell the whole truth about Auschwitz.' These words were spoken by Jozef Cyrankiewicz, Premier of Poland, who was one of the top leaders of the Auschwitz underground.

With each new memoir about that camp a little more of the truth is brought to light, as in the case of Rosa Robota who helped make possible the only revolt there. Yet it was only recently that her role in this uprising became known in many of its details. Y.S.

On Saturday, October 7, 1944, a tremendous explosion shook the barracks of Birkenau (Auschwitz II), and its thousands of startled prisoners beheld a sight they could hardly believe. One of the four crematoriums was in flames! They were happy to see at least part of the German killing-apparatus destroyed; but none was happier than young Rosa Robota, who was directly involved in the explosion. For months she had been passing on small pieces of dynamite to certain people in the *Sonderkommando*. Daily she had risked her life to make this moment possible. Now the flames lighting up the Auschwitz sky proclaimed to the whole world that even the most isolated of Auschwitz prisoners, the *Sonderkommando* Jews, would rise up in revolt when given leadership and arms.

Rosa was eighteen when the Germans occupied her hometown, Ciechanow, in September 1939, three days after they had invaded Poland. She was a member of *Hashomer Hatzair* and, together with other members, was deeply interested in the organization of an underground resistance movement in the ghetto.

In November 1942, the Germans liquidated the ghetto of Ciechanow, deporting some Jews to Treblinka and some to Auschwitz.

Rosa and her family were in the Auschwitz transport. Most of the arrivals were sent straight to the gas chambers from the railway platform. Some of the younger people, Rosa among them, were marched off in another direction and later assigned to various work details. Rosa was sent to work in the *Bekleidungstelle* (clothing supply section). Some Ciechanow girls were sent to the munitions factory, 'Union', one of the Krupp slave-labor plants in Auschwitz, which operated round the clock on a three-shift basis. Rosa, as well as all the women who worked in the munitions factory, lived in the Birkenau barracks.

One day Rosa had a visitor – a townsman named Noah Zabladowicz who was a member of the Jewish section of the Auschwitz underground. As soon as they managed to be alone he told her the purpose of his visit. The underground was planning a general uprising in camp, which included the blowing up of the gas chamber and crematorium installations. For this it was necessary to have explosives and explosive charges. Israel Gutman and Joshua Lifer, two members of the underground who worked on the day shift in 'Union', had been given the task of establishing contact with the Jewish girls in the *Pulver-Pavilion*, the explosives section of 'Union'. But all their efforts were in vain because the girls were under constant surveillance and any contact between them and other workers, especially men, was strictly forbidden. It was decided, therefore, to try to contact them through some intermediary in Birkenau. Since several of the girls who worked in the *Pulver-Pavilion* came from Ciechanow and Rosa knew them and was in touch with them, she seemed to be the ideal person to act as intermediary between them and the underground.

Rosa was only too glad to accept the assignment. Ever since that day of November, 1942, when she saw her own family, together with the rest of the Ciechanow Jews, taken to the gas chambers, the strongest emotion that suffused her being was a burning hatred of the Nazis, coupled with a deep yearning to avenge the murder of her people. Now the underground gave her the opportunity to express these feelings in the form of concrete deeds.

Rosa set to work and in a short time twenty girls were smuggling dynamite and explosive charges out of the munitions factory for the underground. They carried out the little wheels of dynamite, which looked like buttons, in small matchboxes that they hid in their bosoms or in special pockets they had sewn into the hems of their dresses. These 'buttons' would then pass from hand to hand through an elaborate underground transmission belt that led to the Russian prisoner Borodin, an expert at constructing bombs. For bomb casings he used empty sardine cans. The finished bombs then started moving again on the transmission belt to various strategic hiding places in the sprawling camp. The *Sonderkommando* had its cache close to the crematorium compound.

Israel Gutman and Joshua Leifer concealed their 'buttons' in the false bottom of a canister that they had made especially for that purpose. They always made sure to have some tea or leftover soup in the canister at the time of the S.S. inspection after work. Since it was customary for prisoners to save a little of their food rations for later, a canister containing some liquid would usually get no more than a perfunctory glance from the inspecting S.S. man.

One day after work as they were standing in line during the S.S. inspection, Leifer whispered to Gutman: 'I had no time to hide the stuff in the canister. I have it in a matchbox in my pocket.' Gutman grew pale and began to shake all over. The S.S. had been known to look into matchboxes also. He could not stop thinking that they were at the brink of disaster, and the more he thought of it the more nervous he became. So much so that the S.S. man became suspicious and gave him a very close and thorough inspection. Behind him stood Leifer, appearing very calm. Frustrated at having spent so much time on Gutman and finding nothing, the S.S. man gave Leifer a superficial inspection and passed on to the next man. This was one time, Gutman writes in his account of the incident, when nervousness paid off well.[1]

Moishe Kulka, another member, recalls that 'the entire work was carried on during the night-shift when control was not so strict. In the morning, when the night shift left the plant, I waited around. A Hungarian Jew I knew handed me half a loaf of bread. Concealed in the bread was a small package of explosives. I kept it near my workbench and later passed it on to a German Jew who worked on the railway.'

Rosa was the direct link with the *Sonderkommando*. The explosives she received were hidden in the handcarts on which the corpses of those who had died overnight in the barracks were taken to the crematorium.

The *Sonderkommando* which according to plan was supposed to synchronize its revolt with the general uprising, one day learned through underground sources that it was about to be liquidated. For them it was a matter of acting now or never. Not having any other choice they acted. They blew up Crematorium III, tossed a sadistic German overseer into the oven, killed four S.S. men, and wounded a number of others. Then they cut the barbed wire fence and about six hundred escaped. They were hunted down by a large contingent of pursuing S.S. men and shot. (As it turned out the general uprising never took place and the *Sonderkommando* action was the only armed revolt in Auschwitz.)

The political arm of the S.S. immediately launched a thorough investigation of the revolt. They wanted to know where the explosives came from and how they got into the hands of the *Sonderkommando*. With the aid of planted agents, the S.S. in a matter of two weeks came upon the trail of the explosives. They arrested several girls from the munitions factory, and after two days of interrogation and torture released them. The investigation continued and soon other arrests were made. Four girls were taken to the dread Block 11 for questioning. Three were from 'Union'; the fourth was Rosa Robota.

Gutman, Leifer, Noah, and others whom Rosa knew now expected to be arrested at any moment. They had full faith in her trustworthiness, but they also knew something about the torture methods the S.S. employed in Block 11. At one point they considered suicide. They feared that what might happen to Rosa under questioning could happen to them too.

In the meantime they watched from a distance how Rosa was being led daily to Block 11 for questioning. Her hair was matted, her face puffed up and bruised beyond recognition, her clothes torn. She could not walk and had to be dragged by two women attendants.

One day the underground decided on a daring step. Moishe Kulka was acquainted with Jacob, the Jewish kapo of Block 11. He asked him if he would be willing to let someone see Rosa Robota in her death cell. Jacob agreed and asked that the visitor bring along a bottle of whiskey and salami. Her townsman Noah was chosen to see her. The kapo introduced him to the S.S. guard as a friend of his. The two plied the S.S. man with drinks until he fell to the floor unconscious. Then Jacob quickly removed the keys from the guard and motioned to Noah to follow him. Noah describes the incident as follows:

> 'I had the privilege to see Rosa for the last time several days before her execution. At night, when all the prisoners were asleep and all movement in Camp was forbidden, I descended into a bunker of Block 11 and saw the cells and the dark corridors. I heard the moaning of the condemned and was shaken to the core of my being. Jacob led me through the stairs to Rosa's cell. He opened the door and let me in. Then he closed the door behind me and disappeared.
>
> 'When I became accustomed to the dark I noticed a figure,

wrapped in torn clothing, lying on the cold cement floor. She turned her head toward me. I hardly recognized her. After several minutes of silence she began to speak. She told me of the sadistic methods the Germans employ during interrogations. It is impossible for a human being to endure them. She told me that she took all the blame upon herself and that she would be the last to go. She had betrayed no one.

'I tried to console her but she would not listen. "I know what I have done, and what I am to expect", she said. She asked that the comrades continue with their work. It is easier to die when one knows that the work is being carried on.

'I heard the door squeak. Jacob ordered me to come out. We took leave of each other. It was the last time that I saw her.'

Before Noah left Rosa's death cell, she scribbled a farewell message to her underground comrades. She assured them that the only name she mentioned during the interrogations was that of a man in the *Sonderkommando* who she knew was dead. He, she had told the interrogators, was her only contact with the underground. She concluded her message with the Hebrew greeting of *Hashomer Hatzair*, '*Khazak V' Hamatz*' – Be strong and brave.

Several days later all the Jewish prisoners were ordered to the Appel-Platz to witness the hanging of the four young women – Esther, Ella, Regina and Rosa.

Yuri Suhl (ed. and trans.), *They Fought Back: The Story of the Jewish Resistance in Nazi Europe* (New York: Crown, 1967), pp.219–23. Reproduced by kind permission of Beverly Spector. For information about the author, Yuri Suhl, see 19. 'And the Earth Rebelled'.

NOTE

1. Israel Gutman, *Auschwitz Zeugnisse und Berichte* (Frankfurt am Main: 1962), pp.276–9. For information about Yuri Suhl, see 19. 'And the Earth Rebelled'.

37

Mordecai Anielewicz and His Movement

EMANUEL RINGELBLUM

An Essay

He was a young man, about twenty-four years old, of middling stature, with a thin, pale face, long hair and a pleasant expression. I met him for the first time at the beginning of the war, when he came to me dressed in sports clothes and asked me to lend him a book. From then on he often came to me to borrow books on Jewish history and especially on economics in which he was very interested. Who was to know that this quiet, modest, pleasant youth would, three years later, be the most important person in the ghetto, and that his name would be spoken of with veneration by some and with fear by others?

Hashomer Hatzair, of which Anielewicz was the leader, was one of the groups to which the thinking sections of the youth were drawn – that is, those whose spirit of idealism and of readiness to sacrifice themselves for the public and its interests, was still alive. Immediately after the outbreak of war, *Hashomer Hatzair* began to establish study circles and cultural groups that encompassed hundreds of young people. The cultural activity was carried out at the refugee hostel at 23 Nalewki Street, where hundreds of its members from smaller provincial cities had found accommodation. *Hashomer Hatzair* did not only concern itself with the provision of its members' material needs, but did great things for their intellectual education too. Study circles and seminars sprang up in which the youth received a general and a Jewish education. In the more advanced classes for the older members, they trained leaders for the younger groups of *Hashomer Hatzair*.

Hashomer Hatzair's activity included, apart from Warsaw, the provincial cities as well. The Movement's group leaders endangered their lives by travelling about the country with forged documents – some of them as Jews, but mostly as 'Aryans'. They distributed the Movement's illegal publications and activated local *kenim*. There were special seminars to train leaders for the groups in the smaller cities. Young boys and girls came to these seminars not only from the area of the 'General Gouvernement' (that area of Poland administered as conquered territory – Trans.) but some even stole to Warsaw from the 'Reich' itself [i.e. from that part of Poland which was made into an integral part of Germany – Trans.] – from Sosnowiec and Bendin, etc. Some of them went on foot for weeks until they reached Warsaw. Only someone who knows the dangers involved in travelling by train can appreciate the heroism of this youth, for which no hindrances existed.

I lectured several times to seminars of *Hashomer Hatzair*. These lectures which I gave to youth which held the flag of idealism high, in the sea of barbarism around it, became some of my deepest experiences. When I saw the entranced faces of youth, thirsty for knowledge, I would forget that there was a war going on in the world. The activities of these seminars used to take place in a building facing the German guards who watched over the gates of the ghetto. The young *Shomrim* felt so much at home in their clubhouse that we would often forget what was going on around us. The mob of young people would often dance a *hora* to the accompaniment of Hebrew or revolutionary songs. Once the singing attracted a German *gendarme*, who came and asked what it was all about.

Mordecai was extraordinarily devoted to the members of *Hashomer Hatzair*. He thought about them and worried about them day and night. He managed to obtain foodstuffs for the kitchen of the *Shomer* kibbutz from all sorts of sources.

As long as it was possible, the 'Jewish Self-Help Organisation' aided them under the cloak of aiding refugees. The supply department of the Jewish community also gave the *Shomrim* support, mainly thanks to one of the department's members, Shmuel Winter. However, most of its expenditure was covered by *Hashomer Hatzair* itself from the wages of its members. They worked in various places and used to pay all their wages into the common treasury.

Mordecai Anielewicz's loyalty to his comrades was unusual, and only very rarely can its like be found. He was prepared to go through fire and water for a comrade. I will give you this example which I myself witnessed. It was the case of Zandman, a member of *Hashomer Hatzair*. It took place in Halman's factory in Nowolipki Street, where I had taken to living after the first deportation. The time was 1943. The fighting organisation had carried out several acts of reprisal against people who were guilty of acts against the Jewish population of Warsaw. Sulphuric acid was thrown over them as a punishment. They poured sulphuric acid over an ex-policeman in Halman's workshop. All those responsible managed to get away, but Zandman, who was connected with the sentence, was arrested by the house-guard. The latter also told the Germans in charge of the factory of Zandman's arrest.

When the matter was revealed to Mordecai, he arrived at Halman's place that same day, and together with the leaders of the fighting organisation and I, elaborated a plan to free Zandman. At four in the morning, five armed, masked members of the organisation broke into the factory-guards' rooms, freed Zandman and, at the same time, took the guards' documents and badges. It took place only a few hours before the January deportation. Zandman was picked up again and taken to the assembly spot, from which he was once more freed by members of the Movement. Zandman's case was not unique. Mordecai was prepared to go through any danger for his comrades, just as they were prepared to endanger their lives for him.

Such a tie between a leader and his followers can only rarely be found. It was the kind of loyalty which is found in secret underground organisations where the members consider themselves to be brothers and are prepared to sacrifice themselves for the others. Such mutual aid and loyalty could then be found only in workers' organisations, which organised aid groups, not only in the factories but even in work-camps of the S.S.

Mordecai and the other members of the *Hanhaga Rashit* had had a clear consistent political line since the beginning of the war. This policy was maintained and explained in all the seminars and in all the organs that were published in Hebrew and in Polish. '*Neged Hazerem*' [Against the Current] was the name of their Hebrew organ. One cannot but be impressed by the consistency and strength of character of the *Shomrim*, who were able to maintain their own political line against the bourgeois circles from which most of them came. Their line did not please the General Zionists at all or the Right *Poale-Zion* either. *Hashomer Hatzair*'s orientation was pro-Soviet – believing in the victory of the Soviet Union and its army. The only Jewish party which took a similar political stand was Left *Poale-Zion*. In accordance with this line they made contacts with the P.P.E. – the Polish Workers' Party – and were prepared to do anything for a Soviet victory. Hundreds of members of *Hashomer Hatzair* all over the country therefore joined partisan groups. With all that, we must remember that this attitude did not in the least weaken their view that the Land of Israel was the solution to the Jewish Problem. The programs of the secret seminars of *Hashomer Hatzair* can bear witness to this.

Even before the war, Mordecai had maintained good relations with the Polish Scout Movement, 'Harcerz Polski'. It was one of the rare instances where a Jewish organisation cooperated with a Polish organisation. These relations were of advantage to *Hatshomer Hatzair* in the present war. In Vilna, those relations with the Polish Scout Movement gave the *Shomrim* a path to the Polish priesthood, which aided the general activities of *Hashome Hatzair*. As a result of this, some of the *Shomrim* were hidden in Polish homes near Vilna.

I saw modest, quiet Mordecai in his role as leader of *Hashomer Hatzair* only once. It was in the winter of 1941/2. Mordecai wanted to assemble all the members of *Hashomer Hatzair* just once, in order to increase their feeling of collectivity and to prove what a force *Hashomer Hatzair* was. Without taking notice of the danger involved, I allowed *Hashomer Hatzair* to use the second floor of the Jewish Scientific Institute, where the public department of the 'Jewish Self-Help Organisation' was housed. A license had been obtained for the meeting on the grounds of its being a literary function. In the hall, a large stage was made out of tables, and benches were placed in rows. That evening about five hundred *Shomrim* and *Shomrot* appeared. The girls all wore white blouses. The literary and artistic part of the program was carried out by members of the Movement. The standard was very high. After the program, there was a ceremonial parade of the whole *ken*. At the same time, a graduation ceremony took place, from one age group to the next, which was connected with a public declaration of loyalty to the Movement. A member of the Polish Scout Movement was present at the parade. This activity showed me what love and respect was felt for Mordecai by members of *Hashomer Hatzair*. People felt the same way about him afterwards too, when he took on the task of Commander of the Fighting Organisation. However, power did not make him drunk. He remained modest as always.

Once, during the interval between two lectures at a seminar of *Hashomer Hatzair* (I was lecturing on the history of the Jewish Labour Movement), Mordecai and Yosef called me to the yard of Nalewki 23, took me into a small room and showed me two pistols. Those pistols, the two explained to me, were to be used to train the youth how to use weapons. It was the first step which was taken by *Hashomer Hatzair*, even before the establishment of the Fighting Organisation.

Hard times began. Tragic reports began to flow in from the whole country. The first reports were of the dreadful slaughter in Vilna, which were brought by Arieh Vilner of *Hashomer Hatzair* and Salomon of *Hanoar Hazioni*. Afterwards, we received reports of the slaughters in Slonim and other towns of eastern Poland. Mordecai understood that all the Jews of Poland were doomed to liquidation. From the moment that Mordecai and his friends decided to fight, no other questions were considered, and all the study circles and seminars ceased. The cultural work was suspended. Everyone began to concentrate on the struggle.

Mordecai, who had matured quickly and who had rapidly become the Commander of the Fighting Organisation, was now regretting bitterly that he and his comrades had wasted three years of the war on cultural and educational activity. 'We did not understand the new situation which was being created'; he blamed himself, 'we should have trained the youth to use all kinds of arms. We should have educated them in a spirit of vengeance and struggle against the greatest enemy of the Jews and of all humanity.'

Mordecai put all he had, all his energy and all his enthusiasm into organizing the defence. Together with other groups and parties, the Jewish Fighting Organisation was established, as was the Jewish National Committee and the Coordinating Committee of Polish Organisations. Mordecai was placed at the head of the Fighting Organisation. He was the soul of the Organisation. He was not one of those leaders who send others to the front line and stay well away from it themselves. As early as January, 1943, he took an active part in the fighting. German victims were felled by his hands. He once aimed his pistol at a German *gendarme*'s head, but something went wrong with the pistol and it did not fire. He barely escaped with his life, and that he did was thanks to a friend who rescued him at the last moment.

The time for revolt had come in the Warsaw Ghetto. After leading much heroic fighting, Mordecai was killed some weeks after the outbreak of the Revolt. At the time, he was with the Fighting Organisation's staff in the bunker in Mila Street. It was the bunker with five entrances. The fighters would carry out sorties from there against the Germans. S.S. and Wehrmacht men entered the bunker from all five entrances after throwing gas bombs into it. Mordechai fell together with his closest companions from the Organisation.

The Labour Movement should remember well that Mordecai Anielewicz was one of those people who, from the very first moment, placed their lives at the service of the Jewish people, its honor and dignity, at the service of the world revolution and the first workers' State in the world.

Emanuel Ringelblum, 'Mordecai Anielewicz and His Movement' in

Sefer Hashomer Hatzair and in *The Massacre of European Jewry. An Anthology* (Kibbutz Merchavia, Israel: World *Hashomer Hatzair*, English Speaking Department, 1963), pp.200–6. Originally part of Emanuel Ringelblum's *Oneg Shabbat* Archives, reproduced by kind permission of David Amitai, *Hashomer Hatzair* Institute for Research and Documentation, Yad Yaari, Givat Haviva Archives, Israel, of the Jewish Historical Institute, Warsaw, Poland, and by *Commentary* magazine. For information about Emanuel Ringelblum, see 29. *Jewish Children on the Aryan Side.*

NOTES

Mordecai Anielewicz, the beloved young leader, born in 1919, fell in battle on 8 May 1943, in the command bunker on Mila 18, attaining his last goal to die as a fighting Jew. Mordecai and his remaining companions took their own or each other's lives, not to be captured alive by the Germans.

Ziviah Lubetkin, one of the prominent leaders of the Warsaw Ghetto Uprising who survived, wrote in part, in 1947:[1]

> Finally, the Germans began to send gas into the bunker ... A terrible death faced the 120 fighters ... Aryeh Wilner was the first to cry out: 'Come, let us destroy ourselves. Let's not fall into their hands alive!' The suicides began. Pistols jammed and the owners begged their friends to kill them. But no one dared to take the life of a comrade. Lutek Rotblatt fired four shots at his mother but, wounded and bleeding, she still moved. Then someone discovered a hidden exit, but only a few succeeded in getting out this way. The others slowly suffocated in the gas. Thus the best of the Jewish fighters met death, one hundred in all; among them was Mordecai Anielewicz, our handsome commander whom we all had loved. Twenty-one had escaped; of those, eighteen were fighters.

For information about the Warsaw Ghetto Uprising see 38. *The Last Wish of My Life Has Been Granted* and 42. *Jewish Resistance in the Warsaw Ghetto.*

1. Ziviah Lubetkin, 'The Last Days of the Warsaw Ghetto', *Commentary* (May 1947), p.407. Reprinted by permission of *Commentary*. See also, S.D. Kassow, *Who Will Write Our History: Emanuel Ringelblum, the Warsaw Ghetto and the Oyneg Shabes Archive* (Bloomington, ID: Indiana University Press, copyright © 2007 by Samuel D. Kassow), pp.362–5, 383–5; and 38. *The Last Wish of My Life Has Been Granted* and 42. Jewis *Resistance in the Warsaw Ghetto.*

38

The Last Wish of My Life Has Been Granted

MORDECAI ANIELEWICZ

A Letter

This letter was written by Mordecai Anielewicz, the Commander of the Warsaw Ghetto, on 23 April 1943, in the middle of the revolt. It was the last call for help from the dying Ghetto to the outside world.

Now it is clear that everything that has happened is far graver than we had anticipated. We did more than we could in resisting the Germans. But our strength is being exhausted. We are on the threshold of oblivion. Twice we forced the Germans to retreat, but they have returned in greater force.

One of our groups held out for forty minutes; another fought for six hours. The mine we planted in the area of the brush factory has exploded. Then we attacked the Germans and inflicted heavy casualties, while our losses were slight. This, too, is an achievement. Z fell at his machine gun. I feel that we have dared to do great things, which have enormous value.

Of necessity we are changing our tactics today to partisan methods. Tonight six patrols are going out to accomplish two tasks: reconnaissance and capture of arms. Remember that short-range weapons are of no use to us. We use such weapons only rarely. We need a lot of rifles, grenades, machine guns and explosives.

I cannot describe to you the conditions in which the Jews of the Ghetto now live. Only a few could possibly withstand such suffering. The rest will die sooner or later. Their fate is sealed. For although thousands are hiding in nooks and ratholes, there is not enough air in those places to light a candle. You who are outside – are blessed. Perhaps we shall yet see each other by some miracle. This is very, very doubtful. The last aspiration of my life has been fulfilled. Jewish fighting resistance is a fact. Jewish self-defense and Jewish revenge are a reality. I am happy and contented that I have been among the first fighters of the Ghetto.

Y. Shilhav (compiler) and S. Feinstein (ed.), *Flame and Fury*, translated by D. Kuselewitz (New York: Jewish Education Press of the Board of Jewish Education, 1962), p.31. Based on a publication of Yad Vashem, Holocaust Martyrs' and Heroes' Remembrance Authority, Jerusalem. Reproduced by kind permission of Yad Vashem Martyrs' and Heroes' Remembrance Authority and Barbara Kessel, the Board of Jewish Education of Greater New York. See also 42. 'Jewish Resistance in the Warsaw Ghetto'.

39

To Arms!

The Proclamation of the Rebels in the Ghetto of Vilna

Jews, defend yourselves with arms!
The German and Lithuanian hangmen have approached the gates of the Ghetto.
They have come to murder us! Soon they will be leading us in droves through the gates.
Thus hundreds were led away on Yom Kippur!
Thus were led away our brothers and sisters, our mothers and fathers, our children.
Thus tens of thousands were led to their death! But we shall not go!
We will not stretch out our necks to the slaughterer like sheep!
Jews, defend yourselves with arms!
Do not believe the lying promises of the murderers. Do not believe the words of traitors. Whoever leaves the Ghetto is sent to Ponar, (a Vilna suburb where Jews were murdered in tens of thousands).
Ponar means Death!
Jews, we have nothing to lose; sooner or later we shall be killed. Who can believe that he will survive when the fiends are exterminating us with calculated efficiency? The hands of the executioner will ultimately reach everyone; escape and cowardice will save no one.
Only armed resistance can possibly save our lives and our honor.
Brothers, it is better to die in the battle of the Ghetto than to be led away like sheep to Ponar! Lest you forget – there is an organized Jewish fighting force that will rebel with arms.
Help the Rebellion!
Do not hide in hideaways and shelters. In the end you will be caught like rats in the traps of the murderers.
Masses of Jews, get out into the streets! If you have no arms, raise your hammers! And those who have no hammer let them use iron bars, even sticks and stones!
For our fathers!
For our murdered children!

As payment for Ponar!
Kill the murderers!
In every street, in every yard, in every room, in the Ghetto and outside kill the mad dogs!
Jews, we have nothing to lose; we shall save our lives only when we kill the killers.
Long live Liberty!
Long live our armed resistance!
Death to the murderers!

Command of the United Partisan Organization, Vilna Ghetto, 1 September l943.

Y. Shilhav (compiler) and S. Feinstein (ed.), *Flame and Fury*, translated by D. Kuselewitz (New York: Jewish Education Press of the Board of Jewish Education, 1962), pp.43–4. Based on a publication of Yad Vashem, Holocaust Martyrs' and Heroes' Remembrance Authority, Jerusalem. Reproduced by kind permission of Yad Vashem, Holocaust Martyrs' and Heroes' Remembrance Authority and by Barbara Kessel, The Board of Jewish Education of Greater New York.

40

'Shlomo Jelichovski'

ITZHAK KATZENELSON

A Poem

Sing, earth and heaven, sing God, sing Jews,
Sing all below and above, sing,
Sing all worlds, sing the name Shlomo Jelichovski.
He ennobled man and the earth, he ennobled everything.

Rise, Homer, great blind singer,
And David, son of Jesse, too,
Take your harps, and play a song of praise
To Shlomo Jelichovski, the Zdunska Vola Jew.

Zdunska Vola is astir, there is a bustle,
It is the eve of *Shevuoth*, the feast of the Giving of the Law.
The *Ghetto* has been opened to non-Jews all around.
Even the Germans are preparing to celebrate this day of awe.

They have flung wide open the gates of the *Ghetto*.
There is going to be something grand
For the sightseers who come.
In the market place ten gibbets stand.

The Jews have been chased out of their homes into the market place.
The Germans have come into the fenced-off *Ghetto*-town.
They are reading from a list ten names,
The names of ten hostages, chosen and marked down.

Shlomo Jelichovski! – the name rings out,
The name of this Jew, in every German ear,
And one of the ten lifts his head, in answer.
This is the man! You cannot mistake him for any other here!

Shlomo Jelichovski of Zdunska Vola!
It is the name of a hero! Like one of the heroes of old!
A heroic Jew, whose face shines with courage,
Self-sacrificing, defiant, bold.

Shlomo Jelichovski! It sounds like the beginning of a song,
Like the opening words of a Psalm, a song of praise!
Here he is, standing ready at the gibbet,
As though he were the Cantor at the Synagogue dais.

Shlomo Jelichovski, the Jew, with everything about him Jewish!
Through the Zdunska Vola market place this Jewish name goes
    ringing!
Give him a cup of wine, for he is making *Kiddush*,
He is singing the Sanctification, at death's gate he is singing!

He is not singing alone! Together with him
All Israel is singing, every Jew in the world sings!
From his throat sing all the Jewish generations!
And over his head beat *seraphim* wings!

No! He was wrong! Nobody else is singing!
Even these Jews at the gibbet are dumb.
'Why are you silent! Lift up your voices,
Lift up your heads, come, sing with me, come!

'Why are you sad, why are you disheartened?
Why do you stand here so lost, in despair?
Summon up courage! Strengthen your faith!
There must be no melancholy here!

'It is *Erev Shevuoth* Jews! Tomorrow
We shall receive our holy old Torah again!
Let us rejoice, we who will not live to see it,
We more than all others, before we are slain!

'Let us rejoice! To die thus is a privilege!
We should be proud they chose us to be hung
For *Kiddush Hashem*, for the Sanctification!
Lift up your voices, Jews! Let's have a song!'

Then he raised his noble head to heaven,
High above the Germans, ignoring them,
And in the market place of Zdunska Vola,
He sang the song of Jerusalem!

'When I remember, O God, how every city
Rises on its hill in state,
And how our holy city
Lies desolate!

'My heart faints,
And my eyes grow dim.
Yet however they prosper with their lies,
To God alone we turn our eyes!'

So he sang, with his head held high,
This Jerusalem psalm.
And to the Jews in the market place of Zdunska Vola
His voice was balm.

They lifted up their heads.
Their hearts grew strong.
And God Himself smiled happily
When He heard Shlomo Jelichovski's song.

'This is a man after My heart'
Said God. 'When the world began,
I had him in My mind,
When I created man.'

Sing Shlomo Jelichovski, sing!
As you sing, you grow!
All the Jews of Zdunska Vola
Envy you now.

They wish they had been chosen,
Like these ten to hang,
To have the privilege of being martyrs,
Like this man who at death's door sang.

A German wild beast with a face like lard,
Walks up to Shlomo Jelichovski with measured tread,
And as he is singing his song of Jerusalem,
Hits him over the head.

But Shlomo Jelichovski sings on.
He does not feel the blow.
His eyes are turned to heaven.
He does not see this beast below.

He sings on, and the other nine hostages sing
Ecstatically, on only their singing intent,
Among them an apostate, and a former Bundist.
'Forgive us, God', they pray, penitent.

Now the hangman has dropped the nooses
Over the ten necks.
And they stand firm like ten strong pillars,
Like rocks.

'Rejoice!' cries Shlomo Jelichovski, 'Be glad, Jews!
It is *Erev Shevuoth*, and we are going to die,
We are going, singing, to God
Dancing up to the sky!'

He flung out his arms in exaltation.
And so did the nine other Jews.
And as they stood there with arms and eyes uplifted,
The German hangman drew round each the noose.

Sing, earth and heaven, sing God, sing Jews,
Sing all below and above, sing,
Sing all worlds, sing the name Shlomo Jelichovski.
He ennobled man and the earth, he ennobled everything.

Sing to him a song of praise,
Sing to him a high song under the sun,
For such a man as Shlomo Jelichovski,
Do you know like him anyone?

Sing his praise, land and sea,
Forest, river, hill,
God Himself sings his praise.
He has done God's will.

Sun and moon and stars all sing.
The light sings his praises – whose?
The praise of Shlomo Jelichovski,
The hero of the Jews.

He never destroyed a town,
This heroic Jew.
He never bombed defenceless folk,
No sword from its scabbard drew.

Sing to him, this hero of a poor small town,
Who went singing to God,
The hero of Zdunska Vola,
Where the ten gibbets stood.

J. Leftwich (compiler, translator and ed.), *The Golden Peacock: A Worldwide Treasury of Yiddish Poetry* (New York: Thomas Yoseloff, © 1961 by A.S. Barnes and Company, Inc.), pp.519–23. Reproduced by kind permission of Professor Feliks Tych, director, Jewish Historical Institute, Warsaw, Poland and Julien Yoseloff, publisher.

NOTES

Itzhak Katzenelson, a writer and poet, wrote primarily in Hebrew. But when the Germans invaded Poland in 1939 and drove the Jews into ghettos and death camps, K., who was himself in the Ghetto, took to writing in Yiddish. His poem 'Shlomo Jelichovski', found after the war in the underground Archives, was first translated for *The Golden Peacock*.

The 1942 hangings in Zdunska Wola, a small town west of Lodz are examples of the diabolical cruelty of the Germans all over the conquered lands. In May 1942, the Jewish Council of Zdunska Wola was ordered to select and turn over to the Germans ten Jews. The community was in mourning. They remembered well that on Purim of that year, when ten Jews were selected, they had been executed by hanging. Ten pious and notable men were arrested, among them Shlomo Jelichovski. The entire Jewish community, including children, was forced to attend. On their last night, Shlomo led the condemned men in prayer, and according to eyewitnesses, on the day of their execution he lead them to the gallows singing their prayers. Reports by survivors inspired Itzhak Katzenelson to write the poem 'Shlomo Jelichovski'.

The name Shlomo Jelichovski has been transliterated in different ways, including Zhelochovski, Zhelichowski and Zelichowski. The editor, as a Polish Jew, believes his first name might have been originally spelled Szlomo.

For additional information on Itzhak Katzenelson, see 26. 'The First Ones'. See also the following:

1. I. Neuman, with M. Palencia-Roth, *The Narrow Bridge; Beyond the Holocaust* (Urbana and Chicago, IL: University of Illinois Press, 2000), pp.83–94. Rabbi Neuman, a Holocaust survivor from Zdunska Wola, provides a very moving description of the condemned men's last hours.
2. S.D. Kassow, *Who Will Write Our History? Rediscovering a Hidden Archive from the Warsaw Ghetto* (New York: Vintage, 2009, paper edn), pp.300, 327.
3. M. Gilbert, *The Holocaust: A History of the Jews of Europe During the Second World War* (New York: Holt, Rinehart and Winston, 1985), pp.299, 350.

41

The Letter of the Ninety-Three Maidens

Some weeks ago, the Annual Conference of the Jewish Orthodox Rescue Committee received a letter from Chaja Feldman, one of the ninety-three Jewish girls, pupils, and teachers of the Beth Jacob Schools, who had been jailed by the Gestapo, then given a bath, stripped of all their clothes with the exception of their chemises and told that they would be visited by German soldiers. The girls said their last prayers (the Vidui), took poison and died, 'in order to sanctify the name of God by their death as well as by their lives'. Their letter, as it appears below, is based on a Hebrew version of it by Hillel Babli, which was published in Hadoar, Volume XXIII, No. 12, and was translated into English by Bertha-Badt Strauss. Dr Dora Edinger has added the significant note on the source of the inspiration that led to this great act of Kiddush Hashem by the Ninety-Three Maidens.

Editors, *The Reconstructionist*

We washed our bodies and we grew clean.
We purified our souls and we grew quiet.
Death does not terrify us; we go out to meet him. We served our God while we were alive;
We shall know how to sanctify Him by our death.
We made a covenant in our hearts, all the Ninety-Three:
Together we learned the *Torah*, together we will meet our end.
We read the Psalms together, we read and we felt relieved.
We confessed our sins together, and steady grew our hearts.
Now we feel well prepared and ready to breathe our last.
Now may the Unclean come to defile us; we are not afraid.
We will drink the cup of poison and perish in front of their eyes.
Pure and undefiled, as is the Law with the daughters of Israel.
To Mother Sarah we will come and lovingly clasp her knees:
Here we are! We stood the test, the test of the binding of Isaac!
Arise and pray for our people with us, for the nation of Israel:

Pity oh merciful Father! Oh pity the people that knew thee!
For there is no more pity in men.
Reveal Thy hidden kindness and save Thy downtrodden children:
Save and keep thy world!
The hour of *Neilah* is come, and quiet grow our souls.
One more prayer we utter: Brethren, wherever you are,
Say *Kaddish* for us, for the Ninety-Three daughters of Israel.

A FOOTNOTE TO THE LETTER OF THE NINETY-THREE MAIDENS

In 'Salute to Valor' Linton Wells says: 'The destruction of the Palembang oil fields was undoubtedly the largest voluntary sacrifice in the history of the world, with the sole exception of the demolition of the Dniepprostroy Dam by the Russians.' Yet the sacrifice of the young students of the Beth Jacob School should be recorded for the future history of our times, in testimony of how the Jews reacted. I have met people that could not believe this sacrifice to have been offered in the way it has been reported. Since I have been in the Beth Jacob seminary, I am perfectly convinced that these Jewish girls proved, in this last test, that they were true to the spirit of their education.

In 1932/33 I was in Cracow to deliver some lectures. The seminary was then located in a tall, unfinished building, in the midst of the Kazimierz, the Jewish settlement of the medieval town. It was overcrowded by young eager students from poor and isolated communities, who had moved in even before the floors had been laid. The first Beth Jacob school had started in the private home of Mrs. Sara Schenierer. She had come to Vienna as a refugee during the First World War, and there found access to Jewish learning, frowned upon by Orthodox educators, who opposed the teaching of Torah to girls. But Mrs. Schenierer had realized that, in the precarious situation of East European Jewry, the spirit of Jewish womanhood was the dam that might save it. First in her modest home, then in an apartment, she taught her young students, and finally moved to the seminary where I spent unforgettable days. The Friday night service was conducted by Mrs. Schenierer; no men were present. Advanced students gave proof of their ability in lectures or rather sermons on the *Sidra*. The entire school organization from kindergarten to seminary took care of about 30,000 students, many of them so poor that they later paid back their tuition out of their meager salaries.

Every summer former students were reunited in study camps in the Carpathian Mountains, and the spirit of devotion and faith, in the presence of often insurmountable odds, kept this unique organization full of its amazing vitality. It was not the spirit of ascetic nuns. Mrs. Schenierer herself, and many of the teachers that had been educated by her were married, and they were fully aware that their teachings might, at any moment, meet the supreme test. Even in the comparatively normal conditions of Jewry in Poland between the two great wars, the existence of the Beth Jacob School organization had the startling effect of a miracle, a flame kept alive by the power and burning faith only. Its sublime victory should be remembered as a pledge of the ultimate victory of the spirit over might and power.

Dora Edinger

The Letter of the Ninety-Three Maidens, translated by Bertha Badt, including an introduction by the editors and a footnote by Dr Dora Edinger, was published in *The Reconstructionist*, 2 (5 March 1943), pp.23–4. Based on a Hebrew version of it by Hillel Babli, which was published in *Hadoar*, XXIII, 12 (22 January 1943). Reproduced by kind permission of Rabbi Richard Hirsh, editor, *The Reconstructionist*.

42

Jewish Resistance in the Warsaw Ghetto

VLADKA MEED

An Essay

Fifty years have gone by, and I can still see before my eyes the flames from the burning Jewish houses leaping over the ghetto walls, and through the clouds of thick smoke, I can still hear the sound of explosions and the firing of Jewish guns. In their glare, I see the Jews of Warsaw. I see their life, their struggle, and their resistance during all the years of Nazi occupation. For it was the Jews' daily struggle, their vibrant drive for survival, their endurance, their spirit and belief, which the Nazis failed to crush, even with their most dreadful atrocities. This was the foundation from which resistance in all its forms was derived. For Jewish armed resistance in the Warsaw ghetto, when it came, did not spring from a sudden impulse; it was not an act of personal courage on the part of a few individuals or organized groups: it was the culmination of Jewish defiance, defiance that had existed from the advent of the ghetto; and its significance is diminished if it is remembered only to glorify the honor of those who perished.

Today, many efforts are being made to learn more about the Holocaust, to understand it, to introduce Holocaust studies into the schools. Scholars are searching through documents in the newly open archives of Moscow, Riga, and Kiev. Teachers are being trained; seminars and exhibits are being organized. Well-known photographs of life in the ghettos and concentration camps, of emaciated Jews near barbed-wire fences, of half-naked beggars in the ghetto streets, are being displayed. Most of these pictures were taken by the murderers themselves, whose very purpose it was to demonstrate the helpless, spineless inadequacy of those whom they were planning to destroy. Of course, we survivors know that the pictures are real. They are seared into our memories and into our hearts. But we also know that they present only one part of what occurred under the German occupation, that beyond the murder and destruction, there was life. Yes, life, filled with meaning, with loyalty, even with holiness, of which hardly any photographs remain and all too little is known. The life of the individual Jew, who, in his day-to-day painful struggle, created a universe for himself, and sought to survive with his self-respect. He was overshadowed by the dreadful events around him. He was, most likely, ground to dust in the gigantic murder machine. He is still waiting to be Storyed from the abyss of darkness.

I recall the streets of my ghetto, Warsaw, crowded with starving people. I remember the corpses covered with papers, lying unclaimed on the sidewalks, the carts loaded with books, and children, swollen from hunger, begging for a crumb of bread. The typhus epidemic reached into almost every house. I see my own home, my mother, with eyes puffed from hunger, hiding a slice of bread from us hungry children for my little brother's teacher, the *melamed*. I can see our neighbor, Mrs Ziferman, hurrying with her little girl to a secret class. I recall the sounds of a sewing machine, amidst the hushed voices from a nearby hidden 'shul' (synagogue), and, suddenly, the piercing voice of our ghetto clown, Rubinstein, calling aloud 'Yingl halt sich' (translated freely, 'Hang on, boy!'). Names come to mind, faces of friends, young and old people. There are the teachers; Virowski, Lindner, Rosa Synchourer, Emanuel Ringelblum, and so many others, whom I met at secret ghetto meetings. They were the ones who, together with the youth from various political groups, organized the extensive relief and cultural activities in the ghetto. Over 2,000 house committees came into existence, together with hundreds of public kitchens, in order to fight starvation. At the same time, a Jewish cultural organization, 'Zkor', promoted a broad, clandestine program. There were secret schools which thousands of children attended, a nursing school, courses on agriculture, *heders, yeshivas*, synagogues, hidden libraries, and choral groups. In addition, various political organizations in the ghetto conducted a vigorous traffic in underground publications. Let me recall a lecture, held on a cold winter's evening in 1941 in one of the soup kitchens. We were a group of youngsters, 15–16 years old, huddled together for warmth, and despite the hunger that gnawed at each of us, we listened to the leader speak about the writer I.L. Peretz. Later, we had to spread out to various houses, to talk on the same subject. My assignment was on No. 30 Pawia Street. I managed to get there before the curfew. I remember the large room, in which 40 occupants of the house had gathered. The windows were blacked out. A guard had been stationed outside the room, in case of a surprise 'visit' by the Germans. My talk was on the Peretz story, 'Bontshe

Shveig'. I do not recall the discussion, but I can never forget the wonderful atmosphere, the feeling of being able, even for a short time, to get away from the bitter ghetto reality.

I see the twin sisters, Pola and Zosia Lipshyc, happy, dancing girls, full of life and enthusiasm. They became the souls of the so-called 'children's corners' in the ghetto houses. Together with other youngsters, the two girls worked diligently, teaching children to write, and to sing. They staged performances of operas – which they themselves had learned before the war. They brought a bit of joy, of spirit, to the starving youngsters until they were caught in the Nazi vice.

The historian Emanuel Ringelblum, one of the cultural leaders of the Warsaw ghetto, formed the so-called '*Oneg Shabbat* Group' of writers and scholars; they did research on, and documented what was happening to the Jews.

Acts of violence against the Germans – prior to the uprising – were not committed because we in the ghetto did not believe that such acts would serve our purpose. The Germans enforced a diabolical method of collective responsibility: for every German killed by a Jew, hundreds of Jews would be killed. Our aim was to survive, to live, to outwit the enemy and witness his destruction. Every effort that lent strength to this goal, I see as an act of resistance. Our determination to resist derived from our desire to survive as a people: we refused to allow our spirit to be crushed

But the Germans weren't satisfied with the slow pace of Jewish deaths from starvation, typhoid, and casual persecution. They had different plans. The carefully coordinated Nazi machinery of mass murder eventually went into operation.

Blitz deportations: Suddenly, streets and houses were surrounded by soldiers and police and fast, fast, with the sounds of blows and shots, we were forced to line up. I can still remember the thousands and thousands in those lines. The German officers standing at the head of the lines, pointed with sticks – left, right, left, right. I can still feel the fear as I stood in that line, left to the trains, right to a few more days of ghetto life. I still see them – our ghetto Jews – among them my dearest ones, walking on their last march, to the trains, in silence. As their footsteps echo in my mind, I can hear their unuttered outcry to God, and to the world that allowed this to happen.

Yet even then, many of those remaining in the ghetto still nourished the hope that those who were deported would somehow survive. Even I, who learned from my work in the underground the actual destination of the trains, could not believe, when my mother, brother, and sister were taken away, that they would be killed. I found myself hoping that maybe, after all, they had been sent, as the Germans claimed, to another city for resettlement. How could our people, who believed in human values, imagine such utter madness as an enemy who planned our total annihilation?

How could we grasp the scope of such a huge killing apparatus – installed by German scientists, operated by trained military and civilian squads, supported by German industry and the German people?

The deportations from the Warsaw ghetto began on July 22, 1942; soon after, a clandestine meeting of representatives of all the illegal ghetto organizations took place. Although reports of the killing of Jews in other ghettos had already been received, the majority attending that first meeting opposed an immediate Jewish counteraction in Warsaw, arguing that it would serve as an excuse for the Nazis to kill all the Jews. Painful as it is, some argued, 'it is wiser to sacrifice 70,000 Jews for deportation, as the Germans demanded than to endanger the whole ghetto, the lives of half a million. The Germans will not dare to do the same to the Jews of Warsaw, the capital of Poland, as they have done to the Jews of smaller towns.'

Months passed before the ghetto residents started to recognize and believe the terrible truth of the gas chambers – a truth brought back by individuals who had somehow escaped the death camps. These reports, plus the sight of hundreds of thousands of Jews being deported, hammered into the minds of those who remained, the brutal fact that the Nazis would spare no one.

Then, only then, did the idea of armed struggle – the determination to go down fighting – come into its own.

In October 1942, the coordinated Jewish Fighting Organization of Warsaw, ZOB, was formed. I, a member of the Jewish Labor *Bund* underground, was ordered to live among the Poles outside the ghetto in order to obtain arms for our fighters' organization. More than 500 fighters were organized into 22 units. Other Jews also formed other armed groups. The core of the armed resistance was made up of the various illegal youth organizations: Zionists, Socialists, Bundists, Communists, and remnants of the pre-war political youth movements. Most of the fighters were in their teens or early twenties and they were imbued with a spirit of idealism and a determination to act.

Those who say that organized Jewish armed resistance came too late in the ghetto would do well to remember that it was the earliest uprising of its kind in Europe. The other underground movements launched similar uprisings only when the Allied armies were practically at the gates of their major cities, so as to insure their success. This was true of the French in Paris and, later on, of the Poles in Warsaw. But the Jews, the most persecuted group in Europe, in the most hopeless position, were the first to revolt. On January 18, 1943, as soon as we got hold of a few revolvers, the first German soldiers fell in the Warsaw ghetto. The surprise act forced the Germans to halt the deportations. January 18 marked a turning point, for on that day, the ghetto dared to strike back in an organized fashion.

By setting fire to German factories, by carrying out death sentences against informers and collaborators, the Jewish Fighting Organization won the support of the remaining Warsaw ghetto Jews. Through bulletins placed on the walls of ghetto buildings, the ZOB informed non-combatant Jews of the aims and work of the underground. The ZOB imposed a tax on the wealthy and on the remaining ghetto institutions. Money and jewelry were collected. Bakers and merchants secretly supplied bread and food to the Jewish fighting units. Those who still had possessions of value had to contribute them for armaments. 'Resist! Don't let yourself be taken away' – was the call.

'I no longer have any authority in the ghetto', Mark Lichtenbaum, the head of the German-appointed Jewish Council, admitted to the Nazis when he was ordered to supervise further deportations. It was the Jewish Fighting Organization that expressed the will and the feelings of the remaining 60,000 Warsaw ghetto Jews.

Our biggest problem was obtaining arms. We sent out desperate pleas to the outside world, begging for guns, but in vain.

I can still recall when, as a courier, I came to one of the ghetto's fighting units in Swietojerska 32 and my young friends would repeatedly ask me about our relations with the Poles, with the outside world. 'When will they send us help?' they would ask. 'When will we receive arms; hiding places for our ghetto children?' And I would stand there, forlorn, unable to give them the answers they so desperately sought. Pitiful was the response from the Polish underground.

And so, our own Jewish resistance organization had to find its own way. I will never forget when Michael Klepfish, our armament engineer, and I together tested our first homemade Molotov Cocktail in a big factory furnace outside of the ghetto walls. It worked!

With mounting excitement, some of us smuggled chemicals and some dynamite into the ghetto. I remember one incident. After a long search outside the ghetto, we were able to secure 10 pounds of dynamite, and I was entrusted to smuggle it to the Jewish fighters. Through a secret telephone, the ghetto underground was informed and arranged for some of my friends to wait for the dynamite at a location near a part of the ghetto wall where Polish smugglers sometimes bribed the guards to allow them to bring food into the ghetto. Against the ghetto wall, on the non-Jewish side, stood a ladder; we paid the Polish ringleader and waited our turn. It was necessary to climb quickly, cross over the top of the wall and descend to the ghetto side. As I reached the top, shots rang out from the street. A German patrol was approaching. In an instant, the smugglers snatched the ladder away and took cover. There I was, sitting on top of the wall, holding my parcel. The ghetto wall was over 3 meters high. I was afraid to jump because the explosives might go off. The shooting came closer and I was sure that my time had come. Just then, I heard shouts from the Jewish side of the wall: 'Wait, we'll help you.' Three of my ghetto friends came running to the wall. They had watched me from their hiding place. In a moment they had formed a human ladder, snatched my bundle, and helped me descend. In no time we ran away from the wall. Other colleagues were not so lucky.

On my missions, I could hear the sounds of hammering: Jews were secretly building bunkers and hiding places. Shots rang out; young people were learning to handle firearms. The whole ghetto was preparing to face a new deportation. The historic role of the young at that time has to become better known. None of them expected to survive a Nazi attack. Nor did we expect to influence, in the smallest way, the outcome of the war. But we were fueled by the conviction that the enemy must be fought.

On April 19, 1943, Passover, the German soldiers marched, in full gear, into the Warsaw ghetto, to make it '*Judenrein*'. Suddenly, they came under fire. From buildings, from windows, from the rooftops of houses, Jews were shooting. The enemy withdrew. They set up artillery around the ghetto walls and systematically bombarded our positions. We were so poorly equipped; only a small number of grenades and revolvers and primitive Molotov Cocktails against the combined might of the *Wehrmacht*. In the first days, the Jewish combatants tried to fight from fixed positions. Then they shifted to partisan methods. Groups would emerge from the bunkers to seek out the enemy. In these encounters, whoever saw the other first and was the quickest with a weapon, was the victor of the moment. Inexperienced, untrained civilians fought against a well-trained army. A primitive Molotov Cocktail against a tank, a gun against a flame-thrower, a revolver against a machine gun. One side of the street against the other. The Germans set fire to block after block, street after street. The fires that swept through the ghetto turned night into day. The flames, the heat, and the suffocating smoke drove the Jews from their houses and bunkers. Men, women, and children jumped out of windows and ran through the burning ruins, looking for places where they could breathe. But where could they go when *everything* around them was burning?

At that time I was on a mission outside the ghetto. I can still smell the stench of burning houses and hear the agonizing screams for help. In this flaming hell our Jews fought until the entire ghetto was charred rubble.

General Jurgen Stroop, who was in charge of destroying the Warsaw ghetto, stated in an official report that the Jewish uprising came to an end on May 16, after four weeks of struggle. We know, of course, that after that date the ghetto was unable to continue organized resistance, since most members of our military organization had been killed. Many others were burned to death. But for long weeks after May 16, Jews remained hidden in the still-smoldering ruins and bunkers and would not give themselves up. For weeks after the 'official' end of the uprising, shots were still heard in the ghetto.

General Stroop in another report informed his superiors that he blew up or gassed 631 Jewish bunkers. This means that there were at least 631 bastions of Jewish resistance. No one knows exactly the number of Jews who perished in the bunkers. No one can describe their last hours and their death. Those final days united them all, those who had fallen with arms in hand, those who were gassed, those who suffocated in the smoking ruins, and those who were burned to death. They were all united in one great chain of resistance against their enemy.

During the days of the uprising, members of the Jewish underground stationed outside the ghetto radioed information to our representatives in the Polish government-in-exile in England. We pleaded for ammunition, for help. But the world sat silently by. During the final days of the uprising, outside the ghetto, not far from the ghetto wall in Krasinski Square, a carousel was turning, music was playing, children frolicked and the joyous atmosphere of Easter was in the air. None of the visitors to the square seemed to pay attention to what was going on behind the ghetto walls. Our people were entirely alone, abandoned. Those of us who survived can never forget the feeling of desertion we experienced. We shall never be able to find justification for having been forsaken in our last hours of struggle. Only one year later, after the ghetto rebellion, I was in the Polish uprising in Warsaw. I remember at that time, the planes flying over the city, dropping arms and medical supplies for the Polish fighters. But when our ghetto fought, the skies over the ghetto were empty.

In the months after the ghetto rebellion, we learned that other Jewish uprisings were taking place. The news of the battle of the Warsaw ghetto had spread over the wall and through the barbed wire to other ghettos and camps.

What must be remembered is that, throughout the Holocaust, every Jew in his or her own way resisted the Nazis; each act of resistance was shaped by its unique time and place. The soup kitchens, the secret schools, the cultural events in the ghettos and camps, constituted forms of resistance, the goals of which were survival with dignity, with '*menshlechkeit*'.

The Warsaw ghetto uprising erupted when we knew that the Nazis would spare no one. Our objective then became to choose how we would die, and the choice was to die with weapons in our hands. For other Jews, dying with dignity meant going to the crematoria wrapped in talisim and reciting a prayer. Their self-assertion and our armed resistance intertwined in the chain of Jewish resistance, a chain that grew, link by link, through the long years of the Holocaust.

Yes, we now stand at a distance from the events which shaped our lives and which reshaped history; and, standing at a distance, we look back and remember. For our memory is the ringing warning to all people in all times.

Vladka Meed, 'Jewish Resistance in the Warsaw Ghetto', in *Dimensions: A Journal of Holocaust Studies*, 7, 2 (New York: Braun Center for Holocaust Studies, 1993). Reproduced by kind permission of Vladka Meed, Dr Steven Meed and *Dimensions*, The Anti-Defamation League.

NOTES

Vladka Meed was a young woman at the outbreak of the Second World War. Her book, *On Both Sides of the Wall; Memoirs From the Warsaw Ghetto*, first published in 1948, in Yiddish, was one of the first authentic eyewitness reports about the Warsaw Ghetto uprising, about the destruction of Polish Jewry, the children on the 'Aryan side', the betrayers and the friends.

Still in her teens, Vladka served as a courier between the Ghetto and the 'other side of the wall', finding hiding places for Ghetto escapees, for children, delivering money, testing Molotov Cocktails, never resting or failing her comrades. She lived to write about it. She describes not only the heroism of the fighters, but the dignity of individual Jews in unbearable conditions, and her words breathe truth.

Mrs Meed is the Director of the Holocaust and Jewish Resistance Summer Fellowship Program. She chairs the Education Committee of the American Gathering of Holocaust Survivors, is Vice President of the Jewish Labor Committee and is the director of the JLC's Yiddish Culture and Holocaust Programs.

Other Voices:
Testimonies of Those Who Helped

43

A Pole in the Ghetto

RUTH BAUM

A Biographical Vignette

'At the moment of creation of the Jewish quarter, I have become, unexpectedly, its resident, as the owner of the pharmacy 'Under an Eagle', at Plac Zgody 18 ...'

With these words Tadeusz Pankiewicz opens the introduction to his book *The Pharmacy in the Ghetto of Cracow*, published in Cracow, in 1947.

A second edition, considerably expanded and supplemented, appeared in 1982, also in Cracow. In his introduction the author quotes the above mentioned sentence, adding:

'Imputed by certain circles to be friendly to the Zionists, I experienced unpleasantness from some of my compatriots, who so erroneously judged my activities and duties performed in the nightmarish days and nights of Hitler's occupation ...'

Mgr Tadeusz Pankiewicz's pharmacy was the only one of four pharmacies on the Cracow Podgorze to find itself in the Ghetto area. When, after a while, this fact was noticed by the Germans, they categorically demanded of Mgr Pankiewicz to leave the location. They offered him, instead, a previously Jewish pharmacy on the Aryan side. Pankiewicz, however, was successful in bribing them, greatly aided by his personal charm, for he was uncommonly handsome, eloquent, and, most importantly, well familiar with the weaknesses of the 'Master Race', who considered drinking the height of happiness. And a pharmacy, of course, never lacked spirits. Pankiewicz was the only non-Jew living in the Ghetto, and his pharmacy the only one in Poland within the walls of a Jewish district.

Even later, whenever he was in danger of having to close the pharmacy and to leave the Ghetto, alcohol and bribes of money were effective. And, probably also the proverbial bit of luck, when, through an error, he was driven along with thousands of Jews to the Plac Zgody, from where the transports departed for the death camps, he was successful, at the last moment, in convincing the Germans responsible for the operation, that he was a Pole.

Why did he decide to remain in the Ghetto? What guided his course? Was it sentiment for his family's property (he inherited the pharmacy from his father, also a pharmacist)? Fear of the Germans not keeping their promise? Or a personal reluctance to change his location?

In the introduction to his book, the author suggests: 'I clearly realized that the Germans would lose the war, my pharmacy in the Ghetto would be destroyed, and I would be obliged, after the war, to return someone else's property to its rightful owner or to his family ...'

Then, at the outset, he did not yet know he would be a witness to the greatest homicidal event ever known in world history. That before his own eyes an entire nation would be annihilated, first imprisoned by narrow walls, defenceless, haunted, starved, decimated by disease, then murdered by the savage brutality of the Germans: the final liquidation of the Jews of Cracow, on March 13, 1943. The tragedy of those condemned was also his own; he suffered with them, feared for their lives, and yearned to help them. But how? He was under the continuous surveillance of the Germans. They would have preferred to see him outside the Ghetto walls. The very existence of a pharmacy in the Ghetto was against their 'historic mission' of annihilation of the Jews, since medications prolonged their lives, while they were meant to die as soon as possible.

And yet Pankiewicz found ways to lighten, at least to a certain degree, the lot of some of his dearest friends. He was helped in this endeavour by the self-sacrifice of three pharmacists, his co-workers: Mgr Helena Krywaniuk, Mgr Aurelia Danek-Czortowa and Mgr Irena Drozdzikowska. To begin with, they served, along with him, as links between the ghetto's imprisoned Jews and the outside world. They carried letters to and from families, smuggled forbidden printed literature, which was, later, in the back area of the pharmacy, discussed at great length by Mgr Pankiewicz's guests, who invariably believed in the imminent defeat of the Germans.

He recalled, with pain and shame, that when, at the request of the Jews in the Ghetto, he visited Polish friends, requesting the return of valuables given to them for safekeeping, he was met with brutal refusals. But he also, with satisfaction, underscored the magnanimity of other Poles, who offered even their own belongings.

Mgr Pankiewicz dispensed drugs free of charge (he was financed by wealthy Jews), distributed hot meals, obtained documents 'on the left side', and made efforts to find accommodation on the Aryan side for Jews who had decided to leave the Ghetto, and, most importantly, during the increasingly frequent 'actions' he concealed as many of his friends as possible in a secret room adjacent to the pharmacy. He also tried to free acquaintances imprisoned by the Gestapo, using every possible contact with the Germans, and not skimping on bribes.

'We shall not survive, but you must write about our tragedy', the Jews implored 'so this murderous bestiality will not go unpunished.' He kept his word.

He wrote not only about the murder of helpless and defenceless people by the German bandits, but also about the unbelievable, under those conditions, bursts of energy and rebellion by youths, not always successful, and unfortunately often ending with the deaths of many of them. He recorded the names of those heroes, immortalizing their deeds of valour in his book.

Irena Halpern (now Cynowicz) relates:

> We were driven, in a chaotic crowd toward Plac Zgody for deportation, beaten and prodded by rabid Germans. As we passed Pankiewicz's pharmacy, an inspired thought suddenly occurred to me: to jump inside. If successful, I thought, the noble Master would not betray me. Of that I was certain. I knew him, and used to purchase drugs from him for my ailing mother. My escape was successful, and perhaps thanks to him I have survived the war. I was so young then, and so determined to live!

Irena came in contact with him after the war, in 1947. Travelling one day by train (she lived in Germany at that time) she noticed the title of a book read by a woman in the opposite seat: *A Pharmacy in the Cracow Ghetto*. Author: Tateusz Pankiewicz. Irena asked where she could purchase the book. The stranger gave her the book, claiming she no longer needed it. Irena wrote to him, reminding him of herself, and they have maintained a regular correspondence ever since. In 1957 she also initiated his trip to Israel. He spent two months there. Irena believed that he deserved a tree on the Avenue of the Righteous Among the Nations of the World, and regretted being unable to arrange for it during his visit.

Dr Ignacy Pancewicz, a Haifa physician, was also of the opinion that this noble Pole had suffered an injustice. In Dr Pancewicz's words:

> He helped not only then, but also after the war. When I returned

from Russia, he took me into his apartment, fed and cared for me till I could stand on my own feet. Before the war we were fellow students in a gymnasium in Podgorze, and I knew his family. I knew his father, a liberal and a democrat who loved people, regardless of their creed. His son inherited from him this love of mankind. We were good friends before the war. I appreciated his artistic interests, his fantasy, and the vigour and spirit by which he lived. He had visited Palestine in 1938 and told about its wonders. He is a great humanist and a remarkable man.

Dr A. Mirowski, a Haifa resident, recalled Tadeusz Pankiewicz from the ghetto years. He remembered visiting his pharmacy along with other physicians, marvelling at his courage and ability to win over many of the Germans whose support he needed. After plying them with liquor into near-oblivion, he frequently succeeded in drawing out of them the date of the next action. He then warned the people, and many of them would be absent from the Ghetto, or hidden in ingeniously arranged hiding places.

'Living among us, he was constantly exposed to dangers, but it did not terrify him. Full of compassion at our tragedy, he wished to help us from the bottom of his heart', reminisced Dr Mirowski. 'He took very hard the death of every man, woman and child.' And adding, sorrowfully: 'While he was here in 1957, we were unable to bestir ourselves about a tree in his name on the Avenue of the Righteous. More is the pity!'

I have before me the manuscript of Tadeusz Pankiewicz's speech, delivered to the Academy on the fourteenth anniversary of the liquidation of the Ghetto of Cracow. The ceremony was observed in Tel Aviv, on March 13, 1957. Pankiewich, in moving words thanked those present for the honour and privilege of participation, and for their warmest welcome. He maintained, modestly, that he did not deserve such whole-hearted cordiality, since he did little during those ghastly years ... And then immediately addressed the thought rankling in his heart.

I quote from his speech:

'I found two kinds of answers to these questions. First, I tried to portray the mood accompanying each deportation. I tried to describe the days of anxiety and agitation preceding the roundup and deportation. I talked about the psychosis of fear enveloping the Ghetto several days before the expected action. I strived to convey, as faithfully as I could, the dread, terror and tension of the night, when units of German police tightly surrounded the Ghetto walls, and then the entry of armed-to-the-teeth SS formations, the barking of their dogs, the screaming of soldiers, the echo of first shots … I tried to transmit the entire nightmarish situation, the wrestling of children from their mothers' arms, the barrels of rifles pointing at them, the beatings by whips, the trampling of people, the killing on the spot – the many faces of death. Anyone not present in the Ghetto at those moments, anyone who did not live through all that, cannot, or, unfortunately, does not want to understand, and will forever ask: Why?'

I continue to read:

'I also asked: Why, in these annihilation camps, such as Auschwitz, Gross Rosen, Buchenwald and many others, where besides Jews went to their deaths tens and hundreds of thousands of Poles and people of other nations, frequently officers, young people – why did these people go, often to their death, like the Jews in the Ghetto? Why, I asked, were there no revolts? After all, there, as well as in the Ghetto, was abused human dignity, and death. There can be no different truths for different peoples …'

Pankiewicz emphasized that he never saw self-abasement or degradation by Jews on their way to their deaths. Paralyzed by fear, emaciated by hunger, ill and defenceless, they were in no condition to rebel. But never, with the exception of a few rare incidents, were they devoid of some desperate, unexplainable, instinctive pride.

I stayed briefly in Warsaw in 1939 under the German occupation, and saw the Germans again in prisoner-of-war camps in the Soviet Union. In my book *The Thirteenth Month of the Year* I wrote about them:

Judyta saw the Germans for the first time as defeated people.

'All of them, without exception, bowed obsequiously before every Russian, military or civilian. Their complaisance and dumb obedience was simply embarrassing. They have lost face and self-respect in their desire to insinuate themselves into the good graces of their former enemies and present masters …'

And they were not threatened with deportation, slow agony or death …

How would this 'Master Race', these murderers of women and children, behave if locked in ghettos, under the same inhuman conditions they imposed upon the Jews?

Tadeusz Pankiewicz lives in Cracow. He receives many letters from his Jewish friends, dispersed throughout the world (some of whom he has visited). He dreams about visiting Israel again. He is old, his health declines. Such things should not be delayed. And his friends look forward to welcoming him again, and to planting a tree in his name on the Avenue of the Righteous. He certainly deserves it.

Ruth Baum, *Syn Dziedzica i Inne Opowiadnia* (Lodz: Oficyna Bibliofilow, 1999). Reproduced by kind permission of the author, Ruth Baum and Marek Szukalak, publisher. Translated from the Polish by Hava Bromberg Ben-Zvi.

NOTES

After the publication of the story *A Pole in the Ghetto* Tadeusz Pankiewicz was awarded the title of The Righteous Among the Nations of the World, and a tree was planted in his honour on the Avenue of the Righteous by Yad Vashem, Holocaust Martyrs' and Heroes' Remembrance Authority in Jerusalem. He lived to see it. Mr Pankiewich passed away a few years ago, in Cracow. R.B.

Ruth Baum was born in Poland, where she wrote for the *Maly Przeglad* (Little Review), a children's magazine. Through the years of the Second World War, in Voroshilovgrad (today Lugansk), in the Soviet Union, her stories appeared in the local press in Russian translation. Returning to Poland in 1946, she contributed to literary editorials for the Polish radio. In Israel since 1957, she has been writing for Polish language literary periodicals in Israel such as *Nowiny-Kurier* (News-Courier) and *Kontury* (Outlines) and for the Hebrew press.

Works: *Zycie Nieromantyczne* (The Unromantic Life, 1974) stories; *Trzynasty Miesiac Roku* (The Thirteenth Month of the Year, 1977) a novel; *Syn Dziedzica I Inne Opowiadania* (The Squire's Son and Other Stories, 1999) and *Ogrod na Wulkanie* (A Garden on a Volcano, 2007) a novel.

44

The Hiding Place

LEON WELICZKER WELLS

A Memoir

The barn in which we were hidden housed a cow, an ox, and a horse. There was also a separate corner for hogs. By pushing aside the straw on which the hogs lay, one came upon a small trapdoor in the floor that led to our hiding place. The hogs were good cover because the sound of their breathing was very like that of a human being. Our hiding place housed twenty-four people, three of whom were children; five were women and the remainder men, sixteen of us, the oldest of whom was sixty-two. At first it was difficult for me to understand how so many people could fit into such a tiny space – it was about ten feet wide by thirteen feet long – but somehow we managed.

When Korn and I slipped through the opening in the floor into the basement, we were received with curious stares by the cellar's inhabitants. The owner had already told them about our coming. We were brought water and clean underwear by the owner so that we could wash ourselves and change our clothes. From now on we, as did everyone else here, dressed only in our underwear, for in spite of the fact that it was November, and a cold and wet one at that, it was very hot in the basement. One can imagine how hot it must have been on warm, muggy summer days.

After washing and dressing we sat down on the bed and whispered a short version of our story to the others. We answered the few questions put to us briefly, for there was a strict law of silence.

After a bit we heard steps above us – no one stirred. The small trapdoor then opened, and we could see an arm lowering a pail, which one of us took. Then a bag was dropped down. This was our dinner – bread and soup. After dinner we continued our whispered discussion for a while, and then lay down to sleep. Two men stood guard all night to make sure that none of us made a noise in our sleep. The trapdoor was left slightly ajar at night so that we could get a little air. Even the smell of the hogs and the urine and other liquids from the stable dripping down on us through the open trapdoor could not make us forego the precious cool air.

In one corner of our basement hung a curtain with a pail behind it – this was our toilet. Every night the pail was taken out and emptied by Kalwinski, the owner.

The first night I slept restlessly, dreaming about SS men, hills of sand, and corpses; and I had to be wakened by the guards every few minutes, for I moaned loudly in my sleep. After a few nights I quieted down.

Before I fell asleep the first night, I heard the others complain about me. 'He is so big and heavy; in his place we could have taken in two people', one said. And another: 'He doesn't know how to sleep. He could be abnormal from the work he has done, and this could mean trouble for us.'

I should explain that when I came to this hiding place I weighed about 230 pounds – I am five feet, ten and a half inches tall. This weight was owing to the plenitude of food we had had in the last few months in the Death Brigade. Because food had been so scarce these last few years, one ate as much as possible.

At five-thirty in the morning we were wakened; we washed very quickly. An hour later our breakfast was brought. We had to hurry because we wanted to turn off the light as soon as possible; someone walking past Kalwinsky's back yard might possibly see the light. At this time suspicions were easily aroused. If an unusual light came from a stable, or even if a Gentile was noticed buying more bread than usual, it could be enough to make the Polish neighbors suspect there were Jews hidden nearby. The neighboring Poles kept an exact account of who had been taken away to be killed by the Germans. But one Jewish family in the neighborhood had not been accounted for – and this made it even more dangerous, for the neighbors suspected they were hiding. Therefore we kept the light on as little as possible, and lay or sat in the dark. Two of us always had to sit on the 'toilet', since it was impossible for us all to lie down at the same time. We took turns, changing guard every two hours, day and night, to prevent those sleeping from making too much noise. It was very hard while on guard duty to keep awake in the heat and the darkness.

At about 11:00 a.m. a pail of soup was lowered. The man on guard duty picked it up, turned on the light, and when everyone was awake we had our lunch. At 4:00 p.m. we had another light meal, and about 10 p.m. we had our dinner. This timetable was not always adhered to – very often one of the meals dropped out altogether or was delayed by a few hours. After dinner we kept the light on for a few hours. This was possible owing to the 10:00 p.m. curfew. We knew that people couldn't be on the street at that hour, so the risk that someone might see the shaft of light from our basement was minimized.

The old man – we called him Grandpapa – acted as the barber, cutting our hair. After dinner some shaved, while others read the newspapers. At about 11:00 or 11:30 p.m. our host came down. Everyone listened breathlessly to his whispered account of outside happenings. He gave us an exact tally of how many trains had gone through the town that day and also the exact number of railroad cars that had gone east and how many had gone west, and what these cars had been carrying. From the number and direction of the trains we drew our own individual political conclusions. Of course, everyone had a different opinion. The women usually had none – for what did they know about war strategy! Grandpapa and Korn were our experts; they knew more than anyone else, for they had been soldiers in World War I – Korn had been in the artillery.

During these political discussions the man on guard duty had to be very alert to stop the whisperings from becoming too loud, and only one person was allowed to whisper at a time.

Among the occupants of the barn cellar was the Holtz family. For many years Mr Holtz had been an owner of a bar in this neighborhood. Everyone knew him, and he had many friends. His children had become completely assimilated, and the whole family was considered to be just like anyone else's family – Polish, not Jewish. When there was talk of the big liquidation Aktion in August, 1942, Holtz had hidden in this cellar. Mr Kalwinski had known Mr Holtz from childhood on. The refuge was to be a temporary one until after the Aktion. But when the ghetto was created, Mr Kalwinski agreed to continue to hide him instead of sending him into the ghetto. Holtz had two sons and two daughters, and he had managed to talk Mr Kalwinski into giving shelter to these four young people, too.

The Kalwinskis had taken Holtz's younger daughter into their own house to help cook and do the laundry for the three Kalwinski men. She worked in the kitchen, and if anyone approached the house she would hide in the kitchen closet that had been prepared for her.

Holtz's other daughter and her two children, aged six and eight, were first hidden in another farmer's house, while the daughter's husband was working in a 'good place.' They were hidden there temporarily for the 'August 1942, Aktion time', but when the Aktion was over they tried to remain in the shelter longer. They managed to prolong their stay for a few

more weeks, but the owner didn't want to keep them indefinitely. Holtz
had pleaded with Mr Kalwinski, and finally the latter agreed to take them
in, too.

One of Holtz's sons had been in love with a girl, Malke, who was still
in the ghetto. He had begged Kalwinski to let her come here too. A com-
bination of compassion and a romantic heart convinced the farmer, and
he agreed to increase the number of people he was hiding to eight.

These people had very little money, and of course Kalwinski couldn't
support eight people indefinitely, even though he was well to do. The
Holtzes then thought of Malke's cousin, Harry Feig, who was single and
fairly well off. He, too, joined the group in the cellar. But being well-
to-do and having available cash proved to be two different things, and it
quickly became clear that someone besides Harry Feig would be needed
to support the by now nine people.

A Mr Held who had a wife and a seven-year-old daughter now
appeared on the scene in need of refuge. He agreed to pay all expenses,
and now there were eleven in the basement, as well as the girl in the
kitchen. Mrs Held had one surviving brother, Bernard, and he joined the
group. Bernard, who was a very quiet man of about thirty-seven years,
had lost his wife and child. One day the husband of Mr Holtz's daughter
lost his 'good job', and he, too, came to the cellar.

Now everything seemed to be peaceful and complete for the cellar
dwellers – except for the fact that the end of the war was not in sight. The
German armies were still advancing.

The political situation made Mr Held restless; he feared his money
would not last.

One of Holtz's sons, who occasionally went out to the city in the
middle of the night, knew a place where a doctor and a lawyer and their
wives were hiding. The Gentile who hid them was by then too frightened to keep them any longer, and wanted to be rid of them. But how
could this be achieved? If he handed these people over to the Germans
to be killed, he, as the owner of the place, would get into trouble for
'breaking the law', though probably he would not get a death sentence.
If he evicted them they could be caught, and under torture they might reveal their hiding place. If the matter should come out in this way, he could
be hanged in the marketplace in the city. There was a third possibility, and
this had the least amount of risk involved – he could simply kill these
people.

Once someone undertook to shelter a Jew, it wasn't so easy to change
one's mind.

Holtz's son got in touch with this Pole, and took the doctor and lawyer and their wives to our place, keeping it a secret from the Pole where these couples were being taken. The two additional families were able to help the group pay the bill for its upkeep.

Holtz's son-in-law had two brothers in the concentration camp, one in his forties, and the other, a prizefighter by profession, in his thirties. Knowing that their brother and his family had found a hiding place, they escaped from the camp two weeks before our escape, and were hiding at Kalwinski's son's house. Their fate there was similar to ours, and under the same circumstances, and for the same reasons, they were brought here. Korn and I were the last to arrive, and no one else joined our group afterward.

Mr Holtz, whom we called Grandpapa, was a quiet man, happy that he had been able to save his entire family. He recited his prayers every morning, and because of his seniority he had the best place in which to bed down.

Next was Mr Held. For a while, being the sole supporter of the group, he had considered himself superior. He was most unpleasant. For example, he would not drink his tea in a cup, but must have a proper glass. He must also have a metal handle for this container, because he might burn his fingers on the hot glass. In addition, he refused to stand guard; his brother-in-law or his wife had to do it for him. He believed that the later arrivals should be squeezed together and that he should keep the original space he had been allotted.

His wife tried to keep all of her husband's obnoxious traits as unobtrusive as possible. Her brother, Bernard, was a very quiet man, who well understood the deadly seriousness of our situation.

The wives of both the doctor and the lawyer came from the same town in the southern part of Poland; both were from rich families, had known each other since childhood, and had been rivals since then. They were attractive girls, married to professionals.

The lawyer was a boy from a poor home who had worked his way through school and achieved his degree. He had married his wife shortly before the war.

To the lawyer's wife the doctor and his wife seemed to have a higher social standing within our group than she and her husband had. We all liked to ask medical questions, of course, and naturally some medical problems arose among us. In addition, the women in the group felt deep pity for the doctor's wife. She had a one-year-old boy whom she had given, for safety's sake, to a Gentile couple to be raised. It would have been too dangerous to hide in a basement with such a small child. A few months before our arrival the child had been discovered by the Germans, and killed. One of the reasons for their discovery of the child was that he had been circumcised. Everyone in the cellar, including the doctor, knew about the child's death, but the mother hadn't been told. She half sensed what had happened, but when she asked about it everyone gave evasive answers. Hopes and uncertainties were fearful things to live with, all knew, but they were afraid to tell her because in her first reaction she might cry out.

Because the lawyer's wife felt that the doctor's wife was getting more attention than she, she went about becoming the center of attraction in her own way. First her sleeping place – the doctor's wife had a better one, which she wanted. Though the exchange was finally made, it didn't help because the better place 'followed' the other woman. Next she began to have choking fits, but this didn't get anyone's attention as long as the 'choking' was done quietly. Because the lawyer's wife knew she wouldn't get far making noise the next step was to insist that when she felt a choking fit coming on, we should open the small door to get air for her. She didn't care that this would be dangerous for us all.

When, after repeatedly demanding that we open the door, she was at length firmly told that she could either choke quietly or we would help her choke, she stopped. Now her energies were turned against her husband. She said that he didn't care whether she choked or not, that he didn't even take her side, and that he didn't care how much other people took advantage of her and pushed her around. All of us could see that he didn't care about her, she claimed, and that this was why they threatened to choke her. The poor husband not only had to bear her harping but also the fact that the others told him that it was all his fault because he didn't know how to handle her. This mad situation between the lawyer and his wife continued until our last day together.

Another problem was Holtz's son and Malke, whom he loved and had brought here. Their love was not mutual. She looked down on him as being a simple, non-educated, boorish man, and didn't even want to speak to him. Taking into account that he was a member of our 'family' here, the whole group was hostile to Malke. Abusive words were directed at her; she could never take part in any discussion, and would be immediately silenced. Her cousin, Harry Feig, whom she tried to rely on, was not of much help.

I don't know how intelligent or how smart Malke was, because in the entire eight months we were together I never spoke a single word to her. I can say, though, that she was neither friendly nor shrewd, and was most inflexible. First the boy began maneuvering to get her to lie next to him; this wasn't difficult, because the family helped. However, when he tried to embrace and kiss her, she tried to escape him by climbing over the other people in the darkness, and this made noise. People were annoyed by the whole thing, and didn't care who was in the right; they knew only that noise was dangerous.

Holtz's whole family soon began to resent her more and more, because, it was clear, the boy really loved her. Wasn't their brother and son good enough for her?

With each new event her life here became harder. Now, when in the dark the smitten boy tried to kiss her she still fought back, but quietly, without trying to escape. When he threatened to scream if she resisted, she gave in. But it didn't end with kissing, and a few weeks later he tried to rape her. Again he threatened that if she didn't give in he would scream, and when she paid no heed to his threats, he let out a loud yell.

Everyone was stunned by the noise; the lights were turned on, while the frustrated lover sat shaking nervously. Silence. No one said a word. Fearfully we lay down again and the light was turned off. That night, after dinner, when the first shock was over and we were sure no one had heard anything outside the basement, the two brothers who had escaped from the concentration camp stated that if this were repeated they would leave. They refused to remain at the mercy of one man, a lovesick boy. They stressed that if anything similar were repeated, they would leave.

These two brothers beckoned Korn and me to a corner and talked about the advisability of actually departing. From then on, I became a member of the four 'tough' ones.

By now my background and schooling had given me a certain 'standing' in this society. To leave now, I told the other three, would be a big risk. The owner wouldn't stand for a few leaving because of the great risk he would run if they were caught and under torture revealed his 'crime'. He might, I continued, be tempted to kill anyone who tried to leave. We four finally decided it would be the wiser policy to stay.

There was another group, not belonging anywhere, and with no 'social' standing – Malke, her cousin Harry Feig, and Joe.

Harry, a thin little man about forty, was peculiar. If he didn't like a dish he wouldn't eat it, even if he had to fast for several days. If he didn't like something in the soup, he would fish all of it out and lay it on the rim of his plate. He was very easily offended, and when his feelings had been hurt he wouldn't speak for days. He had set ideas, and nothing could change them. He was very serious, never smiled, and worried not only about the present but also about the time when he would be liberated by the Russians. His hope was that the Russians should suffer a defeat someplace, allowing enough time for the Western Allies to come here even if it had to take another year.

Holtz's daughter, the one working in the kitchen, was in her twenties, lively and pretty. The Holtz family wanted Harry Feig to marry her, yet Harry never exchanged a single word with her during her visits to the basement. The family, of course, realized that Harry and she would not make a suitable pair. The reason they kept an eye on him was that they thought it was possible that no Jewish men would be left after the war, and even though he was clearly abnormal, he was still honest; furthermore, he had real estate. The occupation by the Russians would be only a temporary one. This was not doubted by anyone in our cellar, and we all believed that after the war Poland would resume as a national state with a democratic form of government.

Joe: About the same age as Harry, he was a little under average height, stocky, with a round face wreathed in smiles. Friendly to everyone, even to those who didn't want his friendship, he tried hard to make the Holtz family like him. He showered compliments on their daughter. Right or wrong, the Holtz family was always right in Joe's opinion; but no one paid any attention to his opinions. He was always denigrating Harry, trying to tell the family that Harry didn't know how to appreciate what they did for him. Harry never talked to Joe.

The days passed slowly in the darkness and terrible heat. The monotony was interrupted only by short-lived excitements. From the heat and the hours of lying about we developed big red spots all over our bodies. A few days after Korn and I came to this shelter Korn got sick. In the beginning he had hiccups, but after a while he began to regurgitate his food, and this became progressively worse. We did not know then how serious this symptom was.

To keep my mind occupied, I memorized a few pages from Grandpapa's prayer book and kept repeating them while lying in the dark. The only outside book I could get was a Christian catechism, and so I learned the whole catechism by heart. The idea of survival was still very dim in my mind, practically an impossibility, but at the same time a dire necessity to hold onto. The concentration camp and the Death Brigade showed how little value life had. The thoughts of how my parents had prepared for their old age, how even when my sisters were infants my mother and father began saving for their dowries symbolized the futility of thinking about the morrow. The world as a whole had no reality or meaning.

At certain moments I would try to believe in the idea that you fight your enemy by trying to achieve the reverse of his purpose; in this case by surviving. Putting my memoirs together in order to tell the world what had happened, wasn't this too the normal desire of any teenager to keep a diary? All the goings-on in this hiding place proved to me the tenacity of the will to live.

I recalled listening in the concentration camp to a discussion between a father and his son after they were both put behind the barbed wire, which meant they would, beyond any question, be shot. That evening they got their dinner ration – a little piece of bread. The son wanted to eat it up right away, while the father thought they should divide it, a piece for now and a piece for the morning. The son's argument was that they would most probably be executed by the morning. The father replied, 'But we will be taken to the "sands" to be shot, and on our way there we can still eat it up.'

This discussion was much calmer than one between a father and son on how a ballplayer should have handled the ball in a minor-league play.

I didn't think about the future, or what I could do after liberation, if ever I were liberated. Never, during the time of hiding, or for the two years before, had I any dreams or thoughts about the future – after the war. I didn't even know whether I cared about being liberated. For whom and for what? Perhaps a feeling of guilt lingered on in me; why should I be chosen to survive? The few people here in the hiding place didn't count anymore. On the outside everyone was an enemy, a potential murderer.

Monday, December 6, 1943; in the evening.

As usual the owner came down, but this time he seemed very nervous. We realized immediately that something was amiss. He told us that in a neighbor's house, the Juzeks, only a few hundred yards from there, thirty-two Jews had been discovered. The hideout had been reported to the Germans by Juzek's own brother-in-law. From the thirty-two, twenty-six were from the Death Brigade, and among them was our leader, Herches. While they were being led to the truck, they had made a sudden attack on the Germans, and twenty-eight of the thirty-two escaped.

Juzek and his wife had been arrested and the next day publicly hanged in the market.

Our host was very much afraid that the discovery of Jews in this neighborhood would lead to a search of all the houses. A small search did go on during the following few days, but nothing happened in our house.

I should like to tell about the Polish and Ukrainian underground. On the whole, the Ukrainians in this section of Poland, in the beginning, joined the Germans, and took a very active part in the murder of the Jews. After a time, seeing that the Germans were not going to give them an independent Ukraine, a group of them became partisans, under the leadership of one Bandera; for this reason they were known as the Banderowcy. Their fight was not against the Germans but for a 'General Peace Conference.' Their aim was to prove that they were an absolute majority in this area. To become an absolute majority they had to get rid of the Poles. The Banderowcy would catch an important Pole, cut him to pieces, and place him in a public place for other Poles to see, and take note; they wanted to force the Poles to move out of this part of the country. The Jews were even more afraid of the Banderowcy than of SS men.

The Polish underground in our area was a nonfighting group; they published an underground paper, did some radio work, spreading propaganda among the people, but did very little sabotage. Their underground paper was widely read. As a whole, the Polish partisans never accepted Jews, and very often some of its members would hand over Jews to the Germans. The underground paper and radio never came out with strong condemnation of their fellow Poles for helping in the massacre of Jews, and not even against the Poles who informed on the few Poles who were hiding Jews. Anything would have been of help to us. The few Poles who did hide Jews got no moral support – not even the cold comfort of believing that, if a fellow citizen informed on him, the informer might one day be punished.

One can see how shocked I was to read in January, 1960, in the political section of a leading American weekly, about the 'hero' Bandera, a fighter against Communism, who lived in Munich and was killed there. He was pictured as a hero in this magazine, when he was really a murderer. How fitting for Bandera that the city where Hitler got his start should give him refuge!

Christmas, 1943, was approaching now. It was getting harder for our host Kalwinski to obtain a large enough food supply for so many people without calling attention to the size of the purchases.

Christmas passed. It was now the New Year. At the start of the year 1944, all-night shootings began between Ukrainians and Poles. This made our host very nervous. Each day now we awaited the Russian offensive. We never tired of calculating and recalculating how many days and hours the Russians would need to get from their present front line to Lvov.

At last Tarnopol, only eighty miles from Lvov, was taken by the Russians. But in the next weeks it changed hands several times. These changes led to new rumors, and every time something good happened it was spoiled for us by the malicious gossip of the local people. Stories about the Jews were one of their favorite pastimes.

One story circulating at the time was that when the Russian Army came into Tarnopol a group of Jews came out of their hiding place in a Polish house. A few days later, when the Germans returned, this Polish family was hanged for hiding Jews. This story made our host ponder just how long he should keep us in the cellar after the Russian Army had liberated Lvov. Other stories about Poles hiding Jews resulted in new searches for Jews by the Germans. All the houses in the neighborhood were very thoroughly searched except our house, and this was due only to the fact that our host was the chief representative of the local farmers to the German officials. We were just plain lucky.

The Russian offensive posed another problem. In some sections the Germans forced certain families to evacuate with them. If that should happen to our host, who would then take care of us? In some places people left voluntarily, not wanting to be at the front line. If our host didn't do what the others did, everyone might begin to suspect him. Our minds were not only occupied with the military events of the day but also in seeing to it that we were not killed, not now, not after such a long, hard struggle to stay alive.

In February, the German Army took over many rooms in our neighborhood to house their soldiers. In our house, they requisitioned a few rooms to serve as their headquarters. They even put two horses in the stable under which we were hiding. From this day onward, until they moved out four weeks later, we got a meal but once a day, late in the night, and we considered ourselves very fortunate indeed even to get this. One can well imagine how we felt, constantly hearing the Germans talking and stamping heavily about in their army boots right above our basement. We were afraid to breathe. Because our host didn't come down at all, we now were without any information as to what was happening on the outside.

This too passed. It became a little easier again – the news of the Russians was all good. All of us now tried mentally to prepare ourselves for liberation, for being reborn. We had to remember to keep in mind the 'labor pains' which could be deadly for us.

It was April, and the Russian Army was coming nearer, ever nearer.

In the Jewish cemetery twenty-eight Jews, hiding among the tombstones, were discovered by the Germans. The first bombs since 1941 now began to fall on the city. Every day became increasingly longer for us.

May again brought bad news. A group of twelve Jews were discovered on Balanowe Street, only one block away from where I used to live. A daughter informed on her own mother, telling the Germans that she was hiding Jews. The mother was hanged, and the Jews were killed.

Lvov had now become the front line. One day we heard many

244 Years of Flame and Fury

German soldiers come into the stable. They were going to use it for some purpose or other. To make it fit for this unknown purpose, they planned to pull out the whole floor above us. We heard the entire discussion. We sat paralyzed, staring into the darkness of the basement. The work began; then suddenly an order came for the soldiers to move out. Again we were saved at the last second.

At last the Russians arrived! Our host rushed in with this news in the middle of the day. The light went on, and everyone sat up and quietly listened to details of the news. We still could not talk loudly or make any noise because we were still afraid that the neighbors would find out that we were hiding here.

No one really knew where he would go or what he would do. We were too estranged from the world to have any plans. Everyone must get out and see for himself where and how to start anew. It was planned that we would leave in the early hours of the next day, so that no one would see us. Even now our host asked us not to come back to visit him, or for any other reason; it would go hard for him if it were known that he had hidden Jews.[1] Many of the Poles didn't like the idea that even a few Jews had been saved. These survivors could be witnesses that the Poles had collaborated with the Germans in destroying the Jewish population. Others, who had taken over Jewish houses and belongings, were afraid they might have to return them.

The only plan that I could make at the moment was a vague one; I would join the army and fight the Germans.

Next morning, about five, one by one we began secretly to leave the place. It was the first time in eighteen months that I was dressing to walk on the streets. The women and children, as well as Grandpapa, were staying until the next day, waiting for their men to find them a place to live.

NOTE

1. How sad was the situation in Poland that when a man proved he possessed high, idealistic qualities, he should be ashamed and unpopular for doing such a great deed!

Selected text from the updated 1999 edition of the The Janowska Road, by Leon Weliczker Wells, published by and used with permission of the US Holocaust Memorial Museum, Washington, DC (pp.247–63). Previously published in 1963 by the Macmillan Company as The Janowska Road and in 1978 by the Holocaust Library as the Death Brigade. See also 48. 'Liberation' and, for information about the author, see 6. 'Time of Peace'.

45

Polish Friends

VLADKA MEED

A Memoir

It must be stressed that not all the Poles with whom we dealt were treacherous blackmailers or calculating mercenaries. Most of the Gentiles did, indeed, demand cash for any service rendered. But there were also those who were kindhearted and sympathetic to our sufferings. Some even risked their lives to rescue Jews. Without the cooperation of this handful of friendly Gentiles, the Jewish underground on the 'Aryan side' would not have been able to accomplish much. At crucial moments and at times of great peril, these friends enabled us to carry out our missions.

Wanda Wnorowska was the first Gentile with whom I had any contact after I left the ghetto. The widow of a Polish officer, she was in her forties and belonged to the so-called 'better' Polish society. She operated a dressmaker's shop where I found employment almost as soon as I crossed to the 'Aryan side'. Not only was I assured of a job and warm quarters during the winter, but I also had an important front for my underground activities.

When I was called upon to devote all my time to underground work and had to give up my job as a seamstress, Wanda gladly accepted in my place friends of mine who had just succeeded in getting out of the ghetto. She welcomed them all warmly and paid them relatively good wages. Wanda made friends with her new employees, took an interest in their difficulties, and endeavored not only to give them advice but also help them through her contacts with other Gentiles. Gradually she became one of our confidantes.

Before long, Wanda's home at Wspolna 39 became a secret meeting place for Jews, especially for those who came from Piotrkow and were passing as Gentiles. Generous and kind, she opened her heart as wide as her door to the frantic, despairing Jews who sought her help and counsel. Whatever the problem, be it living quarters, documents, or anything else, Wanda usually knew the right contact to solve it. She would take me aside to discuss 'her' poor Jews, insisting that more help must somehow be obtained for 'her' people.

I managed to transfer considerable sums of money to her from funds of the underground organization, and she in turn distributed these funds in accordance with our instructions. She never asked for anything for herself, and was offended when we offered her money to ease her own strained circumstances.

'You are in worse straits than I am', she said with dignity, declining our offer.

Another compassionate Polish woman who ran great risks for Jews hiding from the Nazis was Juliana Larisz, who before the war had worked for the Zilbergs, a Jewish family in Praga (a suburb of Warsaw). When the *Aussiedlung* began, the kindhearted Juliana, responding to the pleas of her Jewish friends, began cautiously to smuggle them out of the ghetto. With her help, twenty-one of them escaped. Some were hidden in her own house at Brzeska 7; eight were with a friend at Targowa 38. Iza Blochowicz, a three-year-old Jewish girl, was sent to a friendly Polish family in Radzymin, while one Jewish woman with Aryan features was put up elsewhere.

Juliana operated a prosperous meat supply business, with most of the profits providing food, clothes and books for the Jews in hiding. This splendid woman was constantly preoccupied with Jewish affairs, running from one secret hiding place to another seeking to lighten the burdens of the unfortunates. She helped them observe the Jewish holidays and even lent a hand in baking the matzot for Passover.

To divert the attention of her neighbors from the huge baskets of food she sent to the hidden Jews, Juliana invited her Polish and German customers in for snacks. Through the thin walls of their hideout, the Jews eavesdropped on the German and Polish conversations, often hearing venomous anti-Semitic remarks.

For some months, everything went smoothly. Then, early one morning, the German police knocked on Juliana's door. The Jews in hiding managed to conceal themselves in time and nothing suspicious could be found. Juliana quietly and calmly answered all the questions of the Germans, but they persisted; they demanded to be taken to the house of her friend on Targowa Street. On some pretext, Juliana managed to slip away from the guards and telephone her friend. Thus, when the German police arrived there, they found no one at home. Later, Juliana learned that her own employees, suspicious of her activities, had trailed her to the hideouts and reported her to the Gestapo. Undismayed, she continued her work of mercy until the end of the war, sheltering refugees until new hiding places could be found for them.

I used to make the rounds of Juliana's hideouts, supplying the Jews there with forged documents. Of these Jews, seventeen survived: three Blochowiczes, three Ziffermans, four Zilberbergs, four Miedzyrzeckis, and three Goldsteins.

Pero, a middle-aged Gentile clerk in a Polish hotel on Marszalkowska street, was another friend. He had become our ally through a Jewish woman named Mala Piotrkowska and her thirteen-year-old daughter, Bronka. Compelled to leave her hideout in broad daylight, Mrs. Piotrkowska, who looked Jewish, wandered about with her daughter in search of lodging for the night. Eventually a band of Gentile hoodlums recognized the unfortunate woman as a Jewess. They tried to snatch her pocketbook, pursuing her with shouts of, 'Zhydowa! Zhydowa!'

Mrs. Piotrkowska ran straight into the arms of the Polish police, who took her and her daughter to the German authorities. Mala had obtained forged Aryan documents for herself and Bronka and decided to carry on the deceit, although she had little confidence in her prospects. Interrogated about their origins, and about their knowledge of Christian prayer and custom, the daughter gave acceptable replies, but the mother fumbled. Both were kept in jail overnight. They were told that unless they could produce a Pole who would vouch that he had known them before the war and that they were real Christians they would be executed.

Pero was the only Polish friend they knew who might be willing to give them such a testimony. It was evening. There was no telephone in Pero's home, so they had to pray that he could still be reached where he was working. Even so, would he risk his life perjuring himself on their behalf? In any case, he was their only hope.

Pero came to the Gestapo headquarters the next morning, swore that he had known the Piotrkowskas for quite some time before the war, and that they were Christians. When the Germans warned him that perjury was punishable by death, Pero assured them in flawless German that he would never run such a risk, and asserted once again that the Piotrkowskas were good Christians. Convinced at last, the captors released Mala and her daughter and apologized to them for the inconvenience to which they had been put. Should Frau Piotrkowska ever be molested in the future, she had only to report the incident to the Gestapo to be cleared!

Though his own home was under surveillance, Pero allowed the Piotrkowskas to stay with him. Later, we persuaded him to give shelter to still other Jews. All the Jews who found asylum with Pero survived. He himself died as a Polish officer in the general Warsaw uprising of 1944.

Helena Sciborowska of Krochmalna 36 was another dedicated worker for the underground. A small, dark-skinned widow with children of her own, she neglected her own household while she was busy helping Jews. Though her house had been raided because informers had reported her to the authorities, she still occasionally sheltered some desperate Jews there or tried to persuade her Gentile friends to accommodate Jews, often overcoming resistance by cajolery and persuasion. Each time, she hurried to our secret meetings to tell us joyfully of her latest success.

She lived in poverty but whatever money she accepted for her efforts she immediately spent on the Jews under her care or for sheltering of Jews with other people. She sold her jewelry and donated the proceeds to needy Jews. Many Jews owe their survival to the efforts of this dedicated little woman whose kindness and compassion were pure and selfless.

Unfortunately, there were very few like her. Had there been more Gentiles among the Poles with hearts and conscience such as hers, many more Jews might have survived.

Vladka Meed, *On Both Sides of the Wall; Memoirs from the Warsaw Ghetto*. Translated by Dr Steven Meed (New York: Holocaust Library, 1979). First published in 1948, in Yiddish, the book was one of the first eyewitness reports about the Warsaw Ghetto uprising. Reproduced by kind permission of the author Vladka Meed and Dr Steven Meed. For information about Vladka Meed, see 42. 'Jewish Resistance in the Warsaw Ghetto'.

46

Their Brothers' Keepers

PHILIP FRIEDMAN

An Essay and Biographical Vignettes

During the Nazi reign of terror in Cracow, a Jewish mother brought her small boy to St Lazarus Hospital. The boy had a broken leg. Both mother and child had 'Aryan' documents, but Dr Lachowicz, the chief physician, and the admitting nurse both took note of the fact that the prospective patient was circumcised. The Germans would deem his presence at the hospital a crime punishable by death. However, the doctor and nurse admitted the boy but sent the mother away. The boy's leg was treated, and his belly bandaged as a precaution against Gestapo visits. During one such raid, Dr Lachowicz refused to remove his young patient's bandages, pleading with the Gestapo that the boy was a Christian, assuring the Germans that on their next visit he would show them proof. Two weeks later the Gestapo returned, but the boy was no longer on the premises. The staff had removed him to a convent in the neighborhood of Miechow. The Germans, who did not neglect making periodic searches among the nuns also, found the boy and threatened to execute him. The nuns insisted the boy was a Christian. They presented an official statement, signed by Dr Lachowicz, explaining that a bad fall had so injured the boy's foreskin and his leg that an operation was later performed to save his life.

Jewish children were hidden by their mothers or by Gentiles in baking stoves, garbage bins, and boxes. In Warsaw this writer saw a child who had been kept in a box concealed in a dark cabin. The child was almost totally blind; the muscles of his limbs were atrophied, and he could not walk. His speech was a series of inarticulate sounds. This six-year-old Jewish boy, reared in a world of darkness, was not under-nourished; his foster mother had simply taken all necessary precautions for their mutual safety.

The Gestapo was constantly on the alert for the thousands of Jews who seemed to burrow into the ground like moles. Among their allies were collaborationists, professional informers, anti-Semites, drunks, and prattlers. To anyone turning in a Jew, the Gestapo usually paid one quart of brandy, four pounds of sugar, and a carton of cigarettes, or a small amount of money. Incidentally, the prices varied at different places and times. The host was usually executed on the spot, or hanged in a public place as an object lesson to 'Aryans' who entertained the notion of hiding a Jew.

In 1942, when the Germans ran amuck slaughtering the Jews of Tarnopol, several desperate men and women pleaded with a Ukrainian doorkeeper to let them hide in the large, abandoned attic of an office building. They were aware that the ground floor of the building was occupied by the Gestapo, but they were surrounded; all avenues of escape were closed. The old doorkeeper agreed and led them upstairs. He did not reveal the terrible secret even to his wife. He bought food for his 'tenants' from his own money and took it to them after office hours, when the ground floor was empty. One day, unable to sustain the burden of his secret, the doorkeeper revealed it to his wife. At a party, after several drinks, she whispered the intelligence to her brother, who hated Jews. The brother threatened to go to the Gestapo, and the doorkeeper tried dissuading him. They quarreled, fought, and as the brother-in-law started for the door to summon the Gestapo, the doorkeeper grabbed an ax and killed him. After the German retreat and the return of the Russians, the doorkeeper helped his twenty-one Jewish 'guests' to settle in Zbaraz. One day he came to his friends and pleaded with them to hide him because his wife and her family were seeking to avenge the man he had slain. When the Jews made preparations to emigrate, the old doorkeeper joined them.

The Lwow cattle dealer, Jozefek, met a different fate. He was hanged in a public square for concealing thirty-five Jews. His body was left dangling for several days as a warning to others. In Athens twelve Greeks were publicly hanged for helping a group of Jews to escape. On occasion, Jewish guests, fearful of the consequences to their hosts if they were caught, left the places of safety of their own free will, often to commit suicide. 'We are trailed and hunted', wrote Francisca Rubinlicht of Warsaw. 'We can no longer find a place to hide. Our money is gone. We cannot stay here any longer because we have been threatened with being reported to the Gestapo. If this happens, our protectors will suffer as well. We cannot commit suicide in this place because our protector will be victimized. So we have decided', the note goes on to say, 'to surrender, in the knowledge that we can swallow the (suicide) pills that now constitute our only, our priceless possession.'

The good, generous, and godly people who hid Jews feared not only the wrath of the Nazis; they also had to contend with anti-Semites among the local population, and terror organizations that preached the gospel of hatred even after the war. There are numerous recorded instances concerning Poles who gave protection to their Jewish countrymen and later were shot by terrorist groups. Andrzej Kowalski of Parczew, Poland, who had concealed six Jewish families without remuneration during the war, was forced by anti-Semites to leave his home and settle elsewhere. Two Polish families of Bialystok who had put their lives in peril by helping Jews during the Occupation were forced by their neighbors to look elsewhere for home and sustenance. They left for West Germany, and then were helped by the Jewish Labor Committee to immigrate to the United States. In 1946 the Jewish Committee of Bialystok was aiding 180 Christian families who were being persecuted by illegal Rightist groups for their generosity to Jews during the evil time of Hitler. In bidding goodby to two Jewish women they had hidden in his place until the Nazis were driven out, the Polish beggar, Karol Kicinski, pleaded, 'Please don't tell anyone I saved you; I fear for my life.'

THE SMALL NUNNERY. A BIOGRAPHICAL VIGNETTE

The small nunnery was located not far from the Vilna Colony railroad station. During the German occupation there were only seven sisters in this Benedictine convent, all from Cracow. The Mother Superior, a graduate of Cracow University, was a comparatively young woman of thirty-five at the time when the Jews were driven from their homes. Although the convent was too far removed from the ghetto for her to hear the cries of a tortured people, the Mother Superior seemed always to be gazing in that direction, as though she were waiting for a summons. She found it hard to keep her mind on the work that had previously claimed all her time and love, the ministering to the poor and the miserable.

One day she decided that the time had come to act. She summoned the other nuns and, after prayer, they discussed the subject of the ghetto. Not long afterward, as a result of this conversation, a few of the sisters appeared before the gate of the ghetto. The guards did not suspect the nuns of any conspiratorial designs. Eventually contact was established between the convent and the Vilna ghetto, and an underground railroad was formed. The seven nuns became experts in getting Jews out of the ghetto and hiding them at the convent and in other places. At one period it seemed as if the small nunnery were bulging with nuns, some with features unmistakably masculine.

Among those hidden in the convent were several Jewish writers and leaders of the ghetto Underground: Abraham Sutzkever, Abba Kovner, Edek Boraks and Arie Wilner. Some stayed a long time, others returned to the ghetto to fight and die. When, in the winter of 1941, the Jewish Fighters' Organization was formed, the Mother Superior became an indispensable ally. The Fighters needed arms, and the Mother Superior undertook to supply them. Assisted by the other nuns, she roamed the countryside in search of knives, daggers, bayonets, pistols, guns, and grenades. The hands accustomed to the touch of rosary beads became expert with explosives. The first four grenades received gratefully by the Fighters were the gift of the Mother Superior, who instructed Abba Kovner in their proper use, as they were of a special brand unfamiliar to him. She later supplied other weapons. Although she worked selflessly, tirelessly, she felt that not enough was being done. 'I wish to come to the ghetto', she said to Abba Kovner, 'to fight by your side, to die, if necessary. Your fight is a holy one. You are a noble people. Despite the fact that you are a Marxist (Kovner was a member of *Hashomer Hatzair*) and have no religion, you are closer to God than I.'

Her ardent wish to enter the ghetto to fight and, in the end, to die the martyred death of the Jews was not realized. She was too valuable an ally, and was prevailed upon to remain on the Aryan side. In addition to supplying arms, she also acted as a liaison between the Jewish Fighters' Organization inside the ghetto and the Polish Underground with which they were desperately trying to establish a military partnership. The partnership was never achieved, but this failure was not her fault. And although the battle was lost, she was not the loser. Her heroism was enshrined in the hearts of those who would remember.

JANINA BUCHOLC-BUKOLSKA. A BIOGRAPHICAL VIGNETTE

Janina Bucholc-Bukolska was employed in the small firm of Rybczynski on Miodowa Street in Warsaw. The tiny office, which specialized in translations, was always overcrowded. Papers and documents were piled on desks, shelves, and cabinets. The papers were not even remotely connected with translations; they were, in fact, birth certificates, marriage records, school diplomas, food ration cards, letters of recommendation from employers, and all manner of documents and forms. Mrs Bukolska was a large woman, awkward in movement.

Wearing the thick glasses she depended on, she sat calmly in the midst of this chaos of papers and attended busily to her work. Her work, among other things, consisted of supplying false identification cards to Jews. A German policeman would sometimes pass outside the window and gaze curiously at the picture of industry and prosperity inside. Customers were always coming and going. The males among Bukolska's clients invariably wore bushy mustaches and the women displayed peroxide-blonde hair. In fact, not one person entered the office that did not have a Nordic appearance save Mrs Bukolska herself, and she was the only Gentile in the crowd. All the others had been Aryanized, in appearance at least, before they came to her. They brought with them photographs, fingerprints, and other pertinent information, most of it spurious. Janina Bukolska then had the Aryan identity papers known as *Kennkarten* made up by an expert.

The customers entered her office as Jews and left as Gentiles. But they seldom went out without consulting with Bukolska about a possible place to hide in the Aryan sector. She took down their names. Finding places for the new Aryans to live was one of Bukolska's occupations. This was far from easy, as the Germans offered ten pounds of sugar and a pint of vodka as a reward for surrendering a Jew hiding in the Aryan sector of the city. The punishment for hiding a Jew or helping one to find a place to hide was death.

Mrs Bukolska shrugged off all obstacles placed in her way. After a busy day at the overcrowded office, she spent her evenings visiting around, ringing doorbells, inquiring whether the good people of Warsaw would consider giving shelter to one of her new Aryans. On occasion she met with a bit of good luck, as she did when Dr Jan Zabinski, director of the Warsaw zoo, offered her clients some cages vacated by animals that had perished for lack of food. But in most instances she met with reticence, refusal, and abuse; often she was threatened with the Gestapo. Her labors continued, however, and her 'business' prospered until the last ghetto hovel had been put to the torch by the Nazis and the last Jew murdered. And even then Pani Janina carried on, for her work was not finished. It came to an end only when the Hitler hordes were driven out of her beloved country.

SOPHIA DEBICKA, JADZIA DUNIEC, IRENA ADAMOWICZ, JANINA
PLAWCZYNSKA AND RENA LATERNER. BIOGRAPHICAL VIGNETTES

A roll-call of heroic women who risked their lives to help a cause that appeared lost would not be complete without the mention of Sophia

Debicka, Jadzia Duniec, Irena Adamowicz, Janina Plawczynska and Rena Laterner. Sophia Debicka came from a family of Polish intellectuals and was related to the veteran Socialist leader, Stephanie Sempolowska. She hid several Jewish women in her house, camouflaging them as nurse, seamstress, cook, and maid. She seized a little Jewish girl from a transport, declaring the child was her daughter. Her home became an operational base for the Jewish Fighters' Organization of Warsaw. She alerted her friends in the Postmaster's office who examined letters addressed to the Gestapo, to intercept those containing tips from informers about Jews hiding in the Christian sector.

Jadzia Duniec, a Catholic girl of Vilna, did not leave behind a long record of deeds that would memorialize her. She died too young. But for a brief period before the Gestapo captured and executed her, Jadzia served as a courier and liaison between Jewish underground organizations and the outer world. She supplied weapons to the Szeinbaum fighting group in Vilna, and she was often sent to Kaunas and Shavli on errands for the Fighters. She died as she lived, courageously. Her name deserves to be remembered, for she was one of a small, valiant group.

Irena Adamowicz belonged to the same small group. Irena was not so young as Jadzia. She came of a pious, aristocratic Polish family, and before the war she was an executive of the Polish Girl Scouts. During the German occupation she became a courier between the ghettos of Warsaw, Vilna, Kaunas, Shavli, Bialystok, and other cities. Along with several other Christian women, she volunteered for this work that meant certain death if she were captured. Among her co-workers, though Irena probably never met them, were two wrinkled old ladies, Janina Plawczynska and Rena Laterner. Both these venerable ladies were in their seventies. They carried messages between the Fighters and the Polish Underground in Warsaw. After the collapse of the *ghetto* uprising, they sheltered ten Fighters in a bunker they erected. They perished with the ten Jews.

Philip Friedman, *Their Brothers' Keepers* (New York: Crown, 1957), pp.16–19, 26–30. Reproduced by kind permission of Dr Sophie Balk.

NOTES

Among the selfless heroes never to be forgotten is Staszek Jackowski. See Ruth Gruber, 'The Heroism of Staszek Jackowski', in *Saturday Review*, 15 April 1967, and Wladyslaw Bartoszewski and Zofia Lewin, *The Samaritans; Heroes of the Holocaust* (New York: Twayne Publishers, 1970) for documented evidence of Polish assistance.

Among organizations to be remembered is Zegota, the Polish Council to Aid Jews. Zegota, in spite of its limited funds provided money, false documents and safe houses. Philip Friedman (1901–1960), a historian, lecturer and educator, was born in Lwow, then Poland (today Lviv, Ukraine), and earned his PhD from the University of Vienna in 1925. He is renowned for his research and writings about the Holocaust, based mostly on his personal experiences as a Jew in German occupied Poland during the Second World War. His wife, daughter, mother, brother and sister all perished in concentration camps.

In 1946 Philip Friedman served on the Joint Distribution Committee, aiding Holocaust survivors, was an advisor on Jewish affairs at the Nuremberg trials, and, later, after emigrating to the USA, worked as a lecturer at Columbia University and as director of the Yivo Institute for Jewish Research in New York.

His books recorded Jewish experience and the heroism of those few who helped them in their darkest hour. His books: *Martyrs and Fighters* (1954), *Their Brothers' Keepers* (1957) and *Roads to Extinction* (1980) remain basic sources for the study of the Holocaust period.

S.D. Kassow, *Who Will Write Our History? Emanuel Ringelblum, the Warsaw Ghetto and Oyneg Shabes Archive* (Bloomington, IN: Indiana University Press, copyright © by Samuel D. Kassow).

47

Survival on the Aryan Side

MIECZYSLAW ROLNICKI

Vignettes

WITHIN THE GATES

My sister Hanka returned home very distressed. This is what happened to her. As she stepped down a tramway, she was approached by a young man, who demanded she enter a gateway with him, because she was a Jew. Inside the gate he ordered her to open her purse, and took away all her money. There was little. In farewell, he kissed her hand and left.

THE GERMANS AND THE GOOD COLLEAGUE

My sister Hanka worked in a canteen as a waitress. My brother in-law, Ludwik, had no steady occupation, and was busy, off and on, with trade. They managed to earn enough for a very modest existence. We lived close to each other, I in a sub-let room, and they, a few houses away, in a small room, near the caretaker. We met every day. Every passing day brought us closer to war's end and increased our chances of survival. Every coming day was pregnant with danger of unmasking and exposure, and exposure meant death.

I lived on Dobra Street, when Hanka, trembling, woke me in the morning, and told me about the tragedy that befell them the previous day. They failed to notice they were followed returning home. A few minutes after their return two men entered their room: one in a German uniform, the other in civilian clothing. They followed Hanka and Ludwik, because of suspecting them of being Jews. A most threatening suspicion. When Hanka and Ludwik denied being Jews, the Germans ordered Ludwik to take off his trousers, to inspect if he was circumcised. The result of their examination was negative(!). Evidently, they knew nothing about the matter. Nevertheless, they ordered the couple to accompany them, for they wished the Gestapo to hear them out. They went into the street together, but on the way, Ludwik broke down under the increasing pressure, and admitted his 'guilt.' They all returned to the room they had left a few moments ago. At the order of the German blackmailers, Hanka and Ludwik packed all their clothing into two suitcases – that was their 'wealth.' The Germans took their plunder and left.

Hanka and Ludwik were robbed of everything. Hanka in one dress, Ludwik in slacks and a shirt. It was summer. In 'farewell', one of the Germans said (they both spoke Polish): 'We are not taking you, but everyone knows now you are Jews. You will perish anyway ...' His prophecy was fulfilled.

Without money and clothes they had to leave immediately the 'burned' apartment. They found a temporary shelter in a boarding house near Otwock. Money became a critical problem. They needed new documents. They needed money to pay for the boarding house, and to eat. I earned very little, and my assistance had no real value. The most valuable possession I had was my father's used suit, brought from Lvov.

Even before the blackmailer's 'visit' we have decided to sell the suit. It was useless, being too big for me. My sister's colleague, a co-worker, purchased the suit, promising to bring the money in a few days. Following the 'unmasking', my sister could not come to work, and the burden of obtaining the payment for the suit fell to me. I repeatedly called at the correct address, and was always informed that the debtor was not at home. My last visit ended not only with failure, as before, but with a threat. A man sitting in front of the house warned me clearly never to come again, since I was already being investigated. I followed his 'friendly' advice, which liberated Hanka's colleague from the duty of paying her debt. Perhaps the money gained from the sale of the suit might have given my sister and her husband a chance to survive. This chance was ruined, or, rather, corrupted.

Was my sister's colleague aware, by appropriating the suit, that her dishonesty shattered the possibility of rescue of two young people?

Mieczyslaw Rolnicki, *Krzak Gorejacy* (The Burning Bush: Notes of the Years 1939–1944) (Jerusalem, Lublin: przy wspoludziale [with the assistance of] Wojewodzkieg Domu Kultury w Lublinie, 1999), Part II:: 'W Bramie' (Within the Gates), pp.51–2, and 'Niemcy i Kolezanka' (The Germans and the Good Colleague), pp.57–8. Reproduced by kind permission of the author, Mieczyslaw Rolnicki.

NOTES

Mieczyslaw Rolnicki was born in Poland in 1925. He survived the Second World War in Warsaw on 'Aryan papers'. His stories reflect his true experiences. Living in Israel since 1957, Mr Rolnicki is a contributor to the literary magazine *Kontury* and to *Nowiny Kurier*, published in Israel, in Polish. Works: *Mysli, Aforyzmy, Fraszki, Opowiadania* (Thoughts, Aphorisms, Trifles, Tales) (1996) and *Krzak Gorejacy: Zapiski z lat 1939–1945* (The Burning Bush: Notes from the Years 1939–1945) (1999).

Part III
To Live Again

48

Liberation

LEON WELICZKER WELLS

A Memoir

I WAS OUT IN THE OPEN

Korn,[1] everyone, had left the hiding place, each going his own ways. Feeling very weak in the legs, my mind a blank, I walked in the direction of the city's center. The streets of Lvov were still empty, except for a few groups of Russian soldiers I passed, and army trucks lumbering by. I tried to speak with a group of soldiers, but they were not interested in talking to me. When I met a Russian Army officer and asked him where the army headquarters were, he asked me what I wanted there. I explained that I had just come out of hiding, that I was Jewish, and didn't know where to go and what to do. His answer was that all the Jews were killed, that only a few German-Jewish collaborators had been spared, and that I must be one of them; there was no other explanation, for him, as to why I should be alive. When I tried to impress on him that I had been in hiding, his answer was short and simple: One does not hide from the enemy; one fights him, he told me. He gestured with his hand – a gesture of contempt – and turned away from me.

I continued walking, without a destination, for hours. I was getting weaker and weaker – and ravenously hungry. Because I had gone so many months not wearing anything on my feet in the cellar, my shoes blistered the soft skin of my feet, and they began to bleed. Finally, I couldn't walk any farther. I sat down in the middle of the sidewalk, took off my shoes, and could not get up. My feet were covered with blood.

I sat ... my head in a whirl; I drowsed off for a while, how long I don't know. Passers-by stopped to look at me. Some stopped only for a second, others for a little longer. They talked among themselves. The only thing I heard them saying was, 'It is a Jew'.

I shook myself out of my stupor. A group of people were standing around me, staring as if I were something never seen before. I spoke to no one and no one spoke to me. They whispered to each other, gaping at me. What should I do? I didn't know anyone in the city. I didn't even have a *grosz*. When we escaped from the Death Brigade I was able to take very little money; part of that I had turned over to Juzek, at the first hiding place, and the rest to our second host, Kalwinski. To go back to Kalwinski was impossible, for he had asked us not to return. The only place I could think of going to was the apartment where I used to live. After all, the whole apartment house once belonged to my parents. This was the last place I ever wanted to see again, but what could I do?

So, slowly, barefoot (I could not put my shoes on at all now, for they were so swollen), I walked in the direction of my house. The street where I used to live, which was once inhabited by Jews, practically all of whom I once knew, looked completely strange now. It is hard to describe my feelings. When, until yesterday, the problem had been to escape being killed, survival dominated one's every thought; today this was not a problem anymore. Today the anguish for those who had been killed flooded over me.

The tortures of the family, the way in which they were killed, began to prey on my mind more and more. The street looked so barren to me.

I was now guilty in the eyes of the people and of the Russian officer for being alive. The only question anyone asked me was, why was I alive?

With such thoughts I approached the house in which I used to live. I stopped at the entrance for a while and pulled myself together. I walked into the first apartment, where a woman, the janitor, lived. She recognized me at once, and told me to sit down. She asked me questions. I felt as though I were under an anesthetic. She gave me a plate of soup. I ate it. She told me with an authoritative voice that she kept telling her friends all the time that the Germans hadn't killed all the Jews and that there must still be some in hiding. I was proof of what she knew all along, she said. She tried to get me out of her apartment, telling me that the shoemaker who used to live across the street, and whom I should know, was now living in our old apartment one flight up. There were only four people, he and his wife, a daughter and a son, she said, so that I can find space there to stay. After all, she continued, it is your apartment; the furniture that your parents left is still there.

I went upstairs, knocked at my apartment door, and, without waiting for an answer, walked straight in, straight through the kitchen into the living room, and sat down on my own old couch. The shoemaker and his family already knew of my presence. Without even greeting me, the shoemaker told me that this was their apartment now; after all, there was a war on; they had had to leave their own place with their furniture, too. (They previously lived in a one-room basement apartment.) He said I shouldn't think that only the Jews had had a hard time; true, his family had not been killed, but 'we didn't have it too easy either'. He told me about high taxes and curfews.

I told him that I hadn't come to reclaim my own things, but that I would have to stay somewhere until I could find a place or until I could start to walk. I showed them my feet. They calmed down, and made up a bed that was once my father's, and brought a basin with warm water. I closed the door, washed up, and lay down on the bed. In no time I was asleep.

So passed my first day of liberation – the day that so many had waited for. I had lived to see it.

Selected text from the updated 1999 edition of the *The Janowska Road*, by Leon Weliczker Wells, published by and used with permission of the US Holocaust Memorial Museum, Washington, DC (pp.265–8). Previously published in 1963 by the Macmillan Company as *The Janowska Road* and in 1978 by the Holocaust Library as the *Death Brigade*.

NOTES

The author, Leon W. Wells, describes his days of hiding in a bunker in detailed, painful terms in 'The Hiding Place'. The end of the war and liberation proved to be a shocking experience for many survivors, who found a world devoid of families and friends, frequently facing hostile neighbours who were afraid of having to return homes and other possessions to their rightful owners.

In outbursts of violent Jew-hatred, attacks and murder of Jews were not unheard of, even after the war, culminating in the attack in Kielce, on 4 July 1946, in which forty-two Jews were killed, including two children and four teenagers. Hundreds of Jewish survivors were murdered in Poland by Poles, precipitating a mass exodus of Jews from the land of their birth. For detailed, heartbreaking information about the

Jews in Poland immediately following the end of the Second World War, see Martin Gilbert, *The Holocaust; A History of the Jews of Europe During the Second World War* (New York: Holt, Rinehart and Winston, 1985), pp.811–28. For information about the author, Leon Weliczker Wells, see 6. 'Time of Peace'.

1. Korn: a character mentioned in 'The Hiding Place'.

49

The First Letter from America

LEON KOBRIN

A Short Story

The first letter from Mirke's daughter Leah has arrived from America, and it is filled with good news. Mirke weeps for joy and begs her Meyshe-Itsye to read it for her, over and over again … Meyshe-Itsye reads it and is so deeply moved that he keeps pulling at his nose and swallowing his tears. Old Avrom-Layzer bends over toward his son-in-law, with his ears well-cocked to catch the words, the end of his flowing white beard clutched in his fist; he is careful not to lose a word of the letter, and his countenance glows with an expression of wonderment. Lea's sisters read the letter, too, in agitated voices, and tears of joy glitter in their eyes. Even little Shlayme is seized with the happiness of the occasion; during the past year he has grown taller, paler, thinner, but he has remained the same mischievous creature as before. And for sheer joy he begins to beg: 'Mama, give me a *kopek*!' And for sheer joy Mirke gives him a *kopek* at once, bestowing the same largess upon the other children, too. Then she seizes the letter and dashes off with a glowing face to the market-place, that the shop-keepers may read the wonderful news.

And somewhat later Mottel is standing before his store, reading the selfsame letter in a loud voice, with Mirke beside him, surrounded by all the storekeepers and the women who own the market stands; all listen to the letter with mouths agape and eyes distended in wonder. Mirke drinks in every word, smiles with enthusiasm, wipes her eyes and every other moment interrupts Mottel's reading. 'Oh, thanks be to God! Do you hear? Well, what do you say to that, ha …?'

And the rest shake their heads, smack their lips and murmur their wonderment.

'My, My! Ay! Ay!'

'Why not confess it', reads Mottel. 'Never in my life have I seen what I saw in the home of my brothers-in-law in New York. On the very sidewalk lay precious things such as I only wish you could have on your table for the holidays. It's only too bad that people step all over them with their feet. And there are golden mirrors there that reach to the ceiling. And there isn't a trace of a lamp in all New York. And at night you press the wall, and a lot of moons in glass cases light up, just like on the ship on which we came across …'

'Well!' interrupts Mottel, 'What do you think of that? Ha …?'

'Do you hear?' adds Mirke, and her whole countenance is one smile of exaltation.

'My, My! Ay, Ay!' chorus the listeners.

Mottel resumes his reading:

'And the walls here are so red and velvety. I touched one of them, and it's so soft and even, and I thought to myself: "I wish I had a cloak made of it!"'

'She knows what's good to have!' called one of the women shop-keepers.

'And as for eating', the letter went on, 'they eat of the very best here. They don't lack even the bird's milk! Roast hens in the middle of the week and so many other dainty dishes that I don't know how to name them …'

'There is a Rothschild existence for you!' interjects Mottel once more, continuing to read:

'And the buildings in New York are so high that even when you turn back your neck you can barely see the roof. And over the roof there fly machines filled with people, and the people aren't at all afraid, and my brothers-in-law tell me that none of the machines has ever fallen down …'

'My, My! Heavens! Ay, Ay!'

'And they rented a home for us in which even a count might live. Six rooms in a fine building. And in three of the rooms, on the floor they've laid down a kind of oil-cloth with such nice squares, and in the hall on the floor they put a big piece of velvet with flowers painted on it. I don't let anybody into the house, because I don't want them to step on it. Then I have got chairs, a bureau and what not else, which they sent in. It simply dazzles your eyes to look at them. And mother-in-law is living with us, and there's water in our home. All you have to do is turn a faucet and water comes from the wall. And you don't need any lamps, either, for when you want light, you simply turn a sort of screw and you bring a match close to it and it gets light. And there is no oven here, either. When you wish to cook you turn another screw and pretty soon the stove is hot and you put your pots on top of it and you make the finest dishes. And my brothers-in-law have taken Orre into their iron factory, where they make iron ceilings and stairs for the buildings, and they pay him, thank god, twenty dollars a week. In our money that's every bit of forty rubles.'

'Listen, folks! Just listen to that!' cries one of the women. 'I could pinch my cheeks …'

'Read on, Reb Mottel!' urges Mirke with ardor, drying her eyes.

Mottel continues: 'Yes, where was I?'

'In our money that's every bit of forty rubles. And later, say my brothers-in-law, he'll get even more.'

Mirke can no longer restrain her sobs.

'Well! Ha? Well!'

'I hope to God that I'll be able to send for all of you, and bring you across. And my brothers-in-law tell me that in New York there are a good many Jewish policemen too …'

'That's so', cries Mottel. 'I heard that long ago, – that Jews over there have equal rights!'

'Really?' asks one. 'And they have Jewish policemen there too?'

'What do you think?' shouts Mottel in reply, his voice ringing with confidence. 'Even Jewish intelligence-officers …'

'You don't say!'

'I would pay to pawn our wives and children and take a trip over there!' jests one of the men.

'And the men too!' retorts one of the women. 'But I'm afraid Berel-Itsye the money-lender wouldn't advance a groshen on them.'

The rest of the women burst into laughter.

'Unless the Gentile butcher would give something for them as impure meat', suggests another woman.

'Shoo, ladies!' exclaims a shopkeeper, and waves his hands at them as if he were driving geese along.

The laughter waxes louder. Both men and women are now guffawing.

Mirke now stands with the letter in her hand, taking no part in the general merriment. She feels provoked that they should not now be talking of her daughter's good fortune. For a moment she remains thus, then she remarks:

'And I, fool that I was, tried to keep her from going …!'

Nobody notices her reflection. Out of envy, they all pretend not to have heard anything that she had said. So she approaches close to one of the women with whom she is wont to quarrel all the year long – Elke, the daughter of Chaye-Dvoshe, a gaunt woman with a crooked nose, wearing a white bonnet under a red, flowery kerchief, – thinking to herself, 'Let her burst with envy!' and she says:

'What do you say to that, Elke? Such a fool I was trying to hold her back ...'

'You never can tell', replies Elke maliciously, 'Maybe your heart told you she ought not to go? Maybe ... Who knows what misfortune may yet befall her there ...!'

Mirke, flaming with rage, almost jumps upon her.

'Tfu! Tfu! Tfu!' She spits out thrice. 'On your head! May it befall your own wicked person! You crooked serpent, you! Burst with envy! Explode with jealousy! Aha! Who's daughter has a husband that makes forty rubles a week? Aha? Burst! Burst! Burst!'

And she dashes into her shop. Elke replies with a volley of curses. The other women set up a clamor. The men hold their sides with laughter, while Mottel cries: 'Livelier, Elke, livelier!'

'Hush! Here comes the lord with the brass buttons ...!'

The sergeant issues forth from the apothecary's, stops and eyes the crowd around the shops.

And when the sergeant disappears, Mottel cries to one of his neighbors, in a voice breathless with wonder:

'And in America there are even Jewish policemen. There's no grief of Exile over there. Full rights ...'

For the next few weeks there was talk of this letter all over the town, and of the 'full rights', and on a certain Saturday morning, when Mottel caught hold of little Shlayme in the synagogue and asked him:

'Well, youngster, are you going to sail to America, too?' Shlayme replied, 'You bet! I'll be a policeman there ...!'

At about this time Sholom the Gentile entered the home of Shmeril the cobbler, whistled mysteriously and held out both his hands.

Shmeril happened to be holding a shoe in his lap, heel upwards, and his mouth was filled with wooden nails; he stared at Sholom in amazement, removed the nails from between his lips and asked quietly:

'What's the matter?'

'From Broche ...' he managed to utter in a stifled voice, making a pitiable attempt to smile, 'She is ... phew ...!'

Again he whistled and brandished his arms.

'Well, what about your Broche? Speak ...'

'Sailed for America yesterday.'

'Yes, yes. Broche, my Broche ... She fell in love in the city, with a rascal of a salesman and he turned her head with stories of America, and go try to talk her out of it ...! I and my wife Gittel rushed to the city, begged of her, wept before her: "What do you mean by this sudden craze for America? To forsake your father and mother, brothers and sisters, – the whole world? What do you mean by it, the devil take your father? Haven't you any pity ...?" But you might as well have spoken to the wall! She went away!'

Leon Kobrin, *A Lithuanian Village*, translated by Isaac Goldberg (New York: Brentano's, 1920), pp.167–74.

NOTES

Leon Kobrin (1873–1946) was born in White Russia, today Belarus. Emigrating to the United States in 1892, he became one of the popular and critically acclaimed Yiddish writers, and the first to portray life in the tenements and the Jewish immigrant experience. Kobrin is, therefore, important far beyond his considerable literary merit – his stories, plays and novels have acquired a historical significance. The above s election from *The Lithuanian Village* faithfully, dramatically and realistically transmits the glory and the agony of 'discovering America'.

50

I Discover America

ABRAHAM CAHAN

Excerpt from a Novel

I set forth in the direction of East Broadway. Ten minutes' walk brought me to the heart of the Jewish East Side. The streets swarmed with Yiddish-speaking immigrants. The sign-boards were in English and Yiddish, some of them in Russian. The scurry and hustle of the people were not merely overwhelmingly greater, both in volume and in intensity, than in my native town. It was of another sort. The swing and step of the pedestrians, the voices and manner of the street peddlers, and a hundred and one other things seemed to testify to far more self-confidence and energy, to larger ambition and wider scopes, than did the appearance of the crowds in my birthplace.

The great thing was that these people were better dressed than the inhabitants of my town. The poorest-looking man wore a hat (instead of a cap), a stiff collar and a necktie, and the poorest woman wore a hat or a bonnet.

The appearance of a new immigrant was still a novel spectacle on the East Side. Many of the passers-by paused to look at me with wistful smiles of curiosity.

'There goes a green one!' some of them exclaimed.

The sight of me obviously evoked reminiscences in them of the days when they had been 'green ones' like myself. It was a second birth that they were witnessing, an experience which they had once gone through themselves and which was one of the greatest experiences of their lives. 'Green one' or 'greenhorn' is one of the many English words and phrases which my mother-tongue has appropriated in England and America. Thanks to the many millions of letters that pass annually between the Jews of Russia and their relatives in the United States, a number of these words have by now come to be generally known among our people at home as well as here. In the eighties, one who had not visited any English-speaking country was utterly unfamiliar with them.

And so I have never heard of 'green one' before. Still, 'green', in the sense of color, is Yiddish as well as English, so I understood the phrase at once, and as a contemptuous quizzical appellation for a newly arrived, inexperienced immigrant it stung me cruelly. As I went along, I heard it again and again. Some of the passers-by would call me 'greenhorn' in a tone of blighting gaiety, but these were an exception. For the most part it was 'green one' and in a spirit of sympathetic interest. It hurt me, all the same. Even those glances that offered me a cordial welcome and good wishes had something self-complacent and condescending in them. 'Poor fellow, he is a green one', these people seemed to say. 'We are not, of course. We are Americanized.'

For my first meal in the New World I bought a three-cent wedge of course rye bread, off a huge round loaf, on a stand on Essex Street. I was too strict in my religious observances to eat it without performing ablutions and offering a brief prayer. So I approached a bewigged old woman who stood in the doorway of a small grocery store to let me wash my hands and eat my meal in her place. She looked old-fashioned enough, yet when she heard my request she said, with a laugh:

'You are a green one, I see.'

'Suppose I am', I resented. 'Do the yellow ones or black ones all eat without washing? Can't a fellow be a good Jew in America?'

'Yes, of course, he can, but – well, wait till you see for yourself.'

However, she asked me to come in, gave me some water and an old apron to serve me for a towel, and when I was ready to eat my bread she placed a glass of milk before me, explaining that she was not going to charge me for it.

'In America people are not foolish enough to be content with dry bread', she said, sententiously.

While I ate she questioned me about my antecedents. I remember how she impressed me as a strong, clever woman of few words as long as she catechised me, and how disappointed I was when she began to talk of herself. The astute, knowing mien gradually faded out of her face and I had before me a gushing, boastful old bore.

My intention was to take a long stroll, as much in the hope of coming upon some windfall as for the purpose of taking a look at the great American city. Many of the letters that came from the United States to my birthplace before I sailed had contained a warning not to imagine that America was 'the land of gold' and that treasures might be picked in the streets of New York for the picking. But these warnings only had the effect of lending vividness to the image of an American street as a thoroughfare strewn with nuggets of the precious metal. Symbolically speaking, this was the idea one had of the 'land of Columbus.' It was the continuation of the widespread effect produced by stories of Cortes and Pizarro in the sixteenth century, confirmed by the successes of some Russian emigrants of my time.

I asked the grocery-woman to let me leave my bundle with her, and, after considerable hesitation, she allowed me to put it among some empty barrels in her cellar.

I went wandering over the ghetto. Instead of stumbling over nuggets of gold, I found signs of poverty. In one case I came across a poor family who – as I learned upon inquiry – had been dispossessed for non-payment of rent. A mother and her two little boys were watching their pile of furniture and other household goods on the sidewalk while the passers-by were dropping coins into a saucer placed on one of the chairs to enable the family to move into new quarters.

What puzzled me was the nature of the furniture. For in my birth-place chairs and couch like those I now saw on the sidewalk would be a sign of prosperity. But then anything was to be expected of a country where the poorest devil wore a hat and a starched collar.

I walked on.

The exclamation 'a green one' or 'a greenhorn' continued. If I did not hear it, I saw it in the eyes of the people who passed me.

When it grew dark and I was much in need of rest I had a street peddler direct me to a synagogue. I expected to spend the night there. What could have been more natural?

At the house of God I found a handful of men in prayer. It was a large, spacious room and the smallness of their number gave it an air of desolation. I joined in the devotions with great fervor. My soul was sobbing to Heaven to take care of me in this strange country.

The service over, several of the worshipers took up some *Talmud* folio or other holy book and proceeded to read them aloud in the familiar singsong. The strange surroundings suddenly began to look like home to me.

One of the readers, an elderly man with a pinched face and forked little beard, paused to look me over.

'A green one?' he asked genially.

He told me that the synagogue was crowded on Saturdays, while on week-days people in America had no time to say their prayers at home, much less to visit a house of worship.

'It isn't Russia.' He said, with a sigh. 'Judaism has not much of a chance here.'

When he heard that I intended to stay in the synagogue overnight, he smiled ruefully.

'One does not sleep in an American synagogue', he said, 'it is not Russia.' Then, scanning me once more, he added, with an air of compassionate perplexity: 'Where will you sleep, poor child? I wish I could take you to my house, but – well, America is not Russia. There is no pity here, no hospitality. My wife would raise a rumpus if I brought you along. I should never hear the last of it.'

With a deep sigh and nodding his head plaintively he returned to his book, swaying back and forth. But he was apparently more interested in the subject he had broached. 'When we were at home', he resumed, 'she too was a different woman. She did not make life a burden to me as she does here. Have you no money at all?'

I showed him the quarter I had received from the cloak contractor.

'Poor fellow! Is that all you have? There are places where you can get a night's lodging for fifteen cents, but what are you going to do afterward? I am simply ashamed of myself. "Hospitality", he quoted from the *Talmud*, "is one of the things which the giver enjoys in this world and the fruit of which he relishes in the world to come." To think that I cannot offer a Talmudic scholar a night's rest! Alas! America has turned me into a mound of ashes.'

'You were well off in Russia, weren't you?' I inquired, in astonishment. For, indeed, I had never heard of any but poor emigrating to America. 'I used to spend my time reading *Talmud* at the synagogue', was his reply.

Many of his answers seem to fit, not the question asked, but one which was expected to follow it. You might have thought him anxious to forestall your next query in order to save him time and words, had it not been so difficult for him to keep his mouth shut.

'She', he said, referring to his wife, 'had a nice little business. She sold feed for horses and she rejoiced in the thought that she was married to a man of learning. True, she has a tongue. That she always had, but over there it was not so bad. She has become a different woman here. Alas! America is a topsy-turvy country.'

He went on to show how the New World turned things upside down, transforming an immigrant shoemaker into a man of substance, while a former man of leisure was forced to work in a factory here. In like manner, his wife has changed for the worse, for, lo and behold! Instead of supporting him while he read *Talmud*, as she used to do at home, she persisted in sending him out to peddle. 'America is not Russia', she said. 'A man must make a living here.' But alas! It was too late to begin now. He had spent the better part of his life at his holy books and was fit for nothing else now. His wife, however, will take no excuse. He must peddle or be nagged to death. And if he ventured to slip into some synagogue of an afternoon and read a page or two he would be in danger of being caught red-handed, so to say, for, indeed, she often shadowed him to make sure that he did not play truant. Alas! America was not Russia.

Abraham Cahan, *The Rise of David Levinsky* (New York: Harper and Row, 1917), pp.92–7.

NOTES

Abraham Cahan (1860–1957) was a journalist, editor, novelist, teacher and community leader. Steeped in the Jewish tradition, in European and Russian literature, and influenced by socialist ideology, Abraham Cahan pioneered modern Yiddish journalism in the United States.

He noted the lack of a Yiddish newspaper and the needs of the masses of Yiddish speaking immigrants for education, information, literature, beauty, pleasure and an introduction to their new life in America. The *Forward*, under his direction for nearly fifty years, met that need and expressed their soul. With talent, vitality and energy he contributed to other publications as well, and his novel *The Rise of David Levinsky* is a splendid example of literature reflecting the Jewish immigrant experience in New York.

51

'The Sweatshop'

MORRIS ROSENFELD

A Poem

So wild is the roar of machines in the sweatshop
I often forget I'm alive in that din!
I'm drowned in the tide of the terrible tumult
my ego is slain; I become a machine.
I work and I work without rhyme, without reason,
produce and produce and produce without end.
For what? and for whom? I don't know, I don't wonder –
since when can a whirling machine comprehend?

No feeling, no thoughts, nor the least understanding;
this bitter, this murderous drudgery drains
the noblest, the finest, the best and the richest,
the deepest, the highest that living contains.
Away rush the seconds, the minutes, the hours;
each day and each night like a wind-driven sail;
I drive the machine as though eager to catch them,
I drive without reason – no hope, no avail.

The clock in the shop, even he toils forever
he points and he ticks and he wakes us from dreams.
A long time ago someone taught me the meaning:
his pointing, his waking are more than they seem.
I only remember a few things about it;
the clock wakes our senses and sets us aglow,
and wakes something else – I've forgotten, don't ask me –
I'm just a machine, I don't know, I don't know!

But once in a while, when I hear the clock ticking,

his pointing, his language, are not as before.
I feel that his pendulum lashes me, prods me
to work even faster, to do more and more!
I hear the wild yell of the boss in his ticking,
I see the dark frown in the two pointing hands.
I shudder to think it: the clock is my master!
He calls me 'Machine!', 'Hurry up!', he commands.

But when there's a half-hour lull in the uproar,
at noon, when the boss turns his back on us, then,
Oh then, the sun slowly rises within me,
my heart reaches out and my wounds burn again,
and tears that are bitter and tears that are seething
soak into my thin little banquet of bread.
I choke on the food – I can't swallow a morsel –
Oh bitter to be neither living nor dead!

At lunchtime the shop's like a grim field of battle,
the cannon are resting, I look all around –
wherever I turn I see nothing but corpses;
the blood of the innocent shrieks from the ground!
One moment, and soon an alarm will be sounded,
the corpses awake, they return to the fight;
the dead rise to battle for strangers, for strangers,
they strive and are stricken and sink into night.

I look at the bloodbath with rage and with horror,
with grief, with a vow to avenge what I see.
At last I can hear the clock rightly, he wakes us –
'An end to enslavement! An end let there be!'
He ticks back to life my emotions, my senses,
and points to the hours that are hurrying past.
As long as my lips are sealed up I'll be wretched,
as long I am what I am I'll be lost.

The man who had slept in me slowly awakens,
the slave seems asleep that was wakeful in me.
The hour, at last the right hour is striking,
an end to misfortune! An end let there be!
But in comes the boss with his whistle, his bugle;

I'm lost – I forget what I am, what I mean.
Such tumult! Such battling! My ego goes under.
I know not, I care not – I'm just a machine...!

E.J. Goldenthal, *Poet of the Ghetto; Morris Rosenfeld* (Hoboken, NJ: Ktav, 1998), pp.150–1. Translated from the Yiddish by Aaron Kramer. Reproduced by kind permission of Edgar J. Goldenthal and the Dora Teitelboim Center for Yiddish Culture, sponsor of *The Last Lullaby: Poetry of the Holocaust*, edited and translated by Aaron Kramer (Syracuse, NY: Syracuse University Press, 1988).

NOTES

Morris Rosenfeld, considered by some 'The Crown Poet of Immigration' was born in 1862 in Buksha, close to the town of Suwalki, at that time part of Russian Poland, and spent some of his childhood years in Warsaw. He began to write at the age of 14. Self-educated, he read some of the great works of world literature in English, German and Hebrew. Emigrating to America at the age of 24, in 1886, he worked in a sweatshop as a tailor. In his own words: 'It was in the damp, dark sweatshop of New York where I learned to sing of oppression, suffering, and misery. During the day I worked and at night I wrote my poems' (Goldenthal, *Poet of the Ghetto*, p.2).

Morris was the son of his people, and he wrote for them and about them. Steeped deeply in tradition, he understood the immigrants' history, experience, fears, joys, needs and hopes. His poetry in Yiddish was embraced, loved, sung and published. *Songs of the Ghetto* was published in 1898, and a second edition followed in 1899, published by Professor Leo Wiener of Harvard University.

He sang of the sweatshops, and the workers:

> His eyes see the workshop with loathing,
> from morn 'til the hours grow late.
> His tears soak themselves in his clothing
> as he mourns at his pitiful state.[1]

He sang of his constant hunger:

> Bread and tea and bread and tea!
> What a menu! Woe is me![2]

He sang about his family, and is best known for 'My Little Son', whom he sees only at night, when the little boy is asleep (translated by A. Kramer, p.200–1). Morris Rosenfeld lived a full life. He loved his four children, his pen and his people, remaining the voice of the poor Jewish immigrant, and one of the fathers of Yiddish literature in America. He died in 1923.

1. Edgar J. Goldenthal, *Poet of the Ghetto: Morris Rosenfeld* (Hoboken, NJ: Ktav, 1998), p.147.
2. Ibid., pp.163–4.

'Bread and Tea'

MORRIS ROSENFELD

A Poem

Bread and tea and bread and tea!
What a menu! Woe is me!
I ask you, God, is this a joke,
to fix it so I'm always broke?
Can't You spare a few sardines,
a slice of lox,
a can of beans,
a little milk, a piece of cheese?
Just bread and tea and bread and tea?
What a menu, woe is me!

Is this a judgement You've decreed,
just to make me come and plead?
Haven't I sought You day and night,
praying that you ease my plight?
Yet here I am, in fifth floor flat,
and You care less than does my cat!
Apparently, God, it must be true;
things are not so 'extra' with You.
Are You, Yourself, in trouble too?

E.J. Goldenthal, *Poet of the Ghetto; Morris Rosenfeld* (Hoboken, NJ: Ktav, 1998), pp.163–4. Translated from the Yiddish by Max Rosenfeld. Reproduced by kind permission of Edgar J. Goldenthal and Jack Rosenfeld for the translator, Max Rosenfeld. Information about Morris Rosenfeld is found following 51. 'The Sweatshop'.

'Yiddish'

MORRIS ROSENFELD

A Poem

There are rhymesters who complain, all
say our tongue is banal,
it has no flowers, shades or class,
and scrapes the soul like broken glass.
They say it's common, plain and dry.
They cannot sing and wonder why.

They say our language lacks allure,
the noble word, the rich and pure,
it circumscribes their singing.
They hear but harsh words ringing.
They say it's just a stick, a sabre,
to chill a heart or hurt a neighbor.

Oh, dear! To so delude the world is wrong,
it's rude to so abuse your mother-tongue
and so demean yourself with lies.
Oh Yiddish! To your portals my heart flies!
How rich you are, how holy too,
what songs can't I create with you?

Your range of colors makes others pale,
the prettiest flowers on hill or dale
I sharply paint. My palette's full.
The poet's heart and love can pull
the colored threads of sound, and conceive
from language heaven-large a tapestry to weave.

Life could give me nothing if I could never sing.

My language, wide as all the seas,
put images and memories
like May in bloom and children heard in gleaming cantos of the soul,
its thousand-colored flames enhances the poet's role.

E.J. Goldenthal, *Poet of the Ghetto: Morris Rosenfeld* (Hoboken, NJ: Ktav, 1998), p.277. Translated from the Yiddish by E.J. Goldenthal. Reproduced by kind permission of Edgar J. Goldenthal. Information about Morris Rosenfeld is found following 51. 'The Sweatshop'.

54

In the Catskills

ABRAHAM CAHAN

Excerpt from a Novel

Dinner at the Rigi Kuhn on a Saturday evening was not merely a meal. It was, in addition, or chiefly, a great social function and a gown contest.

The band was playing. As each matron or girl made her appearance in the vast dining room the female boarders already seated would look her over with feverish interest, comparing her gown and diamonds with their own. It was as if especially for this parade of dresses and finery that the band was playing. As the women came trooping in, arrayed for exhibition, some timid, others brazenly self-confident, they seemed to be marching in time to the music, like so many chorus-girls tripping before a theater audience, or as a procession of model-girls at a style display in a big department store. Many of the women strutted affectedly, with 'refined' mien. Indeed, I knew that most of them had a feeling as though wearing a hundred-and-fifty dollar dress was in itself culture and education.

Mrs Kalch kept talking to me, now aloud, now in whispers. She was passing judgment on the gowns and incidentally initiating me into some of the innermost details of the gown race. It appeared that the women kept tag on one another's dresses, shirt-waists, shoes, ribbons, pins, earrings. She pointed out two matrons who had never been seen twice in the same dress, waist, or skirt, although they have lived in the hotel for more than five weeks. Of one woman she informed me that she could afford to wear a new gown every hour of the year, but that she was 'too big a slob to dress up and too lazy to undress even when she went to bed'; of another, that she would owe her grocer and butcher rather than go to the country with less than ten big trunks full of duds; of a third, that she was repeatedly threatening to leave the hotel because its bills of fare were typewritten, whereas 'for the money she paid she could go to a place with printed menu-cards.'

'Must have been brought up on printed menu-cards', one of the other women at our table commented, with a laugh.

'That's right', Mrs. Kalch assented, appreciatively. 'I could not say whether her father was a horse driver or a stoker in a bath-house, but I do know that her husband kept a coal-and-ice cellar a few years ago.'

'That'll do', her bewhiskered husband snarled. 'It's about time you gave your tongue a rest.'

Auntie Yetta's golden teeth glittered good-humoredly. The next instant she called my attention to a woman who, driven to despair by the superiority of her 'bosom friend's' gowns, had gone to the city for a fortnight, ostensibly to look for a new flat, but in reality to replenish her wardrobe. She had just returned, on the big 'husband train', and now, 'her bosom friend won't be able to eat or sleep, trying to guess what kind of dresses she brought back.'

Nor was this the only kind of gossip upon which Mrs. Kalch regaled me. She told me, for example, of some sensational discoveries made by several boarders regarding a certain mother of five children, of her sister who was 'not a bit better', and of a couple who were supposed to be man and wife, but who seemed to be somebody else's man and wife.

At last Miss Tevkin and Miss Siegel entered the dining room. Something like a thrill passed through me. I felt like exclaiming, 'At last!'

'That's the one I met you with, isn't it? Not bad-looking', said Mrs. Kalch.

'Which do you mean?'

'Which do you mean! The tall one, of course; the one you were so sweet on. Not the dwarf with the horse-face.'

'They are fine, educated girls, both of them', I rejoined.

'Both of them! As if it was all the same to you!' At this she bent over and gave me a glare and a smile that brought the color to my face.

'The tall one is certainly not bad looking, but we don't call that pretty in this place.'

'Are there many prettier ones?' I asked gaily.

'I haven't counted them, but I can show you some girls who shine like the sun. There is one!' she said, pointing at a girl on the other side of the isle. 'A regular princess. Don't you think so?'

'She is a pretty girl, all right', I replied, 'but in comparison with that tall one she's like a nice piece of cotton goods along a piece of imported silk.'

'Look at him! He is stuck on her. Does she know it? If she does not, I'll tell her and collect a marriage-broker's commission.'

I loathed myself for having talked too much.

'I was joking, of course', I tried to mend matters. 'All girls are pretty.'

Luckily Mrs. Kalch's attention was at this point diverted by the arrival of the waiter with a huge platter laden with roast chicken, which he placed in the middle of the table. There ensued a silent race for the best portions. One of the other two women at the table was the first to obtain possession of the platter. Taking her time about it, she first made a careful examination of its contents and then attacked what she evidently considered a choice piece. By way of calling my attention to the proceeding, Auntie Yetta stepped on my foot under the table and gave me a knowing glance.

The noise in the dining room was unendurable. It seemed a though everybody was talking at the top of his voice. The musicians – a pianist and two violinists – found it difficult to make themselves heard. They were pounding and sawing frantically in a vain effort to beat the bedlam of conversation and laughter. It was quite touching. The better to take in the effect of the turmoil, I shut my eyes for a moment, whereupon the noise reminded me of the Stock Exchange.

The conductor, who played the first violin, was a fiery little fellow with a high crown of black hair. He was working every muscle and nerve in his body. He played selections from 'Aida', the favorite opera of the ghetto; he played the popular American songs of the day; he played celebrated 'hits' of the Yiddish stage. All to no purpose. Finally, he had recourse to what was apparently his last resort. He struck up the 'Star Spangled Banner.' The effect was overwhelming. The few hundred diners rose like one man, applauding. The children and many of the adults caught up the tune joyously, passionately. It was an interesting scene. Men and women were offering thanksgiving to the flag under which they were eating this good dinner, wearing these expensive clothes. There was the jingle of newly-acquired dollars in our applause. But there was something else in it as well. Many of those who were now paying tribute to the Stars and Stripes were listening to the tune with grave, solemn mien. It was as if they were saying: 'We are not persecuted under this flag. At last we have found a home.'

Love for America blazed out in my soul. I shouted to the musicians, 'My Country', and the cry spread like wild-fire. The musicians obeyed and we all sang the anthem from the bottom of our souls.

A. Cahan, *The Rise of David Levinsky* (New York, NJ: Harper and Row, 1917), pp.421–4. For information about A. Cahan, see 50. 'I Discover America'.

55

The Name (Yad Vashem)

AHARON MEGGED

A Short Story

Grandfather Zisskind lived in a little house in a southern suburb of the town. About once a month, on a Saturday afternoon, his granddaughter Raya and her young husband Yehuda would go and pay him a duty visit.

Raya would give three cautious knocks on the door (an agreed signal between herself and her grandfather ever since her childhood, when he had lived in their house together with the whole family) and they would both wait for the door to be opened. 'Now he's getting up', Raya would whisper to Yehuda, her face glowing, when the sound of her grandfather's slippers was heard from within, shuffling across the room. Another moment and the key would be turned and the door opened.

'Come in', he would say somewhat absently, still buttoning up his trousers, with the rheum of sleep in his eyes. Although it was very hot he was wearing a yellow winter vest with long sleeves, from which his wrists stuck out – white, thin, delicate as a girl's, as was his bare neck with its taut skin.

After Raya and Yehuda had sat down at the table, which was covered with a white cloth showing signs of the meal he had eaten alone – crumbs from the Sabbath loaf, a plate with leavings of meat, a glass containing some grape-pips, a number of jars and so on – he would smooth the crumpled pillows, spread a cover over the narrow bed and tidy up. It was a small room, and the disorder which reigned in it aroused pity for the old man's helplessness in running his home. In the corner was a shelf with two sooty kerosene cookers, a kettle and two or three saucepans, and next to it a basin containing plates, knives and forks. In another corner was a stand holding books with thick leather bindings, leaning and lying on each other. Some of his clothes were hanging over the backs of the chairs. An ancient walnut cupboard with an empty buffet stood exactly opposite the door. On the wall hung a clock that had long since stopped.

'We ought to make Grandfather a present of a clock', Raya would say to Yehuda as she surveyed the room and her glance lighted on the clock; but every time the matter slipped her memory. She loved her grandfather, with his pointed, white silky beard, his tranquil face from which a kind of holy radiance emanated, his quiet, soft voice which seemed to have been made only for uttering words of sublime wisdom. She also revered him for his pride, on account of which he had moved out of her mother's house and gone to live by himself, accepting the hardship and trouble and the affliction of loneliness in his old age. There had been a bitter quarrel between him and his daughter. After the death of Raya's father the house had lost its grandeur and shed the trappings of wealth. Some of the antique furniture which they had retained, besides valuable objects, crystalware and jewels, the dim luster of memories from the days of plenty in their native city – had been sold, and Rachel, Raya's mother, had been compelled to support the home by working as a dentist's nurse. Grandfather Zisskind, who had been supported by the family since he had come to the country, wished to hand over to his daughter his small capital, which was deposited in a bank. She was not willing to accept it. She was stubborn and proud like him. Then, after a prolonged quarrel and several weeks of not speaking to each other, he took some of the things in his room and the broken clock and went to live alone. That had been about four years ago. Now Rachel would come to him once or twice a week, bringing with her a bag full of provisions, to clean the room and cook some meals for him. He was no longer particular about expenses and did not even ask about them, as though they were of no more concern to him.

'And now – what can I offer you?' Grandfather Zisskind would ask when he considered the room ready to receive guests.

'There's no need to offer us anything, Grandfather; we didn't come for that', Raya would say crossly.

But protests were of no avail. Her grandfather would take out a jar of fermenting preserves and put it on the table, then grapes and plums, biscuits and two glasses of strong tea, forcing them to eat. Raya would taste a little of this and that so as to please Grandfather, while Yehuda, for whom all these visits to the old man were unavoidable torment, and whom the very sight of the dishes aroused disgust, would secretly indicate to her by pulling a sour face that he just could not touch the preserves. She would give him a placatory smile, stroking his knee.

Grandfather meanwhile insisted, so again he would have to taste at least a teaspoonful of the sweet and nauseating stuff.

Afterwards Grandfather would ask about all kinds of things. Raya did her best to make the conversation pleasant, in order to relieve Yehuda's boredom. Finally would come what Yehuda dreaded most of all and on account of which he had resolved more than once to refrain from these visits. Grandfather Zisskind would rise, take his chair and place it next to the wall, get up on it carefully, holding on to the back so as not to fall, open the clock and take out a cloth bag with a black cord tied round it. Then he would shut the clock, get off the chair, put it back in its place, sit down on it, undo the cord, take out of the cloth wrapping a bundle of sheets of paper, lay them in front of Yehuda and say:

'I would like you to read this.'

'Grandfather', – Raya would rush to rescue Yehuda in his distress – 'but he's already read it at least ten times.'

But Grandfather Zisskind would pretend not to hear and would not reply, so Yehuda was compelled to read there and then the same essay, spread over eight long sheets in a large, somewhat shaky, handwriting, which he almost knew by heart. Its subject was a lament for Grandfather's native town in the Ukraine that had been destroyed, and all its Jews slaughtered, by the Germans. When he had finished, Grandfather would take the sheets out of his hand, fold them, sigh and say:

'And nothing of all this is left. Dust and ashes. Not even a tombstone to bear witness. Imagine, of a community of twenty thousand Jews not even one survived to tell how it happened ... Not a trace.'

Then out of the same cloth bag, which contained various letters and envelopes, he would draw a photograph of his grandson Mendele, who had been twelve years old when he was killed; the only son of his son Ossip, chief engineer in a large chemical factory. He would show it to Yehuda and say:

'He was a genius. Just imagine, when he was only eleven he had already finished his studies at the conservatory for music, got a scholarship from the Government and was considered an outstanding violinist. A genius! Look at that forehead ...' And after he had put the photograph back he would sigh and repeat, 'Not a trace.'

A strained silence of commiseration would descend on Raya and Yehuda, who had already heard these same things many times over and no longer felt anything when he repeated them. And as he wound the cord round the bag the old man would muse: 'And Ossip was also a prodigy. As a boy he knew Hebrew well, and could recite Bialik's poems by heart. He studied by himself. He read endlessly, Gnessin, Frug, Bershadsky ... You didn't know Bershadsky; he was a good writer .... He had a warm heart, Ossip had. He didn't mix in politics, he wasn't even a Zionist, but even when they promoted him there he didn't forget that he was a Jew ... He called his son Mendele, of all names, after his dead brother, even though it was surely not easy to have a name like that among the Russians ... Yes, he had a warm Jewish heart ...'

He would turn to Yehuda as he spoke, since in Raya he always saw the child who used to sit on his knee listening to his stories, and for him she had never grown up, while he regarded Yehuda as an educated man who could understand someone else, especially seeing he held a Government job.

Raya remembered how this change, as a result of which it seemed as if his mind were confused, had come about in her grandfather. When the war was over he was still sustained by the uncertainty and hoped for some news of his son, for it was known that very many had succeeded in escaping eastwards. Wearily he would visit all those who had once lived in his town, but none of them had received any sign of life from his relatives. Nevertheless he continued to hope, for Ossip's important position might have helped to save him. Later, when Raya came home one evening she saw him sitting on the floor with a rent in his jacket and in the house they spoke in whispers, and her mother's eyes were red with weeping. She, too, had wept at Grandfather's sorrow, at the sight of his stricken face, and the oppressive quiet in the rooms. For many weeks afterwards it was as if he had imposed silence on himself. He would sit at his table from morning to night, reading and re-reading old letters, studying family photographs by the hour as he brought them close to his shortsighted eyes, or leaning backwards on his chair, motionless, his hand touching the edge of the table and his eyes staring through the window in front of him, into the distance, as if he were turned to stone. He was no longer the same talkative, wise and humorous grandfather who interfered in the house, asked what his granddaughter was doing, gave her moral instruction, tested her knowledge, proving boastfully like a child that he knew more than her teachers. Now he seemed to cut himself off from the world and entrench himself in his thoughts and his memories, which none of the household could penetrate. Later, a strange perversity had got into him that it was hard to tolerate. He would insist that his meals be served at his table, apart, that they should not enter his room without knocking on the door, that they should not close the shutters of his window against the sun. When they transgressed these prohibitions he would flare up and quarrel violently with his daughter. At times it seemed that he hated her.

When Raya's father died, Grandfather Zisskind did not show any signs of grief, and did not even console his daughter. And when the days of mourning were past it was as if he had been restored to new life, and he emerged from his silence. But he did not speak of her father, nor of his son Ossip, but of his grandson Mendele. Often during the day he would mention him by name as if he were alive, and speak of him although he had seen him only on photographs; as though deliberating aloud and turning the matter over, he would talk of how the boy ought to be brought up. It was hardest of all when he started criticizing his son and his son's wife for not having foreseen the impending disaster, for not having rushed him away to a safe place, not having hidden him with non-Jews, not having tried to get him to *Eretz Israel* in good time. There was no reason in what he said, which would so infuriate Rachel that she would burst out with, 'Oh, do stop! Stop it! I'll go out of my mind with your foolish nonsense!' She would rise from her seat in anger, withdraw to her room, and afterwards, when she had calmed down, would say to Raya, 'Sclerosis, apparently. Loss of memory. He no longer knows what he's talking about.'

One day – Raya will never forget this – she and her mother saw that Grandfather was wearing his best suit, the black one, and under it a gleaming white shirt; his shoes were polished, and he had a hat on …. He had not worn these clothes for many months, and they were dismayed to see him. They thought that he had lost his mind. 'What holiday is it today?' her mother asked. 'Really, don't you know?' asked her grandfather. 'Today is Mendele's birthday!' Her mother burst out crying. She followed suit and ran out of the house.

After that, Grandfather Zisskind went to live alone. His mind, apparently, had become settled, except that he would frequently forget things which had occurred a day or two before, though he clearly remembered down to the smallest detail things which had happened in his town and to his family more than thirty year ago. Raya would go and visit him, at first with her mother and, after her marriage, with Yehuda. What bothered them was that they were compelled to listen to his talk about Mendele his grandson, and to read that same lament for his native town, which had been destroyed.

Whenever Rachel happened to come there during their visit, she would scold Grandfather rudely. 'Stop bothering them with your masterpiece', she would say, and herself remove the papers from the table and put them back in their bag. 'If you want them to keep on visiting you, don't talk to them about the dead. Talk about the living. They're young people and they have no mind for such things.' And as they left his room together she would say, turning to Yehuda so as to placate him, 'Don't be surprised at him. Grandfather's already old. Over seventy. Loss of memory.'

When Raya was seven months pregnant, Grandfather Zisskind had not yet noticed it in his absent-mindedness. But Rachel could no longer refrain from letting him share her joy and hope and told him that a great-grandchild would soon be born to him. One evening the door of Raya's and Yehuda's flat opened, and Grandfather himself stood on the threshold in his holiday clothes, just as on the day of Mendele's birthday. This was the first time he had visited their flat, and Raya was so surprised that she hugged and kissed him as she had not done since she was a child. His face shone, his eyes sparkled with the same intelligent and mischievous light as in those far-off days before the calamity. When he entered he walked briskly through the rooms, giving them his opinion on their furniture and the arrangement of the flat, and joking about everything around him. He was so pleasant that Raya and Yehuda could not stop laughing all the time he was speaking. He gave no indication that he knew what was about to take place, and for the first time in many months he did not mention Mendele.

'Ah, you naughty children', he said, 'is this how you treat Grandfather? Why didn't you tell me you had such a nice flat?'

'How many times have I invited you here, Grandfather?' asked Raya.

'Invited me? You ought to have *brought* me to you, dragged me by force!'

'I wanted to do that too, but you refused.'

'Well, I thought that you lived in some dark den and I have a den of my own. Never mind, I forgive you.'

And when he took leave of them he said:

'Don't bother to come to me. Now that I know where you're to be found and what a palace you have, I'll come to you ... if you don't throw me out, that is.

Some days later, when Rachel came to their home and they told her about Grandfather's amazing visit she was not surprised, and said:

'Ah, you don't know what he's been contemplating during all these days, ever since I told him that you're about to have a child ... He has one wish – that if it's a son – it should be named ... after his grandson.'

'Mendele?' exclaimed Raya, and involuntarily burst into laughter. Yehuda smiled as one smiles at the fond fancies of the old.

'Of course I told him to put that out of his head', said Rachel, 'but you know how obstinate he is. It's some obsession that has got into him and he won't think of giving it up. Not only that, but he's sure that you'll willingly agree to it, and especially you, Yehuda.'

Yehuda shrugged his shoulders. 'Crazy. The child would be unhappy all his life.'

'But he's not capable of understanding that', said Rachel, and a note of apprehension crept into her voice.

Raya's face grew solemn.

'We have already decided on the name', she said. 'If it's a girl she'll be called Osnath, and if it's a boy – Ehud.'

Rachel did not like either.

The matter of the name became almost the sole topic of conversation between Rachel and the young couple when she visited them, and it infused gloom into the air of solemn expectancy that filled the house.

Rachel, midway between generations, was of two minds about the matter. When she spoke to her father she would scold and contradict him, flinging at him all the arguments that she had heard from Raya and Yehuda as though they were her own, but when she spoke to the children she sought to induce them to meet his wishes, and would bring down their anger on her head. As time went on, the matter of the name, to which in the beginning she had attached little importance, became a kind of mystery, concealing something fore-ordained, fearful and pregnant with life and death. The fate of the child itself seemed in doubt. In her innermost heart she prayed that Raya give birth to a daughter.

'Actually, what's so bad about the name Mendele?' she asked her daughter. 'It's a Jewish name like any other.'

'What are you talking about, Mother' – all Raya's being rebelled – ' a Ghetto name, ugly, horrible! I wouldn't even be capable of letting it cross my lips. Do you want me to hate my child?'

'Oh, you won't hate your child. At any rate, not because of the name ...'

'I should hate him. It's as if you'd told me that my child would be born with a hump! And anyway – why should I? What for?'

'You have to do it for Grandfather's sake', Rachel said quietly, although she knew that she was not speaking the whole truth.

'You know, Mother, that I am ready to do anything for Grandfather', said Raya. 'I love him, but I am not ready to sacrifice my child's happiness on account of some superstition of his. What sense is there in it?'

Rachel could not explain the 'sense in it' rationally, but in her heart she rebelled against her daughter's logic which had always been hers too and now seemed to her very superficial, a symptom of the frivolity afflicting the younger generation. Her old father now appeared to her like an ancient tree whose deep roots suck up the mysterious essence of existence, of which neither her daughter nor she herself knew anything. Had it not been for this argument about the name, she would certainly never have got to meditating on the transmigration of souls and the eternity of life. At night she would wake up covered with cold sweat. Hazily she recalled frightful scenes of bodies of naked children, beaten and trampled under the jackboots of soldiers, and an awful sense of guilt oppressed her spirit.

Then Rachel came with a proposal for a compromise: that the child be named Menachem. A Hebrew name, she said; an Israeli one. By all standards. Many children bore it, and it occurred to nobody to make fun of them. Even Grandfather – she said – had agreed to it after much urging.

Raya refused to listen.

'We have chosen a name, Mother', she said, 'which we both like, and we shan't change it for another. Menachem is a name which reeks of old age, a name which for me is connected with sad memories and people I don't like. Menachem you could call only a boy who is short, weak and not good-looking. Let's not talk about it any more, Mother.'

Rachel was silent. She almost despaired of convincing them. At last she said:

'And are you ready to take the responsibility of going against Grandfather's wishes?'

Raya's eyes opened wide, and fear was reflected in them:

'Why do you make such a fateful thing of it? You frighten me!' she said, and burst into tears. She began to fear for her offspring as one fears the evil eye.

'And perhaps there *is* something fateful in it …' whispered Rachel without raising her eyes. She flinched at her own words.

'What is it?' insisted Raya, with a frightened look at her Mother.

'I don't know …, she said. 'Perhaps all the same we are bound to retain the names of the dead … in order to leave a remembrance of them ….' She was not sure herself whether there was truth in what she said or whether it was merely a stupid belief, but her father's faith was before her, stronger than her own doubts and her daughter's simple and understandable opposition.

'But I don't always want to remember all those dreadful things,

Mother. It's impossible that this memory should always hang about this house and that the poor child should bear it!'

Rachel understood. She, too, heard such a cry within her as she listened to her father talking, sunk in memories of the past. As if to herself she said in a whisper:

'I don't know ... at times it seems to me that it's not Grandfather who's suffering from loss of memory, but we. All of us.'

About two weeks before the birth was due, Grandfather Zisskind appeared in Raya's and Yehuda's home for the second time. His face was yellow, angry, and the light had faded from his eyes. He greeted them, but did not favor Raya with so much as a glance, as if he had pronounced a ban upon the sinner. Turning to Yehuda he said, 'I wish to speak to you.'

They both went into the inner room. Grandfather sat down on the chair and placed the palm of his hand on the edge of the table, as was his wont, and Yehuda sat, lower than he, on the bed.

'Rachel has told me that you don't want to call the child by my grandchild's name', he said.

'Yes ...' said Yehuda diffidently.

'Perhaps you'll explain to me why?' he asked.

'We ...' stammered Yehuda, who found it difficult to face the piercing gaze of the old man. 'The name simply doesn't appeal to us.'

Grandfather was silent. Then he said, 'I understand that Mendele doesn't appeal to you. Not a Hebrew name. Granted! But Menachem – what's wrong with Menachem?' It was obvious that he was controlling his feelings with difficulty.

'It's not ...' Yehuda knew that there was no use explaining; they were two generations apart in their ideas. 'It's not an Israeli name ... it's from the *Golah*.'

'*Golah*', repeated Grandfather. He shook with rage, but somehow he maintained his self-control. Quietly he said, 'We all come from the *Golah*. I, and Raya's father and mother. All of us.'

'Yes ...' said Yehuda. He saw resentfully that he was being dragged into an argument that was distasteful to him, particularly with this old man whose mind was already not quite clear. Only out of respect did he restrain himself from ejaculating, 'That's that and it's done with! –'

'Yes, but we were born in this country. That's different.'
Grandfather Zisskind looked at him contemptuously. Before him he saw a wretched boor, an empty vessel.

'You, that is to say, think, there's something new here', he said, 'that everything that was there is past and gone. Dead. Without sequel. That you are starting *everything* anew.'

'I didn't say that. I only said that we were born in this country ...'

'You were born here. Very nice ...' said Grandfather Zisskind with rising emotion. 'So what of it? What's so remarkable about that? In what way are you superior to those who were born there? Are you cleverer than they are? More cultured? Are you greater than they in *Torah* or good deeds? Is your blood redder than theirs?' Grandfather Zisskind looked as if he would wring his neck.

'I didn't say that either. I said that *here* it's different ...'

Grandfather Zisskind's patience with idle words was exhausted.

'You good for nothing!' He burst out in his rage. 'What do you know about what was there? What do you know of the *people* that were there? The communities? The cities? What do you know of the *life* they had there?'

'Yes', said Yehuda, his spirit crushed, 'but we no longer have any ties with it.'

'You have no ties with it?' Grandfather Zisskind bent towards him. His lips quivered in fury, 'With what ... with what *do* you have ties?'

'We have ... with this country', said Yehuda and gave an involuntary smile.

'Fool!' Grandfather Zisskind shot at him. 'Do you think that people come to a desert and make themselves a nation, eh? That you are the first of some new race? That you're not the son of your father? Not the grandson of your grandfather? Do you want to forget them? Are you ashamed of them for having had a hundred times more culture and education than you have? Why ... why, everything here' – he included everything around in the sweep of his arm – 'is no more than a puddle of tapwater against the big sea that was there! What have you here? A mixed multitude! Seventy languages! Seventy distinct groups! Customs? A way of life? Why, every home here is a nation in itself, with its own customs and its own names! And with this you have ties, you say ...'

Yehuda lowered his eyes and was silent.

'I'll tell you what ties are', said Grandfather Zisskind calmly. 'Ties are remembrance! Do you understand? The Russian is linked to his people because he remembers his ancestors. He is called Ivan, his father was called Ivan and his grandfather was called Ivan, back to the first generation. And no Russian has said: From today onwards I shall not be called Ivan because my fathers and my fathers' fathers were called that; I am the first of a new Russian nation which has nothing at all to do with the Ivans. D'you understand?'

'But what has that got to do with it?' Yehuda protested impatiently. Grandfather Zisskind shook his head at him.

'And you – you're ashamed to give your son the name Mendele lest it remind you that there were Jews who were called by that name. You believe that his name should already be wiped off the face of the earth.

That not a trace of it should remain ...'

He paused, heaved a deep sigh and said:

'O children, children, you don't know what you're doing ... You're finishing off the work which the enemies of Israel began. They took the bodies away from the world, and you – the name and the memory ... No continuation, no evidence, no memorial and no name. Not a trace ...'

And with that he rose, took his cane and with long strides went towards the door and left.

The newborn child was a boy and he was named Ehud, and when he was about a month old, Raya and Yehuda took him in the perambulator to Grandfather's house.

Raya gave three cautious knocks on the door, and when she heard a rustle inside she could also hear the beating of her anxious heart. Since the birth of the child Grandfather had not visited them even once. 'I'm terribly excited', she whispered to Yehuda with tears in her eyes. Yehuda rocked the perambulator and did not reply. He had long been indifferent to what the old man might say or do.

The door opened, and on the threshold stood Grandfather Zisskind, his face weary and wrinkled. He seemed to have aged. His eyes were sticky with sleep, and for a moment it seemed as if he did not see the callers.

'*Shabbat Shalom*, Grandfather', said Raya, much moved. It seemed to her now that she loved him more than ever.

Grandfather looked at them as if surprised, and then said absently, 'Come in, come in.'

'We've brought the baby with us!' said Raya, her face shining, and her glance traveled from Grandfather to the infant sleeping in the perambulator.

'Come in, come in', repeated Grandfather Zisskind in a tired voice. 'Sit down', he said as he removed his clothes from the chairs and turned to tidy the disordered bedclothes.

Yehuda stood the perambulator by the wall and whispered to Raya, 'It's stifling for him here.' Raya opened the window wide.

'You haven't seen our baby yet, Grandfather!' she said with a sad smile.

'Sit down, sit down', said Grandfather, shuffling over to the shelf, from which he took the jar of preserves and the biscuit tin, putting them on the table.

'There's no need, Grandfather, really there's no need for it. We didn't come for that', said Raya.

'Only a little something. I have nothing to offer you today ...' said Grandfather in a dull, broken voice. He took the kettle off the kerosene cooker and poured out two glasses of tea that he placed before them. Then he too sat down, said, 'Drink, drink', and softly tapped his fingers on the table.

'I haven't seen Mother for several days now', he said at last.

'She's busy ...' said Raya in a low voice, without raising her eyes to him. 'She helps me a lot with the baby ...'

Grandfather Zisskind looked at his pale, knotted and veined hands lying helplessly on the table; then he stretched out one of them and said to Raya, 'Why don't you drink? The tea will get cold.'

Raya drew up to the table and sipped the tea.

'And you – what are you doing now?' he asked Yehuda.

'Working as usual', said Yehuda, and added with a laugh, 'I play with the baby when there's time.'

Grandfather again looked down at his hands, the long thin fingers of which shook with the palsy of old age.

'Take some of the preserves', he said to Yehuda, indicating the jar with a shaking finger. 'It's very good.'

Yehuda dipped the spoon in the jar and put it to his mouth.

Silence reigned. It seemed to last a very long time. It was hot in the room, and the buzzing of a fly could be heard.

Suddenly the baby burst out crying, and Raya started from her seat and hastened to quiet him. She rocked the perambulator and crooned,

'Quiet, child, quiet, quiet ...'

Even after he had quieted down she went on rocking the perambulator to and fro.

Grandfather Zisskind raised his head and said to Yehuda in a whisper: 'You think it was impossible to save him ... it was possible. They had many friends. Ossip himself wrote to me about it. The manager of the factory had a high opinion of him. The whole town knew them and loved them ... How is it they didn't think of it ...' he said, touching his forehead with the palm of his hand. 'After all, they knew that the Germans were approaching ... It was still possible to do something ...' He stopped a moment and then added, 'Imagine that a boy of eleven had already finished his studies at the Conservatory – wild beasts! To take little children and put them into wagons and deport them ...'

When Raya returned and sat down at the table, he stopped and became silent, and only a heavy sigh escaped from deep within him.

Again there was a prolonged silence, and as it grew heavier Raya felt the oppressive weight on her bosom increasing till it could no longer be contained. Grandfather sat at the table tapping his thin fingers, and alongside the wall the infant lay in his perambulator, and it was as if a chasm gaped between a world, which was passing, and a world that was born. It was no longer a single line to the fourth generation. The aged father did not recognize the great-grandchild who had not set up a memory for him.

Grandfather Zisskind got up, took his chair and pulled it up to the clock. He climbed on it to take out his documents.

Raya could no longer stand the oppressive atmosphere.

'Let's go', she said to Yehuda in a choked voice.

'Yes, we must go', said Yehuda, and rose from his seat. 'We have to go', he said loudly as he turned to the old man.

Grandfather Zisskind held the key of the clock for a moment more, then he let his hand fall, grasped the back of the chair and got down.

'You have to go ...' he said with tormented features. He spread his arms out helplessly and accompanied them to the doorway.

When the door had closed behind them the tears flowed from Raya's eyes. She bent over the perambulator and pressed her lips to the baby's chest. At that moment it seemed to her that he was in need of pity and of great love, as though he were alone; an orphan in the world.

Aharon Megged, 'The Name', *Midstream*, Spring (1960), pp.61–71, and in *Israel Argosy* 6, edited by Isaac Halevy-Levin, (New York: Thomas Yoseloff, 1959). Translated by Minna Givton. Reproduced by kind permission of the author, Aharon Megged. Also appreciated is the cooperation and assistance of Julien Yoseloff and *Midstream*.

NOTES

Aharon Megged was born in Wroclawek, Poland, in 1920 and came to pre-state Israel when he was 6. He lived on a kibbutz for many years, working in agriculture and fishing. Later, he became a journalist and literary editor, served as a cultural attaché in London, and was writer-in-residence at Oxford and Haifa Universities. He served as president of the Israeli branch of PEN from 1980 to 1987, and has been a member of the Academy of the Hebrew Language since 1980. Megged has published over 40 books.

Among his many literary awards: the Bialik Prize (1973), the Brenner Prize, the ACUM Prize (1990), the Newman Prize (1991), the Agnon Prize (1996), the WIZO Prize (France, 1998), the President's Prize (2001), the Israel Prize for Literature (2003), the Koret Jewish Book Award (USA, 2004), and the Prime Minister's Prize three times, most recently in 2007. He has also been awarded an Honorary Doctorate by Bar-Ilan University (2008).

The Polish Wife

ANNA CWIAKOWSKA

A Short Story

The events described in 'The Polish Wife' take place in 1967 and the following years. It was a time of struggle for power within the ruling Communist Party and its government in Poland, while, at the same time, students, supported by some intellectuals, openly demonstrated against the communist dictatorship.

Israel's conclusive victory over her Arab neighbours who were supported by the Soviet Union in the 1967 Six Day War marked the beginning of a campaign of incitement and persecution, ostensibly against Israel and Zionism, but in fact directed against the remnants of the Jews in Poland. Due to economic pressures, and an atmosphere of slander and vilification, many Jews left their Polish homeland. This hostile environment caused many personal tragedies and was the hour of testing the moral and human values of many mixed Jewish-Polish families.

'What the devil for did I need this Jew?' she screamed, and immediately, with her own hand thwacked her mouth. Spontaneously. This was her habit of punishing herself for uttered stupidities. Her mother taught her that.

When she was a little girl, and happened to say an ugly word, her mother used to wash out her mouth with stinging soap – a penalty for offending Jesus Christ. At dusk, she knelt longer than usually by her bed, under the picture of the Madonna with Child, and begged their pardon for the foolish four letters, thrown in sheer contrariness at the elderly housemaid.

And later, while a marriageable girl, and her mother could do no more than glance with reproof, whenever she spoke other than as was expected of a girl from an intelligent home, she herself, instantly, clapped her hand to her mouth, 'discreetly' but sufficiently for her mother to notice, and acknowledge with a smile of satisfaction.

Times had changed, but little had changed in her family's home. Poland was ruled by communists, but in her circles, in old Cracow, there was an endeavour to preserve old, time-honoured customs.

Father was an expert in his trade, and the communists did not remove him from his pre-war position. What is more: he enjoyed the privilege of special foods allotments. Hungry she was not. Neither did she suffer from the lack of such products as cigarettes or black coffee, never having had the time to sample them. She was hurt, in truth, by the loss of the fur coat, which her mother traded for coal the first winter after liberation, but her parents bought her an inexpensive, pretty fur jacket.

Her golden hair cascading in long curls upon the grey fur, as was the post-war fashion, and she put a bunch of violets in her lapel.

Refreshing, early spring air blew over her, as she stepped into the street. She was as early spring herself, golden and rosy, shapely, fresh, smiling at life.

This was how Tadeusz saw her.

They made contact suddenly. He crossed her way inadvertently, deep in his thoughts. He almost passed her by, murmuring 'pardon me', raising his head, and … was transfixed. Enchanted.

He stood before her like a pillar, barring the way. She stood still. She had never seen a boy as handsome as he was.

She was not naive, she had kissed boys breathless, but she preserved her virginity partly due to her Catholic faith, partly to fear, and partly due to lack of real sexual excitement. Now something strange, a feeling she had never experienced before came over her body. She became hot, and immediately after shuddered. And he stood as if unconscious, motionless, his eyes fixed on her in rapture.

A madman! A thought crossed her mind. Escape!

Moving suddenly, her purse fell from her hand. She bent swiftly, but he was quicker. Their heads collided. And they burst laughing, as if on order. With a loud, healthy, young laughter, full of joy. Now they were happy. They came to their senses.

'Tadeusz Lipowski!' he clicked his heels, saluting.

'Janina Wilczynska', she extended her hand with the elegance of heroines of cinematic romances. He kissed it warmly.

'I beg your pardon', he was embarrassed, 'I have never behaved like that. It is simply … you are so lovely …'

'Nothing has happened to me', she tried to encourage him. 'Are you in the army?' she inferred from his uniform; four stars … aha, officer … 'Captain?'

'Still in the army, but on my way to become a civilian. I am going to ...'

'I won't keep you – you are probably in a hurry', she lied as best she could, praying silently that he not hurry.

'No, no, please detain me. I have muuuuch time to spare', he spread his hands wide, showing how much time he had. 'My affairs I can settle tomorrow. Are you in a hurry?'

'No. Not at all!' She made a decision, fearing he might change his mind. 'I also have muuuuch time', she mimicked his voice, and they laughed again.

'What now? Pastries?'

She hesitated. She feared her colleagues, her mother's friends. They will report it. 'No, better not. Perhaps we can sit in the park?'

They sat for several hours. They talked about everything and nothing, and after analyzing in detail the situation of the world – avoiding, each for different reasons, the situation in their land – after having recited some classical poems, remembered from their school days, after laughing at their pre-war teachers, and having no common subject, they fell silent. He feared she might get up and leave. She was afraid he might click his heels again and depart. To avert that, she carefully put her hand on the park bench between them, and he delicately took it in his large, warm hand. It is hard to say what had happened that day in Cracow. Everything, however, points to Cupid's flying above the town, and his arrow piercing two young hearts. This is how the complex story began. They set a date for the next day, and the next.

After two weeks her parents became suspicious. Their daughter disappeared daily for long hours. Where did she go? With whom did she spend her time?

They spent their time walking, or in secluded little cafes; she was no longer afraid of gossip, she wanted to be with him alone. They fell in love with one another. Each found their first great love; such as happens once in a lifetime, and to most people does not happen at all.

They were aware of it and knew their relationship needed to be given a more lasting form. She decided to introduce him to her parents. He decided to fight for her. On the basis of what was known to him, he was conscious of the difficulties awaiting him. For the role he was to play he did not lack too much. He asked a colleague sharing a room allotted to him by the quartermaster to initiate him into the customs of good, Catholic homes with which he was still unfamiliar. His concern, mainly, was the wedding ceremony. How a bridegroom ought to behave, how to ask the father for the hand of his daughter, what does a prospective bridegroom do during the season of engagement, etc.? He already knew that in her home, these things were meaningful.

She maintained that it would be best to elope, that she would follow him to the edge of the world, but best of all – to the Regained Territories.[1] There they would build a home, raise a family, she would bear him children, and they would be together, till death parted them, in a hundred years.

Not much older than she was, his life experience not equalling that of Methuselah, he did not want to do her harm.

He will take her away, but with her parents' consent, after the wedding.

He was still a soldier, on his 'day out' – joked his commander, a colonel with an equally botanical, pretty name: Adam Kwiatkowski. The captain, Tadeusz, confided in him, that he would probably not escape a church wedding. The colonel thought for a long while, advising not to rush the wedding, but to wait until he was a civilian, and to hold the wedding not in town itself, but rather in one of the little towns, in the vicinity. Because as a civilian, a great career awaited him. The Party officials had in mind a high managerial position for him, in industry. After all, he had completed two years of studies at the Polytechnic Institute in Lvov, during the times of the Soviets. In his new place he would work and enlist as an external student, to obtain the diploma of an engineer. If needed, he might receive a several months' long, paid furlough for his studies. Completing his studies was a condition for the high post, which included the allotment of a beautiful villa, a service automobile and other privileges.

'For such a pauper as you are, this is paradise! You will be the King of Life!' said Adam Kwiatkowski, and as a true son of Lvov, pronounced:

'Brother, with such a future, when you come to your father-in-law, he will himself put his little daughter in your bed, ta-yoy!' – he laughed and winked knowingly at Tadeusz, who understood perfectly. They never discussed it, but a twinkle of an eye, a slight gesture were sufficient for them both to understand.

And so it happened. Daddy Wilczynski, even though not given to putting his daughter into masculine beds, not even Tadeusz's, found his pride in his daughter awakened by the mirage of his future son-in-law's career, and because she had found for herself, not a trifler or playboy, but a real man, with 'life ambitions', as he elucidated to his spouse, in the bedroom, where no one could hear them.

Pani (Mrs) Wilczynska, in turn, succeeded in discovering a noble descent for her future son-in-law.

'Are you of the Lipowskis from the Grodno district?" she half-inquired, half-put the words in his mouth. He understood.

'Yes, indeed, from Milkowszczyzna, we are even related by marriage to the Pawlowskis, the family of Orzeszkowa, but my parents moved into town, my father was a physician and had no future in the country.'

That was true about his father, but the rest of the family genealogy he took from the life-history of Eliza Orzeszkowa, whose books he had always valued and read. To prove his familiarity with facts, he brought up a story, heard in the army from a sergeant from Grodno, handed down to him by his grandfather, how the Grodnians spread and padded with straw the uneven pavement, to soften the road over which the ill Eliza Orzeszkowa was to travel to a doctor in Grodno. Such authentic tales convinced mother Wilczynska that she was not mistaken in regarding her son-in-law as a good, truly Polish boy, who out of necessity joined the Bolsheviks. Tadeusz was, in fact, Polish. He was so very Polish, that no one ever thought it could be otherwise. In an officer's uniform he was dazzling. Splendidly built, light blond with green eyes and a rosy complexion.

'A cavalry type!' decided all the ladies of Mummy Wilczynska's circle.

'How did she succeed to catch such a boy?' wondered her openly hostile girl friends.

Older gentlemen blissfully passed time with him, albeit noticing he was a bit too prone to drinking and brawling.

'Typical Polish faults', they reassured themselves.

Tadeusz soon became a civilian, but did not take off his uniform, and the wedding drew near. It was necessary to hurry, for Janka (Janina) grew somehow dangerously rounded.

'My son', said the older gentleman one day, 'you must take off your uniform. It is also necessary to notify your parents. Let them come, we would like to get to know them.'

Tadeusz was shocked. This he did not expect. The uniform he did not discard, since it was so becoming, and all the girls followed with their eyes an officer so handsome. Well, is there a man whom this would not impress? In truth, he did not possess a civilian suit, and had no idea how to obtain one, but Adek ... Citizen Colonel Kwiatkowski will loan him money for a suit. Whereas the issue of notifying his parents terrified him. He said he would write to them.

He had no courage to reveal to the colonel the quandary that entangled him. He did not sleep a wink.

'Why are you so excited!' laughed a colleague from the bed next to him. 'Are you in a hurry? Soon you will have her whenever you want to! Sleep, you hen-pecked man!'

At night Tadeusz thought about a way out. The following day he stood before his father-in-law for a serious talk, in private. He confessed that out of fear he did not reveal the truth about his parents, namely, that his parents were exiled by the Russians in 1940. He escaped by being in Lvov at the time. He was absent from home. He searched for them for many years, while serving in the army, through the Society of Polish Patriots, wrote even to Wanda Wasilewska, but had received no answer. They have probably perished in Soviet gulags. Pan (Mr) Wilczynski hugged him, in tears: the next day he conducted Tad to the best tailor in town, ordering him to take measurement for two suits for his son-in-law: one dark, for the wedding, and the other of a practical hue, for every day.

The older gentleman would hear of no money from Tadeusz. He understood perfectly that the wedding ought to be small. He selected a lovely little mountaineer church near Zakopane. Only the immediate family was to be present.

Mama Wilczynska experienced the deepest disappointment, but compensated for it by secretly spreading the information about her in-laws' tragic fate, the Count and Countess Lipowski, as she referred to them, and all the ladies viewed the young couple with even greater sympathy.

After the wedding Tadeusz moved into his in-law's home, and soon departed for a great metropolis in the Regained Territories,[1] where he was to assume the promised high position in industry.

In their villa they have found everything needed for comfort for a man in a high position. Even a German maid. Nothing had been looted, for it had been occupied by a high-ranking Russian officer, who, upon leaving, took with him only a few valuable paintings, a stamp collection left in a hurry by the villa's owner, the most expensive liquors from the cellar, and something from the wall safe, but even the maid knew not what.

What remained was lovely, sculpted furniture, porcelain service sets, all household utensils, carpets, even window drapes. The garden was vast and wild. With time, they found a gardener from the Vilno district, who, with real talent, brought the terrain to order.

'Tadziu, what do we lack? Nothing!' Janka was radiant.

'The King of Life!' Tadeusz smiled at the memory of colonel Kwiatkowski. For the present, the King of Life worked like a horse, ten to twelve hours a day. He studied at night. He slept little, was very tired and full of guilt for having so little time for his wife who had followed him 'to the edge of the world'.

Janka rarely felt lonely, being busy arranging her house her own way, following the progress of her husband's career, experiencing the indispositions of a first pregnancy, then childbirth. Mother visited her often, as did her father.

With time she met other women from the neighbourhood villas, and a social life developed. Time passed. They had two children, a son and a daughter. Tadeusz completed his studies, became an engineer, and a director of great works. In the course of years he was valued as a specialist in his field, and seriously considered a doctorate.

I believe he is happy, thought Janka, but she was not too certain She was very happy. His irritation and outbursts of anger she attributed to overwork, and, mainly, to Party duties. Well, nothing in life came free. Besides advancing up the ladder of his career, Lipowski had Party obligations. He was a member of the PPR, then PZPR, and therefore belonged to various committees and commissions of the (Communist) Party, which were always deliberating, sometimes for entire nights.

'What do you do there, all those hours?' wondered Janka.

'They finish off good people, damn them!' Tadek shouted back.

Janka felt he was slipping out of her hands. He had always liked to drink, but now he drank addictively. He frequently returned home drunk, screaming, cursing, falling into bed soiled. In the morning he left home stealthily, not to be seen, and by noon enormous bouquets arrived from the flower shop.

As long as the children had been home, such things did not happen. But now they were not here: their daughter studied in Cracow, living at her grandparents. The son studied in Warsaw, living in a student hostel. Tadeusz drank more and more. She tried to talk to him. He had lost all his spirit, joy of life and strength, previously emanating from him, and which had so positively affected his environment.

The atmosphere at home was sad and hopeless. What had happened to her boy? She wanted to help him, but knew not how.

She decided to tear through these dark affairs, poisoning his life. She searched through his desk to find a trace; perhaps he was being blackmailed. After all, she had always suspected that the story about the Counts from Grodno was not exactly true. It was of no concern to her, she thought, if Tadeusz emancipated himself from some poor, village family. Perhaps his troubles now were connected with that? She found nothing in his desk.

Her eyes wandered, scanning the book spines in the book case. She noticed a few titles, not there before. All about the annihilation of the Jews. Auschwitz. She browsed through the pages, and horrified, inspected the photographs. Putting the book away, something fell out. An envelope. The sender was someone named Zvili, from Tel Aviv, addressed to someone named Aharon, residing in their city, but no street address. She put the strange letter away into its place, forgetting it completely. Particularly, since the home situation had improved. Tadeusz has stopped drinking. Instead, he spent entire nights in front of television. Suddenly, he had plenty of time. He attended Party meetings no longer.

One day he came home early, saying he had secured a furlough. And again, he sat till late at night in front of the television set. This foretold nothing happy. Janka felt an approaching threat. Again, there was talk about the Jews, and this presaged no good. She remembered the German occupation. She trembled. The neighbouring villa had no new occupants as yet. A few days ago she tearfully said goodbye to a Jewish family, emigrating from Poland.

Janka was not a bad person. She was hurt by what was being done to people. And ashamed. She cared not about the battles 'upstairs', Gomulka or Moczar² – they were all the same to her, but why does each one of them attack exactly the handful of Polish Jews? 'Boors!' she commented, consoling herself that this too would pass, and their life would peacefully continue.

One night, after the daily television news, as usual at that time, there was an anti-Jewish broadcast.

This time, it was about the Jews being murderers, that in the concentration camps Jews murdered Poles, that the Jews had murderous instincts. And the like.

Janka felt sick. Tadeusz sat quietly, but she saw his white-knuckled, clenched fists. Suddenly, he started up. He furiously kicked the television set, shouting:

'The Jews are murderers, Whaaaat?! Jews murdered Poles, whaaaat?! My sister was murdered by a Pole, *oberkapo* in Auschwitz, Stenia Starostka from Cracow! From your Cracow! But about Stenia no one talks in Poland!' He turned to her, his face white as chalk.

And he burst into tears. For the first time. He had never wept before. Never. He let her guide him to the bedroom. He sobbed for a long time. When he calmed down, she tried to give him a glass of cognac.

'No, give me a glass of water', he asked, and continued: 'Jasiu,³ how do you feel?'

'Everything is fine. I am with you. I love you.'

'Good, Jasiu,³ then listen, my dearest woman. We have to separate. You will remain here, at home, you will have my pension, your parents will help you a little, you will take one or two boarders, you will manage. Or you will sell it all, and buy yourself a small apartment in Cracow, where it may be easier for you. The children will manage, they are grown. I have to confess to you, but no one beside you will know it. Neither will the children – we should not hinder their lives.'

He got up, sitting by the small table. He took her hand.

'Jasiu, I am not Tadeusz Lipowski. I am Arele *meshumet*.

'A-rele?' she accented it wrongly. 'What does that mean? Arthur?'

'No. Aron. Arele is a diminutive form of Aron, and the word *meshumet* means a convert.'

'Oh, so', she breathed easier, 'your parents have converted?'

'No. My parents perished in Lvov, in the Janowska camp. My sister was killed with a whip by Stenia Starostka in Auschwitz. I heard it from an eyewitness. I searched for this Stenia, to repay her, but was told the Russians took care of her. All my relatives perished, murdered by Hitler's men. My name is Aron Lindenbaum. Linde means lipa, a lime-tree. Baum means a tree. From that they invented for me, in the army, the name Lipowski. The first name I selected_myself. And at home they called me *meshumet*, because I clung to everything Polish. I ran away from the *heder*, the Jewish school, chasing the pigeons with Polish boys. At school I was best in Polish, and no one, anyway, believed I was a Jew, because I looked so very Polish. This, my father laughed, was a family trait, saying that one of our great-grandmothers unkosherly betrayed our great-grandfather – a reason for such Polish types in the family.'

'Why did you not tell me this at the beginning of our *acquaintance?*'

'I was afraid you would not marry me ...'

'I would have married you. Another Jew – I don't know ... May be you did right ... And that letter? From Tel-Aviv?' she suddenly remembered.

'You found it.' He wasn't even surprised. 'Imagine, one of my cousins had survived, the only one. From the entire clan of the Lindenbaums. I became Lipowski in Poland – I have Polonized my name, and he is in Israel. Zvili is the Hebrew version of our name ... That letter had travelled a long way. It passed many hands, until it reached me. I could have told you all this, but now, in this situation, I wanted to spare you. Well, you know everything now. What remains to be said is only this: I was thrown out of the Party. They said I was a

Zionist. I have resigned from my job, rather than wait to be carried
out. Jasiu, a few weeks ago I have reached a decision: I am going to
Israel. You will stay here and continue to live normally. We will invent
a pretext to explain my absence.'

'Well', he sighed, 'Aronek's golden dream has come to an end. The
King of Life ...' he laughed briefly. 'Dearest, pack a bag for me.
Tomorrow I will go to Warsaw. The Dutch Embassy takes care of the
immigration to Israel.' He kissed her and for a long while held her in his
embrace.

She remained still, letting him rock her in his arms. Not everything
she had heard reached her. She needed to absorb it in her thoughts.
And suddenly she wrenched herself free. She took his face in both her
hands. She laughed.

'Tadzinku, you must be mocking me? You go nowhere by yourself!
We go to Warsaw together! And together to Israel, or anywhere you
wish! With you to the edge of the world, remember? Our fates are
bound together. What did you imagine?' she raised her voice, 'You
want to abandon me in my old age?! I will not hand my boy to
another woman, put it out of your head!' She pretended to laugh, a
flood of tears streaming down her cheeks.

Everything was settled very fast. Everywhere, in every office, they
seemed to be expected. It was all arranged on the spot. For Tadeusz all
went smoothly. But Janka had one very unpleasant conversation in the
police headquarters. She was summoned suddenly. Tadeusz accompanied her, but decided to wait on the other side of the street. He did not
wait long. She came out in less than an hour, very disturbed. She said
nothing, and he didn't ask.

Only in the evening did she relate that the police officer who
received her with extraordinary courtesy, attempted to persuade her to
leave her husband.

'The Jew will go to his own, and you, a beautiful Pole, will remain
in the land ...' When she replied sharply, he threatened her with
sanctions and blackmail, that the authorities will use this against her
children, as they know everything. And this. And that. He screamed,
pounded the table with his fist, until she stood up, and with the
words: 'Kiss my butt!' left. And wonder! Nothing happened, no one
followed her.

Then there were further complications with relinquishing their
Polish citizenship. That surprise was hidden until the very end,
following the liquidation of all their property, the return of their home
to the housing authorities, even paying for a cracked windowpane in

the kitchen. This the clerk must have pocketed himself – something more to extort from the Jew ...

In the government offices Tadeusz was the first in line for the, so-called, 'Document of Travel', which entitled its holder to leave Poland 'to all countries of the world', and which stated that its owner was not a Polish citizen. But the document itself they had not seen as yet. Later, Janka would declare that she would donate Tadeusz's document to the museum of national shame. Meanwhile, another document was slipped before him to sign. He glanced at it. 'I will not sign it!' he exclaimed.

A door opened. He was invited to enter. Janka followed him. Two pleasant young women clarified that this was no fault of their own. They were very sorry, but were no more than clerks. And that almost every emigrant reacted similarly to that slip of paper. It was a declaration about renouncing, of one's own free will, Polish citizenship. Unless Mr Engineer Lipowski signed it, he would not receive a Document of Travel.

'Sign it', insisted Janka. 'It has no meaning. They did not bestow your Polish citizenship upon you, and they have no right to withhold it. In Poland you were born, and so were your ancestors. You have shed blood, fighting for Poland, were wounded twice. Sign, Tadeusz, this Poland is not worth living in, under such a government!'

She was inflamed. He looked, not recognizing her. He signed, and received that wretched document. She received another, with the right to return.

The children remained in Poland. This was their decision. Together with their grandparents, they accompanied their parents to the Viennese train.

Israel stunned them. Different, strange, unfamiliar. More Eastern, less European.

A mixture of scenery, human types, costumes, smells, colours of skin, languages, customs, faiths ... Janka's head was reeling. She did not know what was happening to her, or why.

From a life of comfort and relative affluence, from a villa in a shady garden, she entered a vibrant, pushing, jostling, hot hubbub. Yellow, blinding sun, a turmoil of sound, sticky, eye-blinding sweat ... Physically, she was incapable of thought. Not even about the nearest future. Tadeusz, not less stricken by all this 'otherness', was unable to assist her. He was totally helpless. With difficulty, he tried to remember some single words in Yiddish, never used, since his parents spoke Polish with their children. They both, however, knew English, and that proved to be very helpful.

From the airport they were driven to the nice, clean city of Ashdod, to a so-called *Ulpan*. In a large building they were assigned a small apartment, equipped with some indispensable furniture. They received their food, and were required to attend lessons in the Hebrew language.

In the beginning, they tried very hard, but Tadeusz, try as he might, couldn't assimilate these foreign sounding words. Janka learned fast and well. After less than three months, she was able to communicate. Tadeusz, concluding he could not keep pace with Hebrew, began to look for work, returning from these expeditions broken, feeling older than he was, a different man than the one with whom she had spent a great part of her life.

'No one needs me here', he said. 'Forty-five years old! I am too old for them. My knowledge and experience are not needed here. This is not the land of Jews, but of Hebrews. Here, they connect with the biblical tradition. Jews arriving from other lands are merely tolerated, considered 'losers', while the locals consider themselves heroes, and have nothing but contempt for us ...'

One day, following a visit to a potential employer, Tadeusz related he was treated in a particularly arrogant manner, was told that an engineer from Poland was not an engineer, that here Western knowledge was required, and that Poland was technologically backward. He was offered a position ... cleaning the factory hall.

What could she tell him? She was in despair. She did not think about her own fate. She looked at him: intelligent, educated, in his prime, an excellent specialist in his profession.

No, she would not permit him to perish! She must act. Carefully, she questioned him about his childhood friends, his colleagues from the army and the post-war years.

'I shall not beg!' Tadeusz wanted to see no one, too embarrassed to be seen needing help. But Janka had already gathered some information. Secretly, she notified several of his friends, residing in Israel for many years. One of them came, complaining loudly for Tadek's benefit about the difficulty of obtaining their address. Somebody told him Tadek was in Israel! He brought another and another. This way, work was found for Tadeusz in one of their factories. Somewhat close to his specialty, but requiring some additional training. Here he was more capable than in learning Hebrew. The income was not high, but was there. He breathed easier, for he now acquired medical insurance. He feared illness, not his own, but if Janka took ill, and he were unable to help her ... he was obsessed with that. Later, he laughed about it. This was one of his Israeli secrets he revealed to no one.

Janka found work as well, to suit her exactly. As a companion to walk, talk and read aloud to an old lady, wealthy enough to pay. The elderly woman had been born and brought up in old Polish schools, and was happy to find a suitable companion, such as Pani (Mrs) Janina.

'Pani Engineer Lipowska', she introduced her to her friends. Janka was amused, but she had already had time to get used to the snobbery of the Jewish women from Poland in Israel. She remembered, besides, her own mother's stories, in Cracow, about the 'Counts Lipowskis'. Common, human weaknesses ...

Once they obtained an apartment on accessible terms, they frequently entertained. There lived, in the vicinity, quite a few Jews from Poland, emigrants of both *aliot*, of Gomulka, in 1956/7, and the last one, of Moczar, in 1968/9. *Aliyah*, or 'going up' in Hebrew, was a reference, with honour, to immigration to Israel.

Tadeusz listened quietly to these elucidations, appreciating the religious, historical and political sense of this privilege, but thinking that for him, personally, the way led down, rather than up: from the heights of esteem – to slight, from creative work – to mechanical function, from a feeling of participation in a common enterprise of building – to a feeling of helplessness.

Such and similar discussions were carried on in the circle of the 'thrown overboard' as the recent emigrants from Poland called themselves. They still felt the need to be engaged, being used to an active life. After meeting the most pressing needs, such as apartment, some furniture, some income-generating employment, they looked around and came to a sad conclusion: they have nothing to do here. Nobody needed them. From originators they became consumers. They eagerly read newspapers, Polish, Hebrew – if anyone knew the language, English, Russian. They listened to radio news. And commented. Slowly, they became Israelis, active citizens, interested in the country's life and events, hurting with bad news, and proud of good tidings.

In their own circles, they criticized almost everything in Israel. While travelling abroad, they did not permit a bad word to be said about Israel, even when their opponents were right. This local patriotism was seemingly subconscious, a kind of solidarity with the land that had accepted them, ideological shipwrecks, with difficulties, but without political reckoning, at a time when no one, anywhere, showed compassion. For, after all, they themselves chose to stay in Poland, and 'throw in their lot with communism'.

Some of them were proud of their past, for 'whoever, in his idealistic youth was not a communist or a socialist, in his old age would not even be a pig' – they repeatedly quoted this sentence by one of the Polish writers. Others preferred silence. They made no calculations. Tadeusz believed these matters needed to be debated no further.

'This', he said, 'is similar to a tragedy of disappointed love. A man loves a woman with all his heart, but she doesn't want him. Is this to be discussed with anyone? No.'

His love, however, did not disappoint him. What disappointed him was the Communist Party which recruited him in his youth, while serving in the army. Like most people his age, he had no traditions of Party life. And his great love was with him. He loved her even more than at the beginning. She was, now, also his most faithful friend. They were good with each other, and their lives assumed some pattern and order. They missed their parents and their children, but were in frequent contact by telephone.

When *Solidarity* exploded in Poland, old interests were revived. A club was established in Haifa, in solidarity with Polish *Solidarity*.

From Denmark someone brought posters with pictures of Walesa,[4] they purchased Hebrew pamphlets about *Solidarnosc* to raise funds for the cause.

The situation in Poland resembled a civil war against the government. Letters were censored. And precisely then, disaster struck. Janka's mother, in Cracow, became ill. 'Come immediately! Mother wants to see you!' wrote her father and daughter, alarmingly.

Frantically searching for information, they learned they must apply through the Viennese embassy, since Poland had severed diplomatic relations with Israel in 1967, and there was no Polish representative. Janka wrote to Vienna for a visa to Poland, enclosing a hospital report regarding her mother's condition. After purchasing presents and packing her suitcase, she was ready to fly as soon as the visa from Vienna arrived.

An answer from Vienna was received. A shocking denial, with a note, that permission for a trip to Poland would be issued after her mother's death. For the funeral. With the embassy's letter in hand, Janka fell to the floor, unconscious.

A few days later her mother passed away. This time Janka received a permit for a three-day visit to Poland. She did not stay even for three days. Immediately after the funeral she took the train to Vienna, and from there a plane to Israel.

While in Cracow, they had discussed the future. Her daughter wished to come to Israel. Her son would stay with his grandfather, completing his studies. Then, they would see …

At the airport Janka wrenched herself free of Tadeusz's arms, ran to the nearest building and kissed the wall.

Tadeusz, alarmed, opened a bottle of mineral water, giving her a drink. Probably the *hamsin*, the hot desert wind had caused her erratic behaviour – the collision of the cold of the airport building with the hot air outside ...

No, she had no troubles. She was happy not to be there, even though she was not at all happy to be here.

The arrival of her daughter brought new life to their home. The girl's reaction to Israel was so different from their own, they were astounded. Ilonka was enchanted with everything. To her this was exotic, and she immersed herself in this great adventure. Of course, she had a home, support, while they had to start literally from zero, and carry the burden of years past.

From Ilona she swiftly became Ilana, a very popular feminine name in Israel. She completed her studies at the Tel-Aviv University, and there found a boyfriend. She was not less beautiful than her mother at her age, and the boy was deeply in love. But he was not to her father's liking.

'Romanian!' he snorted. 'She has found herself something, indeed!'

'Tadek', his wife said gently, 'he is as Jewish as those from Poland.'

'Oh, what do you know', he waved his hand, 'a Romanian is a Romanian!'

The young couple decided to get married, and since in Israel such things were arranged by the Rabbinate, they proceeded to the Rabbinate. There they were informed there would be no wedding. For Ilana was not a Jewess. She had a Catholic mother, and is, therefore, a Catholic, and the Rabbinate would not marry a Jew to a Catholic!

The boy asked: 'And if her mother converts to Judaism?'

'Then we can talk ....' With this news they came home. That night Tadeusz suffered a heart attack. Both mother and daughter were at his bedside, in the hospital. Upon his return home, Janina made a firm decision: 'I will convert to Judaism! I will do it for my child. After all, I have not been a practising Catholic for years. We will treat it as a formality. As a new Christening.' She already knew it would be necessary to immerse herself completely in a ritual bath, and before that, a long course of studies on the basics of Judaism awaited her. She had made her decision.

'Over my dead body!' said Tadeusz. And that was the end. His daughter would not speak with him. The boy visited daily, scowling at him. Finally, they broke up, the boy's parents sending him to New York, to practise his profession, and to forget.

Janka wept in corners. The girl suffered a depression. She would not accept a good position, when offered, and spent her time at home, dully gazing at the wall. A few weeks later she volunteered as a teacher in a remote desert community in the Negev.

Tadeusz insisted his wife attend church services on Sundays. Almost in defiance, he accompanied her to a small Polish church in Jaffa. In the church, a Polish priest from an Orthodox Jewish family solicitously looked after his little flock of faithful, while enthusiastically leading tourist groups around Israel.

In a Haifa monastery there lived a famous monk, a Catholic activist, who had been a Jewish partisan during the German occupation of Poland.

'My God, what are you doing with people?' wondered Janka, meaning Jews as priests, as well as her own existence, so strangely out of place, and yet persisting here.

At the start she suffered, disliking local Jews, particularly Jewish women from Poland, arrogant and conceited. The women from oriental lands were foreign to her, and she was fearful.

Her views changed during the local wars. She lived through three: the Yom Kippur War, the Lebanese War, and the Gulf War – the strangest of all wars.

She observed with admiration and wonder the unimaginable discipline of this eternally quarrelsome community, the national solidarity, sacrifice and mutual aid. She knew the joke that Israel will never suffer hunger, for a Jew will eat a Jew. In times of war she beheld a different nation, changed, as if by a magician's wand. And as soon as the wars ended – again squabbles, quarrels, malevolence.

The storm subsided, the land grew calm, and so did their life. It was possible to think about bringing from Cracow the elderly gentleman, her father. The son, after a brief arrest for 'illegal' work for 'Solidarity', soon escaped Poland. To Australia. Not Israel.

Two years later the would-be Romanian bridegroom returned. He found Ilonka, and convinced her. One day they appeared at home, announcing they would go to Cyprus for a civil wedding, arranged by a lawyer and somewhat costly, but the boy brought some dollars with him from the USA.

On a spring evening Tadeusz and Janina Lipowski returned to the airport in Lod. They awaited the older Mr Wilczynski, who was to stay permanently with them.

'Well, Jasiu, we are approaching our goal', Tadeusz nodded his head, when settled in the airport hall. 'A couple of retirees. What happened to me in Poland was unfortunate. A pity', Tadeusz very calmly recalled. 'I still had so much to give. I could have had a richer life. But they didn't want me. And they didn't want me here either.'

'Tadziu, we have everything we need for life ...'

'Is that all? Food and a roof over your head? And where was real life, the feeling of being alive? Did we truly enter the current of this land? We came too late, yes, too late ... Ours was life at the margins ... A pity ...' he sighed heavily.

She tried to say something, began to frame some words about every age having its good and bad sides, that a man must search for a point of light in the dark and in a grey reality. She did not know how to express it ... She opened her mouth to speak, but before she managed to utter a word, Ilonka and her husband stood before them. A sunny, lovely young pair, radiating joy. The girl held an enormous bouquet of flowers, to greet her grandfather.

'Salute, dear fossils!' she greeted her father and mother. 'Did you hear the announcement? The airplane from Warsaw is landing!'

Anna Cwiakowska, *Zony* (Lodz, Poland: Officyna Bibliofilow, 1998). Reproduced by kind permission of the author, Anna Cwiakowska and by Marek Szukalak, publisher. Translated from the Polish by Hava Bromberg Ben-Zvi.

NOTES

Anna Cwiakowska, born in Poland, is a survivor of the Holocaust and of imprisonment in a concentration camp. Following liberation she worked for the Polish radio and television as a publicist, reporter and author of programmes in the areas of literature and the theatre. Living in Israel since 1968, she is a translator and the author of *Zabawy w Chowanego* (Games of Hide and Seek) (1966, 1977); Moje *Credo-Ksiazka o Ben-Towie* (My Confession of Faith – A Book about Ben-Tow) (1997); *Zony I inne opowiadania* (Wives and Other Stories) (1998); *Na Krawedzi Snu* (At the Edge of a Dream) (2001) a translation from the Yiddish of Cwi Ajzenman's poetic prose; *Nieobecni* (The Absent) (2004), a novel, and *Natan Gross* (2006) interviews and critical essays. Ms. Cwiakowska is a contributor to *Nowiny-Kurier* (News-Courier) and *Kontury* (Outlines), Polish language literary magazines, published in Israel. 'The Polish Wife' is one of seven stories in *Zony* (1998), focusing on unusual unions and featuring women as their heroines.

1. Regained Territories: A portion of German territories ceded to Poland after the

Second World War, in exchange for parts of Eastern Poland annexed by the Soviet Union.
2. Gomulka and Moczar, Polish Communist Party leaders.
3. Jasiu: A diminutive form for Janina or Janka, when addressing her directly.
4. Walesa, the leader of *Solidarnosc*.

Glossary

Ab see *Av*.

Action/*Aktion* (German): A roundup of Jews, usually for deportation to death camps or for annihilation by other means.

Aliya (Hebrew): Going up. A term of honour to denote immigration into the land of Israel as well as going up to recite the blessings over the Torah in a synagogue.

Altrohstoffverfassung (German): A compound word, meaning a place of disposition of fabric, cloth, and other raw materials.

Almemar: A raised place (platform) in the synagogue, where the pulpit and the desk containing the Torah is placed, to be read.

Arbeitsamt (German): Labour Exchange. A government office handling matters of employment.

Atonement, Day of: The most solemn day of the Jewish year, the tenth day of the month of Tishri, a day of fasting and introspection, spent in prayer for forgiveness of sins committed against God and man.

Aussiedlung (German): Literally transfer of populations. In Nazi vocabulary, deportation to death or concentration camps.

Av (Hebrew): The fifth month of the Jewish religious year and eleventh of the civil year.

Avenue of the Righteous Among the Nations of the World: An avenue of trees planted in honour of each person who saved a Jewish life during the Holocaust period by Yad Vashem, Holocaust Martyrs' and Heroes' Memorial Authority, in Jerusalem.

Baal Shem Tov: Literally, Master of the Good Name. Israel Ben Eliezer (1700–1760). 'Father' and founder of the influential and powerful movement, Hasidism. He preached deep devotion to God, primarily through love and joy, rather than exclusively through scholarship.

Beis Ya'akov (Hebrew): House of Jacob. A Jewish religious organization.

Belzec: An annihilation camp near Lublin, Poland. According to scholars, 5,000 Jews a day were brought there to perish.

Bet(h) Hamidrash (Hebrew): House of Study.

Bialik, Hayyim Nahman: 1873–1934. The best-known Hebrew poet.

Bund: Jewish socialist organization.

'Burned': A place discovered and useless as a hide out. Term used by Jews in German-occupied Poland.

Calling up: Calling up to the reading of the Torah.

Capo: See Kapo.

Capote: See *Kapota*.

Centos: Acronym for the Polish title, *Centralne Towarzystwo Opieki Nad Sierotami* (Central Society for the Care of Orphans).

Challa or Hallah (Hebrew): Braided or round egg bread, prepared traditionally by Jews for the Sabbath.

Chaver: See Haver.

Cheder Heder (Hebrew): Literally, a room. A room, or school in which young boys, frequently not older than four, were taught Hebrew, the Bible, and other Jewish subjects.

Diaspora (Greek): Lands of Jewish dispersion, outside of the Land of Israel.

Diligence (French): A public stagecoach.

Donner Wetter (German): Thunderstorm. Used colloquially as: damn it all!

Dziennik (Polish): Daily. Reference to a newspaper.

Edomite: Edom, a land in the south-east of ancient Canaan. The inhabitants, according to tradition descendants of Essau, were constantly at war with Israel. The term 'Edomite' was used by Jews in the Middle Ages to denote Christians.

Enlightenment: See *Haskalah*.

Eretz Israel (Hebrew): The Land of Israel.

Erev (Hebrew): Evening. Evening of the day before a holiday.

Fringes: see *Tzitzit*.

Gedud (Hebrew) military: Troop. Regiment, battalion. A group of youths of a particular age, part of the *Hashomer Hatzair*. Plural: *Gedudim*.

Gehenna (Hebrew): The Valley of Hinnom, near Jerusalem, used in Biblical times as a place of refuse. Hell. A place of pain and suffering.

Gepegert (Yiddish): Died. Used only when speaking of animals.

Geschaft (German): Business, trade.

Glupsk: An imaginary town. Name derived from Polish: Glupota, or stupidity.

Golah, *Galut* (Hebrew): Exile, or diaspora. See Diaspora.

Gomel: City in Belarus, at that time in Soviet Russia.

Graff: A title of nobility in Germany, Austria and Sweden.

Grosh (Polish): The smallest monetary unit (a penny).

Habima (Hebrew): 'The Stage'. A famous Hebrew theatre company founded in Russia in 1916. The company emigrated in 1928 from Russia to Palestine, today Israel.

Haggadah (Hebrew): The story of the Jewish Exodus from Egypt, retold on Passover night.

Hanhagah (Hebrew): Management.

Hanhaga Rashit (Hebrew): Executive Committee of the *Hashomer Hatzair*.

Hanoar Hazioni (Hebrew): 'Zionist Youth.' A pioneering youth organization.

Hashomer Hatzair (Hebrew): The Young Guard. A Zionist youth organization embracing Marxist ideology. Active in the resistance movement in the ghettos during the Second World War.

Hasid (Hebrew): Devotee. A follower of the Hasidic movement.

Hasidism: A religious movement founded in eighteenth-century Poland, emphasizing feeling, sincerity and devotion to God above study and learning. Despite opposition, due to its appeal to the masses, Hasidism became strong and influential.

Haskalah (Hebrew): Enlightenment. A mid eighteenth-century movement aimed at bringing rationalism and modern European culture to the Jews. It spread to Poland, Russia and Austria, primarily among middle-class, secular city dwellers.

Haver (Hebrew): Comrade. Plural: *Haverim.*

Heder (Hebrew): See *Cheder.*

Homel: See Gomel.

Jasiu: Diminutive form of Janina. Polish grammatical form used when addressing someone directly.

Judenrat (German): Jewish Council of Elders.

Judenrein (German): Literally: Clean of Jews.

Judenstadt (German): Jewish city.

Kaddish (Hebrew): Sanctification. A prayer, in Aramaic, recited at different times in the synagogue. Also a mourner's prayer, exalting and hallowing His Name.

Kaddish de Rabbanan (Aramaic): *Kaddish* of the Rabbis.

Kalla Maidlich (Hebrew and Yiddish): Marriageable girls.

Kapo: A taskmaster in a German concentration camp, frequently recruited from camp prisoners.

Kapota (Polish): A long, black coat, worn by Orthodox Jews in Eastern Europe.

Karaites: A Jewish sect, founded around the eighth century. They differed from the Jewish majority by accepting only the Bible as the source of philosophy, law, religion, and secular practice, and rejecting the Oral Law and rabbinical interpretations and traditions as being post-Biblical. Some of the Karaites settled in the Crimea, Lithuania, Poland and other lands.

Kazimierz: A city near Cracow, Poland, known as the seat of a Jewish community.

Kehillah (Hebrew): Jewish community. Sometimes the administrative body of the community.

Ken (Hebrew): Nest. The basic unit of the *Hashomer Hatzair* youth organization.

Kennkarte (German): During the Holocaust an identity card necessary for survival.

Kiddush (Hebrew): Sanctification.

Kiddush ha-Shem (Hebrew): Sanctification of God's Name, usually meaning martyrdom, but may denote any act of selfless sacrifice in defence of Jews or Judaism.

Kinderrein (German): Literally: Clean of children.

Kol Nidre (Aramaic): All Vows. A prayer in Aramaic recited on the eve of the Day of Atonement, for the annulment of all vows made during the previous year, excluding, however, vows and promises made to other persons. The prayer may allude to vows of conversion to Christianity made under duress, in fourteenth-century Spain and Portugal, and during other times of persecution.

Kvutzah (Hebrew): Group.

Lorelei: German legend about a temptress who by her song caused sailors to wreck their boats on rocks.

Makkabi, Maccabi: A union of Jewish sports organizations.

Majdanek: An annihilation camp near Lublin, Poland where approximately 500,000 people, mostly Jews, died in gas chambers.

Mahlzeit (German): meal time.

Matzah (Hebrew): Thin unleavened bread eaten on Passover.

Menschlichkeit (German): properties which make one a (good) human being.

Mezuzah (Hebrew): Literally: A doorpost. Also a small case containing Biblical verse (Deut. 6:9 and 11:20) attached to doorposts of rooms occupied by Jews. Intended as a reminder of man's religious obligations, it has sometimes been perceived as an amulet protecting the home.

Mgr.: Magister. An academic degree.

Mickiewicz, Adam: A Polish poet, 1798–1855.

Midrash: Commentaries and interpretations of the Bible, sometimes in the form of homilies and allegories, deriving moral lessons for the needs of the day.

Mitnagdim (Hebrew): Opponents. Opponents of the Hasidic movement.

Mizrachi: A Jewish religious Zionist organization.

Molech or Moloch: A name of a deity to whom ancient Canaanites sacrificed first born children by burning. Even though prohibited in the Bible, the practice occurred and persisted.

Muhrer: Chief of Gestapo in charge of the Vilna Ghetto.

Neilah (Hebrew): Closing. The concluding prayer on the Day of Atonement, referring to the closing of the Gates of Heaven after the fate of men has be sealed.

Nowogrodek: A county town in west-central Belarus, between 1919 and 1939 under Polish rule.

Nowy Dziennik: (Polish): A local newspaper in Cracow.

Oberkapo: See Kapo.

Omer (Hebrew): The first sheaf cut during the barley harvest, offered to the Temple on the second day of Passover.

Oneg Shabbat (Hebrew): Code name for the secret archives established by Emanuel Ringelblum in Warsaw during the Holocaust period. In Yiddish, *Oyneg Shabes*. Literally, 'Sabbath delight'.

Pan (Polish): Sir. A title of respect commonly used, addressing a male.

Pani (Polish): Madam. A title of respect commonly used, addressing a female.

Pentateuch: See Torah.

Phylacteries (Greek): Two small black leather boxes containing passages of the Torah, and worn by Jewish males over thirteen on their left arms and foreheads during morning prayers.

Poale Zion (Hebrew): 'Workers of Zion.' A Zionist Socialist political party, later incorporated into the Labour Movement. It had Right and Left wings.

Ponar or Ponary: An area near Vilnius (Vilna) where, approximately 60,000 Jews were massacred.

Positivism: A movement advocating understanding, unity, and cooperation between different social classes, ethnic groups, and minorities.

Psaltyr (Russian): A book of religious hymns.

Reb or Rebbe (Yiddish derived from Hebrew): Literally: Rabbi. A commonly used title of respect among Jews.

Responsa: Written rabbinical answers to questions about Jewish life and thought, shedding light on the problems and attitudes of its times.

Rofeh (Hebrew): Physician.

Rosh (Hebrew): Head. Leader.

Rynek (Polish): Market-place.

Sabbath of Consolations: The Sabbath after the ninth of the month of Av (Ab), the day of mourning after the destruction of the Temple.

Seder (Hebrew): Order. The ceremonial meal on Passover night, retelling the story of Exodus from Egypt and liberation.

Sefer (Hebrew): Book.

Selichot or *Selihot* (Hebrew): Penitential prayers, asking for forgiveness for transgressions, and for divine compassion and mercy, recited prior to the High Holy Days.

Seven Benedictions: Blessings recited under the canopy during the wedding ceremony.

Shabbat Shalom (Hebrew): Sabbath Peace.

Shames, Shamash (Hebrew): The beadle of a synagogue.

Shavuot (Hebrew): Weeks. Feast of the Weeks: One of the three pilgrimage festivals observed on the sixth and seventh of the month of Sivan, marking the wheat harvest and the completion of seven weeks of the counting of the *omer* (bringing the first fruits to the Temple) beginning on the second day of Passover. According to tradition, Shavuot also commemorates the giving of the Torah (the law) on Mount Sinai, on the sixth of Sivan.

Shema (Hebrew): A prayer. Judaism's affirmation of faith: 'Hear O Israel, the Lord Our God, the Lord is One'.

Shmalcowniki (Polish): The spies who ferreted out Jews in hiding and betrayed them to the Germans, obtaining a reward.

Shofar (Hebrew): A ram's horn, sounded in the synagogue during the New Year's services and at the closing services on the Day of Atonement.

Shomer (Hebrew): Guard. A reference to a Jewish youth organization, active in the ghettos. Plural: *Shomrim*.

Shomeret (Hebrew): Guard, female. Plural: *Shomrot*. See *Shomer*.

Shtetl (Yiddish): A little town in Eastern Europe, where many, sometimes the majority of inhabitants were Jews.

Smorgonie: A little town near Vilna, today Lithuania, famous for its bagels.

Sonderdienst (German): Special duty.

Sonderkommando (German). Literally: Special Command. In Nazi vocabulary: units of prisoners who disposed of the dead, including work in the crematoria. At end of their turn, they were exterminated.

Suke, Sukkah (Hebrew): Tabernacle. A booth built during the Feast of Tabernacles, to commemorate the simple booths the Israelites lived in during their wanderings in the desert. Occurring in the autumn, it is also a harvest festival.

Swabs: Germans.

Talar: Monetary unit.

Tallit (Hebrew): A Jewish prayer shawl.

Tashlikh (Hebrew): Originally a verse in Micah 7:19: 'And Thou wilt cast all their sins into the depth of the sea.' A custom to conduct prayers by a river or a body of water on the first day of Rosh Hashanah (New Year) asking for forgiveness of sins, symbolically throwing the sins into the waters.

Tate (Yiddish): Father.

Tehinnot (Hebrew): Prayers of supplication.

Tefillin: See Phylacteries.

Tochter (Yiddish): Daughter.

Tokhehot (Hebrew): The rebukes and threats in Leviticus 26 and Deuteronomy 28.

Torah (Hebrew): Teachings. The Law. The first five books of the Bible. A term also used to denote the entire Bible, the Talmud and rabbinic literature.

Treblinka: A concentration and mass extermination camp in Poland.

Tscholnt (Yiddish): A dish made of potatoes, beans, meat and barley, put into the oven on Friday, to be cooked and kept warm for the Saturday meal.

Tze'enah U-Re'enah (Hebrew): Stories of the Torah, the first five books of the Bible, with rabbinical commentaries and other notes in Yiddish, written by Jacob Ashkenazi (1550–1626), used and favoured primarily by women.

Tzitzit (Hebrew): A small prayer shawl with fringes on its four corners which every Jewish male is commanded by the Bible (Numbers 15:37–41) to wear under his outer garments.

Ulpan (Hebrew): An intensive course of Hebrew, mostly for immigrants to Israel.

Umschlagplatz (German): An area in Warsaw where Jews were concentrated for deportation by cattle cars to death camps.

Ushpizin (Aramaic): Guests. Traditional term to denote the patriarchs (Abraham, Issac, Jacob, Joseph, Moses, Aaron, David) invited to visit the *sukkot* (booths) during the Feast of Tabernacles.

Vilna: Vilnius, the capital of Lithuania. Formerly, under Polish rule from 1922–39, known as Wilno. Th Jewish population, however, refered to the town as Vilna.

White Paper: British legislative documents of 1922, 1930 and 1939 limiting Jewish immigration to what was then Palestine.

Yad Vashem (Hebrew): A Memorial and a Name. The Holocaust Martyrs' and Heroes' Remembrance Authority, Jerusalem. Institution established in 1953 to commemorate the Nazi annihilation of the Jewish people during the Second World War, through research, preservation and publication of memoirs, testimonies and other documents.

Yarmulka (Polish): Skullcap, worn by observant Jews.

Yeshiva (Hebrew): An institute or seminary dedicated to rabbinical studies.

Yeshivah Bocher (Hebrew): Literally, a young man, a student in a yeshivah.

Yom Tov (Hebrew): Good Day. A Holy Day or day of celebration.

Ze'enu U-Renu: See *Tzenah U-R'enah*.

Zdunska Wola (Vola in poetry): Town in Poland, south of Lodz. Remembered for unusual German cruelty, such as the selection of ten young men and hanging them in the public square, in the presence of the entire Jewish community.

Zegota: Full name: Konrad Zegota Committee. Code name for the Polish Council to Aid Jews. Operated under the Polish Government in Exile.

Zionism: English term derived from Hebrew. A movement to return to the Land of Israel and to establish there a Jewish National Home.

Zopfen (German): Braids.

Bibliography

For additional information, see Acknowledgments.

Abramsky, C., M. Jachimczyk and A. Polonsky (eds), *The Jews of Poland* (Oxford: Basil Blackwell in association with the Institute for Polish–Jewish Studies, 1986).

Aleichem, S., *Old Country Tales*, selected and translated with an introduction by Curt Leviant (New York: G.P. Putnam's, 1966). Copyright the children of Sholom Aleichem.

Apenszlak, J. et al. (eds), *The Black Book of Polish Jewry: An Account of the Martyrdom of Polish Jewry Under Nazi Occupation* (New York: American Federation for Polish Jews, in cooperation with the Association of Jewish Refugees and Immigrants from Poland, 1943).

Asch, S., *Salvation*, translated by Willa and Edwin Muir (New York: G.P. Putnam's, 1934).

———, *Children of Abraham*, translated by Maurice Samuel (New York: G.P Putnam's, copyright © 1942 by Ruth Shaffer, Moses Asch, John Asch and the representative of John Asch).

———, *Tales of my People*, translated by Meyer Levin (New York: G.P. Putnam's, 1948).

Ausubel, N. (ed.), *A Treasury of Jewish Poetry* (New York: Crown, 1967).

Balaban, M., *Historia Zydow w Krakowie i na Kazimierzu* (History of the Jews in Cracow and Kazimierz) (Cracow: reissued by Krajowa Agencja Wydawnicza, 1985; an earlier volume covering the years 1304–1868 was published in Cracow by Izraelicka Gmina Wyznaniowa, 1912).

Bartal, I. and A. Polonsky (eds), *Focusing on Galicia: Jews, Poles and Ukrainians, 1772–1918*, in *Polin. Studies in Polish Jewry*, vol. 12, Littman Library of Jewish Civilization (London and Portland, OR: Vallentine Mitchell, 1999).

Baum, R., *Syn Dziedzica i Inne Opowiadania* (The Squire's Son and Other Stories) (Lodz: Oficyna Bibliofilow, 1999).

Bloch, S. (ed.), *Bergen-Belsen 1945–1965* (New York and Tel-Aviv: Bergen-Belsen Memorial Press of the World Federation of Bergen-Belsen Associations, 1965).

Cahan A., *The Rise of David Levinsky* (New York: Harper and Row, 1917).

Cheichel (Hechal), E. (ed.), *A Tale For Each Month, 1967* (Haifa: Haifa Municipality Ethnological Museum and Folklore Archives. Israel Folktale Archives [IFA]. Publication No.22, 1968).

Cwiakowska, A., *Zony i Inne Opowiadania* (The Polish Wife and Other Stories) (Lodz: Oficyna Bibliofilow, 1999), pp.7–25.

Eber, I., 'Choices: Frankfurt, 1945', in M. Kantrowitz-Kaye and I. Klepfisz (eds), *The Tribe of Dina: A Jewish Women's Anthology* (Boston, MA: Beacon, 1986, 1989), pp.104–22.

Eber, I., 'Four Days in August', *Moment*, 11, 5 (May, 1986), pp.37–46.

Eibshitz, Y. (trans. and ed.), *Yomana Shel Rutka Lieblich*, Women of the Holocaust Series, vol. VI (Jerusalem: Hedva Eibshitz Institute, 1990). *Hotza'at Hamachon L'limud Hashoah*. A sequence of anthologies portraying heroism of the Jewish woman in the most trying conditions during the Nazi era.

Eisenberg, A., *Modern Jewish Life in Literature* (New York: United Jewish Synagogue Commission on Jewish Education, 1952, 1968).

———, *The Lost Generation: Children of the Holocaust* (New York: The Pilgrim Press, © 1982).

Eliach, Yaffa, *Hasidic Tales of the Holocaust* (New York and Oxford: Oxford University Press, 1982).

Eliav, M., *Studies on the Holocaust Period*, in memory of Professor M. Dvorjetski, presented by the Department of Jewish History (Ramat Gan: Bar Ilan University, 1979).

Encyclopaedia Judaica (Jerusalem: Keter, 1972) and Yearbooks.

Fredro, A.M., *Przyslowia Mow Potocznych* (Proverbs in Common Parlance) (Sanok, Poland: Naklad i Druk Karola Pollaka, 1855).

Friedman, P. (ed.), *Martyrs and Fighters; The Epic of the Warsaw Ghetto* (New York: Frederick A. Praeger, 1954) copyright © 1954 by Club of Polish Jews, Inc., New York, NY.

———, *Their Brothers' Keepers* (New York: Crown, © Philip Friedman 1957).

Frishman, D., *Kol Kitvey David Frishman* (New York: Lili Frishman, 1929).

Gilbert, M., *The Holocaust; A History of the Jews of Europe During the Second World War* (New York: Holt, Rinehart and Winston, 1985).

Gillon, A. and L. Krzyzanowski (eds), *Introduction to Modern Polish Literature: An Anthology of Fiction and Poetry* (New York: Twayne, 1964).

Glazer, M. (ed.), *Dancing on the Edge of the World; Jewish Stories of*

Faith, Inspiration and Love (Los Angeles, CA: Lowell House, NTC/Contemporary Publishing, 2000).

——— (ed.), *Dreaming the Actual: Contemporary Fiction and Poetry by Israeli Women Writers* (Albany, NY: State University of New York Press, 2000).

Goldberg, I. and Y. Suhl (eds), *The End of a Thousand Years; The Recent Exodus of the Jews from Poland* (New York: Committee for Jews of Poland, 1971).

Goldenthal, E., *Poet of the Ghetto: Morris Rosenfeld* (Hoboken, NJ: Ktav, 1998).

Gomulicki. W., 'Chalat', in *Z Jednego Strumienia* (From One Stream) (Warsaw: E. Wende I Spolka, 1905; Ludowa Spoldzielnia Wydawnicza, 1960).

Gross, N., 'Cracow Autumn', translated by A. Polonsky, in S. Kapralski (ed.), *The Jews of Poland* (Cracow: copyright by Judaica Foundation, Center for Jewish Culture, 1999), vol.2, pp.9–11.

Gruber, R. 'The Heroism of Staszek Jackowski', *Saturday Review*, 15 April 1967.

Halbreich, S., *Before, During, After* (New York: Vantage Press, 1991).

Halevy-Levin, I. (ed.), *Israel Argosy*, 6 (Autumn 1952, Spring 1953) (Jerusalem: Youth and Hehalutz Department of The Zionist Organization).

———, (ed.) *Israel Argosy*, 5 (1958), 6 (1959), 9 (1967) (New York: Thomas Yoseloff).

Halicz, C., *Ludzie Ktorzy Jeszcze Zyja* (People Still Living) (Warsaw: Roj, 1934).

Hellerstein, K. (trans.), *Paper Bridges. Selected Poems of Kadya Molodowsky* (Detroit, MI: Wayne State University Press, 1999).

Hertz, A., *Zydzi w Kulturze Polskiej* (Paris: Instytut Literacki. Edition et Librairie 'Libella', 1961).

Hochberg-Marianska, M. and N. Gruss (eds), *The Children Accuse*, translated by Bill Johnston (London: Vallentine Mitchell, 1996). Originally published in Polish by The Jewish Historical Commission (Cracow, 1946).

Kapralski, S. (ed.), *The Jews of Poland* (Cracow: Judaica Foundation, 1999), vol.2.

Kassow, S.D., *Who Will Write Our History? Emanuel Ringelblum, the Warsaw Ghetto and the Oyneg Shabes Archive* (Bloomington, IN: Indiana University Press, copyright © 2007 by Samuel D. Kassow).

Kaye-Kantrowitz, M. and I. Klepfisz (eds), *The Tribe of Dina: A Jewish Women's Anthology* (Boston, MA: Beacon Press, 1986, 1989).

Kobrin, L., *A Lithanian Village*, translated from the Yiddish by Isaac Goldberg (New York: Brentano's, 1920).

Konopnicka, M., 'Mendel Gdanski', in *Z Jednego Strumienia* (From One Stream) (Warsaw: E. Wende I Spolka, 1905), pp.5–30; (Warsaw: Ludowa Spoldzielnia Wydawnicza, 1960), pp.189–211.

Korczak, J., *Ghetto Diary* (New York: Holocaust Library, 1978).

—— *The Warsaw Ghetto Memoirs of Janusz Korczak*, translated from the Polish, with an introduction and notes by E.P. Kulawiec (Washington, DC: University Press of America, 1979).

——, *The Ghetto Years, 1939–1942* (Israel: Ghetto Fighter's House and Hakibbutz Hameuchad Publishing House, 1972, 1980).

——, *King Matt the First*, introduction by Bruno Bettelheim, translated by Richard Lourie (New York: Farrar, Straus and Giroux, 1986).

Kramer, A. (trans. and ed.), *The Last Lullaby: Poetry From the Holocaust*. A Dora Teitelbaum Foundation Publication (Syracuse, NY: Syracuse University Press, 1998).

Kraszewski, J.I., *Zyd*, translated by Linda Kowalewska (New York: Dodd, Mead, 1890).

——, *A Clever Woman* or *Jermola*, translated by M. Carey (New York: Dodd, Mead, 1891).

Kuchler-Silberman, L., *One Hundred Children*. Adapted from the Hebrew by David C. Gross (New York: Doubleday, 1961).

——, *Anu Ma'ashimim. Eyduyot Yeladim min Hashoah* (We Accuse: Children's Holocaust Testimonies) third edn (Kibbutz Merchavia: Sifriat Poalim, 1962).

Lazaros, H., 'The March', *World Over*, 7 April 1976.

Leftwich, J., 'Songs of the Death Camps', a selection with commentary, *Commentary* (September 1951), pp.269–74.

—— (trans. and ed.), *The Golden Peacock: A Worldwide Treasury of Yiddish Poetry* (New York: Thomas Yoseloff, © A.S. Barnes, 1961).

—— (ed.), *Yisroel: The First Jewish Omnibus*, rev. edn (New York: Thomas Yoseloff, © by Bechhurst Press, Inc., © 1963 by A.S. Barnes and Company, Inc.).

—— (ed.), *Great Yiddish Writers of the Twentieth Century* (Northvale, NJ: © Jason Aronson, 1969).

—— (ed.), *An Anthology of Modern Yiddish Literature* (The Hague, Netherlands: © Mouton, 1974).

'The Letter of the Ninety-Three Maidens', *The Reconstructionist*, 2 (5 March 1943), pp.23–4.

Lieberman, L. and A.F. Beringause, *Classics of Jewish Literature* (New York: Philosophical Library, 1987).

Luszczyk-Ilienkowa, N., 'Ziselman z Honczarskiej' (Ziselman of Honcharska Street) and 'Rivka', *Regiony*, 1, 96 (2000), pp.14–16, 22–4.

The Massacre of European Jewry: An Anthology (Kibbutz Merchavia: World Hashomer Hatzair, English Speaking Department, 1963).

Meed, V., *On Both Sides of the Wall: Memoirs from the Warsaw Ghetto*, translated by Dr Steven Meed (New York: Holocaust Library, 1979).

Megged, A., 'The Name', *Midstream* (Spring 1960), pp.61–71.

Mendelsohn, E. and C. Shmeruk (eds), *Studies on Polish Jewry*. Paul Glikson Memorial Volume (Jerusalem: The Hebrew University of Jerusalem, 1987).

Mickiewicz, A., *Pan Tadeusz* (with translation by K. MacKenzie) (New York: Hippocrene Books, 1974, 1992).

Miegel, J., R. Scott and H.B. Segel (eds), *Poles and Jews, Myth and Reality in the Historical Context*. Proceedings of an International Conference, in collaboration with the Center for Israel and Jewish Studies, 6–10 March 1983. Sponsored by the Institute on East Central Europe (New York: Columbia University, 1986).

Milosz, C., *The History of Polish Literature* (London: Collier-Macmillan, 1969).

Mortkowicz-Olczakowa, H., *Mister Doctor: The Life of Janusz Korczak*. English translation by Romuald Jan Kruk (London: Peter Davies, 1965).

Neuman, I., with M. Palencia-Roth, *The Narrow Bridge; Beyond the Holocaust* (Urbana and Chicago, IL: University of Illinois Press, 2000).

Nirenstein, A., *A Tower from the Enemy* (New York: The Orion Press, 1958).

Opalski, M. and I. Bartal, *Poles and Jews; A Failed Brotherhood* (Hanover, NH: University Press of New England, 1992).

Orzeszkowa, E., *Meir Ezofovitch* (New York: W.I. Allison, 1898).

———, *Gedali* (Warsaw: E. Wenke i Spolka, 1905).

———, *Silny Samson* (Warsaw: E.Wenke i Spolka, 1905).

——— (ed. and comp.), *Z Jednego Strumienia* (From One Stream) (Warsaw: E. Wende I Spolka, 1905; Ludowa Spoldzielnia Wydawnicza, 1960).

Paluch, A.K. (ed.), *The Jews of Poland* (Cracow: Research Center on Jewish History and Culture in Poland, 1992).

Perez (Peretz), I.L., *Stories and Pictures*, translated from the Yiddish by Helena Frank (Philadelphia, PA: The Jewish Publication Society of America, 1906).

Piechota, J., *Gadki i Klechdy* (Chats and Folktales) (Warsaw: Ludowa Spoldzielnia Wydawnicza, 1982).

'Poems of Children from the Warsaw Ghetto', *The Jewish Frontier* (November 1942), p.26.

Polonsky, A. (ed.), *My Brother's Keeper: Recent Polish Debate on the Holocaust* (Oxford: Routledge in association with the Institute for Polish-Jewish Studies, 1990).

Polonsky, A., I. Bartal, G. Hundert, M. Opalski and J. Tomaszewski (eds), *Poles, Jews, Socialists: The Failure of an Ideal*, in *Polin. Studies in Polish Jewry*, vol. 9, Littman Library of Jewish Civilization (London and Portland, OR: Vallentine Mitchell, 1996).

Prus, B. (pseudonym of Aleksander Glowacki), *Placowka* (Polish) (London: M.I. Kolin, 1941, based on the fourth edn, 1896).

———, *The Doll* (New York: Twayne, 1972).

Reznikoff, C., 'Kaddish', *The Jewish Frontier* (November 1942), p.25.

Ringelblum, E., *Notes from the Warsaw Ghetto: the Journal of Emanuel Ringelblum*, edited and translated by Jacob Sloan (New York: McGraw-Hill, 1958).

———, *Polish-Jewish Relations during the Second World War*, edited by Joseph Kermish and Shmuel Krakowski (Jerusalem: Yad Vashem, 1974).

Rolnicki. M., *Krzak Gorejacy* (The Burning Bush. Notes on the Years 1939–1944) (Jerusalem and Lublin: M. Rolnicki przy wspoludziale [with the participation of] Wojewodzkiego Domu Kultury w Lublinie, 1999).

Samuel, M., *The World of Shalom Aleichem* (New York: Alfred A. Knopf, 1943).

Schultz, B. *The Street of Crocodiles*, translated by Celina Wieniewska; Introduction by Jerzy Ficowski; Introduction translated by Michael Kandel (New York: Penguin, 1977). Originally published in Poland as *Cinnamon Shops* (1934).

———, *Letters and Drawings of Bruno Schulz, with Selected Prose*, edited by Jerzy Ficowski, translated by Walter Arndt (New York: Harper and Row, 1988).

Schwarzbaum, H., *Studies in Jewish and World Folklore* (Berlin: Walter De Gruyter, 1968).

Segel, H.B., *Strangers in Our Midst; Images of the Jew in Polish Literature* (Ithaca, NY: Cornell University Press, © Cornell University, 1996).

Shilhav, Y. (compiler) and S. Feinstein (ed.), *Flame and Fury: Material for Yom Hashoah: National Remembrance Day for the Six Million Jews Who Perished at the Hands of the Nazis*, based on a publication of Yad Vashem, Martyrs' and Heroes' Remembrance Authority, Jerusalem (New York: Jewish Education Press of the Board of Jewish Education, 1962).

Sider, F., *Seven Folktales from Boryslaw*, edited and annotated by Otto Schnitzler (Haifa: Haifa Municipality Ethnological Museum and Folklore Archives, Israel Folktale Archives [IFA], Publication No.19, 1968).

Siegel, B., *The Controversial Sholem Asch* (Bowling Green, OH: Bowling Green University Popular Press, 1976).

Singer, I.J., *The Sinner (Yoshe Kalb)*, translated by Maurice Samuel (New York: Liveright Inc. Publishers, 1933. The work was reissued as *Yoshe Kalb* by Harper & Row, 1965, and by Schocken, 1988). Copyright © Joseph Singer.

Suhl, Y. (trans. and ed.), *They Fought Back: The Story of Jewish Resistance in Nazi Europe* (New York: Crown, 1967).

'Two Eyewitnesses', *The Jewish Frontier* (November 1942), pp.14–15.

Wells, L.W., *The Janowska Road*. The updated 1999 edition published by the United States Holocaust Memorial Museum, Washington, DC (also published as *The Death Brigade* in 1978 by the Holocaust Library, and in New York, by the Macmillan Company in 1963), copyright © 1963, 1978, 1999 by Leon Weliczker Wells).

Whitman, R. (trans. and ed.), *An Anthology of Yiddish Poetry*, bilingual edn (New York: October House, 1966).

Wojcicki, K., *Stare Gawedy i Obrazy* (Old Tales and Images) (Warsaw: Nakladem Gustawa Sennewalda Ksiegarza, 1840), vol. 1.

Zinberg, I., *A History of Jewish Literature*, translated and edited by Bernard Martin (Cleveland, OH: Case Western Reserve University, 1972–78).

Zmorski (Zamarski), R., *Podania i Basnie Ludu* (Legends and Myths of the People) (Warsaw: 1902, 1955).

Zohar, Z., L. Dror and I. Rozenzwaig (eds), *Sefer Hashomer Hatzair* (The Book of Hashomer Hatzair) (Kibbutz Merchavia: Sifriat Poalim, 1956).

Zyngman, I. *Janusz Korczak Bein Ha'yetomim* (Janus Korczak Among the Orphans) (Bnei Brak: Sifriat Poalim, 1979).